CONSORT

CONSORT

THE RIFT BRIDE BOOK I

ADA DART

PAINTED BLIND
PUBLISHING
LITERARY ALCHEMY

**PAINTED BLIND
PUBLISHING**
LITERARY ALCHEMY

Consort: Book I of The Rift Bride
© 2022 Ada Dart
ISBN: 978-1-957469-01-0

Text: Ada Dart
Book & Cover Design: M. F. Sullivan

Ada Dart Online: adadartromance.com
Painted Blind Publishing: paintedblindpublishing.com

The Rift has been with us for two thousand years.

No one knows why, or how.

We have only learned to live with it.

After recovering from centuries of undone progress,
human society has stabilized.

A second industrial era has dawned
across a world now joined
by two new subsets of human:

The altered,
men and women living
with Rift beasts inside them;

and the riftborn,
whose gifts are still not understood.

And I,
Thecla Farrow,
have the dubious fortune
of being both.

PART I

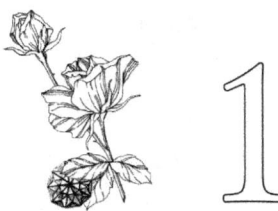

BEFORE FATHER DIED, I knew what Eleison would look like. I even somehow absorbed some impression of his ways, although the vision I received of him was infinity compounded into a moment.

Let me explain.

I was nearly fifteen, and the village of Lescaut seemed as ill-fit for me as a fishbowl for a trout. Most adults treated me like a child; others had begun to speak to me with a discourtesy they never had, expecting more of me than I could accomplish. Still others—men, especially—had begun to study me in manners I found uncomfortable, or, when my father wasn't around, to praise or criticize my appearance in ways that were out of line.

In my environment, as in myself, I became aware of an intense battle between two energies. One drove me to stay home, where life was peaceful and quiet, and where the innocent joys of childhood could still be kindled up like a fire.

But the other energy wished to break free. To abandon everything of that innocent childhood. To leap into the strange parallel reality of adults.

Somehow, the circus captured both.

Nothing was more thrilling than its arrival each autumn. Occasionally a musician would wander through Lescaut's crooked paths, and salesmen or merchants of various kinds were always making rounds for regular matters of trade. The circus, though! It came only once a year, and it held such wild intrigue to us all—for better or for worse.

As soon as the drums echoed out from the distance, metal window shutters rolled high, and the glass panes beneath were thrown wide. Old women who had been lounging on their porches to savor a few moments of safe sunshine, with visible disgust for the encroaching troupe that was doubtless packed with unregistered riftborn, would collect their embroidery and scurry inside.

My half-sister and I, screaming with delight, would fling ourselves up from games or chores or quarrels or lessons and scurry into the street without so much as a glance at the RMS readout glowing on the wall.

What colors! Lescaut was gray, from its streets to its sky— but when the circus came to town, all that changed. Our hands shielding our eyes, we peered down the long road sloping outside our gate, each of us bobbing up and down on our toes. The fanfare grew, with distant neighbors in the outskirts region (a borough even poorer than ours, sad to say) letting up wild cheers and enthusiastic applause.

The beating in my heart matched the drums pump for pump. Some small part of me envied the destitute children who had the special privilege of clapping eyes on the circus before anyone else.

Our turn, however, came soon enough. The timpani increased in clarity, luring more smiling neighbors into their gardens. Sable squealed with delight that increased mine. I held my breath, my focus narrowing to the distant corner of our street.

There: red, and white, and gold. A flashing banner; the cracking of drums; the screams of delight that signaled the pursuing slum children.

Like an overdue river smashing a dam, the circus procession surged into our street and toward the center of the town.

What madness! What delight. We squealed together, our neighbors clapping and crying out in nostalgic joy. The circus itself was a wonderful affair, but their march through Lescaut to the fairgrounds on its southern side was always the sweetest moment to me. Everything was so alive. Jugglers deftly manipulated silver balls and flaming torches; one of these fires was snatched by a tattooed man who consumed the flame and smiled in delight at the gasps; deft female acrobats, sometimes with skill in contortion, sprang alongside the drummers, smiling at all the girls and winking at the boys. Even the horses pulling the carriage were a rare treat— *real* horses. Flesh-and-blood, beautiful white steeds as elaborately ornamented as the coaches they pulled. How a traveling circus afforded them, I could not imagine.

It was all so vibrant, so impossibly merry, that all the motion blended together around the one man walking calmly through the chaos.

I had not seen him in previous visits the circus had made to our little town, but that wasn't surprising. Between the natural tendency of drifters and regular problems like police raids for unregistered riftborn, (one of many reasons my father railed against the tyrannical territory master), I was not sure I had ever seen the same circus twice. The ringmaster, it would seem, was what made a circus a circus; everything changing around him was immaterial.

So, why did this quiet old carnival worker catch my eye? Because he was *so* quiet, I suppose—or, at least, he seemed as such while walking along behind one of the wagons, a cluster of musicians around him to disguise his solitude. Was he blind? I wasn't sure. His eyes, pupils pale white against his dark skin, appeared to scan the crowd with the turn of his head.

And when his attention stopped on me, I knew he *was* scanning the crowd, however blind he seemed. One way or another, he saw me staring. Smiling kindly through the musicians without breaking stride, the old man tipped his hat to me while carrying on with the rest of his band.

I did not think long on the incident until two days later, when Sable and I struggled to talk Father into giving us money to go.

"But you love the circus," I protested. "Why not come with us?"

"The same reason I don't want *you* going yet. Haven't you read the meter? It's— Don't roll your eyes at me, Thecla."

I struggled against the urge to do it again, forcing myself to keep my gaze fixed on his bearded face. "It's been promising a Rift Event for three *days* now, but nothing's happened. Please? By the time the risk level lowers, the circus will be gone!"

"A whole year," moaned Sable, dramatically throwing herself into the sofa of his office with one hand on her forehead. "Can't we please just go for an hour, Daddy?"

"Wait until tomorrow," he said firmly, returning to his repair of the wiring on an electric shutter's control unit for some client of his. While Sable and I groaned in disappointment, he ignored us and soldered on. "We'll bring your mother"—meaning, Sable's mother—"and you two can see the borro taming act."

I waved a hand. "But you let me go to the *market* alone."

"The market is five minutes from here."

"But Uliara said—"

"No," he repeated sternly, disinterested in my anecdote. "And if you ask one more time, you'll be waiting until next year."

Scowling, Sable rolled out of the couch with a noise like a low growl.

"You stink," she said, face down on the rug in protest.

"That's fine," my father replied.

"It's not fair," Sable continued, putting me on-edge in case he meant what he said this time. "Everybody else got to go to the circus the first night!"

"If that were true, they'd only *be* here for one night. I mean it. Don't push me, Sable."

Sighing, I stooped to pull my sister up from the floor. "Come on," I told her, leading her and her glowering face out of father's office. "Maybe the risk will drop sooner, and we can go earlier."

"Maybe," my father agreed.

"Maybe," muttered Sable with a glare over her shoulder— then, as we passed through the living room, an even more hateful expression for the Rift Monitoring System beside our front door.

As was predictable, the rest of the day passed without the least sign of a Rift Event, yet the RMS reading remained stubbornly high. At a 70% chance of a Rift Event, Father would never let us out for more than a quick errand before the circus left town.

And while I supposed I appreciated his concerns, I had no intention of waiting another year.

Perhaps things would have been different if I had endured

more Rift Events in Lescaut, but the truth was that our town was blessed with fair weather most days. On days when it was not, the villagers were grateful to know that even the poorest among them had shutters to be locked against the danger, or friends or organizations that could shelter them if required. As a child, I took my safety during Rift Events as a given.

Of course...I did not consider that I was safe owing largely to the careful oversight of my father. I did not consider anything, in fact, other than that I did not want to feel left behind by the friends around town who had already enjoyed the outrageous performances and wild exhibitions, and who would only spend so long in a state of excitement about it. Soon enough, the glow would wear off and we'd once again be left with our simple lives. I wanted to savor it while it was still bright and gleaming.

So, I did the natural thing. When night fell, and Sable's breathing in the bed on our room's other side had slowed to sleep's peaceful rhythm, I slipped from beneath my covers and peered out the window.

There, on the outskirts of town, the darkness of night was interrupted by a warm aurora of torchlight.

Sable turned over to face the wall, her sleep deepening.

Moving through our room with intimate knowledge of every creaking floorboard, I hastily threw on a clean gray frock and brushed my long hair back from my face. When it was tied back with a ribbon, a shock of electric pink against my natural chestnut, I fetched my small cache of coins from the sock where I kept them from Sable. Then, the hazel eyes of my reflection crinkling as I smiled at my own expertise, I slipped through our room's one window.

The drop from the eave to the ground was made a simple matter by the trellis of trumpet vines my stepmother kept in those days. I always worried today would be the day its wood collapsed under my foot, but, as always, it held, and I sprang from its center to the ground without the least harm.

With but a glance up at my open window, I hurried through our gate and across Lescaut.

Though it was far from a city, Lescaut was not as provincial as I found it to be at the time. In fact, I recall Father once explaining to me that the town was home to six hundred some family lines of varying size, and I felt every one of them as I made my way through the winding streets and unkempt back alleys in the shortest route I knew to the town's other side.

Lescaut itself was oddly quiet that night. Anyone normally out around this time was likely down at the circus, it was true; but, even with that accounted for, the open streets seemed somehow haunting. It was all the shutters, I realized as I at last spied a laughing couple careening back into town and home again. The shutters were all closed. Just in case.

But the risk had hovered at 70% for nearly half a week, and nothing had happened.

I hurried on, my heart throbbing with excitement to at last reach that point where our plain little town transformed into something magical.

There it was. One step past the autohorse repair shop, everything changed. The street had been extended by tents and stands that were arranged in rows, as neatly organized as the very storefronts through which I passed. Colorful pennants fluttered in the night air, their motions cajoled by the warm smoke of torches burning throughout the amusements. Any reticence I felt relaxed at once, and I laughed in delight when a fool near the entrance greeted me with a bouquet that turned out to be attached to a long scarf I could have pulled endlessly from his fist. Gleeful, I carried on through the crowd and eased into the night.

The risk had been worth it. Simply being there, the air dense with happiness, eased something in my mind that I had not realized was growing tense all year. It was a world apart from reality: clearly, the risk of a Rift Event weighed low in everyone's minds. A girl younger than Sable struggled against smiling as the face painter's brush tickled her cheek, while groups of people my age, individuals known to me as the friends of my friends, milled about in front of the row of game booths I knew were rigged. These families, these young people, felt as I did about the likelihood of an Event. It put me at ease, as though our collective will might, in fact, prevent one from descending on the town.

If only.

I had almost reached the other end of the fairgrounds and was about to turn around, having decided on the order in which I would visit the attractions. It was my first time there alone, and the freedom was thrilling as it was overwhelming. With so many choices, I was almost grateful that the circus would call it a night in a few hours. It provided the pressure required to make a decision.

Yet, in the end, my choice did not factor in at all. Having reached the limit, I turned on my heel to double back to a performance by the fire-eater I saw in the procession.

Before I could take more than one step, a man's alerting whistle stopped my foot.

I froze mid-motion, twisting at the waist.

There he was. The pale-eyed man from before, his slight weight poised against a cane I hadn't seen during the caravan.

"Good evening, young lady," he called in a smooth, merry

tone from before his small tent. "Would you like to have your fortune read tonight?"

I sometimes wonder if I ought to have told him 'No.'

Then, the feeling passes, and I can't imagine my life any other way.

AT THE TIME, I laughed at the offer.

"I don't believe in fortune telling," I said, half-aware I emptily parroted my stepmother's opinion without forming my own. "It's all so unspecific—and, anyway, by the time the thing has come to pass, I'll have forgotten the fortune. It won't matter."

"Then what's the harm in it?"

"The harm is I'll have one coin less to spend on more tangible amusements. Anyway—what benefit could knowing my future possibly have? It always turns out badly in the stories I read."

"I could tell you were a smart girl when I caught you looking at me the other day… You don't need to worry. Prophecy may doom the heroes of your books, Thecla; but, if you pay attention, this story will have a happy ending."

I certainly *was* paying attention.

"How do you know my—wait—"

He turned away and ducked into his tent in one fluid motion. Teeth bared, I hesitated with a glance across the grounds. No one drifting around me had noted the exchange, or, if they had, they did not feel it queer enough to stop. I stood alone in a lake of people, up to my neck in isolation.

Annoyed, I strode into the tent and demanded, "Who told you my name? Was it Clarent? This is some rude prank, isn't it?"

The strange man stood on the other side of the open flap. He unfixed it from the structure of the tent and allowed it to fall shut. When it did, the cramped little booth grew eerily quiet. As though the thin tarp had been impossibly proofed against sound.

"Please," he said, gesturing to the small table and one of the two chairs flanking it. "Sit."

"I just want to know who embroiled you in this nonsense, and then I would like to go."

Ignoring my indignation, the man leaned his cane against the table and slid familiarly down into his seat.

"Do you know what the riftborn are, Thecla? You do, don't you?"

I hesitated, but only because it was not often a riftborn even implied they were one. There were, broadly speaking, two types—registered, and unregistered. Those who were born during a Rift Event could be so dangerous that the government, since long before my birth, had engaged in the practice of tracking women through their pregnancy. Those with the misfortune to enter labor during an Event, it was said, were subject to horrors up to and including the confiscation of the child after birth. I wasn't sure that I believed it, since, relatively speaking, Rift births were rare in a town our size, but I did know two things: the government kept a list of riftborn operating within the confines of the law as normal citizens; and some of the riftborn, for whatever reason, chose or were forced to avoid it.

"Of course I know what a riftborn is," I answered after the sense of surprise and slight discomfort swept past me.

"Then you'd ought to know I don't need to ask anyone's name, or embroil anybody in any kind of scheme. Sit. Relax. I promise, you'll have fun."

Lips pursed, I glanced over my shoulder at the shut flap before, with some reluctance, I lowered myself into the offered seat. Smiling, the man set his hands palm-up on the table.

"Pass me an object, please; something in your possession that I may use to divine."

Though I was a little embarrassed to humor him, the thought that this man might be genuinely riftborn eased my resistance. He might have been lying to seem powerful, but that was unlikely. The risks of pretending to be riftborn far outweighed any benefit to a scam artist's circus profits.

And, well...if I was being honest with myself, I really was dying of curiosity whenever I thought of my future.

Reaching back with one hand, I freed the ribbon from my hair and set it gently across his palms.

"Ah," he said, folding his left hand over the right and pressing both, the ribbon between them, to his forehead. "Yes, Thecla... you are an extraordinary girl. An extraordinary young woman."

I laughed at him, hair falling across my back as I shook my head. "I don't know if I would say that. And even if I am, who could be extraordinary in a place like this?"

"You won't always be here...and, regardless of whether you find yourself extraordinary, the men who will love you will certainly find you such."

From the tips of my ears to the base of my spine, my skin tingled. Despite myself, I leaned forward. "Men?"

"Two…no…three. But…the other—"

The old man's eyes had shut, his expression transfiguring into a grimace.

"The other," he said, lowering his hands upon the table and rocking slightly as he spoke, "is only a man as much as a shadow is a man…as much as a male beast may be called a man. Not a man, no. A feral thing. An empty thing, masquerading as a man."

My skin crawled. What did *that* mean? "Would it—will it—hurt me?"

"Would it—yes. Will it—that depends on the others. And I see one…yes, one whose life depends on you, and who would defend you against any threat."

The old man emitted a small gasp. His pale eyes snapped open, those voids fixed unnervingly on me. Could he see, or couldn't he? It was alarming.

"Thecla," he asked, his voice soft, "don't you know?"

My brow furrowed. "Know what?"

Lapsing into silence, the man leaned back in his seat. His hands parted, the right turning down to press the ribbon to the table.

"What a lucky girl you are…one of the fated."

"The fated? Fated to what?"

"Fated to know a bond that few in this world may ever hope to understand. Fated to a connection so intense it could destroy your life—or make it new again."

"What on Earth are you talking about?"

"Give me your hand," he said, turning his right palm up again. "Let me show you."

Another flicker of hesitation; another crest of fear.

Yet, hearing such a thing, desperate to know more, I could not help but fit my hand into the fortune teller's.

When his hand snapped shut, I gasped beneath an inundation of images too clear to be called dreams, yet too visceral to be termed fantasy. The tent around the old man twisted, the colors of his face and the red tent breaking apart into new, more wild colors that assembled themselves into scene after scene.

A man—a dark-haired man who ached me even as I lost awareness of myself as a person and instead became a kind of disembodied observer. There we were in an empty garden, his red eyes blazing with intensity as we discoursed before a towering hedge.

There were his lips on mine, even though I had yet to feel a man's lips, a man's touch. All the same, there it was: true, vivid, burning in my mouth and my heart and my mind, better than I could have ever guessed a kiss would be.

Then, in the window seat of an opulent bedroom, his hands—

I jerked away from the stranger, flushed and shaking.

The fortune teller grabbed me again before I could rise.

The man again, his shadowed gaze fixed upon me, raising a gun as though to fire.

"A monster hunter," I gasped, at last managing to slip fully free of the fortune teller's grip. "Oh! A hunter—"

"And much else, besides."

Sliding back in his seat, the old man smiled.

"I wonder if he will confine his hunting to monsters when… well…" He chuckled and stroked his gray beard. "I don't care to curse it, like in your fairy tales."

I wanted to know what he had meant by this, but my mouth had barely opened when a noise from outside breached the shut flap of the tent.

The Rift siren.

Paling, I looked at the only adult nearby, then back to the flap of the tent.

"You should go," he said. "Hurry—now."

"But, your money—"

"Pay me another day," he insisted, whisking up his cane even though he didn't use it on the short, familiar trek to let me out of the tent. "Get home before the Rift opens…the future I've told you will mean nothing at all if a dharmine comes to snatch you up now."

Shuddering at such a horrific suggestion, I darted into the crowd. "Thank you! I promise, I'll pay you back soon."

The wailing siren echoing across Lescaut mimicked the frantic tones of the crowd. At the very least, it heightened them. Mothers cried out for children who had wandered off; groups of friends pushed and tripped over one another to escape the circus grounds and rush back home. All around, carnival workers put an emergency stop to their shows, shut down their games, and either put down their shutters or retreated to a booth that had them.

My hair whipping around me as the wind picked up, I peered into the eerie night sky that had begun to gather a toxic purple hue.

Dimples rising down the back of my neck, I plunged into the crowd and fought my way through.

For the most part, the evacuees were headed along the same route—but there were those who, for one reason or another, would dash erratically in the wrong direction, or slow the surge of the crowd by fighting back against it. Exiting the circus grounds, a task that should not have taken more than four or five minutes, instead took close to fifteen thanks to narrowed streets and disorganized visitors.

Add to that the fact that I was caught at the far end of the circus when the sirens took up their cries, and it should come as no surprise that the Rift had begun to swirl in right around the time I at last broke free of the crowd and into the open streets.

Though they resembled a violet mist that reduced visibility and colored the whole town, Rift Events were nothing of the sort. In truth, they were intangible intersections with another reality— the Rift. And when the Rift opened, things came through.

Dharmines were the very least of my worries, so far as I was concerned. Though legend told otherwise, my senses insisted a creature that looked like a human could be reasoned with like a human; but the proper animals, like the wild borros, or the stinging swarms of irdels? None of the vicious creatures that stumbled into our universe from the Rift could be negotiated with by any means but violence.

My heart hammered as I hurried through the streets, regretting my choice to leave home. With my every step, the event grew denser. As though the Rift became more real by the second. The hateful purple sheen that had seemed so oddly beautiful as an innocent child now mutilated the darkness and the few lamps that lit it with the insidious promise of otherworldly danger. I hastened my stride, my hair fluttering behind me as I forgot all decorum and half-ran through Lescaut.

I had more than monsters to worry about. I also had my father. Would he pull down the shutters without checking our beds? Did he know I was missing? I had to hurry or risk being locked out—locked out in the Rift, with all the things that lurked there.

My palms grew sweaty. Absurd worries crossed my mind. The window had been left open; would the closing shutter damage the pane somehow? And my ribbon! I'd left it with the fortune-teller. I had to get it back the next day.

If there would ever be a next day.

Something rattled a woodpile alongside a house I'd been about to pass.

Heart stopping, I looked around for but a moment before darting into a dark alley and permitting the shadows to be my cover—whatever good they were, when many Rift creatures were as guided by scent as were Earth's.

What had those visions meant? If they really represented the future, I was certain I would survive the night. I just had to rely on my intimate knowledge of the town. Cutting behind the clinic, I rushed through the breezeway between the homes of the Tanners and the Morgans.

And I was nearly to the other side when I heard it.

The growl was low, and ugly. Hearing it stung my ears, as if my brain tried to warn me it was a sound I shouldn't hear. As if its very frequency was somehow damaging.

I looked over my shoulder before springing into the shuttered doorway of the Morgans' home.

It was no use knocking. They would take me for a dharmine in disguise, stealing their neighbor's voice and face to gain entry under false pretense. They'd be good as dead.

Like I'd be, if I didn't find a way off the street before the lupella scuttling around into the breezeway found me.

All Rift creatures are horrible, but lupella are, to my mind, especially grotesque. It is not that they have many legs but rather that they have so many legs—more than could be counted, and in different numbers, depending upon the specimen. The dense array of limbs with which the pig-nosed entity swept the ground made me shudder, and when I picture them now they fill me with a kind of disgust.

Not as much as did the boar's tusks, gleaming almost pink in the pulsating violet of the Rift.

Though it snuffled along the ground, I had the distinct sense it was searching for me and not some paltry cache of old garbage or unlocked vegetable patches. Every scrape of its tusks along the cobblestones hastened my breath.

And not just that. The sharp, grating sounds it produced drew my attention to the insidious pulses of a headache I should have known to be coming on.

Most human individuals, unlike altered beings, were not sensitive to Rift exposure. There were others, however, generally pregnant women and the infirm, for whom any and all Rift exposure could bring on a number of illnesses. I was one of the so-called lucky ones, although whatever was wrong with me, neither my father nor the doctor to which he brought me could say just what it was. The effects were mild—if a splitting headache that arced across my temples and seemed sometimes to strike me blind could be called 'mild'—and my father and I had come to regard the condition as something like an allergy. Unpleasant, but generally benign as long as I avoided prolonged exposure to the Rift.

Now, though, it was a serious detriment. I shut my eyes for a few moments, yet that seemed to make the migraine worse. It pounded mostly on the right today, which frightened me because that was the direction in which the lupella snuffled, and I suspected that soon I would struggle to see on that side. Did it have my scent? Should I duck out and run while I still had a chance?

In the distance, a garbage can rattled with its upending. The lupella grunted eagerly, its multitude of legs beating out a skin-crawling patter that was more like a unified murmur around it. It rushed away, eager for an easy meal.

I waited until it was out of sight before I darted from the doorway and along the path home.

I hadn't been exposed to the Rift so long in years, let alone by myself. My father religiously followed the RMS's readings, government guidelines, and our house's largely hand-engineered security system. Every day, he announced whether it was safe for us to leave, and for how long. We took advantage of every beautiful day we had, and if an unexpected Rift Event did manage to make its presence felt, Father always knew where the nearest shelter was.

He went to great lengths to give us rich lives that were still safe from the Rift, and because of that, I did not know what would happen to me if I spent too long in its chthonic atmosphere. Whatever it did to me, it surely wouldn't be as bad as the effects experienced by those unlucky altered hunters, but—

"Thecla!"

My heart sped along with my feet, that familiar silhouette in the violet darkness ahead at last emerging through the aura of my headache. I cried out, unaware of how sweaty my palms were until I threw myself in my father's arms and gripped his jacket.

"I'm sorry," I gasped while he held me, his bristly face buried in my hair and his body wracked by a sob of relief. "Oh, Papa, I'm sorry!"

"I'm just so glad I found you. Don't you know what would happen to this family, to me, if you—"

His arms tightened around me with his sharp exhalation, his question answered by his own lips. "No. Of course not. You could never know. Thecla—"

A row of houses away echoed with the snarls of fighting

animals. I started in my father's arms and swore even he braced against the noise.

"Come on," he urged me, wrapping one arm around my back while still wielding a simple pipe with the other. "Let's hurry home. We'll talk more tomorrow."

And we did talk more, rest assured. After arriving home without incident; after waking up the next day; after my stepmother woke up an hour or so later; and even before, to my surprise, we were permitted at last to attend the circus.

"There's no point in punishing Sable," my father said. "And, anyway, I think what you went through last night was punishment enough...don't you?"

He was always gentle with me, my father. Always kind. I made sure to bring my money when we went to the circus, and since I knew he wouldn't be keen on me wandering away, I asked when we arrived, "Can we go settle my debt with someone?"

His brow arched. My stepmother, her hand around Sable's, laughed. "What kind of a time did you have yesterday, young lady?"

I wanted to laugh, but the residual effects of the headache were still hanging on to my skull. "I had my fortune told"—my stepmother's laughter was punctuated by a noise of disgust I strove to ignore, knowing it was so much more than parlor tricks and mirrors—"and the man told me to hurry out of the circus before I paid him...I want to make sure I give him what I owe."

Whatever he thought about the fortune-telling aspect of things, my father approved of my honesty. "All right," he said with a nod and a stroke of his short beard. "Let's you and I go. Sable, why don't you tell Mama about that show you wanted to see earlier...see if you can figure out what she's talking about—"

While Sable, excitable as ever, launched into a rambling explanation of some exhibition her friends had told her all about, Father and I made our way through the crowd. Between the Rift Event the day prior and the circus entering its final day, the attendance was not what it had been during my solitary trip. Even so, that feeling of levity brightened the air and my heart. I was still shaken from the night before, yet I had passed through the ordeal and felt somehow stronger for it. I had proved to myself I could survive one small thing.

But, brave as I felt, the empty ground where once stood the mentalist's tent turned my guts icy with fear.

"Are you sure it was here?"

"I'm sure," I protested with a rapid glance around. Up and down the row of tents, stands, wagons and stages, I saw nothing resembling the small red booth that hosted our consultation. "Yes, I'm sure it was."

"Well, maybe he moved. Come on, sweetheart—let's look around and see if we can find him."

But I knew that we couldn't.

And I was right. We didn't. We searched the circus with one eye open, my father taking in the sights and sounds and more happily reuniting with the rest of our family than I did.

I was busy looking, listening, wondering. That fortune-teller, the things he showed me—all that had been real, hadn't it?

Maybe not. Maybe I dreamed it.

"Smile, honey," my father said to me with a brush of his knuckle against my cheek, drawing me from my thoughts while the contortionist on stage wowed the crowd to outrageous applause. "The circus only comes once a year. Let yesterday stay in the past."

And I wish that I could. But I think of that visit to the circus so often—and not just because of the fortune teller. Rather, I think of it often because it was our last.

Seven months later, my father was dead of blood sickness brought on by a dharmine, and we were three women alone.

AT THE TIME that everything happened, I did not understand my stepmother's motivations. I thought she was incredibly cruel. My father hadn't told me anything before his death, so I simply didn't know.

I would like to think that, if his illness hadn't been so sudden, he might have told me the truth by his own lips; but, inside my heart, I know he would have left it all buried until the very last minute. Out of denial, hope, or some other misguided motivation, nothing but absolute necessity could have prised the truth from his lips.

After all—he didn't even tell my stepmother the whole truth. Just enough to prepare her for the dangers our household would face after his death, if the right precautions were not taken.

"You'll have to start working," she told me three days after the funeral.

"And do what? I have no skills!"

"That's not true at all." Her head reflexively craned toward my father's chair as though to consult him. She stopped midway to the tight purse of her lips, the memory of death distancing her eye.

"Your father," she continued, righting her gaze to me, "taught you writing, reading, and arithmetic, didn't he?"

Reluctantly, I nodded along with her rhetorical question and fought back the stinging of my throat, my eyes.

"That's plenty. If you can do those things, there's no question you can grow skilled enough at weaving to help support the household. The Parson Textile Emporium has already agreed to take you on; Madame Parson is training you herself, so don't act miserable about it."

And that was all there was to it. The matter was indisputable. With the death of my father, my stepmother needed every coin she could get to maintain the household and raise my younger sister. I obeyed her because I had no choice in the matter, though there was a hefty sickness lying deep within me every day I roused to work. Madame Parson was quite pleasant, and all the old ladies who worked with her treated me with kindness, yet every day seemed bleaker than the last.

Was this all I was to be? With my father dead and my education over, would there be no more warmth? No more tenderness to enrich and engage me with life? Every day for the rest of my life, nothing but the clack and clatter of the loom as I swept the shuttle back and forth—nothing but the feeling of tension in my diaphragm as true destitution slavered dangerously at my heels. Worse, I quite enjoyed weaving, or at least I found I enjoyed the way my imagination might boundlessly sore off into some other place while I fell into the rhythm of the work, but the textiles I was tasked to produce were as uninspiring as my wages.

Perhaps I was truly the lost cause my stepmother found me to be. Frankly, I did not blame her. I was an orphan; I stayed in her household by her generosity only.

And that generosity reached its limit when the first red envelope slipped beneath our door.

I paid it hardly any mind but to notice the peculiar color of the paper, which must have been expensive. Only later, when I came down the stairs to find my white-faced stepmother scanning the lines with pinpoint pupils, did unease drape over me like a shroud.

"Is everything all right?"

"Oh—yes—"

Snapping shut the paper, a curious stationary of cream with a red border, my stepmother leaned forward in her seat and self-consciously lay her forearm across both letter and envelope.

"Thecla, would you do me a favor and run to the market before it closes? I just realized I don't have anything for dinner tonight. Go take some of my money from the chest in my room, get a duck. Don't you feel like something special?"

I didn't, not really; but a nice duck did have a way of breaking things up, especially since we'd had to miss out on the circus for the first time I knew. That night, we ate and laughed, and my stepmother had wine, and it was the most normal I had felt since my father's booming presence suddenly left the house so empty.

And it was, somehow, so empty. Even with the three of us, it was changed—and exposed. As one of the preeminent repairmen in Lescaut, he had spent many of his days maintaining our security and monitoring Rift activity; now that was left to my stepmother and me, and after a long day of weaving in the textile plant that represented one of Lescaut's best and only options for my employment as a teenaged girl, I often came home to spend an hour or more troubleshooting battery packs, testing shutters and studying RMS forecasts. I watched over our house as a sleepless hound watched the flock through a night of borro howls.

Which is what made it all the more surprising when my stepmother sat down with me once my sister was in bed.

"Sable's nearly twelve," my stepmother lamented. "I can't believe it. And look at you—not long now, and you'll be seventeen. Do you have any boyfriends?"

I laughed and shook my head, although the same dark-haired man that had plagued my thoughts since the fortune-teller's performance somehow managed to slither into my mind.

"Maybe that's good," she went on to say quickly, looking as though she spoke mostly to herself. Her hands stretched across the kitchen table to take mine. "You've been through so much, Thecla. I'm sorry."

I lowered my head, studying my hand in hers. Would this feel more natural if it were my real mother? I always wondered.

"I try not to think on it too much," I told her. "I want to be a part of the world and feel joy instead of going inside of myself and stoking pity."

Something in her face cautiously brightened. "That's good. I'm glad to hear you say that. Because—Thecla…I think it might be time for you to move out on your own."

The words bolted through me in a shock that straightened me upright. I pulled my hand from hers. "What do you mean?"

"Well, you're making your own money now—and I could use the help, but it would be easier if it were just Sable and me.

Besides…the Leftner family has a spare room over their shop. I'm sure they'd rent it to you cheaply."

A vague sense of illness combated with a kind of excitement. "But how am I to pay for my own things when I'm helping you?"

"You wouldn't anymore. It would be all your money, Thecla—I just think it's best for everyone. For you, and for Sable."

And for my stepmother, too. With two girls hanging around, one almost grown, she wouldn't have a prayer of remarrying. With just one, she almost stood a chance. I tried not to think bitter thoughts, but in that instant I was so blindsided I couldn't help it.

"Are you all right? Thecla?"

Yet—the lure of freedom was too enticing to deny. The idea of living on my own, even if in a little loft, possessed the same seductive qualities as did my memories of wandering the circus alone for that first and only time. Besides…the Leftners' trade was bookbinding. Perhaps, if I wasn't a bother, they might let me do some reading in the evenings.

"Can you come with me to speak to the Leftners tomorrow," I asked her.

Relief eased her features into a broad smile. "Of course," she said with an encouraging pat of my hand. "Of course, Thecla—anything I can do to help."

And, to her credit, she did. She helped me acquire the place at a reasonable rate from Madame Leftner, whom I had known for most of my life to be something of a miser. The discount meant everything, and because of it I was pleasantly surprised at my ability to survive on my own. Granted, I did not exactly thrive—I ate two meals a day and still slept on my old half-bed, moved from my childhood home to this pale, empty imitation of it.

All the same, I *did* eat, and manage to clothe myself, and I even occasionally scrounged up the coins to enjoy a hot meal at one of the town's taverns. When I was eighteen, I met a boy— nothing like the dream man prophesied to me, but nonetheless more accessible. Our relationship was fumbling and brief, yet I got from it the sense that I was a desirable woman—or could be, if I would ease into the confidence of it.

And of course, at least once a month, I returned home to visit with my sister and stepmother.

Despite the shock of being ejected from my home, I truly made the most of it. Before I knew it, seven years had passed. I began to tell myself that perhaps weaving for someone else's business for the rest of my life would be tolerable, so long as I was healthy and able to find a suitable man from somewhere within our cramped village. Madame Parson sold her textile plant to a wealthy entrepreneur from Karris, and he installed machines that made weaving infinitely easier, faster, almost automated, so that each day seemed to breeze by and leave much time for chatter— though, I confess, I missed the loom at once.

It had taken several years, but I had recovered from my father's death in a truly meaningful way, and I was a woman on my own two feet.

Then, the next red envelope arrived.

This time, it was sent to me.

NORMALLY, I WOULD reproduce the letter in whole right away. Yet, to permit the reader to absorb it now would permit them an unfair advantage over my twenty-four-year-old self.

The truth was, even after reading every word twice from start to finish, I could make neither head nor tail of the thing. It was all strange nonsense. There was something in it about my father, mentioning him by name; and something else about a contractual agreement; and it was certainly addressed to me, Thecla of Lescaut, Daughter of Rigel of Lescaut.

But the nature of the contract was so outrageous that I just couldn't parse the meaning of the message.

More confusing still…it referred to me with a kind of casual intimacy as, of all things, a riftborn.

There had to be some mistake.

My brows knitting and unknitting, I examined the paper and the envelope in which it had come. Everything was, now that I had it up close, of a finer quality than ever I had beheld. The smooth paper had the hallmarks of disposable wealth, and the hand in which the letter had been written was so immaculate I would have taken it to be a woman's had not it been signed in the most outrageous flourish of all.

I read the signature lines a final time.

Territory Master Malin Farrow

Territory Master—*the* Malin Farrow? The ruler of Gudrune? A man so dangerous that the Overseer had once tried to uninstall him from his position, and had instead been embarrassed into not just retreating but awarding him an additional stretch of territory in what was now referred to as "The Expansion?" The man notorious for leaving impaled enemies on display during wartime and publicly executing traitors in the modern city streets? Rumors flew about him—that he killed women for pleasure, or had eaten human flesh during the war. I had even heard from some busybodies that he was a dharmine, though that was ridiculous for any number of reasons.

This letter was ridiculous, too.

This had to be some ruse. I set the letter down and studied the seal of golden wax I had broken upon the opening of the envelope. Carefully aligning the greater whole to the dissevered edge, I bent in my little apartment to squint at the sigil.

That notorious serpent, its coils winding beneath the eight petals of an open rose.

I leaned back in my creaking chair, releasing my breath in a stunned hiss.

The territory master? Truly? It seemed unfathomable that he should contact me. Why? I had never seen his face, outside of a grainy picture taken years before my birth and published in a history book my father had used to teach me. And I was supposed to believe he was writing to me, in his own hand? That he even knew I existed?

I was sure of it. This had to be some scheme to wring me dry for what few coins I had…somehow.

Yet, I could not help but read the letter again, one final time. I lifted it, eyes setting on the first line, but I hesitated when the rich aroma of warm sandalwood plumed from the paper to sweeten my head. Strangely drunk on it, I gave the bizarre query one final read-through.

DECEMBER 14th, 4083
Dear Thecla,

The task has been more difficult than I would have expected, but it would seem we have found you at last. Per the terms of our contract, in the event of your father's death, I was to accept you as my ward. I will make the charitable assumption that his demise arrived too abruptly for notice to be sent to my office.

As an unregistered riftborn, you surely understand the debt you owe in exchange for my generosity. Now that we have made contact, please do not delay in coming with Charlotte to speak to me in person. We have much to discuss regarding the terms of my stewardship, and trust me when I say the life you leave behind pales in comparison to what could await you.

I by no means wish to threaten you, but I hope you understand the only alternative to fulfilling your father's contract is the enforcement of those laws I am obliged to oversee; and, as an unregistered riftborn, the law is structured against you quite harshly. Please think carefully, for the sake of your future—and your sister's.

Signed,
Master Malin Farrow
Gudrune Territory

Absolute nonsense, in the truest meaning of the word.

No matter how many times I read the thing, I could make no sense of it. I gave up and shook my head, stuffing the letter back into the envelope with an uneasy laugh.

Whoever had gone to the trouble of orchestrating this, it was quite a *lot* of trouble. Learning my dead father's name, duplicating the seal—

Why, even sending multiple letters over a period of several years.

That was right. With the restuffed envelope in my hand, I remembered my stepmother's ashen features while she scanned a similar missive.

Perhaps some lout had gotten his hands on the census records of the village. I'd heard of stranger things happening, certainly. Shaking my head, I pulled on my shawl and bonnet while checking the RMS's digital read-out. A 60% chance of a Rift Event, dangerous but not deadly—a hundred percent chance of snow, though. I glanced at the window with a derisive little sniff, not needing a machine to tell me that, and made my way out into the windy street of my village.

I wish it hadn't snowed that day! Between the bracing wind that stung my eyes and my preoccupation with the silly letter, I hardly saw a stone of my dear hometown. If I had known then what I knew now—that it would be the last I saw of Lescaut for a very, very long time—I would have held my eyes wide against the precipitation and absorbed every detail, down to the cracks beginning to fill along the cobblestones. I would have kissed the buildings and stopped one by one to embrace my friends and acquaintances.

Instead, I was so distracted I didn't notice the carriage until my hand was practically upon our gate.

It, along with its autohorse, was parked near the end of the block—near the spot I could not see without remembering the bright fanfare of the circus spilling around the corner. Now there was just the snow, and the wind, and this queerly expensive carriage demeaning itself in my family's impoverished little neighborhood.

I ogled the gold accents against its black surface for but a few seconds before, shaking myself free of the spell, I proceeded into my father's—no, my stepmother's—house with only a cursory knock upon its unlocked front door.

"Hello, Mama, hi, Sable! You'll never believe this letter I—"

My hand on the knob, I froze in place.

At the small table in the cabin's main room, a woman I did not recognize rose from her seat.

My stepmother, looking as pale as she did the day that first letter came, (pale—if not green!), regarded me with eyes ringed in obvious terror. Eyes that had been weeping.

Just as I caught a glance of Sable, shell-shocked on the stairs where she had eavesdropped until my arrival, the unfamiliar woman turned an arched brow upon my stepmother.

"Ran away, did she?"

My stepmother said nothing, wringing a kitchen towel between her hands. As I crossed to them, removing the bonnet from my head, I realized how much her fingers had changed over the past seven years—as though the stress of losing my father finally, at long last, began the aging process in her.

I felt myself aging similarly as I asked, "What is this about? Who are you?"

How breathtaking she was! I'd never seen anyone in such finely produced clothes, the slight flare of her black gown beneath her cloak contributing to a figure I'd seen in drawings but never

Lescaut. With a sly smile, this strange woman said, "I don't suppose you remember me, do you?"

I shook my head. Her red lips widened, flashing white teeth behind.

"Of course not…no one ever does. Even so, Thecla, it's a pleasure to meet you again."

While she curtseyed to me, I curtseyed back and said, allowing my confusion to sound in my voice, "Would you remind me where we've met before?"

"At your birth," said the woman.

"This is the woman who midwifed for your mother," said my stepmother hoarsely. "Charlotte."

The name sprang out at me from that bizarre letter.

I fell back a step, my hand raising before me as though to protect me from an assault.

"You remember me now, don't you?"

"From this," I said, raising the red envelope in my hand. "But—what is—"

"Did you read it?" When I nodded, she gestured at it and said, "Then you already know, don't you?"

"But, this must be some mistake. Isn't it?" I looked at my stepmother, laughing a little. "This is clearly meant for somebody else."

Charlotte's immaculate eyebrows contorted above her flashing green eyes. "Was it not addressed to you?"

"Yes, but—"

"Then where's the error?"

"Because I'm not a riftborn, of course!" Laughing at the absurdity, I snatched the letter from the envelope and flung it open. "Look—it calls me that at least two times, but that's ridiculous."

No one else was laughing, though. I realized that when I looked up to see my stepmother regarding me through watering, still frightened eyes. Charlotte, her glamorous yet stern features fixed upon me, did not even crack a smile.

Lowering the letter I had hoped to be my defense, I asked in an increasingly weak tone of voice, "If I were riftborn...wouldn't I know?"

New understanding in her features, Charlotte said with lips that strained against a frown, "Not if no one told you, of course."

My mouth opened, but no sound came out.

I looked desperately to my stepmother, who lowered her eyes from mine on the instant of contact.

As a voice in my head rose to a kind of frightened scream, I once again consulted the letter that fluttered in my trembling hand.

"But—but—if I were riftborn—I'd have powers, then, wouldn't I? Something strange about me—"

"Not all riftborn abilities are immediately apparent, and some are too subtle to notice without long-term observation."

My throat was so unbelievably dry that I felt like I was being strangled. "Observation in a lab," I managed to whisper out.

Nostrils flaring, Charlotte nodded one time. The motion did not so much as threaten the immaculate bundle of dark red curls that had been pinned high and crowned with an artful black fascinator.

"For many riftborn, that's true. You, however...are a very fortunate young woman, Thecla."

Charlotte's eyes narrowed. She prowled toward me, the short heels of her boots clicking ominously upon the innocent floor of my childhood home.

"And now that I see you in person, a grown woman…I think even among the lucky in the world, you can expect to be blessed. Wouldn't you like to meet Master Farrow?"

My stepmother had shielded her brow with her hand. I did not bother looking at her anymore. Instead, I forced myself to meet the predatory eyes of the beautiful woman who now stood perhaps three feet from me.

"Do I have a choice?"

There it was again; the slight dimpling at the corner of her lips as she repressed a frown. Even without the movement of her mouth, some strange sense of pity seemed to flash through her eyes and be gone.

"No," she said. "In truth, no, you don't. If you refuse today—well. I'm sure I don't have to say what's going to happen."

At my shaky exhalation, my stepmother burst into a girlish sob. Even when she wept at my father's death, I had never heard her sound this way. Throwing herself up from the table, she crossed to me and took my hands in her trembling ones.

The letter fell to the floor while we held each other as we never had.

"If you come now," Charlotte went on without outward show of emotion for our embrace, "and you do it without a fuss, I can guarantee that Master will forgive your stepmother's indiscretions. It will all be forgotten, and everyone may move on in peace."

Indiscretions, plural. How many times had the territory master's servants come beating down the door in search of me? How many times had she been forced to lie to the faces of very dangerous people?

How long had she nursed my father's secret to protect me from the knowledge of my fate?

Thecla…don't you know?

The fortune-teller had been right. I'd had no idea of my identity. But, as my stepmother relaxed her embrace and drew me down into the couch, I was startled to realize how hard my family had worked to keep it that way.

"Your parents moved to Lescaut when your mother was already carrying you," she began, drying her tears with that thin little towel and composing herself against her sorrow. "They were very nice people, everyone could tell, but your mother was—sickly. Very sickly with you. I hardly ever saw her…and what I know of that day, I know from your father's lips and not by my own eyes."

"I'm sure I can fill in the gaps," said Charlotte, earning a spiteful glance from me as my stepmother continued.

"From what I understand—the night before you were born, a prolonged Rift Event had been forecast. It began just after her water broke and didn't end until more than twenty-four hours later."

Feeling the blood drain from my face, I whispered, "Why didn't I know this?"

"Because—because—"

My stepmother couldn't bring herself to say it and lapsed into silence, her fist pressed against her lips. Charlotte spoke up instead, drawing our attention—and the attention of Sable, who had descended the stairs and now openly stood upon the landing. I opened my arms to her, accepting her as she dashed into my embrace, while the woman explained.

"Your case was pursued very closely, Thecla. Since your mother was an altered—"

I looked up at Charlotte so sharply that she took all she needed to know from my features alone. Those eyebrows of hers lifted so high I might have laughed on another day.

"What experts on communication you all are," she observed with a wry look at my stepmother.

"Can you blame us?" Insulted, my stepmother straightened up and hammered her fist, bunched tea towel and all, down upon her knee. "What family wants to tell their daughter that she's been bargained off?"

"Bargained," I repeated, dumbstruck.

"That's a crass way of putting it." Charlotte's tone was clipped. "Most parents with a child like Thecla would consider themselves lucky to have her for six hours, let alone eighteen years. Second-generation altered, when they're detected, anyway, are always at least earmarked for potential research subjects—but an altered riftborn?"

She scoffed at the absurdity of it, waiting for the same millisecond I had earlier for someone else to join her in her laugh. Seeing we all stared at her in cold impatience, her half-smile disappeared to leave behind her more robotic facade.

"Such children are too rare and valuable to be left with their parents in most jurisdictions," she summarized colorlessly. "If you were not a citizen of Gudrune—if I had not been the midwife assigned to your case when the doctor tending the birth reported a Rift Event—you *would* have grown up in a laboratory somewhere, Thecla. And you would very likely be dead."

"And now, instead?"

She regarded me with a kind of feline intensity. The sort I have seen cats reserve for a houseguest it has never met—or a small animal it is not sure it can kill, despite its urge to.

"And now," she answered, "we shall see. The agreement between Master Farrow and your father was not with the intention of any specific use. It was simply established that, on your eighteenth birthday, Master Farrow would take custody of you in exchange for permitting you to remain free until that time."

"Why would he do that?"

Drawing a pair of black leather gloves from the pocket of her coat, she said, "Because your father had just lost his wife, and it seemed unreasonably cruel to separate the two of you at the time," in a way that told me it was not even a quarter of the truth. Perhaps that was what moved Charlotte to represent my father in a suitable fashion, but that was not why the territory master had agreed to the arrangement.

While I wondered over the mysteriousness of it all, Sable tearfully looked up from where she'd rested her head upon my shoulder. Would she be as changed by this night as I was by our father's death?

"Please," she begged Charlotte, "don't let him hurt my sister. Don't experiment on her, please, don't."

At last, a frown slipped through Charlotte's cultivated features. Flexing her hand within her glove, she folded her fingers before her waist and seemed to speak to me as much as she did to my sister.

"I am quite sure that Master Farrow would prefer to keep such a rare specimen for himself, although I cannot guarantee anything, of course. Still…I have the feeling he will find something for her to do around his manor."

The tone she used was very strange, as was the look that crossed my stepmother's face to hear it. Charlotte did not feel the need to elaborate, however, and lowered her eyes as she swept toward the door.

"I'll wait for you in the carriage down the street. If you decide to go anywhere else, I'll see you."

"I can't even take my things from my apartment?"

"What do you have? Clothes? Heirlooms?"

Hesitating, I said, "Heirlooms, no, but I do have a few dresses and books."

"Rare books?"

I wished I could lie beneath that intense stare, but I couldn't. I shook my head.

Charlotte turned away, though I caught the edge of something like a smile. "Well. If you can focus well enough to read, I happened to bring one of my own…you're welcome to it in the carriage, and there are plenty more in the master's home. As to clothes…let's not worry about those until we're back safe and sound."

She tapped the RMS meter by the door, drawing our attention to the change it had made at the turning of the hour. The chances now stood at 65%.

"I'll let you say good-bye, but try not to take too long."

Charlotte let herself out, the bracing wind howling through the door until she slammed it shut behind her.

As it closed, my stepmother, Sable and I all burst into tears. We rapidly and furiously embraced one another amid profuse apologies for old slights and omissions, but I would not let my stepmother apologize for keeping the truth from me.

"It's better this way," I said between hiccups. "I'm glad—I'm glad I never knew this day was coming, and that I was able to—to just be a part of our family."

This worsened her weeping when I said it out loud, but it had the strange effect of stilling my own tears. Squeezing her hand, then turning to kiss Sable, I rose and pulled my shawl tight around me.

"I have to go. Please tell the Leftners good-bye, and thank them for the apartment for me. And apologize for the short notice, of course. Oh—"

Sable sprang up to hug me again. "Run away," she urged.

But I shook my head.

"It's not so bad, is it? Working in the territory master's mansion."

"Please," my stepmother begged. "Be careful, and write to us if you can. I've heard things—be careful."

My face numb with a strange combination of fear and thrill, I tied on my bonnet and turned away from my last family members.

"I promise, I'll write to you somehow. Oh—good-bye!" Tears overflowed my eyes again and I found myself rushing for the door, unable to delay another second lest I die of heartbreak. "Good-bye, I love you both so much—"

They called after me as I burst into the snow, but I didn't hear what it was they said. I only knew there was love in it, and it overwhelmed me utterly. Wracked with a sob, I made it two steps away from the familiar little door before my body nearly collapsed. I staggered, one hand over my mouth, and stood there trying to catch my breath. Trying not to weep hideously before the woman waiting beside the carriage down the street.

After a few vertiginous seconds, I composed myself and made my slightly steadier way through the gate. My hand rested upon that comforting wood longer than it ever had.

Of all absurd things, I found myself whispering, "Thank you," to the house as I left it for that last time.

Jaw set, anticipation and fury battling in my heart, I wiped my face with the back of my hand and marched down to Charlotte.

"There's somewhere I'd like to stop," I half-demanded before she opened her mouth, only remembering to tack on, "Please," when I reminded myself who she worked for.

As she had at my birth, she proved not unreasonable.

We stopped at the cemetery on the way out of town, and I said good-bye to my father, and I thanked him for protecting me.

While the ravens answered on his behalf, I returned to my seat in the carriage and watched with a heavy heart as Lescaut disappeared behind us.

CHARLOTTE HAD BEEN right, of course. As emotional as I was, reading was impossible. My mind buzzed with ill-informed future predictions that struggled for attention with strange snippets of my past.

In the broader sense, my father's reluctance to speak about my mother now made sense. How had she been altered? I asked Charlotte after I could no longer endure the absolute silence of our steadily rocking carriage.

"I believe she was spliced with ventil DNA," my chaperone answered, "but don't cite me, please. It was a long time ago, and I didn't think to check any files before coming to get you."

"Ventil—those are the benign ones that are like deer, aren't they? Did she have antlers?"

Charlotte nodded. "When I arrived, she was unconscious, dying. She had no control over her appearance anymore."

I shuddered, the scene of my birth now taking a wholly different form in my mind. Strange to think that, in all this time, I had thought I had never been in the presence of an altered person! They were generally soldiers under contract with various levels of government; if not, they tended to be mercenaries serving similar purposes in private sectors. I had never heard of one retiring alive, let alone having a child.

"Was she a soldier of some kind?"

"I don't know," answered Charlotte, peering out the window and across the snowy mountains through which our carriage navigated. "As I said, I personally know little about you or your family. I only know that your father cared about you very much, and that you should be very grateful to Master Farrow when you meet him."

"What is he like?"

"Peculiar," she said without turning away from the window. "But then again, all rich men are."

"Have you worked for many?"

"Just him."

She was so closed-lipped—so difficult to speak with. "Are you still a midwife? It sounds like you work closely with Master Farrow now."

"I have since retired from that line, you are correct. We always worked closely together, and when he invited me to come aboard his staff, I accepted."

Nothing further uttered from her lips. Annoyed by her lack of voluntary conversation, I sank back into my seat and let my gaze unfix through my own window.

Now that we were more than an hour away from Lescaut, it felt I had escaped some sort of gravitational field. The sorrow left me, my body instead vibrating with intrigue I had never felt.

So *this* was how I left my village.

In the depths of my heart, through every tedious day of weaving and every long night of shivering over books in my cold little apartment, I nursed the spark of hope that the strange man from the circus had given me. I would not always be there, he had said. Not always in Lescaut. But the mystery of how I would accomplish such a thing seemed insurmountable; and perhaps, in another person's life, it might have been.

Charlotte was right. I was extremely lucky, in my own unlucky way. That same ill star that portended the death of my mother also guaranteed me this.

As though my father had bargained with the devil.

Shuddering, I folded my arms across my chest and tried to sleep; but my heart hammered relentlessly in my ears, and my mind would not stop rushing through my childhood in search of all the little clues it had missed.

In truth, there weren't many—but the one matter I kept coming back to was the one of my allergy.

"I've heard it said"—I once more broke the silence of the carriage and stirred Charlotte from the beginnings of a doze, earning an irritated look from the corner of her eye—"that the altered can only withstand the Rift for so long before they are overwhelmed by the monstrous part of their DNA and lose their humanity altogether."

"That is correct."

"Yet I have been exposed to the Rift, and the only ill effects I've noticed are a headache. Violent against me, perhaps—but I have never felt the urge to do harm to others during a Rift Event, for instance."

"I'm not so sure you would feel it in such a way, per se. You would be better off asking Eleison about that. That said, second generation altered are much more stable than their parents. Their genetics are more stable, at least. Their lives—I'll just say again, not all are as fortunate as you."

"So it would seem. Does all this mean"—she had begun to close her eyes and forced them open again, obviously trying not to exhibit the annoyance she felt—"that there's some kind of... power inside of me? What does it mean, to be altered and riftborn at once?"

"It means you had better stay in Master's good graces and keep as close to him as you can," said Charlotte honestly, much to my alarm. "If he decides you're of no benefit to him, you may end up in the possession of someone who will not treat you as kindly."

"But I've heard Master Farrow is cruel."

"The best rulers are cruel and kind, each as the situation requires. See to it that you earn his kindness."

"How much longer until we're there?"

"At this rate? Twelve hours."

I groaned in misery at the thought. Charlotte chuckled, her eyes closing definitively this time.

"Now you see why I was so eager to leave," she told me, settling in for any sleep she could get.

How I tried to follow suit! I willed the landscape whirling past to hypnotize me into slumber; but on and on, my thoughts flew with fright. What use could I be to a territory master? How would I survive in a world that, all this time, had considered me a fugitive? Me, an unregistered riftborn! A second generation altered!

An altered, at all.

I shuddered at the thought. As reviled as riftborn were,

altered were similarly taboo, albeit more respectable. The battle that they waged against their monstrous inner mind was considered a sacrifice made in the service of humanity, although some very hardline monster hunters didn't see them that way.

I did, though. I was glad now that I had never bought into the myth of altered beings as anything less or more than human; I would have struggled with news of my identity much more than I already was.

Still, I was afraid. Altered required a chemical compound after Rift exposure—sometimes even during, depending on the scale of the Event and how acute their sensitivity to the Rift had become.

Never in my life had I taken the drug. Did that mean I was dangerous? Would prolonged exposure to a few more Rift Events be sufficient to make me forget my human identity altogether?

When I did fall asleep, nightmares plagued me. I dreamed of a woman giving birth, screaming as the antlers of her baby tore her womb open on delivery. The blood in the air filled my disembodied mouth with a copper tang, and soon that copper tang was medicine. A lab—they had me in a lab, suspended in a tank of blue fluid while scientists around me took down notes.

My mouth opened to scream, but I couldn't make the sound come out.

"Thecla"—Charlotte's hand landed upon my shoulder to snap me, disoriented, from the hateful sequence of nightmares— "Thecla, you're dreaming."

"Oh—"

Gasping awake, I jerked upright and rubbed my face.

The carriage rocked on around us, the darkness outside a thick and uncanny kind.

We rode on all night, the autohorse dutifully pulling its passengers without need for rest. When Charlotte found out I hadn't eaten dinner, we stopped to eat a picnic in the back of the carriage. Parked on the overlook on the edge of a mountain road, I could just identify a white peak through the early morning dark.

Although my traveling companion was not overly talkative, I had begun to view my situation with some optimism when the alarm rang out.

Exhaling slowly, Charlotte drew a pocket watch from her waist and snapped it open. The digital readout glowed pink, its display flashing with white letters.

RIFT EVENT IMMINENT

My stomach and limbs went cold while Charlotte snapped the watch shut again.

"Is there someplace we can stop?"

"We're two hours from the manor," she said, her eyes shut with irritation as though she spoke not to me but to some deity. "Two hours—no, Thecla, we won't stop."

Leaning down toward the empty seat opposite us, Charlotte opened the compartment that, beneath our seat, had housed the picnic basket full of grapes, sandwiches and tarts.

This compartment, however, held a rifle she casually assembled while thinking out loud.

"As long as the autohorse doesn't encounter a problem, we should make it…but let's not take any chances."

After inspecting the gun, she rested it back in the crook of her arm and once again flipped open her watch. "Call Eleison," she told it, the name ringing familiarly in my ears.

"You mentioned him before."

"He's Master Farrow's lieutenant, as it were. Part valet, part guard, the most formidable fighter I know—"

"Charlotte."

The call had been answered, and the voice on the other side was low and warm—somehow rumbling. Never had a man's voice been so pleasing to me. While I flushed, this Eleison continued, "I just got the alert. Where are you?"

"The girl and I are two hours away," she said over my snort to be addressed as 'the girl.' "Do you think you can meet us halfway and escort us back to safety?"

"Can do—I'll hit the road now. Stay safe until we rendezvous."

"We'll try," Charlotte replied ominously, shutting the watch again. Then, to me: "Can you fire a gun?"

Pale, I shook my head. She sighed and glanced down at her weapon.

"If something happens, stick close to me. You don't want to get lost here during a Rift Event. If the monsters don't kill you, the wilderness will."

Mouth dry, I squeaked out, "Okay."

She patted my hand, but offered no more comfort than that.

The Event did not begin for fifteen minutes.

Until then, the carriage was frighteningly quiet. I sat stock straight, my stomach tight as a drawn bowstring, my eyes fixed on the road through the front window of the carriage. My palms, pinched into fists on my knees, sweated with this new uncertainty.

What would happen? What would happen to me if I was exposed to the Rift for longer this time?

By the time the first crackling signs of violet stormed in the clouds above us, my heart had settled firmly in my mouth.

Charlotte used an interface on her device to close the carriage's shutters, leaving us blind to potential dangers by any means but the feed from the horse's electronic eyes as it played out dutifully on the pocket watch.

I eyed the rifle in Charlotte's other arm, letting out a strange sort of wheezing breath as I asked, "How long have you been shooting?"

She flicked me a glance, then refocused her attention. "A long time."

"When was the last time you used that?"

"Last month."

Her tone was distracted, her gaze focused on the little screen. I watched with her, my body primed for action it could not take within the confines of that little car.

Whoever Eleison was, I prayed that he would hurry.

Once the Rift split open across the sky and the entirety of the camera feed had been transformed from pre-dawn navy blue to that sinister violet that colored all our nightmares, I braced for the worst. Any moment, our carriage would be descended upon by foul harpros, their talons already bloody from whatever kill they'd left for their perceived larger prey; that, or a giganturn would come shuffling through the trees and knock us over with a wave of its fist.

In the end, though, the culprits were less exotic than that, and they did not appear for forty-five minutes.

We were so close to our escort. "Any minute now, we'll meet up with Eleison," Charlotte said to me as the baleful howls begin. "Don't worry. How are you feeling?"

"I'm fine." My hand swept over my forehead. "Usually, as long as I can stay behind shutters, I don't have any trouble."

"Well—"

Her mouth contorted to the side, her eyes fixed on the pocket watch screen. My stomach churned at the black shapes darting through the trees, though they were difficult to distinguish through the horse's eyes until a few had gone by.

"I apologize in advance for what I have to do."

I swallowed down my fear, nodding as a borro darted across the road ahead of us.

"Whatever you have to do to keep us safe," I said, the words rasping with my fright.

She patted my hand without looking up.

Another borro dashed along the road.

"They're flanking us," she said with a shake of her head. "Blast—"

Gritting her teeth, offering me no further apology, Charlotte raised her shutter with a tap of her pocket watch and dismissed the window along with it. Frigid mountain air blasted into our warm little cabin, chilling me to the bone not half as much as the vicious wind that howled along with the borros.

Her hip against the windowsill, Charlotte leaned from the carriage with the rifle in her hands and fired.

A sharp yelp; a collapsing body, large enough to fall audibly as we passed. I cried out with amazement and had to cover my mouth to contain myself when her next round dismissed a second one of the beasts.

She ducked back in and raised her shutter, commanding me to the opposite bench as she did. I hurried to obey, but as my foot set upon the floor with half my weight on it, the carriage gave a violent rock. Even the refined woman behind me, thrown about along with me, cursed at the impact she received, and the pocket watch fumbled from her hand to swing its face against the edge of her seat with an ominous *crack*.

"Damn—"

Teeth grit, Charlotte forced open the window on my side with an emergency latch, first raising the shutter, then shoving the glass out with her elbow. As I scrambled into my new seat, the watch hanging from her waist regained half an image. It was enough to reveal the peaked jackal ears and pantherine eyes of the borro that tripped up the autohorse by biting at its legs in an attempt to drive it from the road.

Her entire upper body out of the window, Charlotte angled her gun sharply down and fired.

She missed.

The carriage rumbled, half its wheels riding on gravel alongside the paved territory road.

"Stand still," she hissed under her breath, hammering the lever of the gun before firing again.

The round struck true.

Too true.

SNARLING AND HOWLING surrounded us.

When I opened my eyes, my skull throbbed so violently I nearly threw up. To help the nausea pass over me, I shut my eyes again. I'm quite sure I cried aloud as I tried to assemble my thoughts, but if it amounted to anything other than a senseless groan of pain, I was unaware amid my reconstruction.

The Rift Event—riding in the carriage. Charlotte, firing the gun.

The borro on the screen, collapsing and disappearing under the autohorse's feet, causing the automaton to stumble and the carriage to upend.

I could hold on to my thoughts for no more than a few seconds at a time, the headache was so intense. My breathing shallow, I forced my eyes open as much as I could bear and lowered my hand before my face.

No blood. No blood! A concussion, maybe—but, more likely, my allergy.

I wasn't sure I could say the same about my chaperone, whose condition looked worse than mine. When I gasped to see Charlotte slumped in the corner with a bloody forehead, I realized two things.

One: I did not see the gun.

Two: We were upside-down.

Quaking with fear, I pressed my hands to my pounding head and tried to think.

Before I could even approach a plan of action, one of the snarling beasts scratched rapidly at the door. I cried out, jerking my feet back when its foam-flecked face jammed into the open window to snap its jaws around whatever it could reach.

Not thinking clearly, I raised my foot and smashed the borro in the muzzle.

While the creature, yelping, withdrew from the carriage, I looked around me. The longer I stayed in here, the more likely it was that these monsters would break through the door. I had to get to the gun if I was going to hold my ground until Eleison reached us…assuming he did at all.

And, looking around the carriage, I only found one plausible solution to the situation.

It was a long shot, though.

The motion more difficult inverted than it would have been upright, I grit my teeth and pushed up against the emergency lever of the still-shuttered front window of the carriage. It slid free, revealing a pane of glass that had been bloodied by the barking monsters smashing their mouths against their meal's container. One leapt into my view, yielding a scream from me—and the immediate impulse that my idea wouldn't work. Soon, though, it lunged toward the already open window, slavering and snapping its jaws while its packmates howled, and I released a shuddering exhalation.

Unhooking the broken pocket watch from Charlotte's waistcoat, I swung it by its tether into the glass as hard as I could.

The glass was sturdy. At first contact with the metal case, it held.

But the second slam came.

The third.

Something cracked, both in the watch and in the window.

I slammed it again, and the crack grew larger.

Leaning back, I raised my foot and kicked against the weak point.

Inch by inch, the crack widened.

My teeth grit, I forced myself to stomp as hard as I could.

The window gave, abruptly splitting into a spider web of defeat. Glass rained in upon me, and I wasted no time. Those seconds more valuable than any in my life, I tore the picnic basket and its leftover breakfast food out of the bench above me and tossed it out of the window for the bloodthirsty creatures.

Alerted by the motion and perhaps the lingering smell of food, four of the snarling beasts bolted after it.

Ignoring the very definite sensation of glass sinking into the heel of my palm, I grabbed hold of the edges of this new opening and pulled myself out of the carriage.

My head throbbed like the Rift pulsing brightly above us. Tears filled my eyes and rolled down my cheeks, but I refused to give into the pain.

There was the rifle. I could see it in the perverted morning light, lying along the road perhaps a hundred yards back.

Before I could even cry out for joy, a low growl drew my attention to my right.

Baring its teeth, the one borro that had stayed behind slowly prowled toward me.

I scrambled up and away from the carriage just as it lunged right for me.

My scream heightened while its massive jaws snapped at my back, grabbing hold of fabric that somehow did not delay me. My shawl—it had grabbed the shawl. As it pulled harmlessly away I sobbed in gratitude, scrambling down the road, dizzy with the throbbing of my headache.

In the distance, another borro inspired the howls of its fellows.

I would not die like this. I would not suffer a grim and bloody end the first time I left my village. I would not, could not, submit to the Rift and become some sort of animal the way an altered would.

Was that what was happening to me? Was that why my head ached so fiercely with the thundering of the Rift above?

I had to hurry and hope I would never find out.

By the time the borro had finished mangling my shawl and come to its senses enough to chase me down, I had reached the gun. As I bent, I made the mistake of glancing once over my shoulder.

The panic overwhelmed me.

Dissatisfied with the contents of the basket, the pack now rushed to catch up with my primary aggressor.

But the rifle was in my hands.

I whirled just in time to use it as a bat against the closest of the monsters.

The hard metal *thud* of the barrel's impact with the monster's jaw rang through my hyper-sensitive ears like an explosion. I cringed, turning on the next and swinging true into its ribs.

Another was on me before I could turn, grabbing at my skirts and snapping past them for my ankles.

Another leapt at my face, barely stopped by the gun I raised between us.

My heart sinking with the slowing of time, I submitted to a great sorrow.

I was going to die.

But then, the snarl of a new borro echoed through the highway.

With a yelp that lowered to a whimper, the one that had been snapping at my face was thrown off of the gun and away to the side of the road. Two of the animals attacking me whirled toward this new threat, raging as they sprang into action.

The scene was pure chaos. With all the limbs and claws and tails and fangs, I could barely follow what was happening.

But, as the fight went on and all the borros got involved, I came to recognize the interloper by a peculiar mark: a band of jagged white arcing up its shoulder and toward its back, like it had survived some grievous injury and the fur had grown back the wrong color.

Was this the altered man Charlotte had mentioned? I marveled, the gun in my hand forgotten as this new borro held off its fellows almost effortlessly. It was clearly not only stronger, but more thoughtful about its approach to the fight, and after gaining the high ground it made steady work of all our aggressors.

The howls and snarls that filled the night were terrifying to me. I hadn't observed wild Rift monsters so closely in my life, and this intervening one made it clear why they were such dangerous predators. The attacking borros dropped one at a time, managing to get in a scratch or a bite but never much more than that.

At last, when the pack had been reduced to a single member, this slightly smarter animal dropped back a few steps, its spine highly arched.

The borro with the white streak approached, head low, fangs flashing in the violet light.

Afraid, the animal turned tail and sprang off into the trees.

Gasping with relief, I hurried toward the great beast that kept its eyes toward its retreating opponent.

"You must be—"

Startled, the borro turned around with its teeth bared.

Before either of us realized what was happening, it had lunged upon me.

Shocked, I raised my hand between us, and its ready jaws clamped down on the soft flesh of my forearm.

"—Eleison," I screamed, lurching forward at the sharp pain of deadly mandibles snapping their fangs through my flesh.

Its red eyes wide, as though it were shocked to find itself called from a trance, the borro relaxed its jaws.

Along with the pain, a strange sensation of rapid chills rushed through my body. They pulsed, worsening my headache—and, of all things, inspiring a tug in my diaphragm that reminded me of the love-jerk I once felt when the old fortune-teller showed me those visions at the circus. A kind of erotic excitement overwhelmed me, but at the time the arousal only made sense as fear. I panted, studying my bleeding arm in disbelief.

Beneath the pounding headache, the chills, and the sight of my own blood, I collapsed before the borro had even begun to return to human shape.

I AWOKE AGAIN.

The room was so unfamiliar to me that I didn't realize I was conscious at first.

Granted...that could have been a concussion, too.

"Oh, what a relief."

That half-familiar voice drew my attention to the door. Charlotte stood with one foot in the room and a book in her hand, and I wonder now if it wasn't the sound of the door opening that drew me from my slumber.

"You're alive," I observed weakly, earning a vague semblance of a smile.

"I'm sure you're overjoyed," she responded dryly, coming to sit at a chair by my bedside. While she settled in, I quickly observed her split lip and bruised temple. "It's a good thing Eleison came when he did...although it sounds like you were holding your own."

"I wouldn't say that."

Talking was difficult. I was dehydrated and smacked my lips, looking down at the bandage around my arm.

Of all things, a streak of guilt shot through me. It really *had* been my fault that I'd been bitten, after all. The altered man, Eleison—he had been keyed up from the battle. I had surprised him in his most wild and instinctive state.

I was lucky he hadn't killed me, quite frankly.

"How long have I been out?"

"We had you kept under to give you stitches and clean your other wounds, a few scrapes here and there. That was at seven this morning, but you clearly needed some sleep. You've been out, oh, easily twelve hours."

Groaning, I tried to sit up. Charlotte gently forced me back down. "Now, don't push yourself. Relax."

"But, Eleison—I should apologize for provoking him to bite me."

Not understanding, Charlotte looked at me with sympathy and said, "You're confused from the anesthetic after your faint. I'll tell you what—promise me you won't sit up until I'm back with something for you to eat. Does that seem fair?"

Somehow, I nodded. With a pat of my unharmed hand, as she had delivered during the onset of the Rift, Charlotte vanished through the door of the opulent bedroom in which I'd been laid up.

It is safe to say I had never in my life seen a bed so lovely, let alone a bedroom. The gold and copper walls had been covered by a tasteful damask that ran down to the wainscoting, its pattern interrupted only occasionally for a painting or a mirror. A ballet dancer on one side; a woman in a tower on the other, her gaze fixed on the knight passing beneath her window. Above me hung a small but lovely chandelier, all its crystals softening the glow of its electric lights.

And there was no question about it. The bed in which I found myself might as well have been stuffed with angel feathers, it was so plush and pleasant. In my lifetime of using the same cramped, thin mattress, I had never realized how comfortable a bed could be.

As helpless and alone as I felt when I thought of where I was, a vague gratitude lay there, too.

When Charlotte returned, it was with a bowl of soup that made me realize how nauseous I was—although, much to my delight, there was no trace of a headache. The brief coma had done wonders for me, and although I was a little unsteady when my soup was gone and Charlotte had me get up to walk around the room, I was more mobile than either one of us expected.

My arm, though.

When she left me to sleep through the night, my arm throbbed with a terrible heat that made it itch beneath the bandages. Sweat dotted my brow and questions flew through my head. Was the wound infected? If so, had the bite and its bacteria reached the bone? I trembled beneath the blankets, all the uncertainty of my situation compounded to more pressing worries about my arm.

That night, as I lay awake, footsteps resonated through the hall outside my room. I wouldn't have thought anything of them, had they not stopped at my door.

I raised my head, anticipating Charlotte's arrival for a midnight check-in of some kind, but nobody entered. Whomever they were, they just stood there for a long moment. As though they were thinking about coming in, or maybe just listening to me breathe.

Then, they went on, their firm footsteps receding from me at that same steady pace. A man's stride, I was sure. My heart raced for reasons unknown, and my thoughts drifted away from my pitiful mortal terrors.

When I fell asleep, it was well after midnight. The next morning, I made good use of the adjoining bathroom while marveling at its features. We'd of course had indoor plumbing in Lescaut, but the water pressure in this place was a precious jewel. The size of the clawfoot bathtub, the softness of the towels, the gleam of the polished mirror hanging above the sink basin—every detail was seen to.

If this was how property was to be treated, I suppose I was lucky chattel.

My mood turned grim as the thought struck me. I put on a robe I found neatly folded in the cabinet with the towels and sat there, contemplating my reflection while I combed out my hair.

What was to become of me, truly? What would happen to me here? I was overwhelmed. I'd seen only two rooms and already I wondered if this place was too good for me—if I would not be immediately seen for what I truly was, and thrown to the wolves.

Or the laboratories.

"How are you feeling today?" Charlotte's pleasant question came as she pulled open the red velvet drapes of my windows, tying them back with their golden cords and cracking open the pane. "The weather should be beautiful—it's only 5% on the RMS. You'd ought to take a walk and stretch your legs a little before the Master calls on you."

"And when will that be?"

"After suppertime, I would expect—he's very busy today. But, then again, he always is, even when he's out here in the middle of nowhere."

Straightening up and seeing me more clearly in the sunlight, Charlotte set her hands on her hips. "What a pale face!"

"I'm frightened of—all this."

"Well...good. You should be." At my sharp look, she spread her hands and turned away to a parcel she'd set upon the chess table of the small but exquisite suite. "It's true. You'd better hear it now than learn it too late. Master Farrow is to be feared— maybe more than the average territory master."

My lips tightened and I nodded. "I understand that he is vicious in war."

"It's true...but not without reason. You mean the Expansion, don't you?" When I nodded, Charlotte assured me, "He was young, and had a message to send to the Overseer and his peers. Now, I would say he's—more subtle than that. He understands consequence. What he accomplishes, he accomplishes not through violence but through the capacity for it."

I shivered. "And other masters still work with him, in spite of his history?"

"Oh, well, he's not some drooling brute. Aside from being born to a line of territory masters, he is exceedingly persuasive. To a certain type of person, he's quite charming. I wouldn't be surprised if you fell into that category, Thecla."

Though I laughed, Charlotte went on while drawing a pale cotton shift from the torn butcher paper of the parcel. "If you want my advice: Let yourself be fond of him, but never too fond. Not if you can help it."

"Why not too fond?"

"Because he will hurt you. Give him your body, if you like"— she ignored my sputtering while pulling me to my feet—"but keep your heart for yourself, and never wholly trust him."

But I was hung up on her casual allotment, and could only stutter, "My—my body—"

"Oh, he is a notorious rake, although his interest never lasts more than a few weeks." Charlotte chuckled to herself in a knowing way that made my face burn. "As I said…he's charming. Be charming back, Thecla; but be wary, too."

I wasn't at all sure what to say. Had I not been brought here to work on the grounds as a kind of servant? Had I misunderstood?

"Before I left, my stepmother—she said that she had…heard some things. About him. I don't think she meant his military history."

"Did she tell you what kinds of things?"

I shook my head, making another slightly shocked little noise as she thoughtlessly stripped me of my robe and raised the shift above my head to dress me as though I were a doll.

"And have *you* heard anything?"

Again, I shook my head.

Charlotte shrugged and let the fabric fall around me like a curtain.

"Then…don't worry about it."

"But—"

"After what you did for me, do you really think I would let you walk into the luptich's den?"

At Charlotte's sharp look, I was given pause. Satisfied she had made her point, she turned away to the parcel again and now withdrew a silvery blue dress.

"Trust me, Thecla, when I say—whatever gossip may fly about the Master, and however dangerous he may be…you're much better off humoring his attentions than spending the rest of your abbreviated life in a government lab."

She was right, of course—but I was still terrified. More terrified, perhaps, because my choices now seemed so desperate. I was not used to amorous men, and the idea that one might want my body as part of some exchange made me feel ashamed. Was that all I was? A specimen? A plaything?

When Charlotte had satisfied herself with my appearance, braiding my hair and tying sections of it back with a lilac ribbon, she asked with a sigh, "Why don't we give you a little tour, then have something to eat? You must be famished."

So much so I would have preferred things in reverse order, but my hunger had a way of evaporating as I was introduced to the extraordinary country mansion from which the territory master managed Gudrune for part of the year.

Everything that was not made from marble was carved from mahogany, or even the ivory of Rift animals who supplied the world with an acceptable stock of the historically objectionable material. The ceiling of the sprawling foyer had been painted with a gorgeous fresco depicting an Expansion battle I didn't recognize, replete with thrashing horses and piles of bodies; the formal dining room's long table gleamed in anticipation of parties; the ball room was so bright and gay it was like something out of a dream. There were music rooms, game rooms, a smoking room, a series of offices. Busy vassals roamed the halls to fulfill appointments, the servants of the manor scurrying among them to and fro to keep the property running like clockwork.

I, amazed, wondered if I had been transported to another world.

The garden was covered in an inch of melting snow, but the sky was blue and beautiful enough to justify Charlotte's walk when the tour was finished. Empty for the winter, the fountain served as little more than the look-out point for a few birds who scattered at our arrival. When I dusted off its edge and settled there for a moment, admiring the hedge maze from a distance, Charlotte pointed to the far edge of the house.

"Look—oh, rats."

All I caught as a man disappeared around the corner was a flash of black hair and the back of a suit.

"That was Master—Eleison, too. No point in bothering them now, but I was hoping I could at least point them out to you...maybe later."

But there was no 'later' for that. By the time we managed to eat, the ache in my forearm had worn me to exhaustion. I retired, realizing only when Charlotte said with a shrug, "You don't need *my* permission," that I had been acting like a prisoner.

I supposed, if I did not want to be treated like a prisoner, I had ought not to think of myself as a prisoner...but it was easier said than done, especially when dinner came around. After a rich winter stew and soft bread so pleasing I wished my family were there to taste it, Charlotte collected the dishware that had been brought to let me eat in solitude.

"Here's your moment, Thecla...Master has requested your time tonight, if you would kindly see him in his study."

I swallowed back my anxiety, nodding while I clambered to my feet. "Will you walk with me?"

"Of course...Thecla—"

Looking at me in that stern way of hers, Charlotte pressed my hand between both her palms.

"Though it's wise to be wary, so long as you are, I swear you'll be fine. Believe me."

And I wanted to believe her. Of course, I wanted to. But the walk across the manor from my guest's quarters to the master's apartments seemed so long that I wondered if it would ever end. In that time, my whirling mind concocted any number of dreadful, deadly scenarios I might be forced to endure. If something about me was displeasing to him, what would happen to me? To my family?

I couldn't think like that.

We stopped before the door of the office and exchanged a wordless glance.

Charlotte knocked for me, listening with her head lowered a few degrees.

"Come in," commanded a man's pleasant bass, half-musical in merry anticipation.

Still moving for me, Charlotte pushed open the office door and stepped aside to let me in.

And, as I entered, I was met with the man from my visions.

OUR EYES LOCKED. My heart, already speeding as we approached the study, now clenched with pain enough to stop it.

This was him: this was the man the seer had revealed to me.

It was all the same! His dark hair, short and elegantly styled to permit the fall of a few locks along his temple; the brooding brows that contorted briefly above his crimson eyes, which roved wildly over me once our gazes separated; even the suit was the same, I realized, although I was not sure I had been conscious of his clothing at the time of those mystical impressions.

I stepped toward him, my mouth open in shock, joy lighting my heart. How gorgeous he was! His pale features were strong and distinct, his nose aquiline and his square jaw set firm, yet his high cheekbones and the bedroom caste to his heavily-lidded eyes awarded him an almost otherworldly beauty. He was a serious man, I could tell, but one with a gentleness about him.

For one second—for just one long, hopeful second I will always carry with me—I thought he had to be the territory master.

Then, with the flare of his nostrils and the rectifying of his gaze, he turned his face away, and I at last noticed the man sitting some yards behind him.

"At long last—Thecla of Lescaut."

That carefully constructed, mirthful tone that had called me into the room—it was the man seated there by the fire who had summoned me.

My heart wilted a little. "Oh," I said aloud.

Master Farrow laughed, his hand smoothing over the fabric of his waistcoat. "She meets her territory's master, and her response is 'Oh.' I didn't realize I was so disappointing!"

Humiliated, I cast one awkward glance at the other man before I hurried to curtsey for Malin.

The fire burned, its eerie red light highlighting his proud brow and lending false color to the dirty blonde coiffure interrupted by a single silver stripe that was, I realized, the continuation of a scar. It trailed down the temple of his forehead, along his brow, and just beyond his cheekbone. From the Expansion?

However he acquired it, it did little to impact his good looks. Master Farrow was considerably older than myself, in his late forties at youngest, but his dark eyes studied me with more contained, more deliberate appreciation than his companion showed. His features were the kind sometimes called 'hawkish,' or 'severe,' with a strong nose and a regal jawline whose mouth was arranged in an expression of semi-permanent amusement.

"I am honored to meet you," I managed once I had consulted his features and dipped low in greeting. "I'm sorry, I just—this is all—"

But he stopped me, waving his hand and reaching out to me. Against all expectation, he took my hand in his warm one and patted my knuckles. The affectation I recognized from Charlotte seemed somehow different from him. All I could think about was how small my hand felt in his; how helpless I was here, in this place, with him.

And with the man from my visions.

"Please, Thecla"—Malin glanced over at his footman, still patting my knuckles as he spoke—"you needn't be so afraid of me. Whatever you've heard, whatever you expect—well, don't let it worry you. All behavior is contextual, isn't it?"

"What do you mean?"

"How a man treats one individual may not be how he treats another...that's all I mean." While I nodded, he gestured to the sofa across the fire from his armchair. "Please, sit. How are you feeling? Eleison was worried about you all night."

Eleison. I glanced over my shoulder at the other man, who stood by the window with his arms folded. But for a hint of reflection in the dark pane, his face was invisible to me. I craved to see it again: to look on him and re-confirm his significance over and over.

"I'm all right," I told them, intending to launch into thanking Eleison for my rescue.

Malin didn't let me, though. He smoothly navigated my attention back to him, asking, "Is your arm any better? Poor girl...I am very sorry you've had such an inauspicious arrival here."

"Given the circumstances"—I forced myself to look in those glittering black serpent eyes that seemed to see through my skull—"I should say it was the arrival I expected. I am a little overwhelmed, sir."

"I would imagine you are. Upset, too. If I were you, I would be very upset to learn my parents had not told me what to expect."

I wanted to blame Malin, of course, and to scream in his face that it was hardly my parents' fault the law was so unjust. My hands bunched into fists in my lap, the right one unbunching when the action aggravated my stitches.

"I am somewhat shocked," I said. "Yes, sir."

"Now, Thecla, please. Let's not act so formally."

"I cannot imagine how else to act with you, sir. In truth, I do not fully understand why I was brought here."

"Well...now, I must admit that, since you walked into the firelight, I have changed my mind on that particular matter."

"What do you mean by that, sir?"

"Thecla—between you and me and Eleison over there, you are a treasure worth killing for." Malin leaned forward in his seat after plucking a glass that looked like whiskey from the small table beside him. He raised it to his mouth as he contemplated my features. "Have you ever heard of a 2nd generation altered roaming free, let alone a *riftborn* one?"

I shook my head. He lowered his glass, waving a little as he said, "There are still many aspects of these things that are unknown, of course, but I'm something of a gambling man...and I would wager someone like you is capable of things we've never seen."

Embarrassed and a little frightened by his blunt interest in powers I didn't have, I caught myself chewing at my lower lip and instead forced myself to respond.

"I'm very sorry to disappoint you, sir, but I just don't *have* any powers. I mean—when I got your letter the other day, I thought it had somehow arrived to the wrong person."

Laughing helplessly, glancing over to find Eleison now watched me with his back against the wall, I pleaded with Malin to see reason.

"There was a riftborn who came through my town with the circus once, and I saw that he had real powers. I'm capable of nothing like that; moreover, far from becoming a powerful beast the way Eleison can, all I have is an allergy to the Rift."

"An allergy, eh?" Listening intently, Malin urged me on. "What allergy is this, exactly? Those headaches of yours?"

I nodded. "I wish I were as powerful as you think I am, but I'm sure it's not true at all. At least...I haven't seen any proof."

"How long have you been exposed to the Rift in your life? How many times?"

The rich, dark voice I recognized from the pocket watch's communication channel rolled into my ear and down my neck in a sensual growl. Afraid to look at Eleison too much—to be seen staring by him, or to displease the territory master by doing it—I turned my head a few degrees and estimated, "I'm not sure how long I was unconscious in the carriage the other night, but I can't imagine I've been out in the Rift for more than an hour or two total in my entire life."

Scoffing a little at a number that was exceptionally low even among most conscientious people, Eleison nonetheless refrained from speaking his thoughts. Master Farrow tutted, finishing his whiskey and observing, "Your father took very good care of you, didn't he, Thecla."

The question brought back such an onrush of memories I had forced myself to neglect that I had to avert my eyes while I fought back the tears. "Yes," I said softly, studying Malin's ringed hand. "Yes—he cared for me very much."

"I can tell he saw to it that you were educated, as well. You have a pleasant speaking voice; do you sing?"

Taken aback by his question, I laughed a little. "When I work, but not—not as a practice…"

"Oh, I'm sure you have a lovely singing voice. Perhaps you should try. I could pay an instructor for you, if you'd like."

This conversation—this week!—grew stranger all the time. "Um"—I raised my eyes to his and smiled, but the uncertainty made the expression weak—"forgive me for asking such a thing, but…why would you do that for me?"

"As we just discussed, Thecla…it is my opinion that you possess a great deal of untapped potential. Here—listen—"

I confess I flinched when Malin rose from his seat, unfolded briefly to his six-foot, six-inch height, and strode across to lounge at my side. He did not touch me, but kept half a cushion between us and settled back against the arm of the couch. Just close enough to remind me he could have easily chosen to sit a little closer.

"Although I understand you are recovering from quite an ordeal, and that you did not necessarily come here by choice, you should consider your time here as an opportunity for mentorship. Do you know the beautiful thing about mentorship, Thecla?"

He waited for me to offer a response, and I didn't have any. I shook my head, and he parted the index fingers that had steepled together while he waited.

"It goes both ways. The mentor is vivified by the youth and fresh ideas of the apprentice, and the apprentice has opportunities to learn and experience what few can. In this case, I am offering you the opportunity to learn whatever you want, to do whatever you want—to get to know a territory master and the people around him, and all the fascinating machinations of social politics that I can see are blurring your eyes with boredom as we speak."

I laughed a little, and so did he. His teeth glittered bright white against his olive features until they disappeared. He leaned toward me, more serious now, his eyes searching mine.

"In exchange," he said, "I would ask that you learn loyalty to me. And that, in times of necessity, you use whatever gifts you develop to enrich myself and the territory. I have, after all, already spared your life and given you a home, and your family's paychecks have resumed—"

"Excuse me?"

"My goodness!" Unfeignedly shocked, Malin looked over his shoulder at his quiet manservant. "They really didn't tell her a thing, did they..."

"Some families like their secrets," was all Eleison said.

As he spoke, he glanced toward the back of his boss's head.

Our eyes met again.

The panic of a caged bird fluttered through my chest and cheeks. I shuddered under that intense red stare, the visions of the circus juxtaposed with the powerful fangs that split my skin and left me bleeding.

This gorgeous man who studied me so intensely knew what I *tasted* like.

The idea was frightening, horrific.

But—somehow so exciting.

"—Thecla?"

To my embarrassment, I realized that Malin had been speaking. I looked at him sheepishly and he raised a hand to my brow, startling me with the cool, rough knuckles he pressed to my flesh.

"Hm," he said, "she's a little feverish...Eleison, go tell Dr.

Singer to arrange for some antibiotics. Charlotte can pick them up. Then go ahead, take the rest of the night off. You're dismissed."

Malin didn't look back to speak to Eleison at all. His relentless eyes were too busy absorbing my cheeks, my lips, my face. Eleison looked at us together and I swore his jaw tightened, but it was hard to tell from the distance. It must have been my imagination.

"Good evening, Master. I'm glad you're up and about, Thecla. See you around."

I opened my mouth to say good-bye, but Malin once more smoothly navigated into the gap.

"Perhaps we should get you a sling to help you keep that arm still...you will tell me if you need one, won't you?"

The door shut. I had missed Eleison's exit and rued the lost seconds in which I could have appreciated anything—any part of him. Even just his back.

Left alone with the territory master in his sandalwood perfumed office, I steadied myself with a somewhat anxious breath.

"Yes, Master Farrow, of course."

"Now, Thecla..." He chuckled, one brow roguishly arching and contorting the scar along with it. "As pretty as the title sounds on your lips, I meant what I said...let's not be quite so formal. Call me anything but that when we're conversing on intimate terms this way."

"All right, Malin."

"That sounds much better...I'll let you call me 'master,' when you've done something wicked."

While my face flushed, he smiled and went on in that steady, warm patter.

"I think you and I are bound to be good friends, Thecla, and

I'm quite sure our mentorship will unfold naturally as time goes on, so I won't bore you much longer today…but I would like you to start thinking early about issues like loyalty. And I hope you will take a critical look at your life, at your past, and ask yourself who has wronged you in these matters."

My face somewhat numb at that last implication, I nodded. Though I didn't agree Malin was somehow blameless, I *was* angry at my father and stepmother. I'd had time to ruminate on the matter, and in two short days I had catalogued all the many instances where some information could have made a difference to me.

"I am"—I leveled with those sharp eyes—"truly grateful, you know, Malin. To know that I was spared—that I got to be with my father even though I ought not to have been…"

My shoulders trembled. I passed my hand over my eyes.

"Excuse me."

"It's perfectly all right, Thecla, please…"

His hand stroked down the back of my bicep, his caress warm and firm through the layers of pale blue fabric that hung from my sleeve. Though I stiffened, still afraid, there was a kind of delight in the fear. Yes, delight in how queerly Malin made me feel—even in the helplessness.

"I know this transition is painful for you," he told me, his voice somehow tender. "But please know, I would very much like you to enjoy your life here with us in the manor. Tell me what you want, and it's yours. I'll give you anything; support you in any task you choose."

"I am not sure how much good I could do around the estate, but I would very much like a way to contribute to this place. The idea of lying around all day doing nothing but taking singing lessons sounds—"

"Like something my mistress would do?"

Once more, the heat flooding my face intensified. As it prickled down my neck, Malin smiled.

"Well, Thecla, I confess I would hardly mind such a fate for you...but I think we could find you something to do around the home, instead. I believe we found you through the tax records of some weaver, didn't we? Do you enjoy your occupation?"

The buy-out at the textile factory...so that was how he found me.

"I do enjoy it, very much—I just found I didn't care for weaving bland, artless textiles for someone else. Sometimes, with free time, I practiced drawing patterns, but I've never been able to actually produce any."

"Well, that sounds promising. Perhaps you could work on a lovely tapestry for the staircase over the foyer. That could keep you busy for a while...until you get comfortable enough here to realize what it is I'm offering you."

"What's that?"

"Security."

Smiling at me in a somehow fond way that nonetheless seemed divorced from the motion of his indecent eyes, Malin absorbed me for another moment and patted my elbow as he stood. He kept his hand extended, offering it to me to help me up.

He really was very gallant, I was surprised to find. Perhaps it was only that, amid the mist of rumor about him, I really had expected a far crueler man.

Contextual, as he said.

"If you don't mind, Thecla, I'd like to see you regularly and get a sense for how you're getting along."

"All right—when?"

"Would every morning suit you fine?"

I blushed as I repeated, "*Every* morning?"

"Of course. I am a very busy man, If I don't make time for the important things in my life every day, I'll never get to enjoy them. Besides…I want to monitor your progress and get an idea of any developing powers. When some appear, I suspect I will need to employ Eleison's help in taming them."

Perhaps I really was running a fever. I certainly swore my body was about to burst into flames, even when Malin opened the door and let me out into the significantly cooler hallway. "And you *will* tell me," he insisted firmly, "if you need anything or come up against any trouble, won't you?"

My throat tight, I nodded—though, at the time, I could not imagine having the audacity to complain about anything in a place so fine.

"Very good. I'll see you tomorrow, then, Thecla."

Taking the hand of my unwounded arm in a gentle grip, he bent at the waist and sent my heart flying with the damp brush of his lips along the back of my hand. When he straightened, his smile was wide as his gaze was knowing.

"Try not to get lost on your way back to your room, now…"

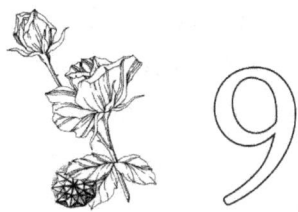

M Y ENCOUNTER WITH Malin left me unexpectedly giddy. Had he really meant what he said? I had the feeling he must have; at the very least, Charlotte seemed to believe his intentions toward me were sincere.

"Mind what I told you," she warned me all the same while taking my measurements for what I presumed to be some uniform of the household staff.

I did, in fact, mind what she had told me, but there was now a lot to think about…and a lot to figure out.

Eleison, for instance.

That whole night I once more lay in my bed, now with my body burning at the mere thought of the altered man. He had been nearly as tall as the territory master, but his dress shirt had hinted at more sharply defined muscles, and his way of moving across the floor was closer to a cat's slink than a man's stride.

Most of all, though—those eyes. Those sharp, sorrowful crimson eyes.

The mere thought of them resting upon me for a second drove my mind to a state of heat I'd never known. It revved from one wild notion to the next, occasionally interrupting thrill with uncertainty. I was pretty in my small town, but was I as glamorous and attractive as, say, Charlotte could be?

And did it even matter?

I may have been young, and perhaps naive, but I was not blind. It was very obvious that the territory master was interested in me—but I assumed, based on Charlotte's advice, that this was typical behavior for him when an attractive young woman joined the manor staff. It did not occur to me that surely not every woman received his knock on her door at the bright hour of seven in the morning.

"Thecla," he said in a tone of true pleasure to see me that first morning, "how are you settling in? Ready for a little fresh air?"

Soon, we were walking through the placid gardens that had been tucked to bed for winter, flowers absent and trees or hedge sculptures covered up. Why a country place, so isolated, in winter? I pondered it as Malin at last broke our thick silence.

"You must think I'm some terrible brute, I'm sure."

"Oh, no! Of course not." I laughed a little, reluctant to admit his reputation frightened me, but I was relieved when he went on.

"You had a life in Lescaut, and I recognize that. But I hope that, as time goes on, you'll appreciate it here."

Smiling in spite of myself, I confessed, "I have *family* in Lescaut, sir. I wouldn't say I had a life, as such."

"A pretty girl like you? You must have been out dancing every weekend."

"I can't dance." While he balked, I laughed and shook my head. "You're right to guess I sing, but I've just never cared to learn dancing...my father wouldn't let me go to gatherings by myself, and when he died, I had to start work at once."

With a more empathetic frown than I might have expected of him, Malin said, "That must have been very difficult, Thecla."

"It still is."

He pondered my profile for a few steps of silence before looking away, his dark eyes passing over the somber landscape.

"I know what you mean. My wife and I were not on very good terms at the time of her death. Though it was years ago, it all still feels so fresh when I let myself remember."

My lips pursed. Without fully thinking about it, I touched his arm.

"One way or another," I told him, "she's probably not worried about it at all anymore."

With a slight laugh of surprise and a glint of black humor that crinkled his eyes, Malin agreed, "I suppose that's a fair point... yes, that's probably true. So..."

Pausing to sit upon a stone bench that gave a broad view of the gardens from the hedge maze to the manor house, Malin patted the space beside him.

"How does a young woman who doesn't dance spend her time Lescaut?"

"Well, aside from designing textiles never to be made—"

"Without my help."

I bit back my smile dared sit beside him, our elbows touching and my nerves quivering with awareness.

"I spent a lot of time reading."

"Oh, really?" With a look of keen pleasure, Malin probed, "What books? What era?"

"Many." I laughed a little, then confessed with a reflexive

look at the sky, "But I rather enjoy reading books and plays—plays, especially—that were written before the Rift. The world seems like it was so much gentler then, even if it wasn't."

"I'm not so sure it was...but, you must like Shakespeare."

Was that how you pronounced it? I perked with excitement, saying, "Oh, yes, I do—very much! The bookbinders who let me stay in their spare room, they ruined a copy of his collected works and let me have it."

Mirroring my interest with his own, Malin asked, "How many plays have you read?"

"Half of them, I think—and a great deal of poetry, though I only remember "The Rape of Lucrece.""

"Who could forget that one... Really, though, half the plays? Let me see if I can guess your favorite—*Measure for Measure*."

I laughed and shook my head. "I could barely finish that one! What tripe."

"Oh, I love it...but, I suppose it helps to see it performed. Hm...*Twelfth Night*."

My tongue digging against my teeth as though to contain my giddiness, I told him, "You're very far off!"

"Well, we could sit here all day listing them off, or you could act charitably toward an old man..."

What a strange thing for him to call himself! He hardly seemed old. Established, perhaps; but not old. I didn't correct him, however, and instead named the play.

His eyes widened fractionally, then narrowed with great interest.

"Is that so?"

"Yes, oh, I just love it. It has such bite. And it's quick, too. Every word has power."

"That is a very interesting choice…it's my favorite, too."

"Really!"

"It certainly is. Be careful where you go flinging that word around, though, dear…bad luck to say it inside a theater."

I laughed and shook my head. "I've never been to a theater, so I won't worry about it."

His brows raised toward the slight widow's peak of his hairline. "You've never been to the theater? My goodness… perhaps I'll take you one of these days. I'm sure you'll love it. The lights go down, and the world vanishes—until it's intermission and it's time for wine and chocolate, anyway."

"Chocolate! My father told me about it. He said he had it quite a few times when he was in his twenties. I understand it's marvelous."

I was so absorbed in a brief flurry of memories of my father's loving descriptions for that nearly sacred luxury of the rich that I almost didn't note the strange, wounded look that passed over Malin's face. It were as though some astonishment gripped him— but there was more.

Something in his bleak eyes, in the tension of his jaw, pierced me through to the core.

He looked as though he wanted to kiss me…or maybe devour me.

When a shudder wracked me beneath his stare, he stood with a tut on his lips.

"A lovely girl like you never having danced, gone to the theater, tried chocolate…I must do something to improve Gudrune's small towns, mustn't I?"

Somehow, I thought I had offended him. We spoke little on the way back to the manor, and just within the doors, we parted ways with another lingering stare of his. It was a gaze I confess I couldn't help but return until, having shrugged his coat from his shoulders and his hat from his head, Malin bid me good day and exited toward the foyer.

He was an odd man. Gregarious in some ways, closed off in others. An artifact of all his years in politics and war, perhaps.

But there was something about him that was thoughtful—even if it was what others perceived as manipulative.

That evening, as Charlotte delivered my dinner, the tray included a small red box tied with a brown ribbon. "Master Farrow wanted to be sure you tried this," she said, leaving it behind while whisking the remains of my dinner away.

Alone in my room, I slid the ribbon away and opened the box to inspect the contents.

Little jewels—no. Little candies. I plucked one out and raised it to the light, its surface dusted with gold powder but showing through the rich, almost black substance of its body beneath.

As the first bite of chocolate flowed over my palate, my eyes widened.

I fell in love.

As the days went on and I began to fear less for my life, my focus instead shifted to the possibilities my new reality afforded me. Day by day, I found I enjoyed the walks we took through the frosty grounds of the estate, and I even went to bed looking forward to them—but I was always somewhat disappointed. I hoped that seeing the territory master would provide a natural opportunity to see Eleison, but it seemed they were not joined at the hip all day. My morning walks yielded no glimpse of the altered man, which would not have been so bad if I crossed paths with him at any other time of day.

But—I didn't. Not for a week, to my astonishment.

In fact, when at last I encountered him pondering the landscape through a second-floor hallway window, it at last occurred to me that he might have been deliberately avoiding me.

But why?

"Excuse—"

Eleison whirled toward me so quickly I had a vivid flash of that borro he also was, whipping around and snapping its jaws down into my flesh.

"—me."

His nostrils flared within the lines of his strong nose.

"What is it?"

I fell back a step, my healing arm pressed to my chest. "I just wanted to thank you. That's all."

Eleison's lip curled in a sneer. He glanced away, asking, "Thank me—for what?"

"For saving me, of course."

"Seems like you would have fared better without me there."

I wasn't sure what I had expected from him, but it wasn't this. Self-consciously hiding my bandages behind my back, every hope I could have had for the interaction already dashed, I fumbled around for some way to politely correct him.

"But it was my fault I surprised you," I said, his eyes fixing upon me again as I leapt to his defense. Fighting against the way his gaze heated my body and my heart, I insisted, "You didn't do anything wrong."

"That's a ridiculous thing to say."

"It's true! I shouldn't have come up behind you. Please."

I searched his face, wondering if it was even possible for this cold man to become the one I had seen in the visions.

"I don't blame you. It really was my fault."

For a second, his eyes softened. Saddened. Then, as though driven by some secret goal to which I was not privy, they intensified again.

"Then maybe you should just stay away from me," he said, brushing past my arm to stride down the hall.

Even as my limb was seared by the passing contact with his jacket, my heart felt it had been shattered.

I also, you may imagine, felt like an idiot.

How was it I was still so childish after all this time on Earth? What the carnival man had shown me could have been anything concocted from the depths of my imagination. Some psychic funhouse mirror, propelling my fantasies back to me. As to how those fantasies matched so well with Eleison, well—perhaps that was just coincidence. Perhaps his face did not actually match with the dream-man's as well as I thought they did, and I had gotten excited over nothing. Or maybe I had seen his face while he passed through town on business once—unlikely, but not impossible— and the mesmerist summoned it up with his unholy powers.

Unholy...there I was, still thinking of riftborn as unholy. At least they still seemed to be human. At least they still treated *me* like a human.

Wounded, I retreated to my room and lay around in my utter humiliation.

From now on, I would wipe the slate clean. I had been a fool to think I merited some kind of instant friendship from Eleison, no matter how hot a flame he kindled in my body every time we breathed the same air. There was so much else to focus on, anyway—like when a brisk knock rang through the door and revealed Charlotte upon my calling out.

"I have something for you, Thecla," she said with a surprising amount of excitement. In the days that I'd been at the estate, Charlotte had been very reserved. Hearing a playful glimmer in her voice excited me, and I sat up in curiosity as she rolled in a mobile clothes rack from the laundry room.

"Oh," I said, a gasp as I shyly eyed the assortment of silk, ribbons, and lace, "they're lovely—do you have a dress for me already?"

"These are all for you!"

"Really?"

"Yes, really. But you have to try them on. I'm the one who has to help dress you until you have a proper girl of your own, after all...I won't be driven mad by some ill-fitting bodice or some little eyehook that never quite hides right. Here"—she shut the door without ceremony while waving me up from the bed—"come on, get up, let's see..."

The idea of clothes like these coming together in five days was insane to me, but the idea that these were *my* clothes was all the madder. I supposed that they were not *my* clothes, per se. No more than the clothes of a doll were really its clothes.

I tried not to be bitter, but it was hard. I wondered how my stepmother and sister were doing, and I reminded myself to write to them the next day. No wonder she pressed me to get a job so quickly after my father's death. All that time, my existence had provided them with a passive income. When she had to begin hiding my existence, she had to supplement that income. In truth, she had done me great favors by first putting me to work, then sending me out from her house, and I was glad.

But there was still a little twinge of frustration. The feeling that I was never loved as an end, but a means. I wanted to feel loved for myself. Not because of what I did for anyone else, or how well I did it, or how I looked at the time.

Although…I must confess, I looked quite good.

The clothing was wonderful, and in a wide assortment of styles. There were trousers for riding and hunting; dresses for every day, simpler cotton or wool frocks with lace around the collar and what seemed to be little pearls embroidered within the bodice as a touch of glamor; gowns for decadent occasions, like the grand red dress that stole my breath but had a way of improving my bust as if in echo of the grand bell shape of the bustle below.

"I feel a little like a birthday gift in this."

"Maybe the cake," Charlotte responded wryly, making me laugh.

Amid our mirth, another knock echoed upon the door.

"Come in," I called without thinking, spinning toward the visitor.

Not even the unexpected presence of Master Farrow could erase my smile, though I was still so intimidated by him I confess it did tarnish a little.

"It's so good to see you having fun," he said, crows' feet appearing to enrich the good looks of the eyes that swept over me. "Do you like your clothes, Thecla? I know they're a little out of fashion…we weren't sure of your taste."

"I love them." I couldn't help my smile. "It's all so beautiful— thank you so much, truly. I can't believe you would do something like this for me."

"It's all my pleasure, dear, please, don't worry about it…"

"It's not the clothes that are beautiful," Charlotte corrected, tapping me in the bicep with a knuckle.

Though I laughed, Malin didn't.

"She's right, you know."

Blushing at his forward comment, I squeaked out a quiet "Thank you" and found his intense study of my face too much to bear. I looked down at Malin's shoes, their black polish gleaming in the light.

"Goodness but that's a lot of clothes." With his focus on something else, I could breathe again. I supposed I was grateful that he didn't stare at me quite as much as some men. He knew when to relieve the pressure, at least. "Now that I see them all on the rack here, I think Thecla will need quite a bit more space. Don't you agree, Charlotte?"

"I should say so."

Shining a brisk smile across both of us, Malin slipped out through the door again with a laid-back wave of his hand. "See if you can't get her moved into the suite near the entrance of the west wing—that has plenty of space."

"As you wish," Charlotte responded, interrupting any chance I had to thank him for his consideration before he left my sight.

Alone with her again, I smooth my hands over the bodice of the gown and turned to smile at Charlotte.

When I saw how serious her expression had become, I worried.

"What's the matter?"

"Nothing...just mind what I said before."

As she turned me toward the mirror to get access to the hooks at the back of my dress again, I told her, "I remember what you said, and I'm glad you told me, though he doesn't seem like *such* a cad. I certainly expected the worst when I first met him."

"Expect it again...the west wing is his apartment."

While the fading blush renewed itself across my throat and

chest, Charlotte pulled open the bodice and stripped it away from me.

"With Master Farrow as your neighbor, I think you'll find life to be quite exciting."

IT GOES WITHOUT saying that I was very nervous about Malin on my arrival to the estate. Between the vague threats Charlotte had made toward my family and the general reputation of territory masters as a whole, let alone Malin himself, I had been very afraid that I would be expected to perform a nefarious service or face vivisection on some gurney.

As time went on, however, I grew more at ease. As much as one could with such a man, anyway. He made it easy in that I did not see him all the time; but when I saw him, it was with the same clockwork regularity he showed in the rest of his life. Every morning, at 7 a.m., the steady rhythm of his knock would lead me from my book. He smiled every time I opened the door, and he never hid the slither of his eyes along my body, but he never let it become excessive or made his lurid thoughts known.

"Good morning," he said merrily each day, his eyebrows raising. "It's beautiful out—would you like to take a walk with me, Thecla?"

I thought it strange during the first week that he always asked, as though I really had the option, or might change my mind about our prearranged meeting time. Soon, however, I began to appreciate that he took the time to ask.

In those questions, as on the walks, I got the sense that Malin was genuinely interested in me and what I thought.

"Thecla is a very special name, you know," he said to me one day, once I had been there about two weeks. We were taking what I had come to regard as our usual route through the gardens, which were at that time dusted in only the faintest layer of snow.

"My mother named me. Father told me my name is very old. I don't know much about it other than that."

"She was a holy woman and a healer. There are some books on the subject in the library, I'm sure. You should look into her sometime."

"I want to visit the library very much, but oh—I don't know."

"I've noticed you hardly leave your suite. You're not a prisoner, you know."

"Just an unregistered riftborn," I said, unable to keep the hint of bitterness from crisping my voice.

Thankfully, he was patient with me at that moment and said only, "That doesn't matter here," without breaking our steady stride over the dusted path. "You were in more danger in your village than you are here on my property, Thecla. Go anywhere you like. If we were less isolated, I would even encourage you to go off the grounds and enjoy activities that don't require proof of humanity or registration, but we are a little remote for that. Even so—I don't want you to feel that you want for anything."

"It's hard to avoid feeling that way. I'm so restless. What am I to do all day? With whom am I supposed to interact?"

"You and Charlotte seem to be getting on well."

"She's lovely, but—well, I don't know. For instance, she takes her lunch with the rest of the staff, and dinner, too. If she eats breakfast, it's even before I get up, and I'm up very early. So I see her, but it isn't as if it's very restful when I do, and I sometimes have the sense I'm in her way."

"What about the courtiers?"

An uncomfortable laugh bubbled up from me at the merest thought. I hadn't even tried entertaining conversation with the noble hangers-on who lurked around the manor waiting for a chance to talk to Malin. "I don't really know how to relate to them," I decided to say.

"With whom do you eat your meals, then, poor girl?"

I shrugged as I confessed, "With no one, sir."

Quite shocked, then shaking his head with the chagrined eye roll of a man who had just realized something obvious, he said, "Of course not…poor thing. Why don't we start having breakfast together? I hate the thought of you spending so much time alone."

My cheeks burned with the cold, or with his offer. "All right—that would be pleasant. Thank you."

"Think nothing of it…I would gladly take dinner with you, too, but it's an unreliable meal for me with all the politicians and petitioners and so forth I always wind up having to meet. You should find someone to share your suppers with, though, Thecla."

"I will, hopefully, if I can get to know somebody better. I really tried eating with the staff, but—I don't know. I'm not one of them, I think I just made them uncomfortable."

"Well," he suggested after a beat, "what about Eleison?"

My heart hammered to hear the name. I glanced away, off to the muttering blue scrub jay that hopped along the bare branch of a cherry tree.

"I don't think Eleison likes me very much, sir."

Malin scoffed. "What? We can't be talking about the same man...Eleison likes you just fine, Thecla."

I laughed a little despite myself. "I really don't know about that. He didn't seem very interested in letting me thank him for saving my life. I've barely seen him around since then."

Which killed me. What was he doing? I always wondered, then hated myself for wondering.

"Well, I can tell you that Eleison thinks you're a very fine woman. In fact, he was the one who told me I would like you as much as I do...and he was right."

"I like you, too," I seized my chance to tell him, the words falling out of my mouth perhaps a little too quickly before I was left blushing in their absence. Malin looked at me with a merry twinkle in his eye, and I smiled despite my embarrassment.

"Thank you," I told him, "for treating me so kindly."

"You're welcome. But, I admit—I look forward to the day when you no longer feel you need to thank me."

So did I, of course...though I didn't know at the time exactly what that day would entail.

I truly *was* grateful to Malin, however. I was grateful for the home and the food and the gowns and the library; I was grateful for his company.

And, in the end, I was grateful for his next decision...even if, at the time, it was extremely irritating.

The next morning, when I had bathed and dressed as usual, opting for simpler day clothes so as not to need Charlotte's help during the start of her day, the usual knock rang out upon the door.

Except that it wasn't usual.

Its rhythm, its heft—everything sounded slightly off.

My heart skipped a beat at the impossibility my mind insisted to be reality. Somehow, it knew before any hint from my senses were required. That knock alone was enough to indicate what—who—awaited me.

I cracked open the door, and that intuition blossomed like a flower whose petals unfolded in excitement, dread, humiliation, anticipation.

For on the other side was not Malin, but Eleison.

ELEISON RESTED HIS forearm against the jamb above his head, leaning into the frame of the door with an expression somewhere between boredom and placation.

"Sorry to disappoint you," he said, jerking his head toward Malin's living quarters. "Malin's got some appointment he's dealing with this morning...he asked me to fill in."

Clearing my throat, I straightened up my posture and smoothed down a few wrinkles on the skirt of my gown. "That will hardly be necessary," I began, weakening my stance considerably when I was once again caught up in the vivid amber glow of his unnerving irises. "Surely you don't think I need an escort through the garden."

"Wouldn't advise going out without one even a few weeks after a Rift Event, really. Not unless you can shoot. Which, based on your decision to use Char's rifle as a cudgel…"

Hiding my humiliation by fetching my coat from the hanger discreetly behind a panel in the wall, I insisted, "But I've never had problems after a Rift Event in Lescaut."

"Because you've got friends, and neighbors, and a whole town full of people who are all equally interested in seeing the latest wave of monsters exterminated within twenty-four hours of the Event. Here, we've got a staff of twenty-six if you include myself and the security contracted by Malin, plus the private servants and security of whatever courtiers or artists he has staying in this house at a given time."

I snorted, recalling a few standoffish aristocrats I had encountered in the game room a few afternoons before (and one of my final attempts to force social interaction). "And I'm sure they're leaping to contribute."

"Exactly. Add to that the isolation of the estate, and you can probably understand why a hungry monster that's been wandering the wilderness could show up at any time."

I exhaled in disappointment. This was probably all some scheme from Malin to make sure I was capable of getting along with Eleison. I would be as polite as I could, but if he decided to get rude with me again, I wasn't sure I would be able to help whatever I said.

"You look nice," he told me even as I had that thought, turning briskly away and disappearing down the hall. "Shall we?"

Flustered by his compliment—so baffled by it, in fact, that I glanced in the mirror on my way after him to see if it had been sarcastic—I shut the suite's front door and hurried to keep in stride with him.

Just before we turned into a corridor that opened to the central staircase, the sound of Malin's voice rising from the western apartment perked my ears. Another male voice answered, though I could detect nothing distinct.

So it wasn't a charade, then…not a complete one, anyway.

Regardless of the intent—regardless of what I hoped would come of it—the walk was agony for the first length into the gardens. His long coat swirling around him in the same uptick of wind that sent his black tie flapping around his throat, Eleison paused outside the doors to light a cigarette. My nose wrinkled in theatrical disapproval, but to tell the truth I didn't really mind the smell. It reminded me of my father's office, and of such simpler times. Strange that a poison could be so comforting.

When he started moving again, I moved, too. We walked side by side, his free hand in his pocket and my hands folded before me, our elbows carefully tucked into our bodies as though to avoid the least contact.

It was clear he detested me—so why did my heart still throb to walk with him? Why did the clove-tinged scent of his tobacco make me want to bury my face in his neck, kiss his lips, wrap myself in shirts that smelled like him?

I decided to try to break the silence. "Are you always so quiet?"

"Unless I have something to say."

"And you have nothing to say to me?"

He looked at me from the corner of his eye, barely turning his head to do it.

"No," he said while, with a glance at tracks that had preceded us through the snow, he selected the route toward the hedge maze. "No, I don't."

Why did it hurt me so much? I clenched my teeth and strained to read the inscription upon a stone bench we passed by too quickly.

"I suppose I must seem very common to you."

He scoffed. "What do you mean?"

"Just that. You're probably waiting for me to do something oafish, like the rest of those—painters and poets always meandering around, wanting to know when the snow will thaw so they can play croquet again."

The short bark of his laugh surprised me. For just a handful of seconds, I caught the edge of his smirk. Then his head lowered toward the cigarette and the expression was hidden.

"I'm just as low-class as you, Thecla…lower."

He was so elegant in his movements and spare speech that I couldn't believe that, but I was grateful he at least tried to placate me. Maybe Malin had spoken to him more directly than I would have thought.

"If it isn't about class," I told him, stopping at the juncture of walking paths just before the hedge maze, "then what is it about?"

"What is what about?"

"Whatever *problem* you have with me!"

He had stopped to face me, and as I said the words, his facade cracked just a little. Eleison's mouth strained, his dark brows knitting and relaxing in a single second.

"I don't have a problem with you, Thecla."

"Well, you've certainly been *treating* me like you do. When I tried to thank you for saving my life, you blew me off completely. Three days ago you started to come around a corner, you saw me speaking to Charlotte, and you *turned around!* You must have used the service elevator just to keep from passing me on the stairs."

"Guilty as charged."

"But *why*?" It was embarrassing to be so emotional about a man I hardly knew, but I couldn't seem to stop myself. "Malin insists you like me just fine—so why are you avoiding me? Why won't you even talk to me?"

"I'm talking to you now."

"Oh, please. This walk has been like pulling teeth."

"You sure do speak your mind."

I sputtered a little, annoyed that now was the moment he took to smile at me. It was more of a smirk, really, but there was a kind of amusement in his eyes that softened the beautiful expression—and enraged me more.

"I certainly do," I told him at last. "And I want to understand *your* mind, because it must be mad. Is Malin lying to me?"

"No," said Eleison. "But Malin is the problem."

"But why?"

Shaking his head as if in disbelief, looking around himself for an audience, Eleison took the cigarette from the edge of his lip and gestured with what was increasingly little more than a filter.

"Why...because Malin is—Malin. I've seen him in action. Many times. I mean...you get it, right?"

There was a certain gruff element to his tone that was protective as much as it was guarded, and it incensed me. "'Get' what?"

"So you *don't* get it."

After contemplating the filter pinched in his thumb and forefinger, Eleison shut his eyes with a short, dark little laugh. His empty hand raised to rub across his brow, his nose, his eyelids, before those eyes opened once again and pinned me like a butterfly to a shadow box.

"Malin is—trying you out. He's trying to decide what do to with you. And, right now, he is seeing if you'd be a suitable wife."

As I, my entire face no doubt a mask of red, initiated a few sputtered, unfinished protests, Eleison shook his head and tossed the extinguished filter into a can at the corner before the hedge maze.

"He's seducing you, Thecla," Eleison summarized. "And you barely know it."

"Of course I *know* it," I insisted, embarrassed to say it out loud—even more embarrassed to say it beneath Eleison's piercing stare.

He didn't bat an eye, and I went on out of a new, quivering sort of anxiety that welled up within my heart and abdomen.

"I can tell he *wants* me. But, for marriage? Surely, no. I'm neither a child enough to miss attraction altogether, nor to dream that some wealthy territory master would want me as anything more than his plaything."

"You haven't heard him talk about you, Thecla. I have. He hasn't mentioned his dead wife in years; suddenly he's floating ideas, like what a scandal it would cause if he showed up with a young, new wife, and whether or not his dead wife's soul will forgive him, and all this...I know what he's thinking, but, at the same time, I don't."

Biting my lip, not sure what to make of all this—whether any of it was even true to begin with—I asked, "Why would he want to marry me?"

"Aside from the usual reasons men want to marry a woman like you...if there's one thing Malin loves to keep close, it's power. And you have a lot of it lying dormant, Thecla."

I shook my head, almost laughing. "You both keep insisting that, but I just can't believe that it's true."

"I'm sure you will, eventually. How old are you?"

"Twenty-four."

"Interesting. You know...I've never met a second generation altered before. I would have expected them to develop their connection to their monster in the beginning of puberty, rather than the end brain development. Guess I was wrong."

"I don't feel much like a monster of any kind—except for when I'm trying to be friendly with you, of course, and you brush me off like a gnat."

"Thecla—you don't understand."

"Then *help* me understand!" I waved my hand, navigating the terse conversation back to the original point, unwilling to be deterred. "You've been so rude to me since I awoke here! I appreciate that you saved me, and I'm sorry you detest me. But even if you detest me, that doesn't mean you have to be so unpleasant all the time!"

Why did he do this to me? Why did my emotions run so high at the thought of Eleison's rejection?

Why was I acting like such a child?

"Thecla..."

Tears blurred his silhouette and obscured his features enough for me to get away. I turned on my heel, my arms wrapped tightly around my body as I strode toward the house.

Before I got more than two steps, he lunged to catch me by the bicep.

A gasp tore from my lips as his hand rested on me, my body reacting with a cringe that was surely imbued with the muscle memory of his bestial bite. Yet, all the same, the mere caress of his hand was a sensual pleasure—even when he grabbed me roughly to keep me from escaping the conversation!

Stopping in his grip, trembling with enjoyment at his touch, I looked over my shoulder

His cold eyes had thawed into an intense sadness.

"Thecla," he said again, a strangely tender note of desperation straining in his voice. "That's not why."

His hand relaxed. I deigned to face him, chest puffing despite the shimmering of my tears.

"Then why?"

Before he could utter a word, someone stepped from the hedge maze.

THE SUDDEN APPEARANCE of a woman from the maze
had me jolting with surprise.

Without hesitation, Eleison whirled toward the source of
my fright while reaching under his arm.

"Woah, boy." The stranger's voice was a low purr that set
my teeth on edge. "Easy, Eleison."

"Vivian…" Exhaling, Eleison lowered his hand from his gun
and said, smoothing his tie instead, "Don't sneak up on us."

She pouted in a way that made me hate her at once, if I might
be excused my kneejerk response. However, this initial impression
was soon reinforced by Vivian's entire character. Her blonde hair
gleaming upon her head, she strode from the maze with a smirk
on her face and a pair of sunglasses hanging loosely from her fist.

"Sorry, Eleison…didn't mean to startle you."

Her boots clicked to a stop before him. Vivian leaned toward
his face while my blood screamed with rage.

Eleison took a step back. While I relaxed, she pouted again. "Don't I get a kiss?"

"Not today, Vivi."

"Ouch! Now that's not very nice. I can't believe I used to think we could be mates...you're such a sourpuss."

"Mates?"

This Vivian woman had apparently forgotten me. Her eyes, dangerous gold with the same sort of glow as showed from Eleison's irises, flicked toward me in impatient derision at my question.

"Who is this?"

"This is Thecla," he said with a gesture.

Eyes widening slightly, the woman smiled in an artificial way. "I know that name...so *this* is the specimen."

"She's not a specimen."

"On the contrary. Dr. Gall is here to speak with Master Farrow about certain pieces of vital information he would like to acquire."

My stomach flipped. While Vivian's immaculately manicured nails rebuttoned her coat and gave me a glimpse of the trousers and black blouse below, I asked, "What kind of information?"

"Information to benefit humanity, of course...nothing too terrible, I'm sure, but who knows. You should see some of the projects the doctor has arranged before..."

"Shut up, Vivian."

Eleison's harsh remonstration earned him a glance of gratitude from me, plus a deep scowl from the doctor's bodyguard.

"What an asshole you are today, Eleison. I'm just making conversation...you're never like this. Everything all right? Under a lot of stress?"

She stopped inches before him, her lips quirked in a smile.

"I'm sure I could help with that."

Her hand raised toward Eleison's cheek.

He stopped her before contact, gripping her forearm and pushing her away.

"It's not a good time, Vivi."

A storm cloud slid across the woman's features to be rebuffed so definitively.

"That's fine," she said, stepping back from him and tearing her arm free of his grip. "I should head inside, anyway...the doctor will be finished soon."

Sparing me hardly more than a flick of the eyes, she strode off toward the house and bumped arms with Eleison in a show of aggression on the way.

He turned to watch her go, snorting a pillar of condensing air through his nostrils.

"We should head back in, too...come on, Thecla."

Before I could stop him, he took off, retracing our path through the gardens rather than taking the direct route after Vivian. I hurried along with Eleison, more frustrated than ever and still at a loss for how to handle such a strange man.

Inside the manor, it turned out Vivian was right. By the time Eleison and I reached the top of the stairs, Malin and his guest were already in the hall. Somewhat unexpectedly, Dr. Gall was shorter than his bodyguard...and really quite old. If he wasn't retiring age already, he would be soon, and his gray hair told the tale. I shuddered to think of whatever experiments such a benign, normal-looking old man could produce when given infinite money and precious little oversight.

"There she is," said Malin, noting me right away and gesturing us over. "Come here, dear, come meet a friend of mine.

Dr. Gall, this is Thecla…Thecla, this is Dr. Gall. He lives and works in Saalast, up in the north side of the territory."

"Very nice to meet you," I said with my curtsey, forcing myself to stare the man down despite the uncomfortable toothiness of his smile.

"And you, my dear…and you, yes, very nice." After he took my hand for a limp handshake, he smiled at Eleison. "I see you're already under the wing of one of my finest jobs."

"Dr. Gall here was the one who altered Eleison," explained Malin.

Obviously unhappy to see him, Eleison ignored the doctor in favor of Malin. "I'll get the car started for your next appointment. It's a long drive."

"Yes, very good, thank you…at any rate, Thecla, dear, we wanted to ask you a question."

I waited for Malin to elaborate. To my surprise, he took my hand before speaking further.

"As you and I have discussed, your existence is something of a rarity, and your kind have been woefully under-studied. Dr. Gall here would very much like the chance to learn a little bit about you, and in a way that is as unobtrusive as possible."

"Just blood draws," he said, leaving me to grimace and look back at Malin. "Maybe the occasional physical or stress test."

"All recorded at home, of course, and transmitted or shipped up to Saalast so you won't have to be inconvenienced…but it would be quite valuable information."

I frowned, searching his inscrutable expression, trying to find some honest essence in those sharp black eyes.

"Is this something I really have a choice in?"

"Yes, Thecla, of course—I mean that sincerely." My surprise

must have shown, for he released my hand with a small but genuine laugh. "Dear, dear, it is your body...if I thought you were more valuable as a specimen than as a companion here in my home, I would have seen to it that you were delivered to the right agency as an infant."

While I shuddered at the casually delivered reminder of the cruelty he could have inflicted—could still inflict—but decided against, Malin continued with his hands folding before his belt.

"The choice is truly yours, my dear. I don't have a stake in it one way or another. Dr. Gall gets plenty of other specimens from our territory, even if they're not as valuable as you. There's no obligation."

"But," Dr. Gall hastened to interject, "think of all the good you would be doing!"

Good—for whom? Good for the government that would have an easier time selectively exterminating or researching people like me? Good for Malin's relationship with the doctor, whose very gaze so disquieted me that I tightened my coat against it as I would against the wind?

"If it's truly all the same to you, Master," I said, enjoying the slight spark of delight the title always seemed to produce from Malin when I insisted on using it, "I would prefer to not."

"There you have it." Malin gestured toward me with an apologetic smile to Dr. Gall. While the doctor frowned, (and I released a slight sigh of relief to find my wishes were respected), Malin went on. "I'm sorry to have gotten your hopes up, my friend...I'll tell you what, though. The next one I find, I'll send right to Saalast."

"Well," said Dr. Gall with a far tighter, far smaller smile than he'd had before, "I certainly would appreciate it, assuming I'm not retired by then…or dead. Oh, but, before I forget—you should come with me to the Torea Festival's inaugural match again this year, Malin!"

"Oh, dear, I'm sure I couldn't…"

"Come on, it'll be a good time! You've turned me down every time since the first time, but you know my box is the best seat in the house. Plus, the dinner afterwards? You'll regret not going when I talk about it again!"

"Well…" Wearing a coy little hint of a smile, Malin studiously avoided looking at me while he suggested, "Perhaps I might bring along a date. Turn it into an occasion."

"That's the spirit!"

While the men shook hands, the doctor turned his somewhat bulging eyes upon me. Though I smiled politely as I could, I also fell back upon my heel so half my body was tucked just behind Malin's arm.

"Don't be afraid to change your mind, Thecla. We can always use new subjects…especially ones as rare as you."

The doctor turned away to walk with his guard to the service elevator.

Somehow, I kept myself from shuddering until he was out of sight.

A S RATTLED AS I was by the doctor, and as confused as I was by Eleison, something else stuck with me from that morning.

Malin.

I had been dubious of Eleison's claim that Malin wanted to marry me, but the territory master's unusual respect for my bodily autonomy made me second-guess myself. It was just as likely that this was all for show, of course. All part of the seductive game he was playing. Yet, despite their differences in station, I got the sense that Malin and Eleison were very close. I didn't think Malin was the type to say just anything to a confidant.

But—if Eleison was right, then that meant Malin, the territory master of Gudrune, really *was* thinking about marrying me.

Me.

It was strange. Immensely strange. A territory master could have any woman he wanted, and this one wanted me? Eleison had explained it away as a desire to keep power close—but if all he wanted was my power, Malin could have assigned me to physical conditioning and made me into one of his security personnel.

The thought that Malin might genuinely crave to *marry* me was so thrilling I could hardly look at him straight-on the next day, and my gaze had to break away into bashful smiles more than once. As apt as he was to notice everything, he quickly noticed that.

"Dare I ask what's gotten you in such a giddy mood today?"

At his question, I could only shake my head. "Just the fine weather."

"Yes, we've had a good run…enjoy it while it lasts, though. Did you see the RMS today? 80%."

I paled a little. In my haze of the past few weeks, I had fallen out of the rhythm of checking. Now the placid sky seemed ominous. My breath quickened to remember the overturned carriage, the raining glass.

Malin touched my elbow, a little spark flying up my shoulder and into my brain along with the warm murmur of his voice.

"Now, don't worry. You'll see how safe the manor is when it's locked down for an Event—you won't even remember anything's happening outside."

I wasn't so sure about that, but didn't argue as we strolled on toward a frozen pond at the far edge of the garden. "I used to know the day's Rift forecast as well as I knew the date…you just made me realize I haven't looked at an RMS panel in two weeks."

"Everyone needs a break from reality from time to time. If

I'm being frank, that's what I enjoy so much about these walks, Thecla...the world feels very peaceful when I'm with you."

Moved, I smiled up at him and dared to rest a hand upon his bicep. He looked quite pleased, one large hand raising to enfold mine.

Then, with an "Ah" that erupted from his lips, he pointed at the lake's edge while a pair of geese took off, presumably for someplace a bit farther south. They flapped away, honking into the distance, their cries echoing across the estate until long after they'd disappeared.

Later, while Charlotte collected the remains of my supper to whisk off on the usual silver tray, I realized a whole day had passed. I'd spent every moment of it replaying the morning.

"Do you really think Master Farrow is all that bad, Charlotte?"

"If I did, I wouldn't work for him."

"I suppose that's true."

"He's selfish and sometimes extremely cruel, but aren't we all. He has his good qualities, and as a ruler or employer, I personally find he is very fair."

"Does he have any children?"

With a queer glance my way, Charlotte set the tray aside and took to polishing off the table. "No, Thecla, he doesn't. His wife left him before they had any children."

"I thought he said she died."

"She did—a few years after she ran away with another man."

How awful! I wondered about that with a frown, then found myself abruptly focused on something else. "Do you know much about altered individuals, Charlotte?"

"Only as much as most do."

"Do you know about mates? I heard someone say something about that recently, but I don't really know much about altereds. About myself, I suppose."

"Well, I'm really not sure." With a quick sweep of the floor, collecting crumbs she dumped into the dirty tray, Charlotte said, "So far as I can tell, it's a biological phenomenon that occurs when two altered individuals…synch up, for lack of a better term."

"What do you mean?"

"I haven't seen it happen, myself, but I've heard that altered individuals can bond and sort of stabilize one another against the Rift."

"So they don't need that drug?"

"Right. No Stabilify required. There was even a study I remember, showing the capacity for physical healing—the repair of wounds, I mean. It's a kind of symbiotic relationship, almost, although I believe there is an implicit aspect of physical attraction. I'm not well-informed."

"Better informed than I am," I assured her.

"I'm sure you'll pick it all up in time, Thecla…the way I see it, you're flourishing more every day."

In part, I agreed with her. After working to keep a roof over my head, the freedom granted by unlimited time and unlimited access to—albeit not possession of—wealth was an incredible dream from which I felt I could awaken at any second. I seized every moment I was alive, reading books and listening in on the sounds of cellos or pianos being brought to life in the music room. I let the library pick up my education where my father's abrupt death had left it off, plunging into history and educating myself on altered biology. My diet was healthier and more well-rounded than ever, and it gave new sheen to my hair, new color to my cheeks.

I *was* flourishing. But two figures cast their shadows across the flower of my mind, blocking the sun and keeping me utterly consumed in a dilemma that seemed sillier all the time.

Malin was falling in love with me, and I with him. I believed that; there was no question of it.

So why did I care about what Eleison had not finished saying? Why did I ponder over his words day and night, his voice ringing out when I passed him in the hall or glanced him from across the estate?

I had to talk to Eleison again. I had to know what it was that drove him to be so unkind to me.

And I had to know why it mattered to me—why I could not shake such foolish girlhood fantasies.

My will was set. The next day, by then knowing something of their schedule, I lurked and brooded about the manor in anticipation of my best chance. Malin tended to dismiss Eleison in the evenings, taking time to himself in his apartments once supper was finished and his final meetings for the day had been adjourned. I assumed he worked late into the night, or at least stayed up a time with his thoughts, for I occasionally noted a maid bringing him a meal or some nightcap when I could not sleep and wandered the manor to settle. So far as I had noticed, once he retired for the evening he did not emerge again until it was time for him to knock on my apartment's door.

I had the whole evening to speak with Eleison, then, and I looked forward to it all day.

Until, around noon, I recognized the telltale signs of an imminent Rift Event.

I emerged from the library, the long-delayed letter to my stepmother at last in my hand and sealed for its recipient, only to find the staff moving much swifter than usual. Some, in fact, half-ran to their destinations, a kind of restrained skip down the hall from window to window amid a rattle I recognized much too well from my own childhood shutters being checked and re-checked.

Yes: all the window panes were shuttered.

My stomach in knots, I hurried down to the parlor where the courtiers liked to gather. Sure enough, they complained miserably about the weather, ignoring me while I studied the RMS.

RIFT EVENT IMMINENT, it read, bearing an estimated countdown of twenty minutes.

As disappointed as I was to see this meant another delay to my letter, I was all the more disappointed when I emerged from the parlor intent on my room. At the bottom of the stairs in the grand house's foyer stood Eleison, his expression serious as he met with other members of the security staff before they braved the storm together.

His eyes flicked over me, then darted back to the focus of his conversation.

I had known a Rift Event was coming, based on my conversation with Malin the morning prior. I just hadn't stopped to think what Rift Events meant for Eleison, practically speaking. In truth, it was the most important part of his job. Everything else he did for Malin was secondary.

Before Eleison was anything else, he was a monster hunter—even if a lot of hardline monster hunters would have considered him a monster, himself.

My heart ached, no doubt for those same mysterious reasons that made me crave his friendship. I hated the thought of him spending time out in the Rift; hated even more knowing the danger it posed him. The longer he was out there, the more control his monster would have over his mind. I'd read just that morning that some altered got so overwhelmed it took a week-long regimen of Stabilify to bring them back to somewhat normal—sometimes, just in time for the next Event. The thought made me sick, and even as the house was shuttered and sealed, I felt more helplessly exposed than I ever had in our little home in Lescaut.

A lump in my throat, I rushed back to my room and made sure my windows had shut.

My relationship with Rift Events had changed overnight. Just as I had become considerably more wary after being caught in one that night with the circus, my latest brush with the phenomenon had left me terrified. I could barely stand to eat, and Charlotte could not persuade me to. Eventually she gave up and took the tray away, telling me, "Just wake me up if you're famished tonight...I'll forgive you this once."

Then I was alone in my suite, my stomach tight and my skin crawling with the nagging awareness of the danger outside.

The danger to which Eleison was presently exposed.

My body was cold even as my mind ran hot with a fever. I filled the bathtub and sank inside, wishing desperately for someone to talk to—for someone to be of comfort to me while the world outside raged and contorted with horrors inexplicable to mankind.

When I finally finished weeping uselessly, the water was cold.

I hated it, but I couldn't help it. Never had I felt such an uncontrollable terror. Such a deep despair. My understanding of myself had changed my understanding of Rift Events, and of what they could do to me. Better in touch with what they could do to *me*, I was doubly afraid for what they could do to Eleison.

The violet evening passed into deep purple night. I gathered as much from the security camera broadcast that played helpfully on the screen in the parlor. The Event showed no sign of abating, but the security force seemed to be doing their job. The whole time I watched, poised on the edge of the sofa, I saw only one creature—a horned, horse-like calfus, which loped by the camera as though on stilts. They were thought, like ventil, to be mostly benign, and though they were killed like all the other invasive monsters, it was always a relief to see them and know they were likely to feed a borro long enough for a hunter to easily put the predator down.

When I accepted that the Event would not let up anytime soon, I retreated upstairs to bed.

Not even the luxuriant mattress could lull me to sleep. Worse, when it began to, a terrible howl pierced the air from somewhere on the grounds. I trembled beneath the blanket, my teeth chattering, my arms folding around myself as I wondered what the creature had been. A luptich? Not quite. They sounded more like women screaming in agony. An odious cry that had lured more than one well-meaning person to their demise.

No, no—I felt certain it was a borro caterwauling in the night. And while at first the thought of such a thing made me terribly afraid, it wasn't more than a moment before I realized, if it *were* a borro howling in the Rift, it could have been Eleison.

My heart sped. Somehow, possibility turned to certainty in my mind. It *was* him—it had to be him. Prowling the grounds in bestial form, staking the territory around the manor against any challengers who might emerge from the Rift for the hunt.

A heat swept my body. My trembling gained a new, albeit different intensity. I felt taut as the strings of the music room cello. With my eyes squeezed shut, I cleared my mind and focused on the rich black depths of my eyelids.

But Eleison was there with me all the while.

Why did he affect me? It didn't matter he was out there, risking his life. Of course not. I owed him nothing beyond the usual level of gratitude one might show for such an act.

But...it was horrible to think what might happen. Horrible to think that perhaps, when the Rift Event was over, everyone in the security detail would return to the manor—but Eleison wouldn't. We would ask what happened, and they would explain he had reached his limit, and that was it. He had finally gone mad, and no amount of Stabilify could retrieve him from the primitive depths into which his consciousness had sunk. They had given the drugs to him with darts; they had sedated him and tested him, and nothing would work. Nothing would bring him back, and he faced life mad in a cage.

They explained to me they had to put him down, like a dog that had been bitten by a rabid rodi or common bat. I wept bitterly—savagely. Wailing as I had never wailed before.

Someone handed me a knife, explaining I was the only one who could do it. When I asked why, they repeated themselves.

As the knocking awoke me, I was still demanding to know.

14

SWEAT DOTTED MY brow, my body trembling as I came to in the dark.

What was that knock that had awoken me? Had a monster breached the manor and caused some commotion in the hall?

The knock came again, gentler this time.

Thank goodness. It was too human for a monster's accidental fumbling—and too close. I sat up in bed, baffled, and looked toward the wall from which the noise seemed to emanate.

"Hello," I called, a little afraid.

"Thecla"—it was Malin! my heart skipped a beat—"are you all right?"

His voice, though muffled, was only as much as it would be through a door. I frowned despite my flutter of excitement, sliding up from the bedside and wandering a few steps into the center of the bedroom.

"I'm sorry, I was dreaming—I feel like I still am."

He chuckled, explaining, "Try the bookshelf," and I gasped. Hurrying across the room, I pulled, then pushed, then at last rolled the shelves aside in a mechanism not unlike that of the hidden coatrack's panel.

"You *cad*," I remonstrated the territory master, trying not to smile as his tired but gently amused face appeared on the rolling away of the shelf. "I didn't know you had a secret passage into my *bedroom!*"

Batting his eyes and offering a quick shadow of a fake pout, Malin said, "You have to be the one to roll away the bookshelf, Thecla…the panel beneath is just there if you care to use it. Really, though—"

He grew more serious, reaching across the threshold to my room, and surprised me into another soft gasp by resting his thumb against my cheekbone.

"Are you all right? Do you need anything? Some company?"

"Oh, no," I began, a little frightened by how excited I was to be touched by him in such an intimate way, "no, I should probably—"

"Then perhaps some tea?"

My nostrils flared. I nodded, the pretense somehow easing my mind. I still couldn't believe his intentions were wholly pure… but then, I didn't really care. The presence of another person—a strong man who had shown me great patience—was a boon with the Rift Event ongoing outside.

A few minutes later, Malin had brought me to a comfortable sitting room within his apartment and settled me into the sofa. I marveled not just at the thought that he had his own kitchen, as I could see from my seat, but that he knew how to make his own tea.

I had always had the impression that men of his station couldn't clip their own nails, let alone do something like boil water. Yet, nothing seemed beneath him. Not even me.

Well…not in a bad way.

"I don't suppose you feel like sharing the contents of this dream you had," he commented while emerging with the tea tray.

"No." I gave a weak smile he returned more organically while bending to fill the cups. "I'm sorry, sir, it's just—"

"Thecla, please…it's you and me, alone in my apartment. You really don't need to call me 'sir.' Not at one o'clock in the morning."

"Is that the time? Oh, I really am sorry—"

"You don't need to apologize. Here." After handing me a cup and saucer, he took up his own and sat in the corner of the sofa beside me.

The night of our first meeting came floating back. This time, in the sofa in his sitting room, he didn't bother leaving any cushion between us.

A fiery tension rose up in me. I'd had a sexual partner, but it hadn't felt anything like this. There had been anticipation, yes. But there had not been this happy fear; this high energy that had a way of pulsing through my fingertips and down my every limb.

I wanted to resist him, because I feared him, and because the childish part of me still clung to those rusty visions from the circus. But, oh, as Malin regarded the slight sag open of my robe around the bosom of my night dress, or as he let his knee brush mine while he leaned toward me to speak, I wished just as badly to give in without a thought.

"Do you have nightmares often?"

"No—I don't, usually. I don't know what's wrong with me."

"Well, now, it's been a transition…and I know you had a difficult experience during the last Rift Event." While I nodded, he leaned back into the arm of the couch and rested his saucer in the lap of his red robe. "I do hope your dream wasn't about Dr. Gall from the other day. I want you to—"

"Oh, no—"

"—to know," he continued, not a man to be interrupted, his eyes sternly finding mine in both a remonstration and an indication of sincerity, "that I won't let anything happen to you. I took on the duty of caring for you, or agreed to do so when your father died. Because of, shall we say, miscommunication, I was late in fulfilling my end of the bargain. The way I see it, I owe you the pleasure of eight years."

He drew from his teacup, his eyes on me while I shook my blushing head. "That's very generous of you, Mast—Malin, but—"

A small chime from the RMS meter on the wall interrupted me, and a pre-recorded voice announced from the built-in speaker, "Rift Advisory Update: Rift Advisory has been extended for twenty-four hours."

My heart sank, and while I lowered my cup back into its saucer, Malin sighed. The voice droned on, engaging in the usual patter about remaining sheltered and how to order emergency rations of food while in shelter, if necessary. Malin set his cup and saucer down altogether, then swiftly crossed the room to set the panel's audio functions to mute.

Alone on the couch, my teacup rattled in its saucer. When he had accomplished the task and turned to find the source of this new sound, I looked down at my own hands and realized, with a startled sort of laugh, just how *much* I was shaking. The tremors from the bed were mild compared to this: I whimpered, struggling to set the saucer and cup down upon the coffee table while Malin breathed my name. He hurried back, sitting close beside me and not hesitating to slide an arm around my waist.

"It's all right, Thecla," he told me warmly, that arm drawing my head down to his shoulder while his other hand caught one of mine. "You're perfectly all right."

"I know—it's just—"

"In the twenty years I've owned this place, do you know how many monsters have breached the security protocols and gotten into the mansion?" I shook my head against him, against the cushion of his warm robe and its rich sandalwood aroma—and the hot, male scent it masked.

"None," he answered me, his broad hand stroking my back. "None have ever gotten in, Thecla. Not even a rodi."

I nodded against his shoulder. "That's good. That's good—I'm glad."

Eleison, out in the darkness of the tainted night.

"I'm still just—" I couldn't find the words. "I don't know. I don't know."

"It's all right, Thecla. I'll keep you safe, just breathe your way out of it."

Slowly exhaling, I took his advice and did my best to moderate my reactions. I couldn't do anything about Eleison; furthermore, Eleison had been patrolling the grounds long before my arrival. Clearly, nothing significant had happened to him. He was still alive and walking. He still had control over the monster inside of him. He would be okay for one more day.

"There," Malin said gently, his hand sliding more slowly up and down my spine. "There, Thecla...that's better..."

I raised my head and realized my cheeks were damp.

Before I could touch one of the tears that had crept from my eyes, Malin rested his hand against my cheek.

His thumb trailed beneath my eyelid, sweeping back toward the temple and along the track of the tear. It came to stop at the edge of my jaw while his eyes, still tender but now dark with something else, bored into mine.

Unhesitating, hungry, Malin captured me.

I gasped, pushing myself against him, my entire body pounding with my heart at the caress of his lips. While his tongue took advantage of my gasp to slip between my lips, my hand slid into his hair and tangled there. The other caught up the edge of his robe. It fell open so that, when his hand upon the back of my neck drew me closer to him, the heat of his bare chest seared my body through my nightgown.

His kiss was unabashed, but also unhurried. As his tongue familiarized itself with mine, far bolder than I could ever imagine myself being, Malin's steady, deliberate attention ratcheted my internal tension up to a degree I'd never experienced. My legs and my feet, my arms and my hands: every muscle was wound tight, yearning for the caress he dispensed liberally upon my mouth.

And it did not take long before he obliged me. My pulse raced as his hand made an experimental slide from my spine to my backside, which he gently stroked and squeezed. When my center of gravity began to shift back, I realized he was resting me back against the arm of the couch. Excited, my entire body a unified flame, I moved at his silent behest and quivered to lay beneath him—even with so many layers of separation still between us.

His breath mingled sweetly with mine, filling my mouth and my lungs with his intense, rich essence. My fingers itched to touch him: to explore his body.

But his hand trailed from my rear to the path of my thigh, and I realized we were swiftly reaching a point from which return would be impossible.

And—what about Eleison?

Panic rushed through me. The territory master's kisses were sweet and intense, and the caresses of his hands had left me yearning for far more than that. Yet, all the same...

I just couldn't.

Not yet.

"I have to go back to bed," I whimpered, turning my face away from his and provoking a faint groan from his lips at our separation.

"Are you sure," he murmured, his mouth pressing against my hair, my ear, my throat. "I have a very large bed in this apartment, you know. Very comfortable."

"There's one in mine, too," I whispered back, my face flush, my stomach in knots for fear of disappointing him.

But then I saw the dark sparkle of lust in his eye.

Did he enjoy being denied? The thought heated my blood for reasons I couldn't explain.

"All right, Thecla," he told me softly, his nose brushing mine and his hand stroking up over my thigh just once more, stealing the memory of my body for his own pleasure. Then, without encroaching for another kiss, he released me. "All right...but don't be afraid to come seek comfort if you have another nightmare, darling. I wouldn't mind it if you woke me up."

THE UNFULFILLED YEARNING stoked by the territory master's petting stayed with me all night, and when I fell asleep it was to dreams far sweeter—and far more lascivious—than the ones that had chased me into his arms. One of the world's most powerful men, separated from me by a bookshelf.

Going over to him would be so easy. I could picture it—did picture it, in dreams. Slipping through that hidden panel, softly wandering through a hall I did not know. By the sound of his breathing, I would divine where he slept. He surely would have left the door unlocked, anticipating my arrival. He might even hear me then, stirring awake with the readiness of the veteran, prepared to take me from the moment I sank into his arms. Could I stop myself from begging for more of his kisses? More of those tender caresses?

Now I trembled from more than fear. I was overwhelmed by the intense static of excitement when I wondered what it would be like to give myself to Master Farrow as utterly as a woman could give herself to a man.

And that made me wonder what it would be like to give myself to Eleison, too. Younger than Malin, but so much more somber. Could he let himself go with a lover?

I had never expected myself to become such an insufferable person.

Why was I still having these thoughts? What had Eleison done since he saved me? Nothing not within his job description— and even that rescue had been an assignment. As I always reminded myself, I owed him nothing.

Yet there I was, laying in bed, ruminating about him as though Eleison were the one courting me, instead of Malin.

But, oh…both were so fine that I wasn't sure a woman who saw them would blame me.

When erotic dreams of ambiguous quality gave way to morning, the rich scent of bacon filled the room. I blearily lifted my head, startled to see the late time—and more startled to realize I had forgotten to roll the bookshelf back into place on going to bed. The panel had been opened, and Malin's apartment lay accessible as it had when he walked me back to my bedroom with one final kiss at the threshold.

Excitement and dread and desire raged through me. Somehow, I had the sense he did not just open the panel and walk away. How long had Malin stood in the doorway this morning, his eyes fixed on me in my final moments of sleep?

Had anything stopped him from crossing the threshold and coming nearer than that?

I followed the scent of breakfast, my stomach knotted with lust rekindled by nothing more than an open door and my imagination. Charlotte had really meant what she said…charming, and dangerous. I had to be more mindful of the bookshelf in the future, unless I wanted to be awoken by the wickedest man on the continent in the middle of some dark night.

Although, now that I thought of it…maybe I did.

"There you are," he told me warmly, not batting an eye to find I had wandered in still wearing my night dress and thin silk robe from the night before. A delicious breakfast spread of potato pancakes, pork belly, peppers, and eggs had been set out by Charlotte that morning, appearing along with the tea service. I took my usual place across from him after he stood to greet me, smiling as he pulled out my chair.

"I hope you don't mind my opening the door for you…I never heard the bookshelf slide back last night, and when you didn't respond to my knock, I thought the smell might wake you up."

"That's all right…I know you just wanted to see me sleeping, you wicked old man."

His nostrils flared above his razorblade of a smile, the darkness of his eyes aglow as though with the burning light in the heart of a coal.

"You do look lovely all flush with sleep, Thecla…though you are quite right. Helpless and oblivious, the thoughts you inspire in a man like me are of the wickedest kind."

A throb of pleasure pulsed through me, his words as effective as any caress in inciting my body's responses. While he raised his teacup, I shivered beneath his gaze until I managed to avert my eyes to my silverware.

"I suppose it's just as well that I left the shelf aside... though"—I laughed shyly down at myself, then smiled at his trim gray suit—"I'm sorry I'm not very presentable. You know I don't usually sleep in."

"I'm sure you needed it after last night, poor thing. Although—"

He bent forward a degree, my heart fluttering. Beneath the intimate table, his knees brushed mine.

"I hope I didn't frighten you."

Savoring the heat he brought to my face, I shook my head and dropped my napkin into my lap. "No, you didn't. Not—last night, anyway."

"So I frighten you otherwise? There's hardly any call for that..." His great hand rested upon the table, enveloping mine before I could pick up my knife. My entire body unwound into bliss at the touch.

"Perhaps, someday, you'll relax around me. I want to see the Thecla that's really in that mind of yours."

Though I wanted to protest that he had seen me, I couldn't. It was fair to say I was keeping myself from him, mostly owing to Charlotte's advice...but also, juvenilely enough, because I was afraid he wouldn't like me. I kept my opinions to myself, afraid to offend him or make him think I might somehow be a danger to his power. I had not yet found it in myself to speak my mind around Malin, however stimulating his presence was for me.

Yet Eleison was stimulating, too—and he had seemed to like my tongue when it was barbed. If only I could get time alone with him! I could use a little practice at once again being myself before I dared to be myself with Malin.

Surely that was the only reason I wanted to be alone with the footman.

Whatever I did or didn't tell myself, the chance came a few days later. When the weather cleared and the manor was able to throw its windows open once again, I waited with bated breath for the return of the security officers. They never arrived; not that day.

"They patrol the grounds for two or three days after a storm, sometimes camping in the forest outside of the property while they hunt the stragglers." Charlotte explained this to me while changing my sheets, by now very used to my interrogations while engaged in tasks around me. "I'm sure they'll be back any day now."

I couldn't seem to rest until they were. All night, I lay in bed with the new, acute awareness that Malin's apartment was just on the other side of my bookshelf; that, any time, I might give in to my desires without effort. And I admit...I was sorely tempted.

I was not a virgin. I'd had sex before, but it was just that— sex. Mechanical, and rudimentary. Although I was attracted enough to the young man at the time, the cold truth was I just wanted to get the first time over and done with. I wanted to be less afraid of it, and of whatever it would make me feel. So, with a suitable partner, I initiated myself into adult mysteries...partly.

There was more to sex than the body. I realized that now with full certainty. It was true that I craved Malin's body, of course—but what I wanted from him was what I had wanted from no man. I wanted Malin to make *love* to me. I wanted him to caress me with terrifying hands that made tea and brokered deals and signed death warrants. I wanted to kiss the scar on his face and wonder how many people he had killed while I felt him inside of me. I wanted to dissolve beneath his attention, fading off in all directions with the weight of his body once more over mine. I wanted him to teach me things I didn't know—things I sensed to be about him, but could not name or describe.

But I dared not. I was too afraid of the dissolution. I was too afraid that, once he took me, there would be nothing left to interest him. Then, there I would be: back in my original, grimmest fate.

I had to resist him, even if I felt my defenses beginning to fail.

Two days after the Rift Event, in the evening, I was summoned to an appointment in the medical office. It was a fine little clinic, and the doctor there—Dr. Singer, a much more pleasant and friendly woman than Dr. Gall had been a man—studied the scar on my arm once she peeled away the remains of the medical glue. A frown crossed her lips.

"Is something the matter?"

"Well, not really. It's healed fine. I'm just—sort of surprised."

"How so?"

"I don't mean to bring up your private business, but you're altered, aren't you? Second generation, right? Maybe that's why... usually, though, altered don't scar."

My lips pursed at the shadow of Eleison's bite, the spread of his fangs so small now that the wound had closed. The scar did not do justice to the trauma of the wound at the time. No one who looked at my arm now would understand the experience.

The only one who could understand was the man who walked into the clinic as if summoned by Fate.

"Doc," called Eleison, the grit of his voice darker and more rumbling than ever above the steps of his agitated pacing, "you got a minute? It's urgent."

His voice like a bolt through me, I straightened in my seat as the doctor spoke. "Oh, yes, of course. One second, please"—she lowered her voice before speaking to me where we were behind the white partition—"wait just a moment, if you could. I have an ointment I can give you to help the scarring."

"I really need it now, Doctor," said Eleison tersely. With a great inhalation, he added, "Or two days ago."

"Of course, of course…"

While she rose, she clumsily bumped the partition aside a few inches with her elbow. Eleison's breath hitched. If his sensitive nose hadn't already detected me, he certainly just saw the shape of my arm.

I clenched my fists, able to guess what would come next.

"You know what? Go ahead and bring it to my room. This little clinic—I can't wait in here another second."

"But—"

The clinic door opened and slammed behind him. Sighing, the doctor made a noise of impatience and went to a tall cabinet of drugs that rose in a corner of the office. While unlocking it, she said, "Some people could use a remedial course on manners."

"Is his short temper because of the Rift exposure?"

Weighing my question with whatever existed of patient confidentiality in a house that was obviously full of gossip, the doctor removed a small tube for me. "Between you and me, Eleison is usually patient…even after he comes in from an Event. This past few weeks, though, he's been so short-tempered it's almost hard to work with him. Who knows why? I don't let it get to me when my patients are testy…no doctor who does can last long."

Dr. Singer may not have known what caused Eleison's foul moods, but I did. I had a vague idea, anyway. Slipping my prescription into the pocket of my dress, I made my way back toward my room until I heard the clinic door open again. Then, I stopped.

In truth, I didn't even know what apartment in the sprawling house was Eleison's. Asking Charlotte would be too transparent and might even merit some intervention; and for most chances I had to follow Eleison, Malin was also awake or somewhere on the grounds.

That evening, though, he had already retired, and the doctor was bringing the prescription as a delivery; so, keeping a corridor length between us when possible, I followed her through the halls to Eleison's room. Every time she rounded a corner, I darted as quietly as I could to her last place; then, peering around into the new corridor, I watched her for the next turn. It went on like this only a short distance. In the north hallway, Dr. Singer stopped at the third door from the end and knocked upon the hand-carved oak.

Their appointment didn't last long. As the door began to open to let her out about three minutes later, I tiptoed back several yards and stood, waiting, in the center of the corridor. Hearing the doctor's footsteps, I fell into casual, unhurried stride and even made smiling eye contact with her when she rounded the corner and we passed ways.

"Hello again," I told her merrily, earning a small laugh and wave.

"Hello," she said, adding, "good night!"

"Good night to you, too," I called, letting out my breath as I was once again shielded by the corner and she was out of sight.

Now, it was just me and the door.

And the man on the other side of it.

Still wondering what exactly I intended to do or say, I rapped upon the oak.

Heavy footsteps echoed over; the door flew open, Eleison saying, "Did you forget—"

His face changed. His eyes and mouth both opened a little, and although his usual cool demeanor resumed, he straightened up perceptibly within the gap of the door.

"Hey." Eleison nodded, looking me over before—much to my surprise—stepping aside. "You want to come in for a minute?"

A minute, at least. I kept my true thoughts to myself and seized the invitation while it lasted, smiling as I passed him. His room was a suite like mine, with a living room, a bedroom and an attached bath, though he also had a kitchen about half the size of the one in Malin's apartment. I confess, I was somewhat envious... but, I supposed that was how Malin wanted it. If I wanted to make my own tea so badly, he probably wanted me to have to do it in his quarters.

"Can I get you something to drink?"

"I'm all right, thank you." I wasn't sure where to sit and found myself wandering a little around the room, my eyes falling on a framed photograph mounted near the front door. Eleison, looking younger—blue-eyed, to my surprise—with a similarly-featured boy quite a few years younger than him. I perked. "You have a brother?"

"I do."

"I have a sister...I meant to send her and my stepmother a letter that I'm safe, but then the Rift happened."

"Well, it's over for now...you can send it tomorrow."

"I suppose. How was it?"

Unable to resist my curiosity, I turned to face him with my hands worrying one another before my dress. He similarly busied himself while watching me, a glass of whiskey in one hand and the other braced against the bar behind him. The difference between him now and the almost hostile man in the clinic was already night and day.

Not that he wasn't still an unbearable jackass, at times.

"How was the Rift Event, you mean?" He looked at me, his expression dry as his tone, before raising his glass for a mouthful of liquor. "It was just great...a regular vacation."

My eyes rolled. "There you go, punishing me for trying to make conversation with you."

"Sorry. I don't like small talk."

"I don't, either, but you also seem to detest medium and large talk."

The dual notes of a short laugh burst from his lips. His somehow canine smile staggered me with its beauty, then disappeared as quickly as it had come. "I guess that's fair to say. But why are you here, exactly, if you feel I'm in the habit of punishing you for conversation?"

As he spoke, he set his drink down and strode through the open door of his bedroom. I followed instinctively, hanging on the threshold and struggling to ignore the rich navy bed sheets that, along with their silver-accented spread, looked very inviting with him nearby.

"For one thing, I'm trying to be friendly. But, well, for another—we never finished our conversation because of that wretched Vivian woman."

"'Wretched!'"

While he laughed, I said, "I'm sorry. I don't mean to insult your friend, but—"

"No, no, you're right...she's pretty wretched. And I'm not really friends with her, either."

Turning his back to me, Eleison worked free the buttons of his shirt. When I realized what he was doing, my skin sizzled and my fingers itched to help him.

"Vivian and I used to...spend time together, when opportunities allowed."

"Why don't you anymore?"

"Why do you care?"

"Just making conversation, as I explained before."

Tossing me another glance with those moody eyes of his, Eleison shrugged off his overshirt. "Well, let's just say that Vivian and I have...moral disagreements, along with personality mismatches." I got a brain full of his broad shoulders before he tugged the simple white undershirt over his head. Then, I held my breath. The taut muscles of his back, dancing through his pale flesh with every movement, were especially highlighted by the stripe of his shoulder scar—black in his human form, unlike the white strip of fur it appeared to be as a borro. I struggled to focus on his words while he went on, "And she's a little—disturbed."

"From working with that awful doctor?"

"Maybe...but I think it's more that her power screws with her perception, makes her think she's superior to everybody else."

"Power?"

"Yeah, this sort of hypnosis thing...she's riftborn."

"Really! And altered? But I thought they were rare."

"Second generation altered, let alone riftborn ones, *are* impossibly rare. But a lot of registered riftborn end up being altered in their lifetime, either due to enrollment in various research programs, or because the only careers that will reliably accept them long-term are military or security service."

I nodded, saying, "I suppose I can see the benefit to alteration in that case."

"There's no benefit."

His words were sharp as serpent fangs. I cringed at the venom in them, trying not to blush as he turned to face me with a new black undershirt clutched in his hand. His body was a finer piece of architecture than the mansion. I struggled to meet his eyes until the moment in his rantings when his head disappeared beneath his shirt. Then, I could lap up every inch of his body. The sharp planes of his pectorals, the dusting of hair across his chest and trailing from his navel down into his trousers, the alluring lines of the Adonis belt that accompanied it down, down—

"You saw me back there in the clinic," he was saying all the while, a monologue my brain was forced to reassemble once he had his shirt on. "Forget the clinic—you *really* saw me, Thecla. You saw me with your blood in my mouth. You saw me forget I was human. I don't even have to be a beast to feel that way. Hell...I don't even have to go outside."

After a second of delay in which he stared at me, drinking me in as I did him, I managed to absorb the weight of his words enough to respond.

"Wait—you don't have to go out in the Rift to be affected by it?"

"Not anymore. Increased Rift sensitivity—it's a condition that occurs with chronic Rift Event exposure, Stabilify or no."

My heart ached. I stepped toward him, amazed how I never grew numb to the sting of the way he cringed at my nearness.

"But—but what does that mean, Eleison? Wouldn't that mean you'll lose your humanity no matter what you do?"

"Tick, tock," he said with a vague gesture toward the wall clock, loping into motion to make his way back to the sitting room. "It's only a matter of time."

"But"—I hurried after him in a panic, only just refraining from grabbing hold of his arm to keep him still—"but what about Stabilify?"

"It barely works for me now. Doc'll be back to give me a dose every day for the next three or four days, given how I feel now."

"How do you feel?"

He bared his teeth in a short, humorless laugh and didn't look at me while picking his drink up from the bar. "Like an animal."

"What does that mean?"

"I shouldn't talk about it."

I hissed an exhalation through my teeth while stepping toward him.

He whipped rapidly around and fell back a step to match the one I had just taken.

My irritation turned to unsympathetic anger.

"Stop doing that! Stop"—I stepped toward him, he stepped away—"stop *fleeing* me, you absolute madman! What is this all about?"

Falling back on my heel, I waved my hand between us and said, "You wanted to know why I came here—as I said. We have unfinished business. What is it about me that you find so repellant? What is it? What's *wrong* with me, Eleison?"

"Nothing. I keep telling you—it's not about that."

He made me feel like a child! A confused and frustrated child: overwrought, overtired, always on the verge of an interminably overdramatic tantrum. My hand slapped over my eyes, I demanded, "Then what *is* it about? Damn you—what is it about!"

"Because I don't want to see you hurt," he said at last, his gaze unflinching as I lowered my hand. "Not by Malin. Not by me."

"What a silly thing to say."

"You really think so, after what I just told you? The Stabilify barely works, Thecla. Do you understand me? Can you try to understand, just for a second, what that really *means?*"

I tried to understand. I looked his body up and down and tried to understand what it would be like to be a man. To be a man with a beast inside of him, wild and hungry, full up of the urges of a beast and all its lack of social culpability.

To be a man with a beast inside of him, alone in a room with a woman.

"I don't believe you could really hurt me," I said, flushed with all manner of illicit ideas. "No—I don't believe it."

"And that's why I need to protect you. I don't want you to be there at the wrong time, on the wrong day. I don't want to get friendly with you, Thecla. If we get friendly, something might happen."

"But—but why don't you find a mate?"

He had been turning away to set his empty glass on the edge of the bar, but he paused with it still in his hand and looked at me sharply. I went on, wishing I could touch his hand in an impulse that ached me for too many reasons.

"Charlotte explained a little of all that business to me, and I read some more about it in Malin's library, though that was vague, too...but that's all Stabilify is mimicking, isn't it? It's a synthetic cocktail of the chemicals an altered's brain releases when they sense the pheromones of their mate...it just lacks some of the more miraculous effects."

Now, when I stepped toward him, he didn't step away, although he looked poised to do so if I tried to bridge the gap any farther. I didn't, instead asking with that space between us, "Why don't you find your mate, then, and stop the process of destabilization?"

Remembering that glass, he finally set it down and left his hand upon it. He examined both, his face illegible to me.

"It's not that simple."

"Surely you have no trouble getting women to fall in love with you, Eleison. What about that Vivian woman?" I was so urgently worried to hear he was in an advanced stage of destabilization that all my jealousy fled me at once. If someone, anyone could save him by any means, that was all that mattered. "She said she used to think you might be mates. Could that be true?"

"It can't be just anyone," Eleison said, adding, "and I hate Vivian, if you really want to know the truth. I can't trust anybody who enjoys our job as much as she does."

"Regardless, there must be something you can do! What about all the maids in this house? Are any of them altered? Or, perhaps—"

"Don't bother, Thecla." He shook his head, his scarlet eyes softened by a pain I wished intensely to see healed. "There's nothing that can be done. I've accepted it. You should, too."

He turned away, obviously intent on getting the door for me—but that great, somehow primitive rage rose through me. Didn't he want to fight for himself? For his life, for his humanity?

Didn't he want to live?

"Malin kissed me," I blurted.

Eleison scoffed, stopping in place without turning to face me.

"Why are you telling me this?"

Because I was angry; because I was helpless; because, against all logic, I was hurt.

"I just thought you should know," I told him, striding past him for the door. "I hope you have a good night, Eleison—and I pray you will feel more like yourself in the morning."

I made it halfway down the corridor before the gathering tears overflowed.

16

SLEEP LOSS WAS growing to be my custom. In the intimacy of darkness, my mind concocted all number of lurid dreams regardless of my waking or sleeping. I therefore chose to enjoy them awake, so I might reason them out and use them to come to grips with my days.

How was it that Eleison—that anyone!—could succumb to such profound despair? He deserved better. The world deserved better. It was made infinitely more beautiful by his glittering presence in it, and his loss to bestial madness would be an unreasonable devastation to the fabric of reality.

Who could want to live in a world without him, even if seen only from a distance?

When I caught myself in such thoughts, I grew furious. Furious at him and at myself, and at that dastardly old carnie who showed me Eleison all those years ago.

How weak was I, truly? How absurdly had the change in my life, from Lescaut to my new unofficial position as Malin's pet, afflicted my mind? Just there, in the apartment adjoining my little suite, rested a man who quite openly desired my mind, my body, and maybe even my hand in marriage—yet my soul endlessly rotated around Eleison, Eleison, as if his tragic fate were in any way my burden to bear!

I sat up, despondent that sleep was not forthcoming, and had just slid from the bed to fetch my slippers for a nighttime walk when a curious *crack* echoed from the apartment adjacent mine.

Along with, of all awful things, a woman's gasp.

My mind, already fatigued from running wild, once again flew into rapid motion. I tried desperately to imagine a plausible scenario that was not the obvious—but the sharp sound came again, and louder.

And I was next seized not by anger, but by confusion.

Was I really hearing what I thought I heard?

Crack.

No—it did not resemble the sound of flesh on flesh, body on body.

Instead, it sounded a great deal more like the cracking of a whip.

My stomach twisted, and the new ringing in my frightened ears made it difficult to confirm the sounds. Soon, though, I pierced that veil of uncertainty and caught another *crack*, and another cry. The woman's cries—they were of pain, I realized at last.

Fingers numb, I found it impossible to do anything but press my ear to the bookshelf and listen.

What was going on over there? Was someone being punished? I didn't realize the manor engaged in corporal punishment—but why?

And, most importantly—why did these whipcracks, the cries of this woman, the location of it all somewhere in the master's apartment, stir in me such a baffling, visceral heat?

Because I don't want to see you hurt.

Not by Malin.

Not by me.

When the cracking stopped, I listened closely for other sounds, but there were none. Only the murmur of soft conversation. No audible kissing, or sounds of sex. Just footsteps. The shutting of a door.

More footsteps.

I realized someone was leaving Malin's apartment and jumped out of my slippers. On bare feet, I hurried through my suite and snatched up a hand mirror on the way. When I got there, I held my breath, nudged open the door, and barely extended the mirror. I'd just tilted it at the proper angle when the grand door to the west wing's luxury apartment opened and a maid stepped out.

She didn't see me, occupied as she was by smiling with love for the gold coins in her hand. But I certainly saw her—coincidentally, that she was roughly my height and only a few pounds lighter than me.

Before she stepped too near the lowered lighting of the hall outside my room, I withdrew the mirror and quietly shut my door. Yet, to have observed her for even the short time I had, she did not resemble someone who had just been given a beating. There was certainly a limp to her step as she launched into motion, and I thought I saw the hint of a wiped tear track still upon her cheek, but as she passed my shut door, she hummed to herself.

The next day, too embarrassed to face Malin, I crept out of my room well before dawn and found Charlotte in the kitchen, already in the process of opening the manor for the morning.

"What are you doing up at this hour?" She fully interrupted her conversation with a scullery maid on seeing me in the doorway, shooing her off with a brisk flick of her hand and turning her attention to me. Her previous question was revised with the arching of her brow. "Did you even sleep? You look like you've been in a fight."

Perhaps, with Eleison, I had been—but it was Malin who ensured I got no rest.

"May I have a moment of privacy with you?" I glanced at a nearby cook who, while bringing a crate of wines from the cellar, pretended not to look at us...or to be intently listening. "*Real* privacy."

A moment later, we were in a dark corner of that very same cellar, my coach leaning against a wine barrel with her arms folded and her expression arranged to exhibit vague impatience.

"This is about a man, isn't it?"

"Yes," I admitted with an eye roll, inspiring one from her.

"I hate talking about men. It's always the same—*they're* always the same."

"I'm not so sure about that. Malin, he—" I became aware of my volume and strove to speak even more quietly, leaning into Charlotte as I did. "I heard some unusual things last night."

When she didn't reply, I clarified as much as I could stand to. "From his apartment."

"Oh."

Just that. "Oh." Perfect comprehension, but without surprise. I pushed on through her wall of discretion.

"Does the manor—punish its employees?"

"No, no...not physically, anyway. You must have overheard Master Farrow's recreational activities." Her expression one of overt annoyance that extended her mouth and pinched her brow, Charlotte said, "I thought he would refrain with you next door to him, but evidently I gave him too much credit."

My mouth opened, closed, opened again, the comprehension slow to settle in. All I had was my naive frame of reference from innocent Lescaut, where the people were simple and the sex was simple, and both were also, I confess, a little dull.

I needed her to clarify, and pressed, "Recreational activities?"

Her lips still poised in that anti-frown she preferred to a true expression of emotion, Charlotte said, "I normally wouldn't worry about this, and would advise you to do the same; but, it would seem that he's courting you, so I think you'd ought to be prepared to accept some things. And if you don't want to accept them, then accept you'll have to compromise."

Face cold and body hot, I fooled with the pearl inlay around my collar. "What things are you talking about?"

Charlotte removed my hand from my neck as thoughtlessly as a governess might correct a child. "Master is an unusual man, with unusual tastes in—how can I say it politely—*aesthetics*. He values ritual. Have you noticed?"

Impossible not to notice. Every day, rousing at the same time, taking breakfast and walking with me at the same time. Retiring at the same time, too. I nodded.

"Well…for some men, their appreciation for ritual extends to the bedroom. They enjoy—incorporating things, or enacting things they find erotic regardless of how tacit the connection to actual sex seems to be. In Master Farrow's case, he has for years—even while married to the late Madame Farrow—engaged in the use of whipping girls for his amusement."

"*Whipping* girls? Amusement! What on Earth—"

"I did recommend you proceed with caution when it came to engaging Master Farrow's interest in you, didn't I…"

"I—yes, but—that's all—this is quite surprising. Didn't his wife mind?"

"Of course, she minded. I'm sure it's one of the reasons she left him, but I have it on good authority that it was a rather complicated scenario. She couldn't stand to endure his amusements, couldn't appreciate his love of rituals, and so she permitted him to rile himself up by whipping a chambermaid before making love to her…but I have no doubt she regretted the agreement, and the jealousy ate her up inside while she looked at a life without ever fully connecting to her husband on a physical level. Quite honestly, I don't blame her for fancying someone who was more to her taste; it's just a pity it all worked out the way it did, and that Master has spent so many years affected by it instead of moving on."

Charlotte ended her abbreviated tale by spreading her hands. "Admittedly, I never knew her—by the time he hired me to the manor's staff, she had been gone for some years—but even while I was a midwife elsewhere, I knew the rumors."

"How awful! Everyone knowing her for a cuckold…"

As grim reality set into my heart—that this manor would think me the very same if I did not take corrective action at once—Charlotte actually laughed.

I scowled at her, unable to appreciate the rare sound given my realization. "What's funny, exactly?"

"It's only cuckoldry if you're as apt to consider whipping a part of sex as he is…perhaps you two *are* a fine match."

Cheeks blistering with humiliation, I crossed my arms all the tighter and stuttered, "I just—don't like the thought of my future husband taking any excitement of any kind in other women."

"That, you'll struggle to avoid no matter the man, for they all have eyes and ears and even noses that commit too much to memory for any woman's comfort...but, if you want to keep Master Farrow's attentions, good and bad, entirely for yourself, you'll have to make that clear to him soon."

"How can I? He hasn't even confessed to me he's interested in me. You, Eleison—everyone seems to know he's courting me except for *me*!"

"Then that might be the real problem. Can you expect any trace of fidelity from an unofficial courtship?"

Sighing in frustration, the anger breathing out of me and leaving me hollow, I wilted beneath Charlotte's stern observation. My shoulders drooped as I said, "I just don't know what to think of all this."

With a purse of her lips and another of those rare looks of sympathy I managed to fleetingly inspire in Charlotte's features, my friend—for I had begun to think of her as such, as well as a kind of teacher in the arts of a dignified womanhood—patted my hand.

"What you need is to eat and sleep. I'll tell Master Farrow you're not able to join him on his walk when I bring him his breakfast today...but as to you, when you've gotten a little rest, come find me again. You need something to take your mind off these matters if you're ever going to decide how to approach them."

Numbly, I nodded and took her advice. Grateful she provided me my usual helping of breakfast and let me eat it at a preparation island on the far side of the kitchen, I then returned to my room on pins and needles of fright that I might run into Malin, or open my bedroom door to find the bookshelf rolled aside—but I had to be the one to do that, of course, so it was in place the same as ever when I collapsed in bed.

Thick, dreamless sleep rushed to take me; the kind of sleep that accompanies illness and distant travel. When I awoke, the sun was bright and the grounds were free of any hint of snow. Nine in the morning—four and a half hours of sleep were better than none, I supposed, and roused myself in a rather gloomy cloud to go meet Charlotte.

"You'll need these." She presented me with freshly laundered riding trousers, a black blouse, and a long-sleeved shirt for beneath. Her own outfit was similar, and I looked at her in surprise.

"You're not working today?"

"Goodness, I'm not *really* an automaton...we all have to take a day off every once in a while."

Smiling weakly, I let her help me out of my dress before hurrying into the clothes she'd suggested. While she touched up her coiffure, I emerged back into the corridor somewhat breathless.

"Where are we going?"

"Do you know how to ride a horse?"

"Uh—" Embarrassed, I shook my head and admitted, "No, not really."

"I didn't think so...so, I made some arrangements."

Ten minutes later, we had exited the mansion and crossed the sizable property to the stables that lay at a distance. There, I realized the outbuilding also consisted of a small residence, presumably for the stable boys. One of them reclined on his stool, his short, bright white head of hair barely touching the haybale behind him as he dozed.

"Kyrie," barked Charlotte, causing the young man to spring out of sleep with a startled noise. "Wake up—it's time for our appointment."

"Wouldn't have fallen asleep if you didn't wake me up at such an ungodly hour to *set* the appointment," he muttered, rubbing his eyes.

His violet eyes.

My eyebrows lifted in surprise, then raised all the higher as I recognized him through the altered features of his hair and irises. This was the older counterpart of the boy from Eleison's photograph.

"You're Eleison's brother!"

"Yeah—and you're Thecla, right?" Kyrie, who was perhaps only a year or two younger than I was but who nonetheless somehow seemed like a boy, strode forward to shake hands before remembering he was supposed to bow. When he straightened, I smiled and offered him my hand anyway.

"Nice to meet you," he said. "My brother's told me a lot about you."

I was getting very sick of hearing Eleison's opinion of me from other people—almost as sick as I was of hearing about Malin's courtship.

"We're done talking about men today," Charlotte mercifully interjected, her teeth bared in her dangerous little substitute for a smile. "Today, we're talking about something much more pleasant...horses."

"I've never seen so many real horses."

Kyrie brightened, nodding and waving an eager hand into the long stable building. Three horses had been kept in from the fields for our ride. The others milled about under the supervision of another attendant, who carried a rifle as a shepherd might once have a crook.

"They're all thoroughbred, too—not that it matters. All

horses are good horses." Proudly, as though they were his very own, the boy introduced me to them one at a time. "You might like this one, Thecla. This is Ambrose."

I stroked the horse's champagne-colored nose, astonished by how gentle a creature so large could seem. "He's gorgeous! Oh, but I'm frightened. I've never ridden a real horse before, never."

"You'll be okay—they won't hurt you, as long as you follow the rules of interacting with them."

At the boy's supportive comment, I laughed a little. "Somehow, I'm more afraid of hurting *them*."

"Don't be, Thecla." Charlotte's patient voice drew my attention as she unlocked the stall of a horse that seemed to know her well. It bowed its mottled gray and white muzzle happily into her hands, ears flicking above its bright eyes. "Do you know why we use horses and horse automatons, even though we could just build engines into carriages?"

I shook my head.

"For a little while, almost two hundred years, we used automated, closed carriages that did not resemble any animal. They were like sardine cans packed with humans, without any decoy or distraction that could potentially save those humans' lives when the Rift first began to come through. Do you see, Thecla?"

I swallowed back the fear at the thought, absently stroking the cream spot on Ambrose's nose. My memory surged with that awful moment of being trapped in the overturned carriage.

"What almost happened to us," she continued, saddling the horse and stroking its neck once she did, "happened very frequently, very violently, when the Rift Events first began. We quickly figured out that things resembling animals were better, because they could distract the monsters...and real animals were best of all, because they'll often take a horse in the open over a family in a carriage. That's why they're so expensive now—why you only see men like Master Farrow and his courtiers owning horses these days."

Or my circus. As sheltered as I had been, these things had never occurred to me, and I pitied the horses so deeply my heart felt it would break.

Even these animals had a way of evoking Eleison. Noble, quiet beasts meant to die after serving—and in service to—us.

"Show her the basics, Kyrie," Charlotte said, boosting herself into the saddle and urging her horse from the stables. "I'll meet you two in a little while."

With a click from the corner of her mouth, Charlotte sent the horse on into the field and very soon had it at a gallop.

How free she looked! I envied her—and her ability to enjoy it. No wonder she didn't care for talking about men...they really did have a way of making a woman miserable.

Yet, so euphoric.

"Hey." Kyrie nudged me with a glance around now that we were alone. "Are you doing all right? Are you comfortable here? Do you feel safe?"

Amazed by his question, I said, "You're the first person to ask me things like that."

"That doesn't surprise me...those weirdos are all off in their own little world." He waved his hand toward the manor before opening Ambrose's little door and guiding him out by a swiftly applied bridle. "Still—are you okay? Eleison's really worried about you."

"Good God! Then I wish he would exhibit it in any way." I felt dreadful at mere mention of the name, in fact, and nearly asked Kyrie to drop the subject of his brother altogether...but I just didn't want to miss an opportunity I sensed Charlotte may have intentionally arranged to take my mind off Malin.

"Is your brother always stubborn and unforthcoming?"

Grinning, Kyrie nodded as he turned to get the saddle. "Pretty much...but he's also a pretty fun person to be around."

"Maybe for you. He's been making *me* miserable—and be sure to tell him I said that." As Kyrie laughed again, I bit back my own smile with little success. "How is it that he's so insufferable, while you seem like a perfectly nice, easy-going person?"

Though the boy smiled on, his brow knit in apology.

"It's probably my fault," Kyrie explained. "He used to be a lot less serious and a lot *more* fun, to tell the truth, but...something happened. Be careful not to stand behind the horse," he added while turning to lead Ambrose out into the sunshine.

I kept in stride with Kyrie, finding him my height almost precisely now that we walked together. Funny—his brother was quite tall. "How could his bad attitude possibly be your fault?"

"I got really sick," said Kyrie with a reflexive frown. I'm sure I mimicked it, because he turned his eyes back to the horse. "I had a blood disease, and I was going to die."

My mouth opened in shock. Before decorum could stop me, I whispered, "A dharmine?"

Grimly, he nodded. "It came looking like our mom...I didn't know any better. I mean—I knew she'd been dead for two years, but I was just happy to see her. A kid, you know."

"How old were you?"

"Ten," he answered, aching my heart. "It's okay. Eleison killed it before it could really hurt me"—a feat for an unaltered man, I was astonished to note on later reflection—"but I still got sick a few days later. It was already just Eleison and me, and we didn't have money for any medicine. Not even for pain."

The boy cleared his throat, bringing the horse to a stop and busying himself by stroking its nose. "It was a really hard time. Really scary."

"I can't imagine how awful it must have been. I'm sorry."

"Yeah, well...I knew my brother would find a way to save me. And he did. A neighbor lady made us food sometimes, and he asked her to look after me for a while. I was so afraid I'd let him down by dying while he was gone."

I couldn't help myself—I touched Kyrie's shoulder, and he lowered his head with an embarrassed yet grateful sort of smile.

"But, the next thing I knew, these guys from the government came. They told me they were taking me to a hospital for a special procedure, to save me. I was really freaked out, but they promised me my brother would be there waiting for me to wake up...and he was."

Kyrie's chest swelled with a smile that was one part pain, one part a depth of gratitude I prayed I would never have to experience—until I realized it was just what I ought to have felt for Malin, whatever his reason for sparing me had been.

"Eleison's eyes were different," Kyrie reminisced on. "And, when I was allowed to get up to take a pee, I found out mine were, too. After the anesthetic had mostly worn off—like, the next day—he explained to me that he had come here, to our territory master, and made a deal. He got on his knees and said he had no money, but would do anything if Master Farrow would pay for my alteration. He had found out by then that it was the only thing that could save my life. And Farrow agreed."

With one small anecdote, my entire perception of Eleison shifted.

No wonder. No wonder he detested being altered, and all that it implied. No wonder he was so pained to think of the beast inside of him, and so nihilistic in the matter of his destabilization.

He must have felt he had sacrificed his life for his brother. And he *had*.

"Is that why you both work for—Master Farrow?"

Kyrie nodded. "We moved in as soon as I was able to leave the hospital, and we've been working here ten years now. It's hard to believe sometimes."

"Will you ever be free to leave?"

Nostrils flaring, Kyrie said with a slight edge, "You make it sound like we're slaves."

"Aren't you? Indentured servants, at least."

"I guess…but it's fair to me, knowing what those procedures cost and that there was no other way to keep me alive. And, I mean—if I have my choice between where we were living before and the life we have now, I guess I'm kind of glad I got sick. I just feel bad for Eleison…and I worry about him going out in the Rift."

Did Kyrie know about his brother's increased sensitivity? Anxiety struck me like a bolt of lightning to think he might not, but before I found a way to tiptoe out of the subject, he did it for me.

"Okay," he said, merrily slapping his hand upon the saddle to banish our somber conversation, "do you know how to mount?"

I was embarrassed to say I did not.

The next two hours really tested the limits of what I didn't know, I can assure my reader that. The one or two times I had been placed astride someone else's autohorse as a child did not in any way equate to the nuanced relationship developed between the rider and her living steed. As horses go, Ambrose was a dream; forgiving and patient despite his obvious power, he reminded me in temperament of Malin.

And it was Malin who, as though summoned, stood in the stables while waiting for Kyrie's partner to bridle a horse for him.

My stomach flipped to see him while we were coming across the field, having packed the lesson in before I lost the ability to retain new information. The horses marched on, oblivious to the look Charlotte shot me sidelong.

"Well," she said, "it was a nice little break while it lasted…"

Yes, it was—but, somehow, even that short green ocean of peace at the end of my raging night of red had been sufficient to change my mindset toward the night's events. Perhaps it was Charlotte's influence, or the understanding that Eleison was not so very bad after all, or the simple notion that I was tired of childish games. Whatever the reason, I didn't feel as much like the field mouse I'd been before hearing him crack the whip against some chambermaid's backside.

If I wanted Malin to be himself with me, I needed to be myself with him in turn.

"Ladies," said the territory master, pleased to meet us and oblivious to my new knowledge—or pretending to be. "How nice to see you! Are you feeling better than you were this morning, Thecla?"

"Oh, yes, sir, much better. My mind is clearer after the last two hours."

"She's a pretty good rider," commended Kyrie while helping me down from Ambrose's back.

"Is she?"

After smiling at the boy as pleasantly as he did at any of his staff, Malin turned his dark eyes upon me.

A hunger grew in them, and I felt sure he'd known I was listening in on him the night before.

"Perhaps, after you've had a few lessons, you and I will go riding together, Thecla...you can show me what you've learned."

"Or maybe you could just teach me." I eyed the crop he tapped against his shoulder as he took his opportunity to inspect my lower half, the riding breeches revealing the shapes of my legs to him for the first time.

"Oh, yes," he said, a slight smile crossing his lips. "Yes, I'm quite sure I could."

"Then let's talk about it later, when you have time to focus on me. Come on, Charlotte—I'm hungry."

Ten, sixteen, twenty yards from him, I still felt his eyes fixed on me. My heart raced.

An approving smile dimpling her cheek, Charlotte nudged me.

"That's more like it."

THE NEXT MORNING, I awoke to a faint knock on my suite's front door. Especially confused, since Malin had taken to knocking on the panel behind the bookshelf, I stumbled up in a bleary haze and belatedly remembered my robe.

When I made it to the door, the corridor was empty of anything but a bouquet of rich roses from the manor's extensive greenhouse.

As red as a woman's lips, as red as my blush when I beheld them—so red I gasped to lift them and their glass vase into my arms. I had never in my life seen flowers so beautiful, and they smiled at me from my dressing table while I bathed, perfumed, and dressed for the morning.

Then, all starry with excitement, I answered Malin's knock with a smile I couldn't manage to hide.

"Wow," he said, inspiring a laugh from me as he stepped aside to let me into his apartment, his eyes fixed on me. "Good morning."

"What on earth was that reaction about?"

"Oh, nothing—only that you have a glow today. What's put you in such a bright mood?"

Not wanting to come on too strong, I sat primly in my usual place and shrugged my shoulders. "Getting outside a little while yesterday must have put some color in my face."

"That must be it…well, let's take a nice, leisurely stroll today while the weather is looking so grand…"

My body smoldered while we ate across from one another, but I refrained from saying anything at all to him. Charlotte had made me realize I was lying to myself—and, in a way, to him. I needed to speak my mind to Malin just as Eleison liked me to.

And if Malin didn't also like it when I spoke my mind, well… that would settle things, wouldn't it?

In the garden, after we had conversed about light matters like my experience with the horses and my scant history riding their simulacra, I at last gave in to my delight from my morning gift while keeping my tone as measured as possible.

"Thank you, by the way—the flowers were beautiful."

Malin looked over at me, faintly smiling until the sentence was completed.

Then, he frowned in confusion.

"Flowers?"

A deep flush enriched that glow he'd commented on earlier. My mouth opened and shut, and I fumbled, "The roses—the red roses at my door this morning. They weren't from you?"

"No. They weren't."

The air changed. For the first time in my weeks knowing him, the territory master's voice had a darkened edge to it. This was a man who had killed other human beings, I remembered at the numbing of my fingers. Malin maintained an attitude of curiosity, but that curiosity extended to an avenue of theorizing that frightened me.

Surely the flowers couldn't be from Eleison, after all...but, if Malin ever thought they were—

"It must have been Charlotte's doing," I suggested before he could lapse into speculation. "Apology flowers, on your behalf."

The little shock worked, I thought. Somewhat forgetting his train of thought, he turned an arched brow upon me.

"She thinks I need to apologize to you, darling? Whatever for?"

Attempting to evoke the housekeeper's stony glance, I peered at Malin from the corner of my eye without turning my head. "Charlotte seems to know how ugly it feels to be courted by a man who flaunts other women at the same time."

"Now...Thecla—"

"That *is* what this is, isn't it, Master? Courtship? Or am I merely a courte*san*—a bauble to be called upon when your real appetites have already been engaged by chambermaids?" While his face grew quite stony, he did not interrupt me, and it relaxed as I continued with hurt seeping into my voice. "It seems to me half the manor believes you seriously interested in me, but I shudder to wonder what the rest of it thinks. And, as to what *I* think...I have not the least idea anymore."

We were well away from the eyes and ears of others, as always, but his prudent hawk's gaze still scanned across the garden. "Why don't we sit down," he said, not unkindly, gesturing toward the nearest bench.

"Thecla," he began again once he'd had that moment to collect his thoughts, "perhaps I really *should* apologize to you."

He paused, waiting to see if I had anything to add; I sat with my hands folded in my lap, patiently waiting, taking lessons from Charlotte—and from Malin, himself—deep into my heart.

"You're quite right. I have not been straightforward with you. I am courting you, in a sense...although I have hardly been able to do so in any official capacity, and I haven't decided how to have the conversation with you. I suppose this is it, eh?"

"It's no wonder no one cares to get to know me," I told him, airing my displeasure just a little. "I feel like your dirty little secret."

"No...that's the maids you mentioned."

"Then I'm your blasted fool, for being the last one to know. Malin—I think of your kiss all the time."

That got his attention. He had been sliding into guilty reflection, or at least consulting whatever aspect of his inner life constituted something like conscience. Now, he turned his gaze directly to me, and the pressure of his attention gathered hot and tight in the center of my body. I let it fuel my speech, which grew molten as my insides and poured out of me in a way I never knew it could.

"Ever since it happened, when I think of you, or smell your aftershave in the halls, I feel your lips on mine again. I *taste* you, Malin, and shiver like your hands are touching me all over...even when you're nowhere to be seen."

His nostrils flared. Perhaps in response to a desire to do just what I'd said, he slid his great hand into my lap and tucked it between my gloved palms.

"I want to make love to you, Thecla," he told me, my blood

shrieking with delight and everything above my thighs stirring wildly at the words. Not just my sex, but my heart and my brain—I was utterly aflame, and I squeezed his hand in my excitement.

"Yes," I whispered. "That's all I want, Malin. Oh, Master—I want to know you absolutely, but—but I'm so afraid."

His eyes began to dim again. At least, they dimmed until I spoke on.

Then, they grew bright and hot as the noonday sun.

"I'm afraid that, even when you make love to me—even if you marry me—I may never know who you really are. After hearing you whip that girl the other night, I realize you've kept your true desires hidden, and I'm afraid you'll hide yourself from me forever. I want to know you, Malin—truly, deeply know you, and to be clear with one another. Please...please, if I let you take me, promise me it will really be *you*. Promise you won't use another woman when you could be teaching me. Promise me you *are* seriously interested in knowing me, and in letting me know you."

"You'll be frightened to know me in the way you're asking to."

"I'm already frightened of you, Master."

His eyes, haunted like the rest of his hungry face, flicked toward my decolletage and its evidence of my speeding respiration.

"That's one of the things I like most about you," he told me, his voice a rich bedroom murmur. His eyes found mine again as he went on. "I love how afraid you are...and I love how it doesn't stop you."

"I don't like being afraid," I told him, my breath hitching as his right arm slid around my back like it had during that fateful Rift Event. "I hate it. But, sir, I love the way *you* make me feel afraid...you make fear feel like something sweet."

His pupils, enlarged by desire, focused my mouth.

"If you can make fear feel so sweet," I went on in a whisper, my body trembling at the dart of his tongue across his lower lip, "then I must imagine there is something exceedingly delicious in experiencing pain at your hands."

"I would like to kiss you, Thecla—right this very second."

"Please," I begged, the word barely free before his mouth swept down.

As incredible as his kiss had been during that late hour in the superficial intimacy of his quarters, the beginnings of our true intimacy transfigured his embrace into something almost transcendent. There was absolute power in Malin's lips and tongue and hands. I recognized it and submitted to it at once, thrilled by the pure command he exhibited over my body, drinking in his breath as every second left me more sensitized. More attuned to—and desperate for—him.

With only a kiss, he could set me on fire. With one hand on my back and the other resting upon the nape of my neck, his fingers just inching into my scalp, he made me moan as though I already lay unclothed in his sheets. With the scrape of his teeth along my lip when his tongue absented itself from my mouth, he promised me what it was to fully love him.

"I will refrain from engaging the maids," he said when we parted, his words breathless, his hand raising from my back to brush a few slightly disheveled locks of my hair back into place. All the while, he studied my face. "They try too hard to please me, at any rate...but, Thecla—"

He addressed me with a stern passion, my ruler and future lover at once.

"If I'm going to make these sacrifices as a consequence of

our courtship, while you sit here making sweet promises of what awaits me on the other side...you must appreciate that I am an impatient man. Moreover...I'm a man who knows what he wants when he sees it."

To my unending shock, Malin slid from the bench and knelt before me.

"I want you, Thecla. Marry me."

"Malin—"

Charlotte's advice was very good, whatever it had done to me. Was I dreaming? Had I gone mad, or had the world? I didn't know; I didn't care. I didn't for a moment stop to consider *truly* 'Why me.' It didn't matter, and doesn't. Not in that moment; not now.

Not anymore, anyway.

"Malin," I gasped, my body and words incensed by desire and delight, "yes—of course, yes, do you mean it?"

He actually smiled to hear it, his hands tightening around mine. "Of course I mean it. I've been a lout, Thecla. Oh! Thecla, angel, don't ever think of yourself as my dirty little secret. Think of yourself only as my beloved. Let me court you properly."

"But—I'm unregistered—"

"And will be registered, as the wife of the territory master. You see, dear, this is the problem I've had...it really is rather all-or-nothing. Either I'm marrying and legitimizing you, or I dare not breathe a word of what's between us. There's no happy middle ground of open courtship."

Now understanding his dilemma, I gasped a little as he slid back into the bench beside me and explained, "Marrying you takes the backlash away. It would be just as if you came from another country, from a legal perspective at the very least. In fact, that may be how we process your paperwork—but, that's for me to worry about. For you, well—rest assured, as my fiancée, no one would dare treat you as anything other than legitimate."

Malin bent over my hands to kiss them, his expression as sincere as I had ever seen from him when he sat back up.

"I'm so sorry, Thecla, that you've had a difficult time adjusting here. It's all my fault...let me make it up to you."

"Yes." I nodded as I spoke, head whirling with questions I dared not ask. "Yes, Malin—yes, I want to marry you. I want to kiss you every day, I—oh—will you kiss me again, please? I'll go mad today thinking of it, but—"

His arms were around me, and his lips were upon me, and the low murmur of my name on his voice flowed through me. I moaned, melting into his embrace, my hands curling around the lapels of his coat while I wished they were scratching the bare skin of his chest.

When we separated, and that burning gaze raged into and through me, I noticed someone standing in the distant mansion's rear entrance.

Eleison watched us a few seconds more, then put out his cigarette and retreated inside.

THOUGH MALIN LEFT me at the rear doors of the manor as he always did, there was real regret in his face to let me release my grip on his arm. He kept his hand over mine while we stood in the mud room, his dark eyes glowing with those strange and frightening male thoughts that somehow delighted my body with their very existence.

"I would so much rather spend the rest of the day with you," he murmured, his head bending over mine. "Oh, Thecla... Thecla— Would you think me an absolute hound if I asked you to see me tonight?"

The air surged through my lungs in a great, reflexive inhalation.

"I want to see you, too. Oh! I'll be afraid all day—I *am* so afraid," I corrected, half-laughing.

That dark hunger deepened in his eyes, and he let me go.

"Good," he said, removing his coat. "I'll expect you at nine. No later, is that clear?"

Frightened and excited that he chose to command me this way only now that our engagement had been settled, I told him, "Yes, Master Farrow."

He stood at the edge of the room, his eyes fixing me to the spot with the arrows of his unspoken lust.

Then, he was gone.

Alone, my heart raced. I sagged back against the wall, my hand upon my chest.

What just happened? *How* had it happened? The manor tilted around me, but it did not dissolve as it might at the end of a happy dream.

This was real. A territory master had just asked me to marry him. Not only a territory master, but Malin Farrow. Certainly among the most highly regarded on the continent, if not among the most powerful.

And just like that, he had responded to my pressure against him as though I, an unregistered riftborn able to exist only through his generosity, were his equal.

I supposed, if I was to be his wife, then he *must* have considered me an equal, or at least a potential equal. But I was no fool, either. I could tell there was far more to his decision than that, and the lust he felt was a convenient pretext for ensuring society could never deny him his secret weapon...whatever that weapon ended up doing, eventually.

I didn't worry over the reasons, however. I was ecstatically happy. There was no question that I was in love with Malin, and although on the surface his affection was reserved, within him lay a growing passion that increased like a wildfire more all the time.

All morning, no matter what I did, I trembled to wonder what that passion would do to me when it was unleashed. My mind overflowed with outrageous fantasies.

Yet, when those fantasies reached sweet peaks, the lurid narratives were inevitably interrupted.

Glowing crimson eyes; Eleison, smoking by the mansion's rear entrance.

Guilt flooded me every time his face appeared in my mind.

There was no reason to feel guilty. I committed to Malin because he was courting me, and because he asked me to commit to being his fiancée in exchange for his own commitment. That seemed normal, and I didn't need to worry over the opinion of some other man. Especially not one who claimed to like me, but didn't behave like it.

A man who, I suspected, gave me the roses that seemed already to be drooping on my return to my quarters mid-morning.

I ran my fingers over their petals, my heart aching for their beauty. No one had given me flowers before—not even Malin, although he had given me so much more. Was it even possible these, so thoughtful and generous, were from Eleison?

I turned the vase around, then noticed a little card that had slid between the stems and the glass. When I managed to pull it out, my heart sank.

Sorry.

Had I read that one word, I would have known the flowers were really from Eleison. An apology note from Malin would have been at least a sentence, and would have been immaculately written in the same calligraphy that had summoned me to the manor. This, one word dashed off in a hasty scrawl, could only be from one person.

I ached, the guilt cresting up in a new, more powerful wave.

There *was* something regrettable about Malin's proposal. It was the shutting of a door: a made choice that sealed off any other possibility.

Yet, maybe this was a sign Eleison and I might learn to be on better terms.

That evening, at eight, I listened to Malin's footsteps trail up the hall and disappear into his apartment. I gave him a minute to get settled before I left, tracing the route I had taken when following Dr. Singer the week prior.

My stomach tightened, the night so full of promise that I wasn't sure if I was more excited or afraid. Certainly, when it came to thanking Eleison for his flowers, I was very afraid...and I was right to be.

When he answered the door, his expression was joyless and his eyes rested flatly on my face before lowering away.

"What do you want."

"May I come in for a moment?"

Exhaling in a noise that almost sounded like the first note of a sardonic laugh, he glanced sharply at me, then stepped away. "I guess."

"You're angry with me," I observed after shutting the door.

"No...I loved watching you kiss Malin in the garden today. And I really loved hearing you got engaged to him. Congratulations, by the way."

My face burning, I tried to smile instead of cringe and did a little of both.

"You could try being sincere for once—you know, not attacking me the second I walk into the room. I came here to thank you for the flowers."

"Yeah...I can tell you must have loved them."

"I did! Good Lord." I sagged back against the door, unable to help my scowl. "They were exceptional—and I thought they were from *him,* until later this morning."

"So you agreed to marry him."

That rage Eleison had a way of inspiring bubbled violently up in me. My hands dropped to my sides, balling into fists at my hips as I said, "The man who was courting me? Yes! Yes, I did. And if you don't like it, why haven't *you* tried courting me instead of just watching him do it?"

"Don't you think I want?"

The glass he had picked up and drained was slammed back down upon the bar so hard that I feared for the integrity of both. When Eleison whirled on me, his eyes red as a fire and just as raging, I found myself standing straighter.

"It's not so simple. I can't control myself around you. Don't you understand? Haven't you *seen* it yet? Haven't you realized that every"—he grabbed the headrest of one of the wingback chairs flanking the bar and toppled it over, hurling across the room while I cried out in fright—"single goddamned time I see you, all can think about is *you?* Wanting you, fucking you, the taste of your blood in my mouth—"

"Eleison—"

"No. You asked to hear this."

My hand had drifted toward the doorknob, but he stormed over and caught me. As I cried out, Eleison pinned my wrist up against the door. His other hand rested in a fist above my head, his forearm inches from my cheek and his nose centimeters from mine.

"You keep asking. You keep wanting to know what the

problem is. Well, I'll tell you. The problem— The problem is that we're mates, Thecla."

The very floor trembled beneath me, rattling at the pace of the pulse that pounded in my wrist beneath his grip. I searched his face, astonished.

Everything about him—what I felt for him, how badly I wanted him no matter how aloof he seemed, how frightened I was at the thought of his pain or suffering—fell into place.

"I knew it the second I tasted your blood," he said, his tone and eyes both softening. A shaky exhalation rocked his frame and, with a glance at my captured hand, he reluctantly released my wrist. I wanted to scream at him to keep hold of me, to do with me whatever he liked, to forget about Malin—but Eleison went on, sorrow in his voice, his hand moving in as though to caress my cheek or my hair before he regained his senses and pushed himself away from me altogether.

"One taste of your blood, and I wasn't an animal fighting for territory anymore. I was myself, looking through an animal's eyes at the most gorgeous woman I've ever seen. Thecla—"

As I stepped toward him, he cringed away from me, one arm braced across his diaphragm.

"Please, Thecla. Don't come any closer."

"But this is wonderful! Don't you see? What you were telling me the other day, about how far your destabilization has progressed—I can help you."

But his head was already shaking.

"No. You can't. You're right to marry Malin. He can keep you safe. He can register you as a riftborn and let you live a life I could never provide."

"But I don't care about any of that."

"You do, and you should. I won't take it from you. But it means—I don't have to say what it means."

"Maybe I could still help you, though. Maybe we could sit together as friends, hand-in-hand, or—"

I knew it was all futile even before he shook his head. "It won't work. What I feel for you—I can't just touch your hand and be done with it. I would go insane, *am* going insane. All I want to do is love you, Thecla—"

My eyes filled with hot tears. "I want to love you, too," I whispered back. "I want to love you, Eleison—I want to help you."

"But you can't, because you're marrying Malin."

There was nothing I could say in my defense. I stood there, heartbroken, feeling like an idiot for the second time in a week.

After regarding me in the sad silence of a few long seconds, Eleison strode into his bedroom and shut the door.

"Eleison—please, wait—"

I hurried up to it, trying the knob. It was locked.

"Oh, Eleison, don't do this. Let me in, please. Let me talk to you. Don't give up this way."

No response rang out from the other side. No sardonic wit. Not even a cold dismissal.

Nothing.

Hand pressing to my mouth, my eyes squeezing shut, I cursed myself, and Malin—and, most of all, Eleison.

"If you would have *talked* to me," I said through the door, wiping the back of my hand across my cheeks, "if you would have just said anything at all, I would not have even entertained his attention."

Perhaps it was cruel to say—but it was true, and I wanted Eleison to know it.

Because...no matter what I had said to the territory master, and no matter what I felt for him, I still found myself wishing Eleison would try to win me away.

That loyalty, though—it was too intense. Eleison was too noble and decent a man to betray the employer who had saved his brother from certain death. It was why he never spoke up: not once from the start of my time in the manor. The thought of losing his humanity was easier to him than yielding to what he regarded as treachery.

Yet, noble as that loyalty was, it enraged me.

"I suppose it's just as well," I said, giving the locked knob a mean little shake for emphasis. "Yes, it doesn't really matter. If you didn't speak up when it counted, it just proves you love Malin's employment more than you love the fulfillment of a mate—more than you could love me."

A floorboard creaked.

Refusing to wait for his defense, I turned around and ran from the room.

The first three letters of my name rang out behind me as I slammed shut the door to the hall.

Fighting back tears, my teeth grinding in my head, I forced my running to slow to a brisk walk at the corner. My fists hung by my sides while I marched to my quarters, my mind whirling with conflicted desires; with impossible hopes.

With fury at myself, at my own audacity—for it was undeniable that, gluttonous, I loved two men in the true sense of loving, and even though I had unknowingly decided between them, I could not seem to stop myself from loving both.

But only one of them had proved himself to me, and now waited for my company.

In my quarters, I didn't hesitate. Lips tight, I rolled the bookshelf aside and operated the panel. I didn't call out as I entered, but looked around for the source of a sound like a shutting book.

There he was, his tall frame filling the open door of the study across from me.

"Thecla—"

I dashed into his arms, the tears exploding from me. The book fell to the floor and he drew me toward his face, catching my cheeks in those tremendous hands and kissing away my tears.

"Oh, dear—Thecla, dear! What's wrong, my darling? Whatever has happened?"

"I couldn't wait," I whispered, my arms flung tight around him. "I couldn't wait."

Inhaling sharply, Malin trailed his thumb along a tear track and down to the edge of my mouth. "Angel...you should have waited. Should have enjoyed your last twenty minutes of peace."

I shook my head. "No, no—I don't want them, Malin."

"Then you should understand that, when you are in this apartment, you belong to me. Completely—every last part of you."

My face flush, I took a shuddering breath and answered, "Everywhere I am, Master, I belong to you."

"That's a dangerous thing to say."

"It is—but it's true. I've never felt this way about a man before. Whenever we're in the garden, I wish you would hold me, kiss me. When I think about that night during the Event, I wish I'd stayed."

"I was sorry to see you go," he assured me, stroking a few loose hairs back from my face and smiling down at me in a way that was as tender as it was menacing. "But, I have you now...and we understand each other better now, too, don't we."

"Yes, sir."

"Good girl. come along to Master's bedroom. I'm going to give you a whipping like you asked for earlier, and then I'm going to fuck you, and it's obvious to me now that you're going to enjoy all of it."

A faint moan passed my lips, inspired by the sharp turn of his normally refined tongue. I nodded, my heart hammering in my ears, unable to reply as his hand settled upon the back of my neck.

With this hot grip, he walked me down the corridor off the sitting room and into the bedroom at the end of the long hall.

All the rooms in the manor were extraordinarily fine, but Malin's bedroom was unquestionably glorious. The canopy over the golden bed tented to the ceiling, which was itself a brilliant mandala of emerald green and copper tiles. With the damask walls above the wainscoting a similar, albeit darker green, the entire room produced the effect of some exotic forest.

And there I was, alone in the woods with Malin.

Though the room was large, and itself contained a tea table, balcony access, and several other doors along its walls, (far busier with paintings, I should add, than any other room in the house), it seemed to me that it was immensely small. It seemed to contain at that moment only the bed—and the crop upon it.

"I couldn't help but notice you eyeing it the other day," he said while I stared. When he approached me, I realized he was sliding a key into his breast pocket, and my body flooded with adrenaline to realize he had locked the door. "It seemed like a very simple place to start…but, if you adapt as quickly as I expect you to, perhaps we'll try something firmer soon."

Making his way around the room to snap on a few of the brilliant glass lamps and ensure I was illuminated, he commanded,

"Take off your clothes, Thecla. I've waited to see you since you first walked into my firelight."

My fingers trembling, I jolted to obey—but, with a deep breath, I straightened up and slowed my movements. When Malin turned around from the final lamp, I had barely loosened my bodice. Only when our eyes met and I was sure he was watching did I free it completely, reaching back to swiftly unclasp its hooks.

With the bodice open, I shrugged my shoulders and arms free, then pushed the silvery dress down to my feet and stepped out of the skirt.

The shift would be soon, but I wore stockings, too. I kept my eyes on him, my body aching for the way his gaze roved over every inch of me. Never in my life had I felt so examined, so absolutely seen, by a man...and never had I taken so much pleasure in being revealed to one's gaze. I made sure he could see my thighs as I sat down at the foot of his bed and extended my leg. With an increasingly steady pair of hands, I rolled down the left stocking, then the right. Soon both lay upon the floor, and I resumed eye contact while standing up.

Without raising the front of my shift, I reached back and instead contrived to remove my panties through the thin fabric. When I managed to wiggle them down past my knees, he gasped softly.

As I stepped out of them and at last began drawing up my shift, he said, "Stop—wait."

I did, my hands relaxing, the fabric falling back to my knees once again.

His expression gaunt with hunger, Malin prowled toward me and kept me fixed with that stare. When at last he stood directly before me, his head bent over mine and one hand raised to the back of my scalp.

I moaned softly, my mouth opening to his kiss, pleasure streaking through my body as his other hand slid down my back and cupped the flesh of my rear.

The absolute thrill of being touched by Master Farrow was secondary to being touched so sensually at all. I was not some plaything; not some fantasy substitute to permit a yokel from Lescaut a few seconds of satisfaction.

I was a desirable, even powerful woman, and a desirable, powerful man wanted to feel my body. To enjoy and appreciate it along with me.

While he kissed and caressed me, the hand in my hair slowly drew out pins and shook free locks until the arrangement into which I'd painstakingly put it fell free. Hair tumbled down my back and around my shoulders and along the neck Malin soon lowered to kiss. I moaned, weak to the erotic caresses of his lips and tongue and even hand there. As his mouth next raised to my ear, I was already so hypnotized I didn't realize he was drawing up my shift until the cold air sent goosebumps running along my exposed buttocks.

"You're going to keep count for me, Thecla. Can you do that?"

I shivered in anticipation, my lip bitten even as my face disappeared behind the shift. His low gasp sounded for what he saw beneath my neck, the background as I whispered, "Yes, sir."

The world reappeared, and the shift floated to our feet. Malin kept hold of my waist, kept my naked body pressed to his through his clothes. Even through these barriers, an objective indicator of his desire prodded my tense stomach. I gasped, consumed by longing as I'd been for no other man, craving his touch along every last part of my body.

"If it's too much," he murmured, keeping his embrace to my waist and the chin he caressed with thumb and forefinger, "tell me...and if it's not enough, tell me that, too. If you want to stop altogether, tell me the name of your village."

I nodded, my voice shaking as I exhaled the word, "Okay."

With a small, cruel smile of appreciation for my anxiety, Malin bent his head and pressed his whispering lips to my ear.

"Do you know why I want to marry you, Thecla?"

"Why?"

"I've been falling in love with you just by spending our mornings together...but it's only today that I understand why. Bend over with your hands on the bed, angel."

Every muscle in my body was a coiled spring wound tight with potential energy. I quivered, his eyes burning along my naked body as I bent with my back straight and my hands flat upon the mattress.

When I was as comfortable as one could be in such a position, he reached past my head to pick up the crop.

"You know, some men like to play games where they whip their girls as punishment...but, I confess, I would prefer to avoid that with you. I want you to enjoy it, after all. I want you to come crawling up to me, my undignified and desperate little bride, begging for a beating and a cock in your ass."

I cried out at the first snap of the crop against my backside, the sting somehow playful but sharp and centralized.

"Oh," I cried with a gasp, the heat giving way to an immediate, pleasurable tingle that was echoed between my legs, "oh—one."

"Good...you remembered."

The second cracked out. I barely kept count as he went on,

the implement's thin rod trailing up and down the curve of my backside.

"Thecla, Thecla—I know we're starting gently, but you're already as perfect as I dreamed you'd be. Thinking of you, so near to me each night, has driven me mad."

"Ah! Oh, three—four!"

He doubled his strokes, each sharp swat of the crop precisely aimed. It would not have had nearly the same effect in unpracticed hands that landed a strike here and there and someplace else.

In Malin's, it was a merciless weapon. Each sharp strike landed in precisely the same spot, deepening the sting until, by eight, my leg unexpectedly kicked up.

"Oh, eight!"

"You are sensitive, aren't you…"

I moaned in protest, shivering as the leather of the keeper trailed along my rear, down between my legs, and teased tenderly along the apex of my thighs. My nerves lit up and I realized how indecently aroused I'd been made by even this light, initiatory whipping. He exhaled, the crop lowering.

A finger replaced it.

I cried out in shock, one of my hands raising from the bed for half a second before I forced it back down. Trembling, I focused on staying upright while the sighing territory master let his finger glide along the flooded cleft that invited his touch.

"Thecla, you harlot…I never expected you to be so desperate for attention this way."

"I never expected to—to enjoy being whipped."

I yielded to another moan as he connected with the nodule of flesh that, manipulated alone in my bed, always delivered the urgent heights to which my previous sexual partner had failed to bring me. Malin caressed it expertly, the sensation so pleasurable it was overwhelming.

"It is very fun to get a good beating, isn't it," he said, coaxing that finger back and forth over my flesh while I, crying out, struggled to remain standing. "And exceedingly intimate... you're right. Too intimate for me to engage anyone but you, if you're truly willing. Feeling you now...you really must be."

Malin's breath was heavy as he enjoyed my gasping, his finger tickling steadily up and down for a time before drawing back altogether.

"Do you think you can take something harder for the last twelve, Thecla? It's all right to say 'no.'"

"Oh, Malin—" His fondling had heated me beyond all measure, and my trembling knees sagged together before splaying apart a bit farther. "Please, yes—I want to learn what it feels like to be really *beaten* by you. Please—"

His belt buckle's jingling filled me with a dread that simultaneously flooded my center with lust. I gasped, my teeth chattering until I sank them into my lower lip.

While he set the crop down and doubled over the belt, he urged me again, "Tell me if it's too much. What do I want you to say if you need to stop?"

"Lescaut," I whispered, the word meaningless in my haze but for the smile I could hear it inspired in his voice.

"Good girl."

I moaned, squirming until, on his command, I straightened out my legs a little to stand stock-still.

The first lash came seconds after I'd steadied myself.

"Ah! Oh—oh—"

"I told you, it was harder..."

"Oh—nine, isn't it—"

While he chuckled at my obedience, I panted through the shocking, far heavier explosion of pain. I almost suspected he had begun with the crop to lend me a false sense of security. The belt had a weight, a density that commanded far more respect...and caused a far more profound, deeply embedded burst of a sting.

"Ah! Ten, ah—"

"Halfway there, Thecla." He paused before the next blow, his fingertips lightly caressing along the heated spot on my rear. "Such a pretty pink...how are you?"

"It stings—ah, oh, Master—"

"Poor lamb...we'll use the other side for the second half, won't we."

I cringed, crying out as he proved good as his word. Now my right side was the center of his interest, the target of heavy blow after heavy blow while my legs kicked and my teeth gnashed. Somehow, I managed to keep count, although the last three in particular seemed like an eternity. At nineteen, while I stood panting and trembling as I prepared myself mentally for one more, he once again stroked the marks he'd made and inspired an erotic dimpling across my flesh.

"I'm very impressed, Thecla...only one more to go."

His finger crept between my legs again. This time, his middle finger teased just so into the source of that flood.

"You know what's going to happen after that, don't you?"

"Yes, sir."

"Well? What's going to happen?"

"Oh—Master—you're going to take me."

"I'm going to fuck you, Thecla."

While I moaned, he drew his finger away and raised the belt.

The last blow was hardest, its snap echoing through the bedroom while I cried out and numbered it, "Twenty!"

The heat was so intense my backside was almost numb. I collapsed upon the bed, gasping, while Malin said with approval, "Good girl...what a very, very good girl. Better than I deserve."

Moaning, I turned over and was met with the hateful sting of my rump against the icy cold of the bedspread. As I hissed, Malin chuckled. I settled instead on my side to watch him undress, my heart racing as he stripped away his shirt and pushed down his trousers.

It was natural to compare Malin to Eleison, if only because I had now seen both men shirtless in the span of about a week; but there was no possibility of competition between the two. Each was beautiful for his own reason, and in truth, Malin was no shirk when it came to muscle mass. But, in the way of older men, there was a padding to that muscle, and a warmth to his body and skin. I wanted Eleison to tear me apart; I wanted Malin to embrace me. To comfort me in exchange for what he had just done to me.

Comfort me, he did.

After stepping from his trousers and enjoying my eye upon the tent in his underwear beneath, the territory master—my fiancé—drew back the covers where I lay and turned to kiss me.

"Get in the sheets with me, darling. Let me hold you." His voice was a low suggestion, the command gone but for implication; it was pure sensuality now, although I confess these days I hear as much sensualism in Malin's commands as I do in his soft-spoken words. "Poor thing, you took that beating so gracefully...come into bed properly with me. Come, lie down."

Grateful, thrilled, I slid beneath the comforter and held my breath as he at last stripped his boxers away. Even with my previous experience, I had never seen a man's anatomy so—exposed. Illuminated. It looked violent, yet its violence excited me. It strained like the neck of a horse, bobbing against Malin's stomach as he joined me in bed and drew me into his arms.

One hand slid down over my rear, patting where he had done the most damage and making me whimper beneath his kisses.

"I'll have to take a look tomorrow morning to make sure nothing bruises...not too badly, anyway...poor dear, does it hurt? Here...let me kiss you, Thecla. Let me kiss it all away—"

When his hand once more rested against the nape of my neck, I succumbed to the consuming power of his kiss. His lips enfolded mine, his tongue a weapon that promised so much more than I had ever experienced. With his hands on me as they were, Malin rolled me over on my back without ever breaking the contact of our mouths. When he lifted from the kiss, it was only to breathe and murmur to me, "If I'd found you years ago—if only you were born ten years earlier, and you had me as a slightly younger man. Ah, Thecla...Thecla, lie there, let me kiss you—"

"Malin—my body is so hot, you give me a fever—"

"I know, Thecla, I know...poor girl, let me kiss it away..."

I gasped, his mouth's tender application trailing far down my neck and over the curve of my bosom. Though his mouth paused to engulf and tease a nipple, he soon surprised me by continuing. His kisses descended and I gasped, my stomach tightening as they showed no sign of stopping.

"Oh—no, Malin, that's so wicked—putting your mouth there—"

"My God...you mean a man has never had his mouth between your legs?"

I shook my head, my lip bitten. Sighing in appreciation,

Malin caressed me with his fingers before lowering his head amid an unheard murmur.

Unheard, or forgotten in the sensation of his teasingly slow kisses as they landed without hesitation between my thighs.

Shocked, arush with all number of sensations—not the least of which being the sore sting of my backside as I lay upon it to receive his attention—I spread my legs a little wider and submitted to him utterly. A sense of absolute trust had developed between us as a consequence of the beating, and it meant I would let him put his mouth anywhere, everywhere—and wherever he put it, it went to great use. Soon his tongue, not just his lips, became intensely involved, and I cried out in astonishment at its rapid battering against my body.

Between his tongue and the sensual beating, I had never felt a heat kindling like this. It took longer for me than usual, I noticed—an artifact of the whippings, I would find.

But another, better artifact revealed itself as that blaze raged greater and greater, soon reaching a point where its vessel could no longer contain it. If he kept on, I felt certain I would die. I cried his name, my fingers curling in his hair, pushing back somewhat against his forehead to try and reduce the intensity of the sensation; but Malin carried on, his tongue merciless, his black eyes sometimes raising to fix upon my face.

It was as our gazes locked that I succumbed, my entire body immolated in the eruption of the blaze.

"Oh! Oh, Malin! Oh, God—Master—"

I was genuinely shocked. My mouth opened, my lips fluttering on soundlessly as my body clenched up with a kind of implosion. Malin kept going, his tongue guiding me through an orgasm that was unquestionably more powerful than the ones I usually managed to give myself. It were as though it came from someplace far deeper—as though the whipping really had enriched the pleasure in some way that I realized at once was as addictive as the pain and humiliation were in and of themselves.

"That was beautiful," he murmured, his head lifting from me and his eyes brighter with love than I had yet seen. Raising himself up over me with his body still poised between my splayed legs, Malin caught my mouth with his for a tender kiss. I moaned at the taste of myself on his lips, the experience somehow only adding to my body's instinctive preparations for what was to come. My knee bent, and I shifted my pelvis for a better angle while he slid against me.

"You really do want it, don't you, Thecla."

I whimpered, nodding, almost screaming as the weight of his organ pressed turgidly against my entrance. "Yes, yes, Malin, please! Master Farrow, I want you. Take me—make love to me— fuck me, fuck me all night, oh—Malin!"

My eyes widened; his brow furrowed with the brief shutting of his eyelids.

Our moans rose up in harmony, his dark bass beside my ecstatic soprano.

"Yes," I begged, nodding, his cock's penetration into my body like the filling of a most exquisite arrow wound. I had not engaged in any partnered sexual activities in several years, and as a result the channel was a tight fit. He hardly seemed to mind, extolling my name as he impaled his length inside me.

"My, Thecla...you're not a virgin, are you? That's right, oh, could have fooled me...doesn't matter, of course. I'm not, either." At his wink, we both chuckled. He sighed, then, his forehead leaning against mine as he murmured, "Oh, Thecla...how tight you are. How fine you feel."

My head thrashed back against the pillow as he rocked his hips, the sensual motion arcing him up into hidden spots of pleasure I never could have reached without the use of some contrivance. I gasped, my legs folding around him, begging, "Yes, yes—deep like that, please—"

"Oh, I can give it to you as deep as you like it, angel…very, very deep…and hard, and fast…"

He demonstrated, his teeth bared in a smile as I screamed in pleasure.

"Master! Yes, yes, don't stop—Malin, please, oh, *please!* Keep going—"

"Thecla, Thecla! You gorgeous little slut… You had better pick carefully when you visit my apartment before we're married. Every time you're here, this is going to happen. More and more." His hand fit alongside my neck, his thumb resting along my pulse and his eyes boring into mine with every stroke. "And when you're my wife, it will be all the time, every day, whenever I see you…you drive me mad, Thecla."

"No, oh, *I'm* mad, I'm the mad one—" I whined, my feet unwrapping from around his body to dig my heels into the mattress and brace my pelvis up against his. "I'm mad because I want it. I want to be taken by you all the time, Malin. I want to be beaten and humiliated by you, then tenderly taken in your arms—like this. Just like this. Hah! Ah—oh, oh, not there, you shouldn't hit me there—"

That spot his strokes aimed toward seemed dangerous now, the pressure inside of me almost abnormally urgent. Embarrassed, frightened, I insisted, "Please, wait—"

"Just relax," he coached me, murmuring against my lips as he delivered kisses through my gasps. "Just relax, Thecla…give in to it. Give in to what my body wants yours to have."

"Oh—oh, I—I—huh, oh, Master! Malin! Yes, yes, hah—!"

All at once, that pressure swelled into a tidal wave. I screamed as though I had been stabbed. At the very least, I was crushed beneath the force of that tsunami and pulled out to a sea where Malin seemed headed, himself. He panted above me, his hand wrapping around my thigh to allow him deep, rapid access to my pulsating body.

"That's it, Thecla...oh, that's it, let it out...scream for me, Thecla—"

"Yes, Malin! Oh, yes—Malin—please, please, I've never felt a man's seed inside me before! Give me yours, Malin—I want to feel you inside of me even after our bodies have separated! I want—I want to carry your heir, Malin!"

It was madness to say it while knowing that Eleison was meant to be my mate, but it was true. The dormant animal in me loved and craved Eleison. But my mind, the feminine spirit in me that begged to find a man worth succumbing to—that heart of me loved Malin, loved and ached for the childless territory master who, the better I knew him, struck me as less a force to be feared and more as an isolated veteran who had already lost a woman he loved with nothing to memorialize her but a tomb.

His mouth descended heavily upon mine. His hand slid around my back and held my belly close to his while he cleaved me in two, his lungs stealing all the air from my body.

When that breath of his lost its rhythm in a hitch, I knew he had reached the peak I longed for him to achieve, and I found myself groaning with delight at the mere thought of his seed spilling in me. Sure enough, he grew infinitely more rigid within and against me, his strokes growing harder and faster—and the look in his eyes, when our lips parted, more animal and intense than ever I had seen. His teeth bared with the clenching of his jaw; his thumb sank tighter into my neck, as if he longed to do far more than caress.

Then, just when I thought my body really would break beneath his strokes, he cried out in an expression of relief and amazement. Not delaying, I reached up to trail my fingers over his scalp and kiss his groaning mouth.

His body shuddered against me, the slowing pumps of his hips gradually coming to rest with our pelvises at ease as one.

For a few long, tender seconds, he lay there in my arms and was content to kiss me. Only when he had come back to his senses somewhat did he manage a smile and a kiss of his own volition.

With a sigh we both shared, he pushed himself up and drew gingerly out of my body. The empty feeling left me to whimper with longing, but I thrilled at the wetness between my legs and all it promised. In fact, the feeling of his hot semen inside of me made me desperate for more of his love on the spot; I resisted the urge to beg. Instead, I made myself content to let him dote on me. He drew the covers up over us and caressed my hair, my cheek, my thigh. I could have purred.

"Yes," he murmured while our eyelids grew heavy beneath the blanket of expelled passion. "Yes—I must marry you, Thecla. No man may take me from you...pray for any that try."

As he kissed me, I found the will to smile.

The expression only faded when he rose to snuff the lights, and could no longer see my heavy heart reflected in my face.

PART II
THREE MONTHS LATER

CHARLOTTE KEPT THE air bright with piano while Malin swung me around the empty ballroom, counting the time of our steps.

"And one, and...you know, dear, I still have to say I'm amazed you don't at least already know how to waltz."

I laughed a little, embarrassed by this hole in my knowledge of feminine arts that, in general, still felt somewhat mysterious to me. "I really just never spent much time going out," I confessed, his hand on my waist sliding down bit by bit toward my hip. "Now that I have all this free time and space, I hardly know what to do with myself."

"I can tell."

I laughed. If my difficulty adapting to life was so obvious to Malin, hopefully it wouldn't be quite as transparent to the rest of the household. "I'm trying to get used to things."

Things like having a dedicated lady's maid to wait on me, arrange my hair, and help me dress.

To always know where I was, and to see if I needed anything at all.

Everyone's demeanor changed overnight with Malin's decision to make the courtship formal. The staff, which until this point had essentially ignored me with the exceptions of Charlotte and Kyrie, now knew they had to serve me as they would the visiting courtiers, at the very least. They certainly knew that if they did not, they would be the next to receive one of Malin's pointed, baleful stares a day or so before disappearing from the manor along with their scant possessions.

In fact, as we approached the spring festival to which we had been invited by that enormously unpleasant doctor, there were several maids in the manor who were newer than I; and I could tell by how much I knew of their business just how well my maid, a young woman named Brea, would keep her lips sealed about *my* private matters, so we never grew close as friends.

I had no friends among them, save for Charlotte and Kyrie.

"I think it would help if you would accept that you deserve all these things I'm giving you," Malin said to me softly, his head lowered and his gaze sincere through the pale lashes of his eyes. "And you ask for so outrageously little to begin with—my dear, release that old mindset. It's perfectly acceptable for you to be with me, and to enjoy being with me, if for no other reason than I say it's acceptable. Don't you agree?"

Slightly flushed, I nodded and let him stop us in the center of the room. Charlotte sensed our pattern's disturbance and glanced over her shoulder, her music coming to a halt.

"I'll go, if I'm no longer needed."

"Thank you, Charlotte," he said, gazing intently into my face. "Skip tomorrow's session, of course—we'll be at the arena."

"Of course. Good day, Master Farrow; Mistress."

I waved to her, freezing when Malin's great hand rested upon my cheek and turned my face back toward his.

"Will you come to my apartment tonight, Thecla?"

The heat of the abrupt question, asked with the door barely closed behind Charlotte, made me dizzy with erotic anticipation. I bit my lip, turning my face down and fixing him with a bashful, upward-angled stare I had noticed made him insatiable. Sure enough, his nostrils flared as I said, "I'm not sure I should, Master, if I'm to sit peacefully in the arena tomorrow and not spend all my time fidgeting about on my—memories."

With a low noise of desire that rumbled up from his chest and curled his lip in a delicious hint of the arrogance I loved to feel unleashed upon me, Malin let his hands wander shamelessly down toward my backside. "Yet that's just the thought I love...come now, you coquettish little nymph, I've never been so tormented by a woman in all my years."

"Whatever do you mean?"

"You know what I mean," he murmured, each word roughened with the same desire that made me gasp to feel him. He pulled me tight against his body, his lips and thereafter nose trailing along the ridge of my brow, the corner of my eye, the edge of my mouth as he spoke on. "You know that I lay in my room wondering all night if you'll come into my quarters when I next invite you. How, when I should be thinking of more important matters, I instead find myself concocting various schemes to lure you across that magical threshold."

It did feel magical, at times. Charlotte was right: he was respectful of ritual and rules above all else, and so between us we had developed a game that pleased us both. His job was to entice me, trick me, or even to force me through the panel and into his chambers with him, where I yielded my body to his every command and thrilled to do it.

My job, however, was not just to decide whether to give in and cross the line.

At first, I had been terribly afraid that Malin would use me once, perhaps as many as three times, and be done with me, so I had visited his chambers very sparingly after the deepening of our affections. But, in so doing, my very existence drove him wild with desire. Knowing what he had already enjoyed and, when married, would enjoy again whenever he pleased, denial of that same treasure was unbearable to a man so spoiled. There had even been times he had awoken me at midnight by knocking on our conjoined door, behaving like a tomcat yowling in the street. He bribed me with fine chocolates and drowned me in flowers.

But when I did not yield, sometimes, *he* would. He would cross the threshold and lose all his control in a way that was so exceptional to me I felt like our little game's victor every time. And there, in the ballroom, with the afternoon sun casting a brilliant grid across the floor and up along our legs, I let him enchant my lips with the implication of a kiss before whispering, "I shouldn't, Master...you've got a mad look in your eye, a wild look!"

"I'm sure I do. I want to drag you upstairs by the hair and whip you senseless for even pretending to refuse."

"So, you're saying you'll be even sterner with me if I agree now..." Giggling despite the genuine fright bolting in me to be so ruthlessly eaten up by those black eyes, I wiggled out of his embrace and skipped back a few steps. "I'd certainly better not give in to you, Malin, if I know what's good for me."

"You wicked brat...you have no idea how you'll pay for these games when you're my wife."

Though I tried, I couldn't long hide my smile. Fingers curling through the hair that fell around my shoulder, I told him, "I can't wait to find out," and turned on my heel.

The air in the manor seemed crisp and fresh with the distant winds of spring, and everyone that day was in a good mood—especially me. The servants who were growing used to me and my more casual ways made polite eye contact, even throwing in a smile from time to time. Birds chirped in the trees through the open windows. The RMS declared the risk of a Rift Event was a comfortably low 5%.

I turned a corner, excited to take advantage of the fine day once I'd gotten changed for riding practice, and stopped short.

It just so happened my riding instructor had come up to the house, and stood there speaking to his brother.

And there it was again.

That guilty tug. That itch along the skin of my scarred forearm, as if the bite were still healing. The ache in my chest at the shape of his back in his dark blue suit, or the edge of his profile, or those sad amber eyes that were forever averting from me since the night of our last private conversation.

Our last conversation, period.

The truth was that it was impossible to wholly avoid Eleison. If I was to be Malin's fiancée, then I had to expect to share the room with Malin's closest servant at least some of the time.

But it never got any easier for Eleison and I to be near one another. Never got any less intense. If anything, it was far worse now. I knew he felt the way I felt, perhaps to an even more frightening degree. We had an unspoken agreement; a means of avoiding one another that became routine after a while. I stayed out of the corridors near his room, and he, while never wholly able to avoid at least passing my door on the way to meet Malin in his private quarters, learned my schedule well enough to stay out of its way.

As happy as I was to be with Malin, I was equally miserable about Eleison.

How strange! I was marrying a man who proposed when he decided he *could* love me. Every day after, he had grown into that love with sincerity and devotion. I felt it raging from Malin all the time now, its heat licking my face and singing my fingers whenever my future husband set eye on me. It had escalated from pragmatism to something unnaturally erotic in a matter of weeks.

And then there was the man who from the start had ached, as I did, with an intense, primal, unexplainable love—and he visibly cringed to scent me on the air behind him. Even before his brother, having glanced my way, could say a word, Eleison turned his head a few degrees in acknowledgement of my presence.

"I'll catch you later," he told Kyrie, nodding and laying a pat on his shoulder.

"See you—hi, Thecla!"

Kyrie, I was glad, had not adopted the informal titles the rest of the house had begun to use for me. At the moment, I was "Mistress." After the wedding in summertime, I would be "Madame." Neither one of them felt particularly suited to me, and my friend seemed to agree. Just hearing my name distracted me from Eleison's disappearance into the busy foot traffic of the foyer.

"It's good to see you, Kyrie. What are you doing up here?"

"Oh, Duke Montagne is leaving today. Had to get his horses up and ready to go…shame, I'll miss them. The horses, of course… not Montagne and his staff."

Though I laughed a little, I wasn't sure I could entirely agree. There was an eerie signal of change to the filtering out of the courtiers, steady since springtime had made the mountain passes safer to navigate. "This place will be empty soon!"

"With all these staff members? Never....anyway, I'll meet you down there in an hour, all right?"

"All right—tell Ambrose I'm excited to see him."

Beaming, the boy enthused, "I will," and headed off back through the doors thrown open to allow the duke's staff to carry out his luggage.

There was no doubt about it. As always, life was changing. That was nothing new. It was simply that it was changing more noticeably and less gradually than ever I had experienced. Malin was right—I did need to accept that I was worthy of the life he provided me—but there was more to it than that. There was so much to learn, and not just about the manor, or the lifestyle expected of me.

There was still much to learn about Malin as a man. He was delicious and sensual, but he could brood for hours over anything that troubled him without breathing a word of it to me...and his solutions to problems were sometimes overwhelming.

For instance: the flowers.

It was obvious in retrospect that discovering someone else had left roses for me had been the tipping point of Malin's decision to make things formal. Knowing he had any degree of competition was obviously enticing to him, and it drove him to obliterate that competition completely. The day after he first made love to me, I returned to my room following an afternoon of reading to find my parlor overflowing with chrysanthemums, forget-me-nots, and splendid pink orchids I had never seen before. The roses from

Eleison had been disposed of without my knowledge and were, I was sad to divine, long gone; but there was no end to Malin's onslaught.

Every day since, more fresh cut flowers had appeared in my room. I meant it when I described myself as drowning in them. Even as I arrived to change for riding practice, my maid was arranging more upon the white, round card table.

It sent a message, both to my suitor and to me. Namely: if they wanted to woo me, they would have to do at least as well as Malin.

I couldn't help but agree...and couldn't help but wish that Eleison would rise to the occasion.

Another guilty thought. How I hated my mind!

It was restless every day, all the time. I felt like a glutton. On the back of my horse, in my chambers re-dressing, in the suppers for which Charlotte had given up and joined me, I was now perpetually preoccupied. I had discovered that within me lay a reserve of bottomless lust, an endless yearning that could not be reasoned away.

What was wrong with me? What was so flawed in me that I couldn't be satisfied by one man? Was I so entitled that I required the attentions of two?

It was a cruel inner voice that said such things to me. I denied its barbs because it was all so much more complex than that. The very problem was that I did *not* feel entitled to the attentions of two men; yet my heart was equally drawn to both, and I could not alter its attachment to either.

Simply seeing Eleison had intensified the ache Malin produced in my belly, and I was sure to leave the bookshelf rolled aside from the panel that night. I ignored, however, every knock; every plea; every promise.

"I know you're awake in there, Thecla...I know you can hear me. Why don't you come play with me awhile? Make good use of the time...I'll make it up to you with a nice, slow fuck when I'm through, angel. Don't worry."

I let the fever overwhelm me as his voice wrapped its coils around my body. As silently as possible, I slid my nightgown over my head and threw it aside. Naked in bed, I lay there listening.

Malin, also, listened awhile. After a time, with a sort of low groan of irritation, he warned, "You're asking me to treat you very cruelly when I *do* have you in hand, Thecla...you make me want to push the limits of your consent, to say the least. Come over here at once."

My eyes fixed on the ceiling through the darkness, I let my hand drift down along my stomach.

If I waited, I would truly win.

If I waited, it would happen again.

"Thecla...I'll give you whatever you want. Just let me put you over my knee for a few minutes. Oh, angel, you have no idea how badly I need to put my hands on you. All day, all the time... Thecla."

A shaky exhalation ghosting past my lips, I shut my eyes and tried to sleep—or pretended I tried to sleep, at any rate.

Malin fell quiet.

The whole manor, in fact, was silent.

The sound of my own breathing lured me deeper, through pretense and into reality.

But the click awoke me.

My stomach tightened with a streak of delight as the panel opened. I kept my eyes closed, willing my breathing to remain steady and slow.

Upon crossing the floor with his own breath held against disturbing me prematurely, Malin rested on the edge of my bed and stared at me—my face, my neck, my naked body curled beneath the sheets.

After an eternity of his stare, he leaned down over me. One wonderful hand drew hair from my throat and face so he could kiss my ear, and all my nerves lit up at this one sensual touch.

"What time is it," I softly begged.

"It doesn't matter." His tone was ragged with desperation, his great hands stroking over my arm and along my back. "Go back to sleep, Thecla...I don't mean to be a bother to you."

"Oh...but you are...you're wicked, Malin."

He sighed. "I know, Thecla...oh, I know..."

The calloused pads of his fingers trailed over my waist, stroked along my stomach, fondled and teased my thighs before slowly easing them apart. I whined softly, turning a playful pout upon him in the dark.

Groaning to see it, he bent his head and kissed it from my lips. As his tongue slid into my mouth, his hand beneath the blanket tickled tenderly along the mound of my sex. Every molecule in my body cried with the stimulation. My mind raced with delight, with victory's high and the winner's pleasure.

For this was what I most loved, in whatever form it took. I lived for those nights when I could resist him at his greatest peaks of passion, for they were the nights he would cross the threshold and take what he wanted, no matter how I played at denying him.

Malin loved it most when I consented everything I had to him; when I opened myself to the sensual pleasure of the lash and the bind, and willingly became the captive of his gilded rooms.

I, though...while I of course more than consented to his

forceful claims of my body, the intensity of my pleasure in my victories came just *from* being so utterly taken. When I was awake and the bookshelf's invitation had been extended, he interrupted any book or letter or prayer that might have occupied me to take from my body what his had been denied.

But when I seemed to be sleeping and he found me there, oh—that was the best feeling of all. Instead of play-fighting him like I would when he found me alert, I yielded utterly, hopelessly. I became like a living doll for his pleasure, and for some reason the sweet intensity of being half-asleep and teased awake by him was addictive to me.

Perhaps it was because he was so tender. The sight of me yielding and helpless inspired something unspeakably gentle in him; I heard it in every soft, admiring breath, just as I felt it in every kiss against my throat.

"You win." His fingers teased back up my stomach, along my breast, and over the bead of one nipple. "You devious girl…"

"You're the devious one…"

"Yet here you are, sleeping naked."

"I was hot."

"I'm sure I know where you were hot, too…"

When his caresses trailed again between my legs, it was with such expertise that I could hardly help parting my thighs. As I remembered a few seconds later to try to close them, he tutted and rolled me back against his chest so he could slide a knee between my legs and keep me available.

"Just relax, darling…"

"Oh…you cad…you dirty man…"

"I know." His kisses once again hovered around my ear while he manipulated that ultra-sensitive center of my arousal, slick with his seduction. "I know, I know, I'm terrible...but I can't resist you, Thecla. Even when you won't come to me."

He lifted his hand to shift his dressing robes away from his waist. Soon his member pressed against me, the strain so great it must have been painful. I gasped, peering back over my shoulder, my eyes finding his. In the veil of night, they looked how I had always imagined the starving eyes of a dharmine.

"But why you resist when you want it so desperately, angel, I'll never know."

"Oh, hm...I wanted to *sleep*, Malin..."

The tip of his spear pressed to my center. I whimpered, swallowed by his gaze, overwhelmed as he teased me.

"If you wanted to sleep, you wouldn't be so eager for me... oh! Thecla—"

"Malin! Ah—"

Slowly, so slowly I wanted to scream, Malin eased inside me. The mere experience of his visitation was so erotic that he might not have had to do much more than that, but even as he slowly rocked against me from behind, his fingers trailed back to that weak point.

"Hm—oh—Malin—"

"Ah...yes, dear, I can see that I'll have to give you a very extensive lesson next time you're in my apartment. I think you need an evening with the rod...maybe then you'll stop lying to yourself about what you want."

I shuddered, arching against him, my hips steadily pumping back against his.

"Or maybe," I whispered, "I'll just try harder to escape you...and you really will have to drag me over there by the hair."

His teeth scraping the lobe of my ear, Malin sped the coaxing of his fingertip until I was overwhelmed.

"Don't tempt me, you harlot...you know you'll regret it."

The next day, I awoke to his stirrings in my bed. It was such a pleasure to awaken with Malin...I leaned against him as I turned over, peering at him through eyes that barely knew they were still seeing.

"Must we go to this festival?"

"Now...Dr. Gall is a perfectly fine friend of mine. I would hate to turn him down last-minute...and, anyway, it will be good for you."

His eyes searched mine with a clarity that implied he had been up for some hours. Brushing hair back from my face, he told me, "I want to take you out of here, Thecla. I want you to see the things in Gudrune—in other territories—that you never thought you could experience before. Thecla, darling, I—my God, I love you, Thecla."

My lips parted. I laughed a little, flush with excitement. I wasn't sure he had ever said those words with such spontaneous abandon before.

"I love you, too. I love it when you say that to me."

"I don't like to say it unless I mean it...but I mean it. And it makes me want to push you in every way. Mentally, geographically, sexually." While I smiled at his lingering stare, he leaned his forehead against mine. "I hope you understand what you've gotten yourself into, winning my love from me."

I had some idea.

There was no doubt that Malin was difficult in some ways. He had exceptionally high standards, and the potential for real violence lurked beneath his placid surface—though, somehow, I never worried it would be directed at me.

Being with him truly was a challenge, but it came with so

many rewards. His love aside, it was an honor to be elevated to the position of a territory master's consort; and, of course, there were the gowns, the jewels, and all those lovely flowers. As my maid dressed me in an elaborate moss green gown with gold accents and wrapped me in a cape of brocaded silk, I could not help but think I was an immensely blessed young woman.

Yet, when I emerged from the manor, intent on our carriage, and found Eleison waiting at Malin's side, I could not have felt more cursed.

THE CARRIAGE RIDE to Pont was close to two hours, and I felt every minute as though through the slow lens of dream-time.

To my right, Malin sat with an arm around my shoulders and a pleasant air about him. Across from me, his knees almost touching mine, Eleison intermittently spoke to Malin and gazed at the miles of vineyards and windmills beginning to show the fine, bright hallmarks of spring. I was acutely aware of the bodies and voices of both, though what they discussed I fear I barely followed, as I was so preoccupied with my own futile longings. Only when I managed to dedicate my focus to the landscape did I follow their conversation, though their voices were both so irresistible I occasionally drifted off.

"I still don't know why you had to drag *me* to this thing," groused Eleison more casually than I might have expected of him.

"Tosh—you know you're worth three men, at least."

"And all three of them hate Gall."

While I dared flick Eleison a glance from the corner of my eye, Malin chuckled and leaned across the carriage to swat him on the knee as though he were an unruly boy.

"Now, you can have your opinions, but there's no question that he's contributed an enormous amount to human society with his refinements to the alteration process."

"Then why isn't *he* altered?"

It was really amazing what Malin let Eleison get away with saying to him, at least in front of me. Having seen the formal way Charlotte behaved, and knowing most lower-level servants of the house kept their distance, I would have expected Eleison to be a little more formal. But, smiling effortlessly on, Malin spread his hands.

"You would have to ask him that, of course…but it's rather personal, isn't it?"

Eleison shot through the window a look that I feared would wither the harvest of the property we passed.

"With all due respect, Malin, some people don't deserve privacy."

"You two have such a strange relationship," I couldn't help observing at last, perhaps spurred on by the Eleison's use of Malin's given name. "This is the most I've ever heard you speak, Eleison."

"Then I'll stop talking," he said without looking at me.

There was no helping my eye roll. "You know what I mean… Charlotte is so formal when I see her address Malin."

"We've been together at least part of nearly every day for the past ten years," explained Malin. "And Charlotte keeps her distance from me for reasons of professionalism—but I notice she's taken quite a shine to you." He nudged me with a smile while Eleison nodded.

"Exactly. And anyway, Thecla, give me a break…you expect me to be servile?"

"I don't expect you to be rude, but you still manage to surprise me from time to time…"

As Eleison scoffed, Malin observed us with a wry sort of smile. "Now, children, don't start bickering before we're even halfway there…someone"—the obsidian stones of his eyes landed on me—"will wind up sorry."

I could feel myself blanching, but did I only imagine Eleison's hands tightening into fists beneath his crossed arms?

"Actually"—now my fiancé had his attention grabbed by the landscape—"we really *are* just about halfway there. Isn't it beautiful out this way?"

While I agreed, Malin smiled slightly and slipped his hand around mine, leaning against me to gaze out the window while he let both our hands rest in my lap. The spark of joy that burst in my heart to be touched so kindly by him was at once vanquished by Eleison's red iris, absorbing information at the corner of his eye. I became self-conscious, a little ashamed—and strangely, cruelly excited, my face warm with pleasure as Malin went on.

"You should see everything a little later in the year, dear, closer to fall. Oh, you'll love it…I have a little house on my vineyard—"

"You own a vineyard?"

"Oh, yes. Several, of course."

"I didn't know that."

"I suppose I don't think of them as often as I should these days, since they're less motivated by necessity…smaller, you know. Private."

The word hung in the air and I inhaled, as afraid of the thought of being completely alone with Malin as I was of entertaining those thoughts with Eleison in the carriage.

Luckily, it was Eleison who controlled the subject by speaking up.

"I don't know if I've ever seen you looking like this, Malin."

"What's that?"

"Happy. *Actually* happy, and not just, 'I'm rich and powerful and am networking with other rich and powerful people at this party'-happy."

Smiling a little, glancing down at himself with an almost guilty chuckle, Malin studied my hand in his. "I suppose that's true...and I am. Surprisingly, I am very happy."

Despite myself, I giggled and dug my elbow back into his ribs. "What do you mean, 'surprisingly!'"

"Only that you're half my age and haven't tired of me yet. That, and"—his eyes glittered with memories, perhaps of the night before, and amorous warmth surged along my limbs—"I have been pleasantly surprised to find us well-matched in a few important ways."

Eleison cleared his throat. Malin, remembering him, had the decency to stop himself with a light laugh.

"Sorry you have to listen to me flirt like a schoolchild, old boy."

"It's fine...and, anyway, you're right. I may hate Gall, but it's important I'm here."

I couldn't help myself. Unable to express the flower of love for Eleison, all I had were thorns that barbed my tongue. "Why *are* you here? It's a 2% chance today. Do we need you?"

As I asked the final question, I made the mistake of looking across at him and getting snapped up in the red-hot grip of that powerful stare.

Oh—it was too much. That ache, that tug, that yearning to at least touch his hand. I swallowed a lump in my throat while Eleison explained, "It's a public event, of course, and we'll be in a box, but it's not really very far from the rest of the crowd. Better safe than sorry."

Perhaps I was silly, or perhaps spending my first three months in the isolation of the country manor lulled me, but it had never really occurred to me that my future husband was a potential candidate for political assassination attempts. Eleison's answer jarred me into a sudden, cold reality.

With no heirs, Malin's removal from the position of territory master could have huge ramifications for the area. Regions had been subdivided for less tumult than that, and the truth was Gudrune was an extensive and controversial territory. It was difficult to maintain, I was sure; but that its maintenance should drum up some political dissent or revive old ones from the Expansion was both natural and alarming to me.

A little chastened, I darted my tongue along my dry lip and failed to keep the alarm from my voice. "Is there any group—or any other such thing—that we should be concerned about?"

Malin tutted, clearly touched by my concern, and patted my hand. "Now, Thecla, no need to fret. Eleison is just a precaution. After all...what if that 2% risk of a Rift Event has shot up by the first hour of festivities?"

He was right about that...but I still found myself wishing I didn't have to feel like this. That I didn't have to sit in the carriage, rocking against Malin but breathing deep the scent of sweetened tobacco alongside sandalwood aftershave.

The bright side of the torture I endured was that the carriage ride—and the subsequent ill-fated Torea Festival to which it drove us—represented the first time I had left the manor grounds since my arrival. I had sent several letters to my stepmother and sister, always receiving one back within the same month, and each time it felt like a little piece of me flew off to be with them; but I, myself, my true self within my heart and mind and body, starved for something else.

It was strange that I felt so restless. I spent my whole life never leaving Lescaut until I was called to, after all…but Lescaut was bustling for its size, with small but busy industries, nosy neighbors, young people growing, the elderly dying, friends and enemies and lovers and the daily turmoil of living. The pure entropy of being-ness, existing for its own sake. Malin's properties, on the other hand, were crafted around the idea of preserving and maintaining the ease of his existence, permitting him to do a better job managing his territory no matter his location.

In other words, the manor was Malin's world. I yearned to go out into the shared one from time to time.

When at last we came to the village of Pont, where a great banner unfurling over the road proclaimed the opening weekend of the month-long Torea Festival, I might have climbed out of the window for as happy as I was to recognize the edges of a town. Yes! Ramshackle houses, small properties, signs of traffic on roads in the distance. Even these precursors were nicer than such things in my hometown, but they paled next to what we found within Pont's heart: clean brick streets, pretty little houses with well-kept solar panels gleaming from the roofs, people busily flowing up and down the roads, and, of course, the stadium.

I had somehow imagined the stadium would stand in the dead

center of town, other buildings clustered around it as I had seen in photographs from cities. Pont, however, with its well-organized and very charming fairy tale aesthetic, had thought better. The area around the stadium was extensive, a park unto itself. The carriage pulled off and Malin helped me out with a hand that slid carefully under my arm; he smiled approvingly when Eleison removed our picnic basket, then pointed out a pleasant restaurant nearby while the footman programmed the carriage to find a place to park itself until it was summoned.

With only a few gawkers quick enough—or wealthy or educated enough—to recognize the territory master's face, Malin gestured toward the short set of stairs that led beyond the brick partition around the stadium's property.

"Shall we?"

Once we made it to the field, I had a much better sense for both the scale and the aesthetic of the stadium. The park rolled down, a smooth carpet that descended at all angles toward the amphitheater's high-reaching open mouth. Spectators crowded in a line that was only a line in the loosest sense of the term. It was more a dense column of people just managing to refrain from violence with one other.

"What do you say we have our lunch here on the grass before going in," suggested Malin with a chipper look up at the sky, then toward the distant crowd. "Fun to people watch."

"I'll leave you to it," said Eleison.

"Nothing for you?"

Eleison glanced sidelong at my question, which had been asked as politely as I could manage. I wished so badly to be sincere with him; tender with him.

"I ate before we left," he answered, striding off fifteen yards to light a cigarette and give us the illusion of privacy.

And give himself some peace, I was sure.

"Dear, dear...you must think I'm blind."

Paling, I whipped my head toward Malin and searched his face. Was he bluffing? Absently speculating?

"You know"—he opened the picnic basket and slid the plates from where they were affixed to the lid—"you needn't be close friends with one another if you don't care to be, but I do wish you and Eleison could bury whatever hatchet you two seem to have between you."

My lungs could work again. I exhaled slowly, managing a small if fleeting smile while picking up a few cucumber sandwiches. That greenhouse was a miracle...it would be all right...what a nice picnic...he didn't know.

"I suppose we're just being professionally distant, as you said of Charlotte," I suggested as ambiguously but truthfully as I could. Dusting off my digits after swallowing my bite, I picked up a few stuffed grape leaves that had been packed in oil and canned the previous fall. They were delicious, but I looked forward to learning how they tasted fresh. There was nothing to worry about. It would be fine.

Just focus on the food, and not on Eleison's back, or the scent of his smoke, or on the memories flooding in to speak of him.

"Be professional, of course—but you two don't have to be cold. Between you and me, Thecla, Eleison is not just among my most loyal employees. He's my closest friend...and I don't lightly bandy about that term."

I nodded. "I can tell. I want to get along with him, Malin—I really do."

"Then do," Malin said simply, smiling and plucking up a few raspberries. "Open."

Flush at his casual, expectant command, I tipped my head back and parted my lips.

Malin's devilish eyes seemed bright in the noonday light as he focused on my mouth. The berries he pressed past my lips burst with delicious ruby juice, and I sighed even before he leaned in to kiss the excess from the corner of my mouth. His tongue just barely slipped over my lip, then drew away, back into his tender smile.

"I have faith in you," he said while turning toward a sudden movement that distinguished itself from the steadily growing sea of arriving or picnicking people. "Ah—"

As Malin rose, Eleison tensed until recognizing the interloper at about twenty yards away.

Dr. Gall hurried up to my fiancé, hand extended.

My whole body went rigid before I realized I had to force myself to stand one way or another. Luckily, as I put down the plate, Malin released Gall's hand and bent to help me to my feet.

Were it not for his help, I would not have cared to put forth the effort to rise.

"Joe," Malin addressed Dr. Gall with an expectant, somewhat mischievous smile that never seemed to reach his eyes when speaking to the researcher, "you remember my fiancée, Thecla of Lescaut."

The man's mouth hung open as he caught my hand in that strange, limp shake I now realized he seemed to reserve for women—or for me. "Oh—*fiancée*! Would you get out of town. I didn't realize you cared about her."

The sentence was so hostile it was almost overt, and when he released me I found myself not just withdrawing my hand, but wiping it off along my dress beneath my cape as though some contaminant might have been passed between us. I did not know why I detested his presence as much as I did, but I could not help finding yet another new reason to feel that way with every word he said.

Maybe it was just Eleison's influence. He had loped over to stand on the edge of the blanket, his eyes leaving the interaction only to acknowledge Vivian's approach with a curt nod. Sunglasses on today, she ignored him entirely and I released a selfish sigh of relief.

Malin and the doctor, meanwhile, had continued talking on, and Malin was so discreet in speech that I was not sure if he had read the same hostility into the doctor's words.

"Who could help themselves but care for her? She is truly a delight. I'd out myself as a dharmine if I kept her under my roof without falling in love with her...that, or just a human as soulless as one."

"It's just unusual to see a territory master of your esteem take a shine to a—to an unregistered riftborn." Whatever he was going to say, he corrected it to a somewhat less objectionable and more understandable concern. "And so quickly," he added while straightening the knot of his loud orange tie.

"If you know, why hesitate? I don't want to take the least chance of anyone else sliding in to woo her out from under me...get the basket together and put it away for us, would you, Eleison?"

I kept my eyes averted, but just seeing his nod in my periphery while that low, rough voice responded, "Yes, sir; are you comfortable with Vivian's protection," made my heart leap to a rapid timpani.

I was so dazed that Malin had to tug me along with him, guiding me by the hand off the blanket. "Yes, of course. Vivian seems to take her job very seriously."

"They're safe with me," she responded, turning away while adjusting the sunglasses higher up her nose. "See you inside, Eleison. You remember where the box is?"

While Eleison grunted the affirmative, bending as he was to take care of the picnic, I bit my lip to stave off the nagging of my guilt. My instinct was to stay and help him.

But then again, I had a lot of instincts when it came to Eleison...and I had to wonder how long I would be able to resist them all.

At that time, I was still so naive and unaware of the ways of the world that I had expected to enter the stadium only after waiting in line for half the day; but, to my great, perhaps childish excitement, Gall led us to a side entrance. The walk was perhaps five minutes, emphasizing the size of the park and the impressive height of the structure. Somehow, the scale of a thing never really settled on me until I experienced a thing; then, it was boggling.

Up-close, the stadium towered with more rows of seats than I could dare guess from without. Even the hall through which we were shuttled by an internal security group was vast, though I understood fairly quickly based on some of the signs we passed at certain junctures that this was because monsters, caged and sedated, were brought in for processing by these paths.

And I grew lost in memory.

"TOREA FESTIVALS? OH, they're awful."

In the halls of the stadium, Father's sad and disgusted explanation came ringing back from many years in the past. An echo from when I was a small child still learning the basics of the world, and inquired, as usual, about a term I'd never heard before that day and had picked up who knew where.

"Back before the Events," he explained grimly, "people used to fight regular animals. Lions and wolves and all kinds of creatures, and then, eventually, bulls."

"They fought them?"

"They didn't just *fight* them, though, Thecla. They tortured these animals to death." While I recovered from my open-mouthed shock, he went on a little more gently, "It was always awful and sadistic—just ugly, I mean—but now that they use monsters for it, they're even more ruthless."

"How come?"

"Because the monsters are animals that don't belong here, and that makes people want them destroyed."

"Don't you?"

"I wish the Rift Events would stop. I wish we didn't *have* to destroy these animals. That doesn't mean they deserve to be tortured to death."

"But they're bad, aren't they?"

"They're just animals, Thecla," he told me, stroking my hair before returning to his book. "They're not doing what they do to be malicious. They're just following their instincts."

I missed my father very much, and was, I admit, more than a little embarrassed to wonder what he would think to find me at a place like this. The past played in my mind while the men, talking and talking, led the way to Dr. Gall's private booth. Our security accompaniment from the stadium paid no attention to anything but our surroundings.

Vivian, however, walked along with me behind the men—and I swore her eyes were on me, but whenever I looked at her, she would look away. Maybe. It was hard to tell just what she was looking at behind those sunglasses, which she wore even in the building.

"Thecla, dear—"

Malin dropped out of step with Dr. Gall to speak to me, sending Vivian up ahead with her employer at a glance. When we were side by side, his voice dropped and he took my hand.

"Are you feeling well?"

I smiled mildly, embarrassed to be so easily read by him. Malin was as studied in a woman's mind as he was in politics, or verse, or anything else to which he set his interest. Nothing could be hidden from him forever.

I was not feeling well at all, in truth.

"I'm just fine! A little tired all at once...don't worry about me. I'll perk back up soon."

The sudden look he gave me—such wondering, such excitement in it. Was he hoping I was pregnant? There was certainly nothing to prevent the possibility... My cheeks were flush at the thought and at his eagerness for it, and I almost didn't notice the slight turn of Gall's head back toward our conversation.

"Let me know if you need anything," Malin said, patting my hand before bringing it to his lips. "We'll fetch you water when we're at the box. Maybe skip the tour, Joe."

"Too bad! I thought you might like to see some of the monsters before they were sent out."

"No," I said, thinly. "No, thank you."

Squeezing my hand one more time, then releasing me to wrap an arm around my waist, Malin announced to the doctor, "This is Thecla's first Torea Festival."

"Is it? Do you know where the word 'Torea' comes from, Thecla?"

The doctor turned with the sort of smug grin adopted by those who loved to 'educate' or otherwise correct others to maintain their sense of superiority.

I was in no mood at all.

"Doesn't everybody know that? It's derived from a word from old Hispanic culture—'toreador.' They used to call their bullfighters that. It *is* 'bullfighter,' really, just in a different language."

Malin turned his own smug smile on Gall, whose expression grew a little tighter. "Yes," Gall said, "yes, that's right."

"I didn't realize there would be a test today," I said dryly to Malin, my hands smoothing over my bodice. "Maybe I should have studied."

"My dear, life is a test...but if I'm marking you, you pass with flying colors."

It was apparent to me, upon seeing Malin compared to Dr. Gall, that the qualities of Malin people read as frightening were not *bad* ones, per se. What they read as wickedness was really intensity. He had intense highs and intense lows, intense hatred and intense love. They saw his history, the hints of his private eccentricities, his scar, his position, and they drew conclusions about his inner life.

But, whatever could or could not be said of Malin, I knew two things. One, he loved me, and had come into that love at a pace refreshingly unhurried in spite of the seeming haste of his proposal; two, even as he wished to own me, to utilize me, to mold me, he also had a palpable respect for me.

Dr. Gall, it was clear, did not.

The box, where we arrived after our march and a short ride up a lift, was arranged in two rows, but because of the size of our group we sat three across. Malin, sensitive to my temperament, helped me into the end seat and took the bullet of sitting beside that odious doctor.

Of course...this meant that when Eleison at last arrived and stood at the corner of the box nearest to the balcony and us, he was not more than five feet from me. I could have reached out and touched him. The mere thought of how easily I might do it heated my body with orgasmic bliss and I leaned back in my seat, my fingers raising to toy with the tree-shaped pendant Malin had given me a few weeks prior.

Eleison's hand twitched, and my blush deepened; especially

as he raised his chin, turning his head toward me with such an imperceptible movement I wouldn't have noticed if I weren't so keenly attuned to his every breath.

Could he detect my desire for him? Did some pheromone, the same that maddened me in silence, seem clearer to his awakened powers? I could not help but wonder what it would be like when I finally came into my own…and whether it would be harder to resist him then.

"So, Thecla—"

I cringed at the doctor's voice and, drawn from my thoughts, lowered my hand from my necklace while leaning toward the conversation.

"How have you been feeling? Malin told me when I came to visit last time that you hadn't experienced the development of any powers. Is that still true?"

It really was a quiz…or an interrogation. "I have yet to experience anything out of the ordinary," I told him, my thin smile artfully walking the line between pleasant and disdainful. "My days have been very peaceful since coming to the manor; I haven't even experienced my allergy."

"Your allergy?"

"When I go out in a Rift Event too long," I explained, pressing my fingertips to my forehead. "I get a terrible headache."

"Interesting. Any other symptoms?"

"No," I insisted. "Just the headache."

"You did black out last time," Malin reminded me, much to my annoyance.

"Yes, but—that was different." The fangs: the burning red eyes of the borro—Eleison—leaping upon me. He inhaled softly at the memory of my flesh as I said, "I was bitten by a borro, and had only just recovered consciousness moments before. It was all very shocking."

"Doesn't sound very fun," said the doctor, whose unempathetic understatement was yet another reason to dislike him.

Malin, coming to the rescue, slid his hand around mine. "How is your scar feeling, dear? Any more issues?"

It still ached occasionally, and had from the time it healed. I smiled at him all the same, shaking my head. "It's fine now—it doesn't bother me at all, really."

I didn't tell him I had refrained from using the cream the clinic doctor gave me. Seeing the marks in the mirror, touching them along my skin—they made me think of Eleison. Of Eleison's teeth, his mouth, on me. I wanted the memory there forever... especially if I couldn't have him there in reality.

The festival filled in very slowly, it seemed, until all at once I looked up and every seat below and around and above us was crowded with spectators. Cheering, waving pennants, wearing in their brightest colors, the tourists and locals who had gathered in the town of Pont were clearly anticipating the Torea more than any event the rest of the year. The seats were elevated, all beginning at the second story. The center of the amphitheater formed a pit, and I could tell, by looking at the walls between the support columns of the vast octagonal space, that the panels around it were doors designed to slide up and away. Only two were not these faux walls and were instead obvious entrances for human beings.

When music started up and the portcullis slid away to permit the band of horn instrument players into the arena, the roar from the audience was deafening.

"Hello," called the master of ceremonies through his

microphone, following the band out and waving at the crowd. "Welcome to the 238th Pont Torea Festival! My name is Winston Garland—but you already knew that."

"I didn't," I whispered to Malin, stealing the opportunity to sneak a kiss beside the lobe of his ear. With a low chuckle, he shifted toward me and slid his leg against mine.

"Winston is an extremely popular monster hunter," he murmured in explanation, "both for sport and for occupation. He runs the Gudrune chapter of the monster hunter's guild, actually."

Nodding, I let him take my hand while the mustachioed man prattled on.

"I'd like to thank you all for your support today. Though our humble festival is relatively new compared to some, the tradition of Torea harkens back thousands of years; it even has its roots in superstition! Legend had it that, if all the monsters were slaughtered without a single injury befalling the star hunter, the area around the Torea would be Rift-free for a year. So...fingers crossed, huh?"

Dry, humorless laughter rippled here and there through the crowd. Malin exhaled in displeasure, clearly waiting for introductions to end.

I didn't blame him. The first part was boring. A speech, then more music. I was just about to ask how long the whole program was to take when, at last, the portcullis opened again.

"Introducing tonight's star slayer, Glenn Stone!"

The man who walked out was somehow not what I expected. With his untamed brown hair and wild eyebrows, paired with muscles that were not just worked but lived, he looked like a woodsman that had wandered in from the forest. Yet, the intensity of the focus in his eyes drove any sense of ferality away from him.

I would have expected him to strut in with his chin high and his chest puffed, but his hard expression held no hint of ego. There was only the intention—the duty—of violence.

The crowd went wild for him.

"Stone is a strange choice," Malin commented.

"They're making a statement," Eleison said, his unexpected speech and displeased tone almost startling me after such a long period of his silence.

I looked between the two. "What statement is that?"

"That altered people are monsters," Eleison answered, his eyes fixed on the scene as, one at a time, the assistants of the star hunter were introduced.

"Stone is a hardline, traditional hunter," Malin explained. "He won't even work with altered individuals…and he has been, let us just say, unpleasantly, publicly vocal about his feelings on the matter."

With a derisive wave of his hand, Dr. Gall insisted, "Give me a break. It doesn't *mean* anything that they have him here. He's one of the most popular monster hunters on the continent at the moment."

"And most people despise the altered," Eleison said, earning an unpleasant glance from the doctor. "You of all people should know that, Doc…you make us."

"Whether or not they show gratitude in the end," the doctor rejoined, his smile as ugly and petty as him.

At last, when the participants had all been named, acknowledged, and applauded, the festival began properly. Though the band disappeared, they continued playing on in a box that amplified their music for the entire stadium. On the ground, meanwhile, the participants exited the arena and the portcullis slid shut.

The wall panels all slid away to reveal the monsters waiting within.

My father had taught me about the many known varieties of monsters that migrated through Rift Events, but it was one thing to know them and another entirely to see them in life. Much like the stadium that was to be their doom, several of the ones I saw from our box were far larger than expected. I sat up straight, leaning toward the balcony, investigating them one by one. To the far left, a gray ypron growled at the light while pacing back and forth upon its stubby legs. Short though it was, its muzzle was far too big to fit through the bars at which it snapped and snarled. While its short, round ears fluttered in frustration, the ventil in the cage beside it bleated in fear at whatever was across from it—or maybe the stadium as a whole. Its head bowing, the springtime blossoms of its antlers long having since wilted early due to stress, the ventil pawed at the earth and helplessly looked for a way out.

Only the oris—a giant, deadly bird that thankfully lacked flight even if it did not lack teeth or the hooked talons affixed to the tips of its intimidating wings—seemed untroubled by the opening of its wall to the light and the noise. It remained seated, tired or hungry or both.

"First up," called Winston, his broadcast ringing out through the stadium, "let's see how our assistants fare against a pack of hungry lupellas!"

While the audience cheered, I was transported back to the night of the circus; to that girl, crouched in the shadows of the doorway while fearing for her life. How I wished I could comfort her now!

And how I, like her, wished I could be elsewhere.

I had thought my father exaggerated somehow when he

warned me about the ugliness of Torea Festivals, but I was shocked from the very start. While the assistants rode in on autohorseback through the open portcullis, one of the gates beneath us ground open. Men could be heard hollering over the noise of the crowd, but only barely, and only because we were almost directly over it.

While the lupellas rippled out, their little legs appearing to shiver as they hurried into the arena, the assistants whooped and cheered. They ran their horses toward the pack, and I expected them to try and break up the group. I expected it to be like normal hunting, but put on display for a crowd.

Instead, the assistants appeared to be deliberately trying to trample the lupella, and at least one of them succeeded. As the monster yelped beneath mechanical hooves, my stomach and mouth both tightened. I thought it was a mistake, but the audience screamed with delight and at least one more of the pack was dispatched this way before they made good their scatter.

Then, each man picking his target, they started in with throwing knives.

I couldn't watch, but neither could I obliterate all knowledge of what was happening. Teeth and hands clenched, I tried to think of something—anything else—that could take me away from this place and the screams, the blood, the cheers for death.

But every time I managed to turn my thoughts to more pleasant fancies, another gate would open, and more monsters would be shouted, beaten, terrified into the light where they were dispatched with great prejudice.

"Are you all right, Thecla?"

Malin's concern couldn't even touch me then, I was so sick and pale to see a pair of borros slaughtered from the corner of my eye. They had been shot by bow and arrow, and this time I was certain I saw Eleison's hand clench into a fist for a few seconds. At least I wasn't alone in my disgust.

"I—I'm sorry," I confessed, "I'm not. "Perhaps, that water—"

"Oh, dear—of course, what a fool I am. Eleison, could you?"

"Coming up," he replied, gladly exiting the box.

His attention unfortunately drawn back to me again, Dr. Gall leaned toward us. "Are you feeling sick, Thecla?"

"No—well—"

On the bloody ground of the arena, the ypron took its first reluctant steps before tensing to see the hunters. When it raised its head to brandish its tusks, I had to look away.

"I just didn't sleep through the night," I lied, not wanting to look weak in front of either Malin or the despised doctor. "And the sun is really quite exhausting today—I've gotten so used to clouds over the winter."

"Are you a virgin?"

Dr. Gall's comment caught me so off-guard that I nearly shrieked, "Excuse me?"

Malin looked like he wanted to say something far harsher, but before he could pair a comment with his baleful expression, Gall laughed it off. "I'm just wondering if it's possible you might be pregnant."

"It's possible," I told him coldly, the scream of the ypron as a spear was hammered down through its neck muscles rattling in me like nails on slate. "But it does not seem particularly likely. Aren't altered children rare, anyway?"

"Sure, they are…but that's because altered agree to various forms of controlled fertility when they sign up for the program."

I scoffed a little. At the second cry of the still stumbling, now raging animal, the oris rose in its cage and snapped the stonelike beak that extended from its feathery face.

"Controlled fertility? You mean you sterilize them?"

"Ones who are enlisted into the program, yes. Volunteers agree to take medication or receive shots for the rest of their lives, and are monitored to ensure they do so."

It astonished me—altered were so valuable, yet so roundly despised they couldn't even breed? I wondered about Eleison, my heart twisting in sorrow for him. Would he ever be able to have a child, (assuming he wanted one), or had that been taken from him when he bargained for his brother's life?

"Tell me, Doctor…"

Making no more attempt to smile, I stared the unpleasant man boldly in the eyes. The ypron howled, staggered by the fourth spear, and the portcullis slid open while the master of ceremonies invited their star hunter to the killing floor.

"If you force them to agree to sterilization, how exactly is someone like me born?"

"That is the question, isn't it…what was your mother's name?"

Stone strode out, his bearded jaw set and a sword at his side. While he drew it from its sheath to the delight of the crowd, the oris began a rapid hammering motion with its beak.

"Why do you want to know?"

"Just wondering if she was one of mine. She probably was… or at least came through my hospital."

"Her name was Giselle," I said, half-distracted by the violence. While the tortured ypron, its tusks impossible to lower for the charge with the spears cruelly extending from its shoulders, backed toward a corner with its breath coming in desperate pants, I cleared my throat. "But I can't imagine you would have much memory for names, since it seems altered mean so little to you as actual patients."

"Now," said the doctor, his expression tightening in an unpleasant scowl, "see here—"

Metal clanged. A woman screamed. The hunter halted his advance on the helpless ypron and twisted at the waist to hear the oris's lock mechanism snap at the base of its cage. While the malfunctioning device ground open, the oris waited no more than a few seconds before judging the space suitable to dash beneath the bars.

Though, crying out, the assistants charged with weapons in hand, the screaming bird ignored them and lunged across the stadium for Stone.

The audience was in chaos, screams of dread and terror echoing out while the oris knocked the sword from his hand and thrust him to the ground with one blow of its body.

Now, I could stand to watch. I sat straight up in my chair, my eyes fixed to the scene, my heart racing as the alien bird brutally trampled the slayer beneath its clawed feet. It was not my custom to wish pain on others—but the sleeping beast in me was euphoric at the sight, and I could only think how good it was that this was happening to such a hateful man. When the assistants surrounded it from all sides, the oris stopped to launch at one claws-first.

The human, perhaps wisely, cried out and steered his robotic horse away…but the oris kept running upon its uncannily speeding hind legs, a hiss of pure hatred sizzling from its beak.

I thought it was running away from the assistants, or perhaps through the portcullis directly beneath us—but, as it drew closer, I realized with a cringe of fear that its golden eyes were fixed upon our box.

"It's coming here," I said, stirring Malin from his own somewhat shocked and intrigued meditation.

"What was that?"

"It's coming *here*," I cried again. My words rose in a frightened scream as the oris sprang up, the rapid flaps of its wings carrying it as high as they could.

High enough to reach the first row of the screaming audience.

While spectators fled their seats, the oris effortlessly overleaped the next two rows.

Malin, unhesitating, lunged from his seat and threw an arm before me.

But the oris wasn't coming for me, I realized in the second before the gunshot.

It was springing at Dr. Gall.

Amid the crack and the stench of gunpowder, the oris hissed with pain and stumbled back over our balcony. I rose up with a cry of fright, clinging to Malin as I searched for the source of the shot. Vivian's gun was barely out of her jacket; but Eleison, his pistol still in his hand, darted past us and vaulted from the box's edge.

His name burst from me in a cry, but I should have known he would be more efficient, more skilled, than any of the hunters we had seen in the stadium. His mere arrival was sufficient to send the oris fluttering back into the center of the stadium, the tall bird screeching with rage and what was surely no small amount of pain for the gunshot wound oozing red into its iridescent plumage

Sliding down the guard rail of the stairs and nimbly springing down into the dirt, Eleison raised his gun.

The oris, wild, charged too quickly for him to take proper

aim. His bullet struck the ground and he rolled aside, narrowly missing a talon to the head.

Slowly, I realized the audience was cheering.

His gun still in his hand, Eleison took one look at the speed of the bird pursuing him and decided to ditch the weapon. While the gun slid away, he took a running dive across the stadium and through the panicked assistants who hurried from his path.

When they cleared, I saw his target: Stone's fallen body, and the sword lying beside him.

With absolute elegance, Eleison snatched up the blade and spun to meet the oris just as the bird caught up. Its sharp beak, snapping as it had at the cage, caught the sword and threatened to break it, or at least tear it from his hands.

Raising one foot, Eleison kicked the beast in the chest so hard that it had little choice but release him or suffocate.

He knew what he needed to do, and he didn't think twice about it. With his muscle memory in the heat of battle evident even to me, Eleison drew back the sword and sliced straight across the feathers of the oris's long neck.

While its head rolled aside, the crowd roared with sheer delight.

Slowly at first, but soon in a great flood, roses were thrown at Eleison's feet from all sides of the audience.

Malin whistled, applauding with a laugh of genuine delight for the feat. I applauded, too.

But I could not smile; I could not laugh. I could not even feel relief.

Somehow, all I could feel was the absurd sense that I had caused what just happened—what just almost happened to Dr. Gall.

And, perhaps more alarmingly, I wasn't sure that I cared.

THAT NIGHT, MY mind was on fire. Every time I tried to see causal links between the event, my emotions, and what happened when both reached a certain peak, I rebuffed myself.

It was impossible that I caused that oris to break free and, of all people in that stadium, attack Dr. Gall—wasn't it?

A little voice, a new voice I hardly recognized, reminded me that I had no idea what my limits were now. Nobody knew what I could do, being both riftborn and altered.

Frightened to be alone with myself, yet desperate to sort out my thoughts, I missed a rare opportunity for supper with Malin and instead bathed in my quarters. When that did not calm my nerves, I toweled off, dressed in a thin robe with a floral pattern, and let myself into my fiancé's quarters with only faint hesitation.

No—not hesitation. A kind of paralytic excitement, as though my body's eagerness to submit to him was a deterrent. So overwhelming it might cause me to faint.

I tried not to feel my own perverse flutter of excitement at the thought of his free access to my unconscious body and edged forward into the apartment, looking all around.

"Malin?"

No answer. I had never been in this situation before. Never been in his room without him. Never been tempted by the shut doors of the apartment I now mostly knew but had not inquired about—then rejected that temptation with a bolt of genuine mortal terror.

I had never lain in his bed without him, waiting for him, the scent of the pillows and bedspread and canopy around me all imbued with his rich, warm essence.

He arrived soon enough, his key fitting into the apartment's distant front door and clicking the tumblers over. While it swung wide, my heart raced. I sat up, the robe falling half-open with the motion, each footstep through the hall echoing in my heart.

As he stepped into the doorway, his eye fell on me, and his brief surprise yielded to a smile that stirred my very core.

He closed the bedroom door, his face turned away.

"I didn't think I'd see you again tonight when you missed dinner."

"I'm sorry, sir."

"That's all right...it's your body. I'll only make you eat if I truly need to." Locking the door for added effect, he slid the key into his pocket and turned to study my flushed face, my undone hair, my revealed body all in turn. "You look like you've had another lover, Thecla."

My blush deepening, I couldn't help but gasp and swear, "Of course not! I just took a bath—"

But that wicked light in his eyes didn't vanish. He wasn't

serious; I could tell that in the way he prowled to the bedside and swept his hand through the fan of my hair.

"I think you have, you brat...no wonder you refused to come to dinner with me, and were in such a foul mood at the festival. Thinking about the fellow you could have been having back here, were you?"

What a thing to say in jest! Especially since the fellow I lusted after had been there with us—the undeniable hero of the night, stopped three times on our way across the park to sign programs for children too young to know him from a real celebrity.

"I want *you*, Master." That same great hand slid down the back of my neck to turn my face toward his. I whimpered on, "Please—I'm not some tart, you know, I—"

"Oh, but you are...you're my hot little tramp, and any man in this mansion would risk castration to fuck you even once. We're going to play a new game tonight...lie face down on the bed."

His hand slid away from me altogether, and I exhaled shakily to do as I was told. While I made myself as comfortable as I could, a drawer slid open somewhere in the room.

"As always, tell me your village's name if you have to get down, or feel ill. Are you *sincerely* feeling better than earlier?"

"Yes, sir. That festival was just—shocking."

"I'm sorry, Thecla. I should have considered how sensitive you are...and how interested Gall would be in you, despite my request that he refrain from treating you like a test subject."

Oddly touched by his apology, I assured him, "That's all right, Master. I was so happy to be out with you...and so proud to be seen with you."

"Yet here you are, skipping dinner with me to give yourself to some lowlife scoundrel in my employ...take your robe off, Thecla."

I exhaled, my fingers trembling to obey, and Malin returned to my side. He rested something heavy there, and I saw only when I had wiggled free of the robe that the object was a coil of dark red rope.

"What's that for," I whispered, excited and afraid and increasingly aflame with desire. "Oh, Master—"

"Just something to keep you still for your interrogation. You're going to sit up a little—kneel for me—and when I tell you, you'll lean forward with my help and lie back down again. Otherwise, sit still. I'll show your body how to move."

I obeyed, flushed to be revealed to him even after all the times he had feasted his eyes on me. Malin took up the rope and bent to kiss me, the coil sliding into his elbow while his hot breath filled my mouth. I moaned, reaching up to stroke his face, and he caught my hands, raising them into the air.

Drawing away from our kiss, Malin doubled the rope and slowly drew it around my ribs, just beneath my breasts.

"The events of the afternoon made me realize something, Thecla…"

The pads of his fingers sent goosebumps down my body, every incidental caress as he wound the ropes into a harness around my ribs and shoulders somehow streaking straight between my thighs and high up into my floating head.

"I'm concerned about you…going about in the world, living a life more independent of me. Especially when we're in the city, as we will be later this season. You need to learn how to defend yourself."

I inhaled sharply, unable to confess the sense I had that the oris *had* been me defending myself. Weaving over my breasts and down my back, Malin went on.

"I was a little late just now because I was making arrangements...I'd like you to take self-defense lessons, and I'd like you to start taking them tomorrow."

I pouted a little despite myself, eyeing him as he came back into view. "Dancing lessons, horseback riding, now self-defense... am I to learn etiquette, too?"

"That's a good idea." Chuckling to himself while my eyes rolled, Malin tweaked my already hardened nipple and made me gasp for air. Though the passion obviously smoldered, that sternness beneath his gaze was unaffected. Absolute truth.

"Now remember, Thecla...our agreement when you came here was that when I told you to do something for me, you would do it out of loyalty. Taking self-defense lessons is for me...I don't want to have to worry about you."

Unable to help my small sigh, I agreed, "Yes, sir...you're right."

"I'm always right."

I gasped as he brought the ropes down over my shoulder and tightened them into a 'v' through the lower half of the harness. "Can you breathe," he asked, and I inhaled with my nod.

"Yes—yes, sir."

"Good girl." With a few more weaves and loops over my back, Malin finished the chest harness and took hold of it with one hand. The other rested against my heart. "Now, lean forward with me..."

Carefully, he eased me down before drawing back my arms. Then, the real work began.

I was not sure how long I was there with him weaving the ropes around me, and the truth was that I didn't mind at all. Quickly, the tight hug around my limbs grew comforting—

hypnotic. Winding and winding, Malin encased my arms in a cocoon that fit against my back and was easily attached to another harness he created around my pelvis. As he worked, his fingertips grazed my thighs and whispered against my labia, but the liberties he took were so slight that they seemed nearly cruel.

When he was satisfied with the progress, he stood on the bed beside me and drew something down from the ceiling canopy. I twisted my head, trying to see it, and failed—only to realize, when he picked me up quite effortlessly from the harness's back support, I was about to be attached to a hook suspended there.

"Oh"—I gasped and writhed as much as I could in the bindings, but real movement was impossible—"oh, Master—will it support me?"

"Your slight weight? Of course...just relax, we're nearly done. You look so beautiful, Thecla...next time, we'll do this in front of a mirror."

True to his word, only one more rope needed to be applied: this, binding one leg back against itself, leaving my foot tucked beneath my bottom. The other leg was left to dangle, my toes just touching the mattress of his bed, my legs unable to help themselves but spread for his appreciation.

And appreciate, he did.

"There, you little tart..." As his eyes roved over me, his hand trailed over my free thigh and seemed tempted to creep higher. "You're drenched, yet you want to pretend you haven't been letting some young fool use your gorgeous pussy all night?"

His language, his teasing, his perverse games, the exposure and control of the ropes—I moaned, and doubly so as his fingers relented to the urge to touch me. "Oh"—I arched my hips as much as I could, swinging on the hook with the motion of my leg—"oh, sir, no, nothing like that…oh, I'm just aching for you."

"Liar."

His hand lifted and, to my surprise, struck against my center in a sharp swat. To my greater surprise, I was flooded with extraordinary pleasure.

"Sir! Oh—"

"Like that, do you…"

He did it again, the next slap harder this time, and I quite literally felt myself flooding in response to the strikes. His mouth found mine and I groaned into him, trembling with the explosive sting and eager rush of pleasure that occurred at every sharp spank of my sex.

"Good." His hungry kiss lifted, his eyes bright with lust. "Maybe if I give you what you want, you'll tell me what I want to know. Were you fucking someone while I dined alone? Yes, or no?"

The quick little volley of spanks left me dizzy with desire. I wanted more—wanted him to touch me more, roughly and gently. More than anything, I wanted him to fuck me.

And, knowing if I didn't play his game, he might punish me by refusing those things, I couldn't help but entertain him.

"Oh," I whined, "yes, Master—"

A soft gasp of excitement passed his lips to find me engaged in his fantasy—in some controlled recreation of the traumas of the past. The steady little spanks grew lighter, slower, gradually growing indistinguishable from long, loving strokes back and forth along my vulva.

"Yes, what?"

"Yes," I gasped, staring into his eyes while he spread my

arousal all across that aching valley. "Yes, Master—while you were at dinner, I let someone fuck me...I gave myself to another man."

"Who?"

I cried out, my toes curling as his finger teased its slow way into me.

"Oh—hm, oh, Master—I shouldn't tell you his name..."

That finger withdrew. He spanked me again, the gem of my bliss taking each slap like a kiss. The immobilization of the ropes was so frustrating, yet so liberating—I couldn't reach him to kiss him at my pleasure, yet there was nothing to do but hang there and *be* pleasured.

And, of course, to pleasure him.

"Who had his cock in you tonight, you little slut?"

"Oh, oh—"

I could think no other name. It was too close to home, too much evidence to incite his suspicions if he already nursed them, but I couldn't stop my mouth—particularly not as his fingertip slid back inside me again, this time teasing deeper.

"Eleison," I whimpered as Malin penetrated me. "It was Eleison—oh, Master—"

A tigerish smile furled across Malin's face. As his eyes flickered to my mouth to telegraph his intentions, a second finger joined the first. I moaned his name, opening my mouth to his sensual kiss, the feeling of his fingers gradually growing so intense I might have tried to close my legs if I'd been untied.

"Here I thought you two hated each other," he said, chuckling above the wet sounds of his rapid coaxing. "It's all a charade, is it?"

"Oh—yes, sir, yes—oh, we meet each other all the time... every chance we get..."

I forced my fluttering eyes open and found him watching me intently, desire written all over his parted lips and inflamed pupils. My voice a whisper, I steadied my trembling lips enough to say, "We—hm—we wait until you're in your apartment, and I go see him…before I see you, of course…I love to—oh—meet him in his room, to feel his cock in my hand…in my mouth."

"I'm sure you love to suck it, you dirty harlot…"

His fingers left me and I whined, wriggling, worried I had taken it too far and said something to upset him.

Far from it. His forehead against mine, Malin unbuttoned his trousers and removed himself.

"He gets so big and hard," I whimpered, looking down at the scepter Malin stroked against my eager center. "And when he fucks me, it's—"

"Animalistic," answered Malin, the pressure increasing.

"Yes," I whispered, "yes."

Pleased to hear my fantasies aloud, whether he knew they were longstanding or thought them improvised for his entertainment, Malin slid himself deep inside me and pressed his mouth over mine. The rapid intensity of his kiss was almost equal to the fervor he showed for fucking me, his hand sliding around my free thigh and pulling it up off the bed until I wrapped my leg around him. I hung fully now, kept still by nothing more than his body and my connection to it.

"You know," whispered Malin, breaking character in the immense intimacy of his organ's penetration, "funny you should pick him…Eleison was the one I was just meeting about your lessons." While I moaned, his kisses trailed down my neck.

"Tell me you didn't…"

"It's good for you." His voice a playful growl, Malin landed a few sharp swats upon my ass in impacts that rang beneath my giddy cries. "I meant what I said...you two should learn to get along. Not so well that he robs me of you, of course, if you understand what I'm saying...but, at least well enough that you won't mind bringing him up during our little games. You must admit, after all, that Eleison is a very fine-looking man."

Despite myself, I laughed, then moaned into the pressure of my fiancé's body. As his strokes grew more intense, I shook in his arms to think of the transparency this sort of amusement offered.

And the duplicity.

Malin didn't know about the angry passion that blazed between Eleison and me. It was so wrong to go along with his games and flaunt it in his face, the same way I protested his flaunting the maids' beatings before I gave myself to him.

Of course, as clearly aroused by the idea of my infidelity as he was, I wondered if it was really all that duplicitous. Wasn't it just idle chatter, after all? To such benefit, too—how hard he was! And how wet he'd made me. I swear I saw stars as he fucked me, one hand tangling in my hair to keep my eyes fixed on his. When he next spoke, his voice was hoarse with desire to hear more.

"Did you let him cum in you?"

"Every drop," I whispered, his strikes home growing all the harder. "His semen was dripping from me when I left his chambers."

Groaning, Malin reached down between my legs to tease that tender nerve even as he worked himself within me. "What a wicked girl you are...perhaps I'd ought to punish you tonight, after all."

"Like what?"

"Like no cumming tonight..." While I moaned in outrage,

he sank his teeth into the ridge of my ear. "Maybe tomorrow morning, if you're a good girl and wake me up in that sweet way of yours."

Morning was my favorite time to have sex, but any time was fine with Malin, really...unless he was denying my climax. Yet, the idea of being refused pleasure while he took his own from me—it left me panting senselessly, my leg tightening around his hip.

"Please, sir, no—please, let me cum tonight, I need it so badly..."

"But just think how good it will feel tomorrow...no, Thecla, I don't think I'm going to give you permission."

While I groaned, he thrust harder. His thick tool hammered intensely against that spot that, I had found, yielded the most excellent orgasms. The most excellent, and the most difficult to resist.

"Please, sir—"

"No. Don't cum."

"Oh—oh, Master, but I'm so close—"

"Then you'd better hang on..."

I inhaled sharply, my stomach quivering as I tried to stave off the looming orgasm. Between his dirty talk and the force of his cock, I was overwhelmed, and the heights my arousal had reached were truly rare even for my recently eager condition. My thigh shook in his hand, my body trembling against his.

"Next time he cums in you," Malin murmured, his mouth brushing mine again, "find me right away...I'll make sure my pretty girl is nice and clean before our next fuck."

"Oh, God—yes, sir, yes, Master—please, I love it when you let me feel your mouth! I love it when you cum inside me...oh, Master!"

He was rigid as steel, and his teeth clenched with the intensity of his desire. As though the line between wanting to take me and wanting to tear out my throat with his teeth was too thin to be observed. While his hips battered mine, I felt my own building orgasm with a kind of fury for it. I didn't want it—I wanted to obey him. More than that, I wanted stay at this high, this absolute ecstasy, forever.

Luckily, with a few more pounds and another intense look in my eye, Malin growled my name before spilling inside me.

Those eyes never left mine. He panted his way through it, that hand still on the back of my neck. The other had shifted to my backside, keeping me pressed tightly to him while he claimed me.

"Thecla," Malin panted, his words ragged, "I truly do love you—oh, Thecla, I love you, I adore you."

While I produced an incoherent little moan, he kissed me.

THOUGH HE MAY have been playing a bedroom game with our shared fantasies, Malin had told the truth about one thing that night.

When I rode to the north side of the property, to the tree line where a shooting gallery had been arranged for the security officers, it was Eleison who waited to meet me.

Even from a distance, I knew his figure.

Was there more to it than that? Was I scenting him somehow on the wind? The panic of the festival flooded back to me. My hands tightened around the reins of the horse.

"I hope he at least warned you."

That low voice, rough and almost amused, broke my heart with the weight of my desire. I kept my expression flat, avoiding all thought of the night before, or of the pain in Eleison's face the night of our great fight, or—anything. Anything at all.

"He did warn me," I admitted, dismounting some twelve feet away and freeing the poor creature of its bridle. While Ambrose made himself comfortable, I examined the trees interspersed with targets stapled to wooden signs. Beyond, the trees thickened to woods. "I would have thought the shooting gallery to be, I don't know—more hi-tech."

"In Malin's manor? No way...you'll note that this spot is as far from the house as it gets."

I smiled weakly, but the smile dropped right away when the feeling of Malin's name on his lips really settled with me. Eleison's amusement fell away, and he looked at me for a long moment before his chest swelled with a hefty sigh.

"I'm sorry for the way I acted before." His voice was soft in its sincerity. "It's not easy for me, but—we can be adults about this. Can't we?"

"I really don't know, Eleison—I don't know."

I trembled just to look at him, dizzied by my desire. The wind plucked at his coat and sent his tie flapping, and I had the strange instinct to touch the chest beneath.

He hesitated, then took a single step forward in what I felt was an almost miraculous turn of events.

"Look, Thecla...if I can't have you, I want to know you're able to protect yourself. You can't even transform during a Rift Event yet. How am I ever supposed to rest if I need to leave you alone? If I go out of town with Malin on business, or run an errand for him? And that's all assuming I'm always around."

"I thought you and your brother were indentured servants."

"That's not really what I meant."

That awful pain; that sickness in my soul again. "It's not as if you'll *die* if you lose your humanity, will you?"

"I'd might as well. I'll be human in name only…a servant of the Rift, unhinged, converted to serve it and feed its monsters. Less stable than a starving dharmine."

He studied the obvious pain in my face, then turned his gaze away.

"I brought you this," he said, taking a pistol from his pocket. "It has a laser sight on it, so it'll help you get a feel for aiming."

"Thank you."

I closed the distance to take the extended weapon, waiting for him to step away like he had before. He didn't, and I suddenly found myself standing within three precious feet of him.

"Usually, you're cringing away from me like I'm diseased," I observed, lowering the gun and meeting his eyes. "What's different?"

"Nothing…but I have to get used to this."

"What's 'this?'"

"Being with you. Talking to you. Seeing you. I have to get used to seeing you."

Seeing me with Malin, he meant.

Inhaling, I nodded and agreed, "You're right, of course. Yes, you're right. So…should we start?"

Although I had been shooting once with my father as a child, I had retained almost nothing practical of the matter except for never pointing the gun at a person. When it came to aiming, recoil, and the positions of my arms, I was somewhat hopeless. The first twenty minutes were miserable, and eventually Eleison fell back on his heel with his arms crossed.

"You can't be so afraid of it."

"It's deadly!"

"It's a tool. Here—straighten your arms."

His hand seared my elbow. I let him angle my arms and my aim until he was satisfied, all the while wishing he would touch me for more than these glancing little adjustments. "You're still nervous," he observed.

"It's because you're standing so close to me."

"And you accuse me of not wanting to be near you...just breathe out."

With a glare at the telltale laser that danced back and forth in demonstration of my weaving aim, I took a deep breath in, held it, and let it out.

As I did, I pulled the trigger.

"Not bad," said Eleison, nodding in approval at the hole pelted through the sign perhaps three inches left of the bullseye. "Pretty good, in fact."

"You're a much more patient teacher than I expected you to be."

"You thought I'd yell at you?"

"After last time, I wasn't really sure."

He winced, his eyes averting toward the trees.

"I'm sorry, Thecla. I wish I'd had it in me to explain what was happening sooner. I just—couldn't betray Malin."

"You're a respectable man—a cavalier." I smiled wanly. "Not many men are as noble as you."

"I'm not sure I'd say that."

"Why not?"

"I agreed to come here alone with you."

My heart, which had almost adjusted to his presence, sped wildly again.

Eleison's fiery eyes bored into mine, reading every microscopic twitch in my face as he said, "I tell myself I'm doing things for you

and Malin, or that I'm trying to get used to being around you...
but, if I'm being honest, I'm here because I *want* to be around
you. I want to have an excuse to hear your voice. To touch you. I
shouldn't even be telling you this, but I want to...so I am. There's
nothing noble about me."

I swallowed my desire as best I could, but I wanted him too
intensely. "You can touch me," I whispered.

"Thecla...I can't."

"I mean—there are harmless ways, aren't there?"

"I'm afraid there might not be."

Shuddering, I turned my face away and took a deep breath.
I knew just what he meant. Every time I imagined him holding me
close to inform my shooting posture rather than engaging in those
brisk adjustments of his, I felt the slippery slope down to other, far
more intense brands of touch.

Before I could speak more on the matter, however, a terrible
noise echoed from the field behind us.

We both whirled, my gun jerking toward the noise while
Eleison drew his from under his arm.

A crios, all its slender torsos tangled together in a heinous
net, had slithered through the tall grass and wrapped around
Ambrose's legs. As the creature—truly a colony of beings, I had
been led to understand—constricted the screaming horse's limbs,
I raised the gun.

Eleison pushed it back down. "You don't want to hurt the horse."

Much calmer than I was, rebolstering his gun upon assessing
the threat, Eleison bent to draw a knife from under his trouser leg. I
blanched to realize how armed he was and wondered what else was
on his person, but there was no time to ponder. He turned the blade
around and offered me the handle, asking, "You want to try it?"

"Maybe the next one."

He shook his head. "Let me rephrase... How about you try it."

"If it bites me?"

"Doc'll give you a few shots and get you patched up...not the first time you've been bitten by a monster, right?"

Teeth clenched, I snatched the knife from him and stormed up to the twisting mass of snub-nosed, snakelike beasts. Ambrose did no small amount of thrashing and had managed to smash at least one head, but the rest slithered, bit, tightened and tangled, all looking for the animal's throat. And they were almost there.

Furious at the panic in the horse's eye—and remembering, as I did, the heartbreaking ypron dying in the arena the day prior—I somehow saw the murderous snakes as a kind of great bush. A collection of roses whose thorny buds needed cutting back.

Narrowly avoiding the bite of one of those hateful heads, I managed instead to snatch hold of the same creature's neck and swiftly end its misery with a clean slice of the knife. Disgust and shame rushed through me, but Ambrose's terror urged me on. I threw the head away and, leaping over a hissing pair of colony members, grabbed another portion of the crios just below its jaw and pulled it taut to be severed clean. Another dead head fell at my feet; another torso within the mass loosened its hold on Ambrose.

Soon it was a simple matter: a system, a meditative task. The shame left me along with the fear, and very quickly the fear left Ambrose. What was once an existential threat was reduced to a nuisance, and I breathed easily for the first time in two minutes when the final dead torso pulled away from the horse it had trapped.

"There," I told Ambrose, throwing my arms around his neck

and holding him as well as one could hold such a great animal. "There—you're safe."

Eleison lowered his eyes, his lips in a knowing smirk. "I didn't think you were as harmless as you claimed to be."

"Well—a bunch of hampered snakes is one thing. But shooting? Combat? I'm just not sure I have it in me...or that I'll ever need it."

"I'd much rather you know and not need than need and not know," Eleison told me firmly. "Life is long. You might not need to know this stuff now, but—"

Sighing, I nodded and agreed, "Yes, yes...you're right."

"So—you think you can stand this? These lessons with me?"

"If you can, I can."

He nodded, then glanced down at the face of his watch and up at the sky.

"The RMS reading is creeping up again. Since we were interrupted, how about we try again tomorrow if the weather's fine?"

I decided not to complain and glanced down at myself, my riding pants spattered in purplish blood that seemed intent on drying black. "If Charlotte doesn't kill me when she sees this, then yes, I suppose..."

"Good."

Those burning eyes fixed on mine, Eleison extended his hand.

The wind seemed to reproduce my breath as I crossed back to him, the handle of the blade before me.

When it rested in his palm, he grabbed my hand, instead.

I hardly knew what happened. My heart raced as he twisted me, his other hand flying up to grab the knife that otherwise would have fallen. Instead, I soon found it glinting in the corner of my eye. In the wild flurry of motion in which he'd caught it, that twist had rotated me around beneath his arm. Maintaining his grip of one hand, pinning me still with that same arm, Eleison used his control of me to keep me pressed tight against his body.

With his other hand, he pressed the knife to my throat.

Unexplainable, unspeakable things rushed through me, my breathing shallow. His lips, or his nose, or both, brushed the top of my head.

"Do you see how easy it would be, Thecla?"

I dared not swallow, let alone speak. His body was so large, his hand and arm instruments of pure muscle as much as the rest of him. That the blade of the knife lay over my pulse was somehow incidental. I feared him far more than any knife.

In response, I inclined my chin as much as I could stand to.

"Don't take it lightly. Don't roll your eyes and forget the things I'm teaching you. You need it—every scrap of information."

The knife lifted slowly from my neck. I released my held breath. As respiration racked my body in an intense shudder, I murmured hoarsely, "I don't know if monsters will prove so adept at disarming me."

Again, a puff of air from his lips sent thunder cracking from the crown of my head to the base of my spine. I wanted to stay in his arms forever! I wanted to be crushed and consumed by him, defeated and taken. His body—his body was so powerful, the scent of it so rich and intense—

"It's not monsters you should be concerned about."

When he released me, he pushed me forward a few steps. As though it were the only way he could stand to let me go. When I whirled to face him, the rubies of his eyes were mad with all the things I wanted to see in them, and his face was a tight mask of lust so overwhelming it appeared as a kind of hostility.

"I'll see you tomorrow, Thecla," he said, bending to wipe the knife free of monster blood. "Go away, please."

I didn't want to. Malin, forgive me, but I didn't want to leave Eleison—because I knew if I stayed, he would take me.

And how I wanted to be taken. I wanted desperately to ease the pressure of his insanity there at the border of the wilderness.

But the fear was also there. The fear, not just of not being able to go back from the action, but of Eleison's intensity. Of my own intensity. Of immolating myself in love without censure.

I backed away toward Ambrose, mounted his saddle, and rode off to leave Eleison alone.

TRAINING BECAME A daily affair, and I must confess I use that word for its evocative connotations. Eleison and I had not even kissed, yet the jaw-clenching, heart-racing power of our mutual desire was so overwhelming that every slight contact between us seemed to be sexual.

I tried to remind myself before each session that it was not, of course. That I was ridiculous and paranoid, ascribing my own meaning when he acted toward me as the instructor acted toward any student.

But I could not lie to myself the way we lied to each other. It was all such a charade. We both knew the pleasure we took in breathing the same air, connecting skin to skin in the most innocent way. Simply looking into one another's eyes. When he coached me how to throw a punch, the hard impact of his palm or chest against my fist was like fireworks in my soul.

And when he had enough of letting me get any kind of headway in our sparring, and he caught me by the wrists, I saw in his face nothing but how intensely he fought the urge to kiss me.

I was lovesick as I had never been, and the shame was unending. Malin trusted me completely. Even after our game the night before the first training session, it never occurred to him that I had been speaking from a place of genuine fantasy—or, if he believed I was, he did not seem threatened by it. He rarely if ever inquired how my training went, being more interested in the books I was reading or the progress I had made in horseback riding.

Yet there was an increasing solemnity about him, and it made me nervous as it grew more apparent over the next two weeks. He became very pensive at breakfast, and I was shocked to find myself for the first time trying to cajole *him* into speech—a strange reversal of our relationship in my first days at the manor.

"Is everything all right," I asked at last, unable to stand it anymore when I came into his apartment one late afternoon to note he had canceled some call to brood in his private office. "Malin—I'm worried about you."

"Hm? Why is that, dear? Come here." Without looking back, Malin extended an arm and waved me over. He stood before a tall window overlooking the garden, the hedge maze, and the country beyond with a thoughtful sort of frown pulling at his lips. Yet I slid into his arm, and he pressed his mouth to mine with such tender intimacy that I almost forgot why I had come in. When his face lifted, his eyes once more held that healthy hint of mischief I had only been able to get from him after dark for the past few days.

"I'm the one who should be worried about you, darling...not the other way around. Don't concern yourself with my moods."

"But—"

"It has nothing to do with you, if that's your concern."

It was, but I didn't want to admit that and merely pursed my lips. "Still—maybe it's something I can help with."

Heaving a sigh, Malin said, "No, no. Just feeling a little restless. You'll get used to me, darling, don't fret. I go through this about twice a year…it's past time to move residences, and frankly I'm not used to wintering in this one from the start, but I've been in a bit of a bind. Too much to do."

"Why *are* you wintering in such a remote house? I've wondered."

"For you, of course," he said to my great surprise. At my expression, he laughed slightly. "I hadn't the least idea of your capabilities or temperament at the time, remember. Besides… if I brought you to the city first, you would have been very overwhelmed."

Or more capable of running away…not that I would have, things unfolding as they were. "Where's your other residence?"

"In Saalast," he replied, turning away from the window to face me fully. His hand, raising to stroke across my cheek and comb back through my hair, settled against the base of my neck while he basked in my face. "I have quite a few properties, but these days I find myself moving back and forth between the place in Saalast and this one. Maybe I should take you away to the vineyard, instead…that's what I really want."

His fingers sank into the flesh of my neck, and that heatwave of desire blossomed through my ribs and pelvis.

"I want to whisk you away, Thecla…oh, darling, I want nothing more than to carry you away for just a little while and be fully lost in you."

That sounded like such ecstasy—and if it would take me away from the temptations of my training, however necessary it was, so much the better. "Please," I whispered, searching his face. "Please, our honeymoon—can't we be completely alone for it, somehow?"

"I'll find a way." My stomach tensed at the low drop of his voice. I nodded, my hands sliding over his chest as his caress trailed down to my rear. "Ah—hm, Thecla, you are a maddening distraction to me."

"Your career is a maddening distraction *from* me," I corrected him with a pout, earning a long, thoughtful smile and a dark flash of pleasure in his eyes.

"I love you fiercely, Thecla...you know, I just filed the first bit of registry paperwork concerning you."

I flushed in delight. "Really?"

"Yes, of course. It shouldn't take too long to process with my people on it...although there may be some review after it's accomplished."

My smile faltered a little, but I didn't need to voice my concerns.

"Don't worry," he urged me, his thumb running up and down the edge of my throat. "There's no risk of it being reverted. Doing so would publicly embarrass me, and not even the Overseer would dare. I believe she learned her lesson last time."

It was not often that I glimpsed the true, bleak evil that dwelled in certain corners of Malin's mind, but I certainly saw it then when his eyes fell away from mine and into his thoughts of the Overseer. I understood little about the Expansion, truth be told, and what I did recall was from my father's broad understanding of the world, despite his claim to have lived only in some other small town before Lescaut. I found myself curious about the events leading up to Gudrune's victory, seeing the look in Malin's eyes, and wondered if the conflict was the source of his scar; but, in matters concerning him and his history, the manor's library was curiously lacking. His history was still a cloud of unknowing to me, layered over with vulgar rumor that I knew to be false. Perhaps he would tell me something of his past sometime.

Before I could draw him from his thoughts with a perhaps ill-advised question, the fatal bell of the RMS tolled out through the sprawling apartments.

My body seized in fear; Malin groaned as the device declared, "Rift Event Imminent: Twenty minutes advised."

With a bleak, fully humorless look in his eye, Malin told me, "I think I'm going to take the next couple of days off. When you see Charlotte, would you tell her to cancel everything I have for the next forty-eight hours?"

Unable to find my voice, I nodded, instead. My eyes darted around, the sky through the window still the ordinary slate color of a rainy spring day.

Over the next twenty minutes, that would change.

"Uh—"

My mouth opened as Malin stepped away from me, fetching his suitcoat and pulling it on to head out.

"Yes, Thecla? What is it."

"Just—may I stay with you? The whole time—during the Rift Event, may I stay in your apartment with you?"

His hands froze mid-motion as he smoothed his lapel.

"Are you sure you want to do that," he asked, still looking away from me.

My tongue darted across my lips. I started to nod before

remembering to say, "Yes, sir. Yes—I want you to do whatever you want to do with me. To me." He exhaled softly, right hand extending to let his fingertips rest at the edge of a side table as polished as the rings on his index and third fingers. "I need you to keep me safe from the Rift—but I don't ever want to be safe from you."

Hand raising to toy absently with the button of his jacket, his thoughts clearly consuming, Malin lowered his head, then turned slightly toward me. "While you're giving Charlotte my message, tell her to put two—no, three days' worth of your clothes in here with me, and ask her to make herself scarce when she serves us for the duration of the Event. I don't think I want to be interrupted with you."

My mouth dry, I nodded. That same fidgeting right hand raised from his button and waved me over. When I was within arm's reach, he caught me around the waist and drew me up into a heavy kiss.

The force with which his tongue commanded the submission of mine made me shudder. I clung to him, afraid I would collapse from the breath he stole.

"You'll have nothing to fear, Thecla…no, not from the Rift."

When he let me go, my heart was in my mouth and my body felt hot with a fever like no other. It was what I wanted. For Malin to whisk me away from everything. From the Rift and from my guilt and my fear.

From Eleison—who, as usual, talked with the rest of the security in the foyer. Our eyes met as I passed above him, hurrying from one wing to another past the grand split staircase. I was sickened not just to think of Eleison endangering himself by going out in the Event and hunting monsters. What moved me was how difficult it would be in his mind, during and after.

And how easy it would be to help him—if I could. If I only could.

He saw the pain in my face and broke eye contact first, turning to answer a question. I lowered my head and hurried down the hall, my mind so occupied that when I found Charlotte I very nearly careened face-first into her.

"You always look like you've come from another planet and it's your first Rift Event," she mused, a wry expression across her lips.

When I relayed Malin's commands to her, her wry smile faded into something slightly more serious.

"Are you sure you're ready to stay with him?"

"It's only two days."

"And he'll be sure to use them."

I blanched. "What concern is it of yours?"

"Just a friendly word of warning…"

She was right to warn me, of course, but it was terribly embarrassing to have the subject broached at even a soft volume and discreet manner in the upstairs corridor like that. I was quite sure that the entire staff was in on Malin's proclivities, at least to the extent any gossip mill would be; and I confess there was no small degree of humiliation involved in the assumptions to be drawn from Malin's sudden decision to forego the maids and marry me.

But it was also a little exciting. I was pleased they knew he owned me, as it were. Though I was eager to be called his wife, I was excited in a different, altogether more perverse way to find myself his pet.

Unable to risk running into Eleison, I took a long route through the upstairs, returned to Malin's apartment, and retired within.

I must have sat there alone for three long hours, my heart and mind racing all the time. Charlotte's entrance to bring my clothes and ask what I wished for dinner made me jump out of my skin.

"I don't know," I stuttered. "What did Malin say he wanted?"

"Malin will not be joining you for supper," she said. An increasing rarity. He had been making more time for me, particularly since the traffic of courtiers had cleared up and the house was mostly Malin and the staff.

And me, of course.

When I settled on duck, it was another long wait before it was delivered to me. I ate every delicious, slightly sweet little scrap, the brussels sprouts the meal came with exotically spiced and to be savored in and of themselves. I had never had a bad meal at the manor, and the food settled my mind's high anxiety for the Event going on outside the shuttered windows...but that anxiety was always secondary.

Without Malin there to distract me, my every worry was for Eleison. Eleison—oh, Eleison! I prayed that not one creature's claw would slice him—literally prayed, desperate on my knees, tears filling my eyes to think of him returning wounded. I tried instead to picture him returning to the manor his usual self. Healthy, calm, unharmed.

In need of my embrace, if he was ever to fully shake off the event's ill effects.

The yearning in my body deepened at the thought. The longer I pondered Eleison, in fact, the more uncontrollable grew the warmth in my body. Unspeakable imagery filled my mind, flooding in without the slightest means to put it to a stop—and each vivid image reflected itself in phantom sensations, in a body that was soon feverish to be loved. I paced to the RMS panel, then to the sitting room couch where Malin first kissed me. Even that artifact could not fully erase Eleison from my mind, and I leaned my head against the cool leather with a sad moan.

Then—miraculously—a key rattled in the front door.

I braced myself, prepared for another disappointment from Charlotte.

And Malin stepped in, his eyes striking me where I lay in a sauna that pursued me every step.

"Oh—"

"At last."

A great, shuddering sigh rose from him as he shut and locked the door. While he slipped away the key, I sprang up to greet him.

"Wait," he said, raising a hand before I could throw myself upon him and plead for a kiss, "wait, now...I've been so busy since I left, I haven't decided just what to do with you first."

"Please—please, sir, at least kiss me! Oh—"

The cry came out more like a moan of pleasure than I would have expected, and the desperation in my tone drew an arched brow of surprise from my betrothed.

"My goodness...you certainly are in a mood, aren't you?"

"I don't know what's come over me." I meant it sincerely and touched my own cheek, which I could see in the mirror over the back of the couch to be as red as if I had painted my face to go out. My pupils in my hazel irises were so great, so black, that my eyes looked like Malin's. "Perhaps it's waiting for you—waiting and smelling you, being in this apartment without you. Please, Master! I need you to take me—I need you to fuck me, please!"

"Well, now..."

Chuckling to himself, Malin slid a hand into the pocket of

his waistcoat. His eyes, further darkened by lust just like mine, drank me up.

"This is very charming. I don't know that I've ever seen you quite like this."

"I don't know that I've ever *felt* like this." I trembled, saying with a glance to the nearest sealed window, "It must be the Rift—the fear. I need you, I—"

"Have you ever experienced a heat, Thecla?"

I looked helplessly at him, shaking my head. "What is that?"

"Poor dear...come here..."

I dashed to him at once, throwing myself into his arms and moaning just to feel his body close to mine. His mouth transformed mine into a sex organ, I was so sensitive: my head swam beneath his passion, and in my dizziness I sank against his chest.

"I've heard that altered women go into heat a few times a year, but I've never seen its benefits for myself...it's Rift exposure that does it, usually, and it's generally thought to be for mating purposes, but it's also not normally quite so...pronounced."

I whimpered to feel his desire pressing against me, palpable even through our clothes. Gazing into his face, I shamelessly ran my hand over the protrusion in his trousers and let it all—my audacity, his low groan, the wild flame in my body—sweeten the pleasure I took in his presence.

"Is there something wrong with me? Please—I feel like if you don't take me, if you don't spend your seed in me over and over as many times as you can...it feels like I'll die, Master! Like I'll collapse into flames and disappear."

"Trust me, my dear...there is absolutely nothing wrong with you. Go on to the bedroom and take off your clothes. I'll be there very soon."

Moaning in grief to be gently unpeeled from his body, I begged, "Please, hurry—I've waited for you so long, oh, I'd do anything—"

"Then do what I tell you, and wait."

Though I whimpered, I obeyed and hurried to undress with trembling fingers. Why this heat, I wondered, and why now? I had never experienced it before—then again, I had not known my mate during previous springtime Rift Events. Perhaps something was changing in me.

Would Malin still love me as passionately when its transformation completed?

Thankfully, he didn't take long in arriving to relieve my fever—or, at least, to try. A thick ribbon of black silk lay in his hands, and as he admired my body, he told me, "Sit up."

I straightened from the headboard where I reclined amid pillows and drapes. His very stride commanding pleasure from me, he came to the bedside and stood just behind me.

"If you need to get up, I want you to tell me. Do you need to relieve yourself? You're going to be here some time."

"No," I whispered. The black silk caressed down my forehead before cutting into my vision. There was nothing there now, and I steadied my breathing as best as I could.

"Let me know if that changes, or if you need to stop, as always... Lie down with your hands above your head, please."

I obeyed, my lip bitten.

After stepping away to the drawer where he kept those ropes, Malin returned and set about binding my wrists: first together, then to an iron that ran along the base of the headboard.

Understanding somewhat better, I moaned as the final knot went into place and kept my arms snugly held above me.

"Are you comfortable?" His hands seared my hips as he raised my pelvis, and I exhaled shakily to feel the pillows he slid beneath my rear.

"Yes, sir."

"Good...let's save your beatings for tomorrow. For now, my poor little pet, let me see if I can do something to ease your suffering."

My breasts rapidly rose and fell with my panted breath. His large hand landed gently upon my thigh and he drew my legs wide, sighing at the sight.

That same sigh telegraphed his intent, the warmth of his mouth preceding the tongue that slid wetly along the length of my swollen vulva and to the clitoral nerve that could never be fully satisfied.

"Oh! Oh, sir—"

While I had not exactly had a plethora of sexual partners before Malin, I had never imagined a man might have such a passionate love for applying his mouth to a woman's sex. Yet, if there was ever an expert on the subject, it was him. Every contortion of lip and tongue tweaked another pound of pressure from my body, and as my abdominal muscles tightened into that sweet condition heralding annihilation, I bucked my hips toward his mouth. His broad tongue left its point of focus only occasionally, only to tease the folds of flesh all the way down to the desperate channel that lubricated them. Then it would writhe back up, slithering against that insatiable jewel, and my legs would reflexively kick up toward me before latching around his head.

But it wasn't enough.

"Sir," I begged, "please, yes, you feel so good, please, though—give me your prick, give me its every inch! I need it so badly—"

"Is this how you are with your lover?" At his question, I moaned. The revival of his wicked game was fraught with peril for my mind—and promised an intensification of my ecstasy along with his. While his fingers replaced his mouth, probing slowly into me, he asked in a husky tone of delight, "Do you kneel before him in the grasses of that little shooting gallery and sweetly beg to suck his cock?"

Moaning, the steady strokes of his fingers exacerbating the fire beneath my belly, I could think of nothing but how sweet it would be to do such a thing: to feel and taste Eleison's prick, and to guide it inside me while those brilliant eyes burned into mine.

"Yes," I told Malin, going along with his game, the filthy dreams pouring out of me. "Yes! I love it, feeling it bump the back of my throat—it gets so hard it throbs, just like yours. Oh, Master! Please—please, let me kiss it, at least, if you won't fuck me with it yet!"

"You are the most exceptionally delicious little slut...open your mouth."

Gasping, I lifted my head a little and obeyed. Malin's fingers left me, regrettably, but as the zipping of his trousers echoed through the room, I quivered with delight.

Then it was there: hot against my lips, firm and heavy and musky with the concentrated scent of man.

Moaning, I pursed my mouth against the helmet before parting my lips to allow the explorations of my tongue. He groaned slightly, sliding just so into my wet mouth before easing back out to do it all again.

"I must confess, as miserable as you are over it, I'm thrilled to find you so eager...we'll see if I can keep you satisfied until the Rift is over."

I wasn't sure he and Eleison could do it both together—a thought that flashed across my mind and sweetened the arousal Malin's anatomy inspired in me. It was too thrilling to taste his hot flesh. To feel the shape of it against my lips and tongue and know that soon he would be fucking me with it—soon, it would be spilling inside me, marking me.

Breeding me.

Yes, it must have been some biological heat. That thought affected me like nothing else. Moaning, my arms yanking fruitlessly at the binds, I turned my face from him and let his hard head rest against my cheek.

"Please—Master, you can't imagine how I feel! Please, fuck me now—fuck me hard, sir, oh, I'll do anything—"

"Poor girl! Oh, it's tempting to keep teasing you...but, I suppose there's two whole days for that."

Chuckling to himself, Malin withdrew. The sound of fabric falling away to the floor filled me with ecstasy. My feet braced into the mattress, my legs still splayed as he'd left them.

Then, he knelt between them.

I'M NOT SURE how many times Malin took me over the thirty-six hours that the Rift had the manor house—and my body—in its clutches. All I knew was that every time he finished with me, I wanted him all the more. The feeling of his seed oozing from me was the most thrilling sensation in the world, and my body was so primed for pleasure that his cruelest canes and sharpest lashes were infinitely sweeter than they had any right to be.

When the Rift ended, he kept me there the final half-day, and I feared to discover I was no less excitable in its wake.

However, when his time off was over and Malin had to go out into the manor again, kissing me apologetically and crooning over my wellbeing before he left, my body eased down at long last. After an hour, two, three alone with my thoughts, I cooled off for the first time since, if I was being honest, just before the Event.

I was still, by far and away, desperately primed to explode at my fiancé's touch, and I craved Eleison as always, but these conditions were normal for me. That feverish peak, that height of consequence-free craving—that was not something I had ever perceived in myself before, and it almost frightened me.

If it were not so thrilling, it certainly would have.

Nursing ecstatic memories of the nights before, I left the apartment for the first time in days and asked Charlotte to move my clothes back.

"Here I thought I had you," said Malin with a pout that night, regarding me from the other side of the open panel between our rooms. I hid my smile, stepping back to ensure he couldn't grab hold of me and pull me in with him. He had looked tempted, and still did. "You should give up and come stay in my apartment with me permanently. Why wait?"

"When we're married," I reminded him, "you'll have me all you want, whenever you want...but we're not married, are we, Master?"

Sighing heftily, Malin leaned his head against the hand he'd braced upon the doorway.

Then, stepping back, he left it open and retired to his bed.

I resisted the call to lie with him that night. I wanted to; but, I held fast to my principles. My resistance was not for religious reasons, as it was for some, but rather the simple reality that I wished to prolong his desire for me—to make him crave me and obliterate any second guesses he may still have had about our marriage, if he had any at all.

But, as sweet as our courtship was, and as great a pleasure as the weekend had made the otherwise hateful Rift Event, Malin was back to brooding the next day. Breakfast was mostly silent again, though he took great pains to ask about my plans for the day and wished me good fun since I had the morning off from weapons training. Eleison wasn't back from his maintenance work around the grounds, it would seem.

I sighed sadly once I left Malin to his day, knowing mine would be off-kilter.

My mood was foul. Restless, I fought the urge to wait in the foyer or seek out word of the security staff. I paced and prayed, the concern for Eleison rising over me as it had before Malin took it all from my mind.

Day passed into night, and I heard no word.

The next morning, however, when I opened the panel to Malin's apartment and stepped through to meet him for breakfast, two unexpected faces were already with him.

"Eleison," I half-cried, trying to moderate my joy into a tone of surprise at the last second. "You're back," I added in a more level manner, turning my attention rapidly from the man seated at the kitchenette's bar. He nodded to me, his face turning but his eyes not. Charlotte was my new focus, anyway, and I smiled at her.

"And what are *you* doing here?"

"We're having a little meeting," Malin announced, appearing at the edge of the dining room and waving me in. "And you're invited…come on. Take a seat."

A lump formed nervously in my throat as I obeyed, sliding into the stool three down from Eleison. With two empty seats between us, I still found myself incessantly imagining how easy it would be to touch him, but the urge was not so great that I had to tighten my hand or slide my fingers under my thigh.

Malin, missing my illicit desire as usual, was busy pacing at the head of the dining room with a mug of coffee in his hand.

"Well, it's no secret to anyone in this room that I have had enough of the country for the time being. I am exhausted, and this place is exhausting me further, but I have several daytrips planned down south to Karris and beyond, and I can't cancel them. They're vital."

Charlotte spoke up from where she stood at the edge of the bar, to Eleison's right. "Then go, and I'll open the apartment in Saalast for you."

"That's the idea, but you know what happened last time you tried to do that alone."

"It was fifteen years ago, and the maids didn't listen to me then. I'm sure things will be smoother now."

"Yes, well, I'm sure you're correct, but you know I prefer to be there to look over the first few days. Have to make sure the staff is functioning before I throw myself into work. *Then*, of course, there's the wedding planning, which should be reaching a peak as soon as possible. And all of this has come together to make me think…"

My stomach dropped even before he suggested it.

"Thecla—if you are to be my partner, I do expect some things from you. I need you to serve as my satellite, darling—someone to go out to Saalast with Charlotte and make sure my authority is being represented."

I bit my lip, glancing sidelong at Charlotte while saying, "I want to, Malin, but will the maids listen to *me*?"

"They've figured out by now that if they want to keep their jobs, they should respect you as much as they do their territory master." His tone grew terse at the thought of their disobedience, his mug raising to his lips. "Therefore, if you are there, I am there. Let's see how you do at managing the staff for the first time;

Charlotte can give you advice, and I can get a feel for how things are going when I arrive in a couple of weeks."

I frowned. "A couple of weeks?" The idea stung my heart, and even Malin's jaw grit in pain.

"We have to get used to being apart from time to time. You can't come abroad with me on every trip; not always. But what will separation do but sweeten our anticipation of the wedding?"

Nodding, I sank my teeth into my lower lip and worried. Would whatever spell of romance my presence cast on him be dimmed when I was away? Would he return to me and find me less favorable than he did?

No—I had to trust that the love he felt for me was as deep as it seemed.

Malin wasn't the problem.

"I'll do whatever you ask of me," I told him, raising my chin to meet his eye. "But please forgive me if something is not quite right, or if I make mistakes."

"Always," he said, while Charlotte assured me, "I'll help you."

Eleison stared out into space, waiting for the meeting to be over.

"So, you'll do it?"

I nodded at Malin's question, and he set down his mug to clap his hands in relief. "Oh! You can't imagine how glad I am that you're willing to help, Thecla. That's a weight off my shoulders. Don't worry about a thing. As she said, Charlotte will help you, and Eleison will be there as security, and—"

The floor dropped down a foot or two, or so it seemed. As I settled on the new level and tuned back into the remainder of his sentence about maids—"no more than that, I assure you, it's not a large place compared in size to this one"—I struggled to smile.

"Do you really think I'll need security, staying in Saalast two weeks?"

Pausing, glancing between Eleison and myself, Malin said with a hint of impatience, "Here I'd hoped your training sessions had helped you two get along better. You're not still having problems, are you?"

"No," I said quickly, while Eleison answered, "No, sir, we are not," in a tone that was deeply unimpressed.

"I suppose I'm just not used to—to always having someone around." I knew it was a fumble, but I struggled to find some way to get Malin on my side.

He wouldn't budge.

"Then I'm afraid you're going to have to get used to it... although, be relieved. As I said, the staff is small. Three or four maids—maybe five now, actually with your girl—and Eleison plus perhaps one or two other security staff members per shift, five total. There are twenty-six staff members here, so it's really a substantial difference, I think you'll agree."

I nodded, given no choice but to go along with his logic as it corresponded to my fictitious concern. "Yes, that does sound better."

He looked at me then in a queer way, nearly glancing away but second-guessing his movement and studying me a heartbeat longer. What did he see in my face?

"Then it's settled," Malin said abruptly, turning to the other two. "Charlotte, I'll leave the matter of which staff members will accompany you to your discretion. It doesn't matter to me...make sure they're ready, I want you all setting out soon."

Charlotte nodded, advising him that, "I believe the break in Rift activity is due to continue through the start of next week."

"Then we'll take advantage of it and send you in the next two days. Eleison, would you prefer I send Dr. Singer with you, or are you comfortable bringing a few doses of Stabilify on ice and self-injecting if you must?"

"I don't mind bringing the drug."

"Very good. Then plan to bring three maids now, Charlotte, and I'll see more come up with me...and the rest of vital security, of course. Eleison?"

Eleison had raised his hand and waved it a little. He now dropped it as he suggested, "How about, since it's going to be a carriage full of big skirts and household gossip, we take a *regular* carriage, and I can drive the horses in the front. Especially given what happened last time Thecla and Charlotte were on the road."

"You can still sit in the front with the autohorse," Malin rebuffed, "and, if I'm being straightforward with you, dealing with horses in the city is such a trial I'd much rather you do your typical stellar job by keeping the women safe *without* relying on Rift monsters' love of horsemeat. Now—"

I had never seen Malin so business-minded and was a little blown away, but neither Eleison nor Charlotte seemed to regard this behavior as anything but normal.

"I will trust you two to do what you need to do from here on out, and you can be ready to head north by Friday. Any questions? Then, you're dismissed."

"See you Friday morning," said Eleison with a nod my way, loping to the door of Malin's apartment while Charlotte stayed behind.

"Your girl will be occupied most of the morning with packing an appropriate wardrobe and other travel arrangements, so please find another maid to help you if you require something today, Mistress."

I nodded, waving weakly to her as she also departed.

Then it was just Malin and me. He picked up his coffee again, stared into it, and at last sighed heftily before coming to sit by me. I turned toward him as he slid into the stool at my right, our knees touching, his free hand catching hold of mine.

"I hope you understand I truly do hate to separate us now—especially when it involves sending you to the city by yourself. You must be very anxious."

Mutely, I nodded. His lips pressed thinner now, and he finished his coffee before setting it on the bar and taking both my hands.

"Thecla," he said, looking into my eyes, "if you're worried about my history, and any temptations I might face while alone—"

"It's not that—"

"—rest assured," he continued sincerely, undaunted and ignoring my interruption, "that I have no desire in my heart for any woman but you. The moment you agreed to marry me, I committed to you fully, and along with you I committed to what you want from me; and what you want from me is fidelity."

I nodded, the motion weak and laden with guilt he interpreted as doubt. His hands tightened affectionately around mine.

"Trust me when I say, Thecla—I will think of you every day, every morning and every night, until we are under the same roof again. I am so happy and grateful to have you in my life now. I will take this separation just as hard as you."

That was just it, though. That was just the problem.

Though I fully dreaded being apart from Malin—not because I did not trust him, but simply because I loved and desired him and did not wish to be away—I could not escape the wild excitement that flooded my belly and rushed into all my limbs.

Two weeks in an apartment with Eleison the only man around.

In my quarters, I trembled, and when the maid scurried in to begin packing my things, I took a long bath to calm my nerves.

There was no difference between being alone with Eleison in this context and being alone with Eleison in our shooting lessons. That was what I told myself over and over, yet I knew it was a lie. It was so different. Malin's extended absence would not dull my love for him, but I was afraid. What would happen if another Rift Event sent me into heat? What if Eleison was the only man around when I once more plunged into that sordid state of desperation— or, what if he simply smelled me, and could not help himself?

The things the thought did to me were not acceptable, rest assured.

I worried all day—but at night, sensing my distress, Malin made love to me with absolute tenderness. The night before we were to leave, he took the cane to me, and made love to me for what seemed like hours, and at last released inside me with a long study of my face, as though he strove to memorize it for later invocation.

When Charlotte, the three maids and I piled into the carriage whose external drivers' seat was filled by Eleison, Malin watched from the window with that same wild look of lust he received just when he could not have me. I teared up; I wished to run inside and find him, kiss him, touch him one more time before we left, but the trip was due to be nine hours or more, and if I lingered on the thought of him much longer, I really would cry.

Fighting back those tears, I blew Malin a kiss, climbed into the carriage, and let somebody shut the door behind me.

26

THE TRIP ITSELF was uneventful, but it had a magical quality to it. Perhaps it was the maids, who bantered in happy excitement about what they wanted to do in the city with their precious off-time over the coming season. Whatever the reason, my mood lifted more by the hour.

Or, as it had been with Lescaut, perhaps the easing of my mood was just a symptom of the distance from Malin. As the possibility of turning around and seeing him at all for the next two weeks diminished with our journey, I was liberated to enjoy my duties instead of feeling the need to pine for him. He had honored me, really, by entrusting me with this task.

And I had to do my best to honor him in return.

We broke for lunch after many long hours, and everyone was numb and stiff. While we limped around, two of the maids' whispering attracted my ears. "Eleison," was the word that had earned my attention, and I followed their gazes to see they watched him smoke a cigarette with his back to us.

"I don't know," whispered the other maid as I tuned in, "but whatever his problem is, I hope he gets over it soon."

"Maybe the city will be good for him...maybe he'll find a girlfriend."

"Don't act like you don't wish it were you, Orena."

Blanching in jealousy, I cleared my throat. The maids whirled back toward me, their skittish posture indicating barely contained fright.

I won't deny I enjoyed it.

"I'm not sure what Master Farrow has to say about fraternization," I told them coldly, my slight guilt outweighed by a combination of power and possessiveness that were both perhaps inappropriate, "but I know I don't advise it."

"Of course," stuttered the first maid. "We were just kidding around, ha-ha..."

Their eyes were on me as I returned to the carriage, but I didn't care. Something inside me raged at the thought of Eleison so much as touching another woman. I found myself reflecting as we resumed our drive north that, if that Vivian ever again tried flirting with him in front of me, I might have been tempted to take his gun from him and shoot her before he could stop me.

There was something else inside of me these days, I sensed. And it was not me—but it was also me.

We made it to Saalast shortly before dark, the orange light of evening rich above us as traffic increased and our emergence around a hill revealed the city towering in the distance. Its skyscrapers made it seem at least as tall as it was wide, although its vastness cannot be understated. Highways curved from it in all directions, and in the valley between us and it, infrastructure old and new gradually thickened into what constituted Saalast.

"Saalast is the oldest city in Gudrune," Charlotte informed me, although the maids quieted their discussion to listen. "It's had quite a few names over the years, but in all its iterations it has been known as a hub of art, culture, and scientific achievement."

"You'll enjoy the libraries and galleries, ma'am," agreed Orena, the scullery maid who had taken too much interest in Eleison and now seemed interested instead in my good graces. "My uncle lives here; he'll be so pleased that I'm in town! We missed our winter visits this year."

"That's a good point...my mother also lives in Saalast." Charlotte pondered through the window; then, hearing my slight laugh of surprise, she turned an arched brow upon me. "What?"

"You're just not the type of person one thinks of as having a mother, somehow."

The maids giggled while their manager's eye gave a visible twitch at some deeply repressed comment. "Now, what's that supposed to mean..."

"It's a good quality! You seem sprung from the head of a god. Self-made."

Her lips twisted in a wry sort of smile, Charlotte shut her eyes and continued, "Anyway—she is quite old, and if you don't mind, I'd like some time to visit her before Master Farrow arrives and requires attention."

My heart skipped a beat. Suddenly somehow more aware of Eleison's presence in the driver's seat outside our carriage, I cleared my throat and said, "Yes, of course. How long do you need?"

"A few days, but I don't have to worry about it immediately. We'll get you settled and the apartment opened up to the master's liking, and I'll make sure I've returned well before he's due."

Weakly, I nodded. "That sounds fine—I'm sure we can manage without you, especially once things are up and running."

Inside, I screamed all the rest of the way to the apartment.

Something cruel had devised this fate for me: I was convinced of it. The apartment was incredible—far more extensive than Malin's emphasis on its small size had made me imagine. Quite the opposite. With seven floors, many amenities, and a rooftop garden, it was bigger than any house in Lescaut and certainly a mansion in its own right.

Yet, in that first hour, I was in such a daze I hardly paid attention to Charlotte's tour.

Was I so weak that I needed to be watched? Would the temptation cripple me and all my good sense to the point of giving in?

And that did not even begin to consider Eleison's independent hand in our future, and what he was capable of if madness overtook him because of a Rift Event raging outside.

I shivered to think of how fine an opportunity such a thing would provide, and excused myself to my bedroom when Charlotte introduced me to it.

The first few days were fine. Wonderful, even. The truth was I had to do very little, and often felt I was in the way—but I *had* twigged to a few of Malin's preferences over the past three months. His taste in fine foods, certain liquors, and the expectation for immaculate environments were all foremost in my mind. Since she had some natural expertise in the matter, and I felt a little twinge of guilt over my treatment of her during the trip, I asked the scullery maid, Orena, to bring me to a boutique liquor store.

The sidewalks were busy, the streets all the busier. I saw at once why Malin wanted nothing to do with real horses in this place, especially given the trains that ran across the city by an elevated rail. You could get anywhere, I had discovered while poring over a map helpfully arranged for me by Charlotte. I felt excited by a sense of independence and a craving for exploration I hadn't known since I was an awestruck girl wandering between circus tents. Upon determining Orena had been visiting her Saalastian uncle every year or so since she was a small child, I asked her for a personal tour. Perhaps eager to get out of her usual duties, she agreed.

After I paid a pittance for both of us to ride the train, she and I sat side by side and gazed out the window. District by district, Orena explained Saalast to me while the train ran its long route. The financial district; the arts district; the tourists' section; the waterfront; the fantastic park, which seemed from the window of the train to be a vast sea of emerald. We passed through all the major areas at one point or another, then transferred to a second train to complete the circuit. She gestured over the bridge when it appeared in the distance, indicating a looming white building poised just beyond.

"There's Sigma Labs—see that building?"

I nodded, and she explained when I didn't see the significance, "They're the ones who do alterations...the original ones, anyway, for just over 100 years. They have three centers: one here, one in Europa, and another in Asia. It's one of the reasons there are so many altered people around here."

"In the city?"

She nodded, but went on to emphasize, "In Gudrune, and some of its surrounding territories. But a lot of altered go wandering once they've paid off their debt to the company, and they end up wherever they end up; that, or they get assigned somewhere else, to somebody else."

"You know a lot about altered."

"I used to fancy one." She blushed, glancing away from me. "It didn't work out, though."

"I'm sorry I snapped at you the other day," I thought to say; though, if I were being honest, I didn't fully mean it.

"That's all right! Master would have said the same thing... but he wouldn't have apologized. Oh! See here?"

Clutching my arm familiarly, then remembering herself and releasing me with a nervous laugh, Orena gestured toward a street lined with marquees.

"That's the theater district. It's my favorite place in the world! I used to get to go to a show every time I visited Uncle, but I don't always have time anymore. Maybe I'll go this year!"

"That sounds interesting. I've read a lot of plays, but I've never been to the theater."

Her lips parted and her eyes wide, Orena said, "A refined lady like you hasn't been to the theater?"

I almost laughed to be called 'a refined lady,' but instead I glowed beneath the appellation. The disguise Malin and Charlotte had crafted for me with silks and jewels evidently worked. The charade was successful: perhaps that was what helped Malin suspend his own disbelief about me, if he had any lingering.

"I lived a very sheltered life," I told Orena, "and the town where I grew up didn't have much to speak of in that regard. Traveling shows came through, but I think they're something different than the kinds of theater you mean."

"Oh yes, mistress, very different. There are plays, naturally, but there's also a lot of opera, and light opera, as well. Oh! And ballet, of course. Whichever kind you go to—whichever *theater* you go to, really!—they're all so fun and glamorous! They have big stages and brilliant costumes, and old shows and new ones. It's wonderful, always wonderful. You'll love them."

Her enthusiasm was so infectious that I knew at once I wanted to see a show. The problem was that I had no idea how to go about it. After I interrogated Orena a little more while she cooked breakfast the next day, I discovered the newspapers listed available shows. One could call to purchase tickets, or simply try to get them at the box office. "But I would call," she said, gesturing with her knife to the pocket watch whose chain hung amid the folds of my dress. "Especially since it's you we're talking about. You don't want to get all the way down there and find they're sold out."

"What are you planning?"

Eleison's low, casual tone tightened my stomach as it surprised me not six feet from my back. I had seen no trace of him since our arrival and was just getting comfortable with the idea of successfully avoiding him for the duration of our unsupervised stay. Now here he was, standing in the kitchen doorway, his arm braced against the jamb as he interrupted our conversation. He wore neither jacket nor tie with Malin elsewhere, and the mere sight of his tensely muscled forearms, exposed by his rolled sleeves, made me feel faint.

"Nothing that need concern you," I said, forcing my eyes from him and back to the tea I nursed while watching Orena work.

"Mistress has never been to the theater," said the blabbermouthed girl, who earned out of me an expression that made her yelp. "That is, ah—"

"So, you're planning on going to a show? By yourself?" He straightened up, loping past me for an apple he plucked from the bowl at Orena's elbow. "I'd say that concerns me."

"It *shouldn't*. Orena and I went out and rode the trains around just yesterday—we were perfectly safe."

"You what?"

Eleison's sharp look sent a ripple of fright through me, his red eyes widening before they narrowed in frustration.

"We've been here—two, three days?—and you've already wandered off."

"I don't need a minder," I told him.

"It's not safe."

"I felt *perfectly* safe."

"You're used to the country," he said. "Small towns, nice neighbors. This isn't that, Thecla. Don't kid yourself about this place and what can happen here."

Clearing her throat a little, Orena said, "Well—he is sort of right." At my stern look back at her, she averted her eyes to her work. "Normally, I'd say it's safe, but, well—it's just that you're important, Mistress, and..."

"And you, like him and everyone else, think I can't take care of myself. Right?"

"No, I—"

"Forget it," I said in annoyance, slapping down my cup as I rose from the counter. "I'm going to the theater, and I'm going alone, and I'm going to have a nice time, and that will be all there is to it."

As I left them behind, my frustration belied a strange sense of empowerment. Though Eleison called out in irritation, "Thecla, be reasonable," nobody there had the ability to call me back and demand anything of me. In fact, if they annoyed me enough, Malin had given me the power to dismiss them back to the manor, no questions asked.

It was tempting to use against Eleison...but I resisted the urge, mostly because Malin would have misread it as a petty, childish sort of slight against his friend.

The only one there in the city apartment who had something resembling power over me was Charlotte, and that was only because I believed she served Malin as an informant when she felt it necessary. I therefore made sure to keep my desires to myself as much as possible while the house got its structure together. When newspaper deliveries resumed, I snuck Sunday's issue into my room to study the tickets available for that week.

What was I going to choose? There was so much to pick from—Orena had been right. I was tempted to try an opera, but I didn't want to go alone for the first time, as I was sure to be overwhelmed by the experience of even regular theater. I would need Malin to navigate something like that...but there was one familiar title that I was excited to see among the others. A very, very old play—that same play, I was amazed to note, that I had named as my favorite when Malin pressed me on the topic of Shakespeare. Given the sheer number of plays in the writer's canon, that this one was available to me seemed fortuitous.

Excited to see it in the list, I tore the advertisement from the page and later, alone in the rooftop garden, I called to reserve a ticket: front row, no less. Malin had seen to it I had more money than I knew what to do with, and though I was not particularly interested in squandering it on fashion or food, the experience of a close seat for my first time at the theater made me all the more eager for the performance.

Then, it was a matter of waiting. I held my breath, watching the RMS every day, willing its percentage to remain low. Even with one chambermaid, one scullery maid, and my lady's maid as the only functional staff aside from Charlotte, all seven floors were soon in tip-top shape. By the end of the first week, the house ran well enough for my purposes that I hardly noticed any flaws.

Deeming it acceptable to her standards, Charlotte knocked on my door the night before the show and stood quite formally before me.

"If you are feeling comfortable, Mistress, I would very much like those days off I discussed with you before."

"Of course—how long do you need?"

"I can make it a few days."

Biting my lip, I shook my head and insisted, "Take the week, won't you? If I were in Lescaut and could see my family, I'd want at least that long. Take until Malin's due. One of us can call the other if we hear he plans to arrive early."

I had only meant to be kind to her, but after the suggestion escaped me, I realized I had set myself up. Though she looked perhaps a little suspicious, her eyes narrowing for just a second, Charlotte lowered her piercing gaze in a nod. "That's very generous, Mistress. Please call me if you find yourself overwhelmed by anything while you're here."

"I don't think I'll need you. Please—don't worry about me. Have a good time."

Nodding, Charlotte let me squeeze her hand before she curtseyed. "Then I'll leave tomorrow morning. Thank you, Mistress."

I smiled slightly and shut the door.

Behind it, my smile grew into a wild, giddy grin.

What an adventure this would be! What a journey! I had been getting nervous that I would have to explain my theater ticket to her. With her gone just in time, there would be no one to question me—nobody to debate or challenge me.

And if Eleison was so worried, then just what was he training me for?

Excitement in my heart, I threw myself into bed and lay awake all night. The theater thrilled me as much as Malin—as much as dreams of Eleison. When the sun rose in the morning, I lay there, listening.

Charlotte's steps echoed through the house from the floor below me, circling down the winding stairs and toward the front door.

That door opened.

It shut.

I squealed like a girl, feeling that the evening would never come, telling myself I was not afraid for everything that would surely unfold after.

And I was not afraid...not completely afraid.

But, I was soon to find, neither was I prepared.

WITH CHARLOTTE OUT and not due back for some days, the environment of the apartment changed at once. I saw Orena sitting down—something I had never witnessed outside of that train, I realized—and for my own part, I felt like I could breathe.

Charlotte was beloved, but there was no doubt that her presence reinforced a sense of structure that was beyond negotiation. The household's relaxation seemed to indicate I was not the only one who felt this way.

But Eleison, locked in his suite on the fifth floor, barely came out that day—maybe not at all.

Not until the evening, as I was preparing to go to the show.

It had been quite some time since I'd gone out to anything other than that vile 'festival,' so I very carefully decided that I did not want to stand out in case I appeared clumsy or anxious—but, still wanting to look as good as I felt when I caught myself in reflection, I selected a somewhat daring dress whose black hem dropped to my feet but whose shoulder straps were thin enough to seem revealing. The accompanying cloak was an indigo so dark it played subtly against the gown. My hair, I left free, pulling it back only briefly to apply my cosmetics.

It was as I sat at the vanity daubing a little red on my mouth that someone knocked.

"Come in," I said without thinking, expecting Orena without contemplating the heaviness of the knock. Like the other maids, (including Brea, unfortunately—my lady's maid had taken the day off without even informing me she'd be leaving), she had relaxed the very moment Charlotte left, and I had expected her to come talk to me before I went out into the butterscotch light of the evening.

To my surprise, my delight, my desire—that demonically charged beast of a man, the only person in the house who had not relaxed, stepped into my room and shut the door behind him.

Chest heaving with my barely suppressed gasp, I regarded Eleison from head to waist for a long handful of seconds before he crossed his arms.

"You need to reconsider."

"Hello to you, too, Eleison." Resuming the fine details of my face, I put away the paint pot with which I'd adorned my lips and plucked up the brush for my brows. Focusing on myself rather than on him made it far easier to speak to him, though his voice still clutched my body and wouldn't let it go. "There's something different about you since we got here, but I can't put my finger on it."

"I've quit smoking," he answered flatly, poised to go on before I spared him some attention and a look from my widening eyes.

"Congratulations…no wonder you managed to sneak up on me in the kitchen the other day. I didn't smell you. How did you do it?"

"Change of scenery. Good time to do it. Don't really want to talk about it."

"I suppose not," I said with a sigh, leaning back to regard my progress and letting down my hair in satisfaction. "I suppose, instead, you'd much rather nag me about going out to have fun."

"You know that's not the problem, Thecla."

My eyes rolled. "What do you *really* think is going to happen?"

"Anything. What if you get lost?"

"I'm not going to get lost, Eleison. There's a map at every train stop, and I know the route is simple from here." In truth, I'd studied and restudied the maps many times, and I was, in fact, very nervous that something could go wrong. I just didn't want him to be right. I didn't want to feel like some helpless waif who needed a man to hold her hand wherever she went. "You know, I'm not some absolute ninny—"

"Again. Not about that. This city is huge, and the wrong places are dangerous. You heard Orena—even she thinks—"

"I don't care what she thinks," I told him sharply. "And as to you—to you—"

"You care what I think, but you don't want to say that you do."

"Shut up."

He looked away quickly, but not quickly enough. I still caught the edge of an irresistible smile that blistered my rage all the hotter. Embarrassed that he could drive me to such a state of emotional exasperation, I was on the verge of telling him to get out when he composed his features well enough to look at me again.

"What about Malin, huh? You care what he thinks, right?"

"Don't you dare go tattling on me like some—"

"I'm not," he said, earning him silence enough to say, rightly, "but if you care about Malin, you should care about what he *would* think, even if he's not here. If he knew you were going out to the theater alone—"

"I don't think he'd *give* me the opportunity to go alone," I answered with a shrug.

"Exactly."

"Which is why, although I do respect what Malin would think, I also respectfully disagree with some of those thoughts. There are things I need. Space." My hand was an unmoving fist I realized I had braced at the edge of the vanity, as though to physically contain my frustration. "Freedom," I said, opening that hand and using it to push myself up from my seat.

"Maybe you should consider that Malin and freedom are mutually exclusive concepts."

"Maybe, if Malin really wants me, he has to be willing to negotiate. He's so good at business and political compromise, after all...he can compromise with me."

Snorting, Eleison's gaze trailed openly over my figure.

"Is it possible to compromise with somebody so stubborn?"

"I find Malin very flexible."

"I didn't mean Malin."

Rolling my eyes, I used my proximity to the door to slap Eleison in the bicep. Even that casual contact made my hand itch for more, my heart screaming to lean against his.

Luckily, as I opened the door, he grabbed my hand.

"Just let me come with you," he told me. "You don't have to worry about me getting a ticket, eating with you, anything like that. I'll walk three blocks behind you. You won't see me. I just want to make sure that you're safe."

The plea in his eyes, his voice—my throat tightened. I wanted more than to capitulate. I wanted him to keep me safe.

But I wanted to prove I could keep myself safe, too.

"I'll call you if I need your assistance," I informed him, slipping free of that grip I wanted to enjoy forever. "Otherwise, I'll thank you to let me have this one evening to myself."

Gritting his teeth, Eleison produced a bestial snarl from low in his chest while I marched on down the stairs. By the time I was on the third floor, his door slammed somewhere above me.

Let him act like a child. I forced myself to remember it was his problem—that I owed him nothing. He might have known Malin better than I did, but I didn't appreciate having my fiancé's name invoked to manipulate me.

Of course—I was a little angry, too. A small part of me, that awful, greedy part of me, was somehow hurt that he hadn't taken the opportunity to turn it into an intimate evening. Instead of telling me *not* to worry about him, he might have framed it in the exact opposite way. A date.

But then, of course, what would have happened? And here I was, accusing him of acting like a child...I was certainly thinking like one.

Anyway, I meant what I said. I had been overwhelmed with people since my arrival to the manor. From my solitary little space over the bookbinder's shop, I had been launched into a world where someone was always a room away to grant me whatever I required—and it was, frankly, exhausting. My only peace was when I was alone in my quarters, and then my mind swirled interminably between lust and love. Between what I presently enjoyed and what I coveted.

But, as soon as I stepped out on the city's walkways, I felt so changed.

There was a staggering amount to see and quite a lot of walking to do, so I had taken advantage of my gown's low hem by wearing comfortable black slippers of patent leather that had been artfully decorated with a panoply of colorful glass beads. I found they were a little loose, and one kept slipping from my heel, but by the end of a night of walking or even sitting in them that would surely change, and it was no distraction from the already breathtaking series of buildings careening to the sky.

I had seen images of Saalast, of course, but I had never imagined the true grandeur of it. In scale alone, it declared to me the untapped possibilities of the world around me. There were heights I had never imagined, because I did not know they existed. Now, with the barest taste of this marvelous place in my mouth, I also dreamed at a scale I never before had.

The restaurant Orena had suggested I try was evidently one made with consideration to my new station. Everyone I passed on my way to my reserved table looked as glamorous as one of Malin's courtier friends, and the service and food were immaculate. I had never experienced a restaurant outside of my town's handful of taverns, and I was grateful for the little time I'd had to absorb Malin's table manners.

That was another reason I wanted so desperately to prove to myself I could enjoy this night. Malin was right. I had to accept that I was worthy of the lifestyle he wanted to provide for me; and if I wanted to truly feel that way, I needed to live that way even when he wasn't around.

What was Malin doing? The thought crossed my mind abruptly and would not be shaken while I awaited my food. Perhaps it was the abundance of couples around my small table. A great longing weighed me down to think of him—along with guilt to realize how little I *had* thought of him over the past few days, except as an adversarial straw man during my latest argument with Eleison.

Funny. For all my complaining and my longing for space, I suddenly found myself wishing that Malin were there with me, and that we were going to the show together. His hand in mine, then around me, then petting me in the privacy of some box. How immensely he desired me! I thrilled at it.

And how I desired him…how I wished I could desire him, alone.

After the bill was settled for dinner, I fixed my lipstick and took the nearest elevated train stop per my plan. Everything went very smoothly, though I'm embarrassed by how rapidly my pulse pounded while I waited for my stop. There was always the remote possibility I *had* gotten on the wrong train, and that I would get lost like Eleison had said—but the digital screen over the door lit up with the announcement of the corner I had memorized, and I bounced in my seat with a childish grin that must have seen very silly if anybody in the crowded car noticed it. I couldn't be bothered to care, however. Alone, I had no one to perform for, no pretentions to maintain. I could resume being that girl I still was before Charlotte took me away, even if for only a little while.

The theater was beautiful, and very old. It looked in some ways like the kind of architecture to which Malin's manor aspired, with a faded fresco of angels and saints crowded into the ceiling.

I tucked my clutch into my lap and craned my neck to admire it, then turned around and studied the crowd.

It was not the largest theater, but it did have a balcony with quite a few rows of seats in addition to the ones on the floor, and nearly all of them were full. Every face was eager; every mouth murmured with excitement. Those that didn't were at least smiling, their expressions and moving fingers illuminated by the lights of the watches whose projected keyboards allowed them to brag to their friends and family about the show they were soon to enjoy.

I envied them their casual connections, but also enjoyed the idea of keeping this experience of mine a secret for now. And, anyway, when the lights went down, the watches snapped away, and we were all reduced to the disembodied observers of another world.

The original story of the play was about a wicked king who gained his crown through blood that refused to wash clean from his conscience. On reading the program before the show, however, I was surprised to find the production had been swapped. That was, all the women had been made into men, and all the men were now women. Even the witches and their goddess, which I found to be very intriguing.

The other interesting detail was the play's modern interpretation: the director had staged the play for the subtle inclusion of the Rift. Whenever Macbeth, as her cursed name was known, encountered strange doings—the trio of witches, or the hateful specter of her betrayed friend—the stage lights grew violet, and fog poured down from the rafters, and the audience would tense in age-old instinct.

It was an incredible show. As fond as I was of the original play, I liked it better as the story of a woman corrupted by her wicked lord and dark entities from beyond the Rift. I realized I was going to have to tell Malin about my outing, because I wanted very badly to see it with him while it was still running. If it excited me so, I imagined he might find it quite stimulating, and he liked the play plenty in his own right.

By the end, I was thrilled and inspired. Perhaps I could weave this variation of the tale into a tapestry—ah! And give it to Malin as a gift. A wedding gift. The idea excited me so that I nearly ran out of the theater, my every atom aglow with the glee that accompanies great works.

But as I stepped out of the theater's bright lobby, its swirling gold and red carpet taken out of time, I was swallowed by the darkness and shocked to find myself in the thick of night.

The hours in the playhouse had transfigured my sense of time and space so that I had somehow been utterly unprepared for the environment at the hour of my leaving. Granted, the darkness of Saalast was different than the darkness of Lescaut—but it was a dense enough cloak that I struggled with street signs until I was near. I found myself a little turned around on the way to the train station.

Not that it mattered.

In my focus on learning the geography to avoid becoming lost, I hadn't paid any attention to details like the hours at which the trains stopped for the night on certain days. What unnerved me about the dark city was not the night but rather the quiet of that night compared to its noisy day; and I realized as I trotted up the station stairs, only to stop short on my heel, that the quiet was due in large part to the absence of trains grinding in the distance.

My stomach sank. I hurried to the information panel dimly lit on the wall of the station platform and groaned to discover my own stupidity labeled clearly on the schedule.

What was I going to do? I had no real idea how to flag down a paid carriage and direct him to Malin's house, and I wasn't even sure I wanted to. The fewer people who knew the house even existed, I felt, the better. Maybe I could have them drop me off somewhere nearby...but I checked my wallet with a hefty sigh to find I'd spent most of what I'd taken with me on the expenses of dinner—and the wine I'd finally treated myself to during the intermission and second half of the show.

Whatever mild high I'd had from the alcohol disappeared into cold, cruel, reality.

I had two choices laid out before me.

I could walk home, all the way across the city, while making use of whatever maps I could find, either at stations or on my pocket watch.

Or...I could give up, and call Eleison to come pick me up.

"Good thing I wore flat shoes," I muttered to myself, drawing up the train of my dress and tying its hem in a knot so that it hung around my shins.

I refused to submit. My pride was foolish, almost inexcusably so—but the idea that Eleison would somehow 'win' our argument was just too much for me to take. I would get home by my own devices, no matter what.

Although—it very soon occurred to me that some methods were safer than others.

For the first six or so blocks, everything was fine. I felt quite secure. Some alleys looked a little dark—conducive to bad doings, perhaps—and there was no doubt that a few of the people loitering about at streetcorners were vagrants or criminals or scam artists of various breeds. Yet, either out of naivete or my impression of the city by day, I was not uncomfortable.

Not until I passed a group of men about my age, one of whom fixed his silver-green eyes on the pocket watch in my hand.

"Hey, honey," he called after me, "you lost?"

That quickly, I decided the watch's small hologram map wasn't worth the attention. I waited about six feet before casually shutting it and slipping it into the pocket disguised in the folds of my dress.

Murmuring to his friends, the man waited for me to get to the end of the block.

When I happened to glance back on crossing the street, he straightened up from the wall and made to follow me.

Panic surged through me. Maybe I should have compromised with Eleison by bringing my gun along. He was right, of course. I had no idea where I was, or even really where I was going, and I certainly didn't know the types of areas I'd have to cross through to get home.

And criminals were just the start. I was lucky I was being followed by a criminal, and not a police officer who wanted to check my identity to ensure I was either an organic human or a registered riftborn.

Not being either, I clenched my fists and told myself that at least one could run from a robber. With the block ahead of me empty of people, I broke into a sprint along a row of buildings broken up by an alley I considered taking. Looking back over my shoulder, however, and seeing the man was now chasing me with an asinine, evil laugh on his lips, I didn't want to be easily cornered. I kept on down the block, took a right at the cross-street, and kept going.

I got six feet when my slipper popped off, my bare right foot landing hard on the dirty concrete mid-stride.

Though I cried out, there was no time to go back for it. I swore my shout echoed all the way back to the alley, which was the source of an altogether different noise, though I really couldn't be sure quite what I heard—perhaps it was my pursuer's mocking response.

Swiftly regaining my pace, I dashed on along a length of stores that looked to be of rather ill repute. Embarrassed even then, I averted my eyes and willed my limbs to carry me through to safety.

It was as I passed the next alley that something whipped down over my head, and even the neon signs went absolutely black.

I tried to scream, but the bag's canvas sucked in against my mouth and was held there by a male's big hand.

Never in my life have I experienced a panic like that. Eleison's lessons on self-defense flew straight out of my mind. All I knew to do was to bite, to scream as much as I could, to flail my limbs and try to fall out of the stranger's grip. I kicked, almost making contact with his groin but hitting a thigh instead and crying out to find it firm with muscle.

This wasn't the same man that had been chasing me.

Were they part of some group?

"Please," I begged as the handcuffs went on, binding my wrists behind my back, "let me go, I have nothing to give you—no!"

Though I screamed and protested and my legs kicked out again, he picked me up and threw me over his shoulder as though I weighed nothing. Amazing—surely our struggle was heard by at least one person somewhere in this contemptible city, yet not one responded.

Despair filled me, and my imagination flew through all the truly awful things that could happen to a woman. Things that had been left unspoken because Eleison had too much courtesy to speak on them. That, or because he didn't want to think of such a thing happening to me.

But now—now, something awful *was* happening, and all I could think was how desperately I needed to call him. If I could somehow just get that pocket watch out—

My abductor grunted to open a door, and a few seconds later I had been tossed onto the floor of some kind of carriage. I wriggled my shoulders, struggling against the bag over my head to no avail, and tears filled my eyes.

Then his hands were on me.

"No," I screamed, "no, stop that, stop—"

Too late. He had patted around my hips and found the pocket watch immediately. I was sick to my stomach as he broke its chain with a vicious yank, then slammed the carriage door shut behind him.

Breathing shallowly, I forced myself upright against the seat, then upon it. Feeling along the wall with my mostly immobilized hands, I turned slowly toward where I suspected the door to be, then patted around in search of a handle.

I found it—locked, of course, much as the carriage's windows were shuttered.

Groaning, I rattled the handle and let out as great a scream as I could manage. No reply came.

Just as I began to bang on the door, the carriage lurched into motion.

My heart seemed about to climb out of my mouth. Where was I being taken? What was going to happen to me? Would Malin and Eleison be able to find me? Could they save me?

Was I going to die?

I didn't want to give my abductor the satisfaction of my tears, but they rolled all the same. I gasped for breath, struggling to fight through my terror in search of a plan.

The moment that door opened, I had to be ready to fight. Kicking hadn't worked on the street, but maybe from a height—or I might use my head, too—

Thousands of different scenarios played out as I readied myself for action. The carriage ride seemed to go on forever, and continued on so long that I began to feel sick with the notion that we were leaving the city.

Until, at last, I swayed as the carriage pulled along the edge of the street.

It was parking.

I had to count my breaths to keep myself from hyperventilating. There was no way to know how tall the man had been, so I had to hope I was lucky enough to kick him in the face or throat.

While the driver got down from the seat at the front, I stood as much as I could on the floor of the carriage. My body was braced against the wall at a half-stoop, my muscles ready.

But when the door opened, the unmistakable click of a gun's hammer echoed through the little space.

I wasn't sure if my hands were numb from the fear, or from the handcuffs, or from both. My face also lost its feeling in that instant, and I realized with a sinking terror that I had no choice but to be compliant or die on the spot.

Tears streaming down my face in silence, I edged toward the open doorway.

The abductor reached in, grabbing hold of my bicep and pulling me out into the night air.

The smells of the city clung stubbornly to my nose. We were still in Saalast, it seemed—but where he could so brazenly point a gun at the back of my head while I was hooded and handcuffed, I didn't know. Wherever it was, it was obviously an area worse than the one he'd abducted me from.

My breathing was shallow. He guided me up some steps and into a lobby that had a faint echo, then down a hall to the right. I heard a button depress.

With a shove of the cold gun into my back a few seconds later, he urged me into an elevator.

I trembled, seizing my chance the second the door closed.

"I couldn't give you anything," I told him firmly again, "but there are people expecting me to come home. They'll know if I'm dead, and then you'll really regret this. You'll ruin your own life. Please—whatever you do, don't kill me."

He said nothing. My shoulders trembled.

The elevator jerked to a stop.

The gun lowering away from me, the man grabbed hold of the back of my neck as though I were a kitten and dragged me from the elevator. I struggled again, crying out in protest as I hooked my foot around the edge of the open doors, but he grunted in annoyance and yanked me free so sharply that I lost my other slipper.

Five steps later, he threw open a door and tossed me onto the hard floor of a room.

Some dungeon, I expected—some prison. I whimpered like a spring lamb, scrambling upright and propelling myself away with my bare feet while the door was shut and locked.

"Stay back," I begged, "please, don't do this—no!"

His footsteps made their inexorable approach. I struggled to my knees, was nearly to my feet, could almost picture myself putting up a struggle so frightful he would lose interest in his evil intentions—

And then he whipped the bag from my head, and I recognized my prison.

It was my room.

UNCOMPREHENDING, I BLINKED tearful eyes against the inundation of light. Narrowing them, I confirmed my location with a glance over my shoulder at the vanity—then at the man before me, who held me by the shoulders and stared me down with his teeth bared.

Eleison's red eyes blazed like embers in the heart of a vicious fire.

"Wh—"

"*Now,* do you get what can happen?"

"What—what—"

"Do you understand? If I were somebody else—hell, if I hadn't been planning to grab you and been there to give that freak a concussion—"

"What is *wrong* with you!"

"—something awful could have happened to you. You could have been mugged, raped—you could have been *killed*, Thecla!"

Mouth agape, slowly realizing the full implications of the last forty-five minutes or so, I looked Eleison up and down before stopping at the wild eyes that kept my heart from the least chance of slowing.

"You're *mad*."

"I'm glad you finally realize! Of course, I'm going mad. I'm going insane. I am so in love with you! So violently in love with you, Thecla. You're all I think about, you're all I want, and you're all I can't have. So I'm mad, yes. I'm going mad without you, literally. And that's why—that's why you have to understand this. Why I'm trying to train you, why I did this tonight."

"You pointed a *gun* at me." I was still unable to believe it, my eyes flicking between his face and the holster visible under his suit coat. "You could have shot me."

"I wouldn't have, but somebody else could have. I wish you would stop going out alone, Thecla! I wish you would listen to me. I wish you would take me seriously when I say you're not safe. That the world's dangerous—and so am I."

"You're hardly dangerous, Eleison," I told him, my own madness blazing in my eyes as I made a claim that defied all evidence. Struggling against my handcuffs, speaking with my hands still bound by them at my back, I told him, "You're as much Malin's pet as I am. Malin's the dangerous one—you're afraid of him."

Growling, Eleison said, "I'm not afraid of him. I'm afraid *for* you."

Tears flooding from my eyes anew, I screamed at him, "Then let me help you!"

Shock filled his face. As though I were a banshee, he staggered back.

"Then let me *help you*," I hissed, my eyes shutting miserably before opening to fix on his. "Damn you—if you're afraid for me, if you want to protect me, if you want to be my cavalier, then let me stabilize you. You don't have to lose your humanity, Eleison! You don't have to live out this sad, empty fate."

My lips trembled. I struggled to keep it together and had to bare my teeth to speak, the words coming out in a kind of hiss as a result.

"You don't have to do this to *me*—don't have to force me to lose you without even being able to express how much I love you."

The words settled between us, as stained with tears as my face.

The face Eleison held when he caught me up and devoured me in a kiss so unexpected, so long-dreamed, that I moaned into his hungry mouth.

His tongue's slide along mine and all its eager exploration soon yielded to my opportunity to do the same, and as I gasped at the sweetness of his breath, his hands slid down along my shoulders, my breasts, my waist, my hips. They were at my backside, now, gripping and pulling me toward the heat of his groin to inspire a cry of lust from me. I gasped his name into his mouth, losing balance at the pressure of his body. We fell together, not quite making it upon the bed and ending up half-supported by its edge. Before I could hit the floor, he caught me by the dress he rapidly jerked away from me. Something tore in the back, and I nearly sobbed to be exposed to him at last.

The wildness in Eleison's red eyes was truly animal, truly otherworldly. He lowered his head and kissed my neck, his teeth sinking into a spot that made me moan.

"Oh," I whined, "no, don't, Malin will see—"

"I want him to see," Eleison rejoined, the words a snarl from the beast inside him. While I moaned, he yanked the remains of my dress down my legs and threw the mass of black fabric to the floor. Wrapping me in his arms, he resumed his kisses along the curve of my breast until his lips and teeth could graze my nipples. "I want him to be ready to fuck you, to take his fiancée, and to find me all over you. I want him to know that he can love you as much as he wants—but you're mine. You're mine, Thecla."

The sentence made me want to scream with ecstasy. "Oh, Eleison—oh, please, I want to touch you so badly—"

"You deserve those handcuffs, you bratty little bitch. I'll let you out when I'm ready to."

Moaning, thrashing with pleasure at his every touch, I gasped his name as his mouth and nose pressed against my panties. His brow furrowed and he cried out, the momentary humanity of his desire yielding to another low, unnatural growl that rose up from whatever of him was from the Rift.

"Oh, Thecla—Thecla, I'm sorry, I can't stand it anymore. I have to fuck you—I'm sorry, I have to—"

"Oh, please! Please, yes, make me your mate, truly! Let me give you everything—let me give you my body."

Groaning, Eleison snatched my panties down and looked between my legs as though the sight caused him physical pain. His hand lowered, and as his eye found mine, his thumb slid over the swollen lips between my thighs.

The contact produced a spark of such intensity I finally screamed, my head lifting as though toward the sensation. He exhaled, his thumb working slowly back and forth along that sensitive path, and I was so overwhelmed by pleasure that I seemed on the cusp of climax almost within seconds.

"Look at you, Thecla…do you get this hot and desperate for Malin?"

"Oh, mm…yes, Eleison"—his eyes flashed with dark jealousy and I smiled—"especially when he tells me to talk about you."

Scoffing, his finger replacing his thumb and gliding around my intensified nerve, Eleison murmured, "When he's fucking you, you mean?"

"Yes, oh—he loves to tease me, to ask me if I'm keeping lovers…I think it excites him, and it certainly excites me. It excites me to think of how nice it would be if, during training, you would wrestle me to the ground and force your cock into me, and take me against my will so I needn't have any guilt about it."

Growling, Eleison lifted his hand from me and stood at the edge of the bed. A swoon came over me as he undressed, his eyes fixed on me as I went on sharing my fantasies. "I get so wet when I tell him about it… And, of course, I go just dotty to think of you still inside me when it's finished—marked by you. Oh, Eleison!"

My toes curled to admire the dark hair over his finely cut chest while he went on to the trousers. "I want you to mark me," I whispered, all sense leaving me in my animal desire for him. "I want you to stake your claim to me and leave the evidence…so at least, if he doesn't know, I do."

He was down to his boxers. I moaned at the shape of what lay within, and, desperate to feel it, touch it, taste it, I forced myself to drown in those ardent eyes.

"If you let me out of these handcuffs," I whispered to him, "you won't regret it."

That beastly noise still rolling like thunder from his chest,

Eleison bent over me and reached around my body to take my wrists.

With a metallic snap and a link that flew off to a distant corner of the room, he pulled the cuffs apart and pressed his mouth savagely to mine.

Crying with delight, I spared no time grabbing hold of his boxers and pushing them down. The monster that sprang free made me gasp. Though Malin was, without debate, exceptionally crafted, Eleison's anatomy was so substantial that I whimpered to imagine what it might feel like. Indeed, I trembled while extending a finger along its length, gazing up into Eleison's eyes as he emitted a low sigh of pleasure.

"It's so big, Eleison! Oh, God—it's going to hurt me, you're going to hurt me with it."

"I'll make up for it," he told me, the words feral grunts between the kisses he breathed against my ear. "I'll do anything if you'll take me as your mate. Ah—Thecla—"

My hand now fully trailed up and down his length, the desperation of its straining truly erotic proof of how deeply he desired me. Beneath it, his trimmed testicles attracted my palm and inspired a new strain of far more tender rumbling from his chest.

Slowly easing himself into the bed, facing me, Eleison slid his hand between my thighs. I moaned, giddy that he explored my anatomy as eagerly as I stroked his. When his fingertip teased along the receptive opening of my channel, his lips brushed mine and he told me, "You're so wet, Thecla...I think I'll fit just fine."

Teeth sinking into my lip, I draped my leg over his hip and pressed myself to him. He gasped heavily, rocking against me, his hands sliding around my backside to keep me close.

"Thecla," he breathed, looking down between us, our bodies so nearly joined. "Are you sure you want to do this?"

"Yes!" I couldn't help the insistence of the word, and he flashed that rare, gorgeous smile at the sound of it. Oh, that smile! It made him boyish, cheeky, carefree—as I had never seen him before. "Yes, please—Eleison, Eleison, I want to be marked by you! I want you to fill me up, take on my scent and leave yours in me—Eleison—take me for your mate—"

"I love you, Thecla."

"I love you," I whispered, gazing into the expression whose intensity never flagged as he pressed the head of that intimidating member to my entrance. "Eleison, oh, yes—take me, take me as roughly as you want! Eleison!"

His eyes flashed with pleasure at the invitation. Fingers sinking into the flesh of my rear, Eleison pushed the bare head of his sword up into me, and I screamed to be spread open by its flared helmet. The visible effects of that pleasure upon me, so great it was nearly pain, only egged him on. He kept his grip of me while rolling me fully onto my back with my leg still around him.

Gazing endlessly into me, the hunter plunged the weapon deeply in and made his victim howl.

"Eleison!" I lost all self-control, my hips thrusting up to hammer him deeper into my body. Almost frightened by how profoundly he filled me, I nonetheless opened my other leg to welcome him into me while he took to a delicious pattern of curving strokes.

The feeling of him inside of me after months of torture—after a decade of dreaming—was so incredible that tears filled my eyes. Seeing them, Eleison bent over me to hold me tightly to his chest. I opened my mouth to his hungry kisses, my hands wrapping around his neck to pull his hair and clutch at his back. He snarled as my nails sank into his flesh, his teeth nipping my lip, but I didn't care.

This man, this man inside of me—I never wanted him to be inside of any other woman again. Him, the pleasure he brought, the privileges of his protective love: it was all was mine. He was mine, now. His body was mine, and I wanted to leave him covered in marks so that he and everybody else knew it.

Maybe even Malin would need to know it.

The thought was insane, summoned in the heat of arousal like so many passing expedients of pleasure, but it hovered with me even as Eleison took what I gave him. In that instant, I wanted Malin to know—I wanted everyone to know. Eleison's body threw mine into a dangerous, all-consuming bliss, and all my thoughts were animal thoughts of dominance and hunger and possession.

And I knew he was thinking the same.

His fingers tangled deep against my scalp, Eleison tugged my hair and made sure I could look nowhere but him.

"You're never leaving by yourself in the evening again. Got it?"

"Oh, Eleison—yes, yes sir, I promise I'll be good. I'll take your help…you can take me anywhere…as long as you promise to fuck me like this, oh, Eleison!"

"I will—don't worry, Thecla." My name on his lips produced a wild moan from me, and my body tightened with an impending orgasm whose approach hastened his. His hips slammed into mine at a pace so brutal I thought I might break, and my brow furrowed to once more find myself on that boundary of pain and pleasure. His strokes grew more focused, too: deliberate, probing, as he paid homage to that pressure point that Malin had also been quick to discover and utilize for both our benefits.

"I'll fuck you whenever I can," he swore to me, driving himself again and again into the spot that seemed to swell in greater invitation every time. "When he's busy, when we have a free moment—when you need it—whenever we're alone—"

"Yes, please! I need it—I need it so badly, oh, Eleison—Eleison, oh, you're so big, you're so, so big, I can't take anymore—"

"Too bad."

My head fell back and I groaned, rocking against the pillows, my pleas only intensifying his assault. His hand fit to my hip to coax my thigh high, and his shoulder took on the support of my knee. I moved at his every least direction, astonished by how overwhelmed I could be by such pleasure. The sharp sounds of our contact at the peak of every pump rang out vividly beneath my cries and his snarls.

But it was drowned, finally, by my scream, the urgent and frantic cry of his name that came with the desperate, silent plea from me to him for a kiss.

As he swooped down to give it to me, he roared my name in turn, his body driving into me with the tide of my orgasm until he was drawn out to sea with me.

THOUGH ELEISON AND Malin could not have been more different as lovers in some ways, in others, they shared affinities. For instance, much as Malin did, Eleison took great pleasure in both putting me to sleep at night and rousing me in the morning with carnal affection. In a similar fashion as Malin had shown during that Rift weekend, Eleison paid an ungodly amount of attention and interest to me, his eyes always watchful upon me, his ears always tuned to my voice; and the nearness of his presence—along with his new availability—set me aflame.

I could touch him now, and I did. That first night, after he had fallen asleep, I rested there without closing my eyes. I couldn't. Eleison was with me, against me. He had just been inside of me. My body was so primed with new energy to lay against his that I simply could not get comfortable, and I found myself chewing the inside of my cheek and shifting over on my side in discomfort.

Still fully unconscious, Eleison's arm slid over my waist as though it were the most natural thing in the world, and minutes later I was fast asleep.

Too soon, it was morning. Too soon, I awoke to the softening of the darkness. Too soon, reality would come to mete justice.

For now, we stirred against one another, neither wholly sure who woke whom. When I felt him tilt his head to brush his nose along my shoulder, I slowly stretched my body against his and stirred a great, hungry sigh of appreciation from his nose.

"Good morning," he murmured in my ear, kissing the sensitive ridge and the soft skin behind it as he came to life. One part of him had already been wide awake, and I gasped softly to feel it fit along the hillocks of my rear. "You awake?"

"Mm-hm…"

His great body pushed against mine, and I realized quickly he was rolling me onto my stomach. Face flush with heat at once, I obliged him and made no objection as he draped himself over me. As his kisses pressed along the back of my neck, his hands slid down the muscles of my back, then down along my hips.

"You're gorgeous, Thecla. Ah—I'm an idiot. I shouldn't be doing any of this."

With our proximity, I could tell with joy, his madness had settled. The tender love of his human soul spoke to me now.

"*We* shouldn't be doing any of this," I corrected him, my hips arching back to allow his hand to slide beneath my pelvis. "No, we shouldn't…but—ah—"

"You're still so wet from last night…"

"Oh—but, like I was saying…strictly speaking, none of this should have happened the way it did. We should have gone to Malin"—much like Eleison, it gave me a thrill to say his name in the other's arms, and the little growl my fiancé evoked from my mate (my *mate!*) sweetened my pleasure all the more—"just as soon as you realized I was your mate."

"You're right...you're right."

"But—I don't regret it. I love you both." I looked over my shoulder at Eleison, defying him to say he didn't want to hear it.

Instead, he raised his free hand to tenderly stroke the hair back from my cheek.

"I'm sorry I put you in this situation, Thecla."

"It's all right—I accept it, whatever consequences may come. Just take me, Eleison—use the time, please, and make love to me again."

Exhaling, Eleison gripped me by the hip and pulled me up a little higher. I rested on my hands and knees, upper half bent forward toward the pillows, and he slid against me from behind. Gasping, my thighs parting to invite him, I reached back between my legs, then stopped short with a laugh.

He paused. "What is it?"

I raised one wrist and rattled the broken handcuff I'd forgotten all about in my absolute exhaustion from his lovemaking. He laughed, too.

We had six days together. Six beautiful days that were truly my delight. The first morning, when the maids showed up a few hours late with enfeebling headaches, (I noticed one of the bottles of liquor seemed to be missing from the rack), I realized we had been granted a reprieve that would not last forever. By the time Eleison and I encountered them, we had agreed to put on clothes and function as we normally did in a given day. I knew this charade would not last long, and our next rendezvous would be an inevitable matter of proximity...perhaps without regard for privacy.

Therefore, while the maids shuffled around in a hungover imitation of their usual duties, I sought Orena. She was, I was coming to see, among the friendliest and best liked of her peers, and had influence over them.

"How was the theater, Mistress," she asked through bleary eyes while sweeping out the kitchen, her smile weak.

The theater? Oh, the *theater*. Somehow, in all the chaos after, I had forgotten all about that wonderful play. "It was exceptional," I told her. "Thank you for helping me go."

"I'm just glad you made it home safe! Eleison was mighty worried about you. We kept telling him to join us for cards, but he didn't care to do anything sociable."

"Yes, well...about that."

I cleared my throat and folded my arms.

Just say it.

"You may...hear some things during these next few days. Ignore them. If the other girls hear...things, tell them to mind their business."

Her eyes narrowed in befuddlement; when I drew my coin purse from my pinafore and paid her for the trouble, they widened. Looking around, she tucked the coins into her apron and regarded me curiously.

"I don't suppose it's any of my business to inquire into your private life, ma'am...but, whatever it is you're up to, be careful."

We couldn't be. We simply couldn't be. From the first kiss, all caution had been obliterated. There was no safety for us. No comfort. There was only irresistible animal connection: an almost painful electric sizzle in the air when at last, unable to bear my own thoughts, I found him throwing darts in the game room.

Not five minutes later, our clothes were off.

We decided not to talk about it. About the future; about the inevitability of this coming to an end. We ignored it all and wildly consumed one another's bodies, our breaths and fluids and flesh all mingling when we could no longer resist to be so close yet remain separated.

For five wonderful days, we made love around the clock; and by the end of the third day, Eleison was marked by a definite change. The circles under his eyes were already so much less prominent, and those crimson eyes themselves were no longer sad, but sharp and sometimes even merry in their typical wry way. He was more talkative, inquiring mostly about my life in Lescaut, my family, my time on my own. He asked about men, of course, and listened carefully as I described my bland initiation; I could not bear to ask about women, for he was too skilled with my body for me to endure the details of his history without also wishing for many deaths.

But though his healthy, human drives seemed to be gaining influence, they were also accompanied by human guilt. Perhaps that was just the result of Malin's return drawing ever closer.

Three times, Malin called me while we were apart. He did not want to drown me, he said the first time, "But I fear I'll throw myself off the balcony if I can't enjoy a few minutes of your voice."

The second time, as if prompted by some psychic link, he happened to call the afternoon after my theater adventure, and I entertained his conversation while leaving my plans unstated. The third call was as I reclined in Eleison's arms after we had made love, and the watch's chime sent me flying out of bed like a frightened cat.

There was nothing sinister to his call; it was just my shame. Malin happened to crave me that day, and he promised me he would be back to me within the week. The month had been almost free of Rift Events, and the weather was projected to stay pleasant for another ten to twelve days. Fingers crossed, he'd make it.

Yes, fingers crossed.

No doubt, I was eaten up by guilt. Every time I spoke to Malin, I grew as eager for his love as I was paralyzed by dread. I wanted him to come back so the temptation might once again be stymied.

But there was no return from the path we'd taken. I had already succumbed to the temptation. Knowing well how sweet its fruit was—how necessary it was to Eleison's survival, and mine—I could never un-know. Nothing would be as it was before Saalast.

And when Charlotte found us in the game room on her return a few days early, laughing together over my inability to throw darts no matter how Eleison taught me, that reality was cemented.

Whatever she perceived in our laughter, it must have been telling. Seeing her, I straightened up from my giggling and smiled. I waved.

She nodded back, then looked at Eleison.

He did not smile, the expression stowed away as if not for public consumption.

"I'll be sure your sheets are changed first thing tomorrow morning, Mistress," said Charlotte, turning to stride right back out of the game room. "You should know that your fiancé will be arriving early; he is trying for tomorrow evening."

My throat tightened. How was it possible for her to divine what had happened with such transparent ease? Had the maids told her? Had we given ourselves away by some sign? We had not even been touching when she came upon us, yet she had known. She had clearly known.

Whatever her means, it was a warning. If we wanted Malin to stay in the dark, we were going to have to look at ourselves, and at what behaviors constituted normalcy to us.

I faced Eleison, still holding a dart, endeavoring to reestablish my smile until I recognized the distance of his gaze.

"Eleison—"

Without warning, he drew me into his arms. I gasped. The dart fell at our feet as I succumbed to his kiss, my body melting into pure sensation while his hands fit firmly but gently against my ribs. When we separated, his face was more serious than I had seen it in a week.

"The past five days have meant so much to me, Thecla."

The things this man did to my heart! Not to mention the rest of me. "I love you, Eleison. I love you, and I'm so glad you're letting me help you."

But he hardly seemed to be listening to me. His arms tightened around me, his hands sliding down to fit into my lower back, that gaze still preoccupied. Only when I frowned and he noted my full displeasure did he speak.

"You know how I can tell you love Malin? *Really* love him?"

"I really love you, too," I insisted, my hands tightening around the fabric of his shirt. "It's—I can't just stop loving—"

"I knew you really loved him when you didn't use him."

I fell silent to recognize that the jealousy in the statement was undercut by an effort to be factual, though I didn't understand what Eleison meant until he went on.

"That night after the theater, when you thought you were being kidnapped—you never once said what anybody else would say. That you were the territory master's fiancée, and that he would have paid anything to get you back in one piece, and blah, blah, blah. You never said anything that would have traded or endangered Malin. Instead, you just fought."

My face drained of blood to remember the click of the gun. Strange even now to think the person pointing it at me had been Eleison, who was already so changed by our days of close contact. I cannot emphasize enough the profundity of his recovery. He was so much more natural—he gleamed with love and tenderness, plagued no more by whatever base, animal thoughts had tormented him before we could express ourselves. I overheard him making the maids laugh one afternoon; he hummed while he shaved on the fourth day, and I loved the sound of it. Best of all, when we locked eyes in the hall, we could do something to express ourselves.

I didn't want to ever go back to the way it was before; not in any fashion. But, as he released me with a hefty sigh and turned away to run a hand over his face, Eleison made a suggestion that stilled my blood.

"Maybe I can talk Malin into severing our contract. Ten years…that's a long time. I'm—"

I made no effort to stop myself from blurting, "What on *earth* are you talking about?"

He looked over his shoulder at me with his eyebrows raised in surprise.

"This is *fatal* to you," I insisted, adding, "perhaps even to me someday, if whatever is in me finally awakens."

He sighed, and now his hand worried over his jaw. His red eyes were so pained I regretted even having said it, but his hand lowered into the pocket of his trousers instead of continuing to exhibit his concern.

"You're right," he said softly. "But—I don't know what else to do. We can't lie to him."

"So—we tell him."

"When?"

My hands ran over my cheeks, fingers extending to rub the temples of my forehead. "I don't know," I said, feeling dizzy just to try to answer the question. "I don't know, I—"

My eyes welled with tears. Lips trembling, I folded my arms over my ribs and turned away from Eleison.

"I feel like a selfish, petty little child."

"So do I," Eleison confessed.

I laughed darkly, my hand raising to my eyelid to collect my tears. His heavy strides echoed behind me as I said, "Because we *are* acting like children. Sneaking around behind Daddy's back like a couple of teenagers...only, oh, it's so rotten. I feel so rotten about it. Why do I want you both so desperately? Why does everyone else have such an easy time with their love?"

"Love is never easy," he said, his hands landing gently on my shoulders and rubbing while I held back more tears at the thought of losing Malin. "Not all the time...but even when it isn't easy, it's sweeter than anything."

I turned in his arms and kissed him, my mouth thrusting up against his in a movement I was coming to know quite well. He leaned me back against the billiards table, his exhalation hot and rich on my tongue while his body pressed to mine.

"Fuck me all night," I whispered, twisting from the kiss to sink my teeth into Eleison's ear. As he groaned, his mouth found the fading bruise on my neck. "Don't let me sleep."

"Whatever you want, Thecla. Whatever I can give you—I'll give you."

But he would have given so much more, if he could have. Oh, it was miserable. We made love ferociously, long into the night, and each time he completed we dozed for awhile before stirring and starting again. It was all a poor substitute for what we wanted. Casual, expressible love. A life where we could pass one another and openly smile. Where I could touch his arm, and he could kiss me.

But how could I ask for that, and still receive the same thing from Malin?

Especially…well. It seemed quite greedy of me to want both men equally, when the reality was I would have been stricken ill to know either one of them had paid attention to another woman beyond, say, the professional relationship Eleison had with Charlotte.

That professional relationship was very well reflected as, the next evening, we all waited nervously for Malin's return. The maids had straightened up their routine as soon as their field general appeared on the scene, and I could not help noticing they made themselves far scarcer that last day than they had in the past two weeks. I prayed Orena would stay true to her word, and that the other maids had been either fed misinformation or plain lied to—threatened, if necessary, to keep their tongues tucked away.

If Malin was going to find out, I wanted him to learn it from me…I just could not fathom how I would express it.

"I hope you have taken suitable advantage of your break from Master Farrow," Charlotte told me casually while I paced in the apartment's first floor parlor, a lovely little greeting room just down the black and white tiled front hall and near enough for me to watch the front door. "He can be quite suffocating at times."

I laughed a little, fondling my neck while I puttered around the piano. Having observed the city fashions resembled something a little more like what the courtiers had worn—that was, blouses paired with (or dresses featuring) a long-tailored skirt that was narrow to emphasize the hips and bust—I had favored what in my wardrobe was close to that, although the truth was that many of the gowns were somewhat old-fashioned. I wondered if they were Malin's dead wife's articles even as I smoothed the red collar rising up along my throat.

"I don't mind Malin wanting my attention when I'm with him, or expecting it regularly...he's very dear to me."

"You might make sure he knows that," she suggested.

Bless Charlotte, I valued so her wisdom and discretion! It was no small wonder Malin kept her in arm's reach. "Since we are in the city now, Charlotte—would it be possible to at last acquire a loom with a bit more ease?"

"It certainly would be, Mistress. I'll coordinate with Master Farrow to pick a room for you to work in. Now would be an ideal time to send one back to the country house, as well."

"Yes..." Rolling wheels and clopping hooves came to a stop on the street outside. Straightening up, I whipped toward the door while saying in a distracted haze, "Yes—and perhaps to the vineyard cottage, if the expense wouldn't be too great. I'm not sure how long he plans to keep us there."

"Yes, Mistress...never mind the expense." Upon setting aside her own rarely indulged hobby of embroidery and tucking it into a drawer out of sight, Charlotte dusted off her gown, rose from her seat, and folded her hands before her. "I do sincerely hope you had a pleasant time."

Smiling faintly, I admitted to her, "Yes—yes, I did. And you? How is your mother?"

Before she could answer, the door flew open, and chaos whirled into the Saalast apartment.

A bevvy of people clomped in one at a time, waving hats and shrugging off coats and shouting orders or intentions to their fellows in a wild orchestra of noise. Upstairs, Eleison's feet thundered down in belated response to the arrival. He had waited as far away as he could stand before he was forced to meet with the security team.

Charlotte, meanwhile, stepped smoothly away from me, too busy greeting and briefing the staff to answer my question.

My smile hung awkwardly on as I stood at the edge of the parlor, my heart speeding so fast I could actually feel it thumping in my chest. There was Eleison's face in the crowd, his eyes darting toward me—then he was gone, squeezing past a servant who hauled in several of Malin's bags. Others slipped out to collect more items from one of what was evidently three carriages that had formed the caravan to Saalast. The shouting continued, and boots tromped all over the beautiful black and white floor.

But then, after what seemed like forever, a highly polished pair of black oxfords stepped over the threshold, and I stumbled forward a few steps with a cry on my lips.

"Malin!"

"Ah—! Thecla—"

Empty-handed save for his hat, Malin fobbed even that off to the nearest half-ready servant and parted the crowd with his motion through it. I hovered excitedly, throwing myself into his arms at the first available opportunity, an ache I hadn't fully known I'd felt relieved after two weeks of sustained tension. As his sandalwood mingled with the sweat of his long day and blossomed deep in my lungs as sweetly as a field of flowers, Malin caught my face in his great hands and tipped my head back to kiss me.

Though there was obvious exhaustion in his face, the passion and hunger of his mouth echoed through me to the very root of awareness. My heart lurched with love, and shame. I knew at once that he had restrained himself, just as he had promised.

And I had failed to extend the same courtesy.

"I have *missed* you," he murmured as we parted, his eyes fixed on mine and his hands keeping me from leaning back more than a few inches. "I was so tired before I saw you—I'm still tired—but you, you're here, oh, Thecla...come with me."

Malin caught my hand in his and pulled me away with a tender smile. "You look stunning."

"I'm so happy to see you, Malin." My stomach flipped as he guided me to the service elevator that had been Eleison's way of disorienting me, since I usually used the stairs. How would I tell him? I focused on Malin's presence with me, his love for me, and tried to save my shame for later. "I thought about you every day."

"Keep saying things like that, angel...you'll keep me alive. Take the next one," he said, putting a hand in front of the staff member who was just about to bring the bags up the empty elevator car. Smiling apologetically, I allowed Malin to hustle me in and hit the button for the seventh floor, his private quarters.

Then, as if that very act signaled some great unwinding, his eyes rolled with a mighty sigh of relief. Malin sagged back against the wall of the car, saying, "I won't bore you with the tiresome details—the trip was mostly smooth—but of course just an hour ago the blasted forecast leapt to 75%."

I bit my lip, somewhat relieved I had avoided spending a Rift Event potentially in heat with Eleison...and quite disappointed, in that guilty way. "I'm glad you made it before something happened."

"Yes, well, you can imagine we pushed it. Not well advised with some of those roads, but here I am...and here you are. And here"—he sighed fondly, stepping out into the foyer as the doors slid open—"is my apartment."

While he strode out ahead of me, giving a smiling tut of appreciation for the champagne and note of welcome Charlotte had left on the center table, I wandered out into the only floor I had yet to visit in the Saalast home.

Everything in that apartment was of the most beautiful, well-kept wood, gleaming new even though I sensed it was all quite old. The walls were artfully paneled with enormous rectangles of hand-carved mahogany, and the floor of the foyer resembled a chessboard of alternating red and blond. That center table, which Malin thoughtlessly defiled on passing with the coat I found myself plucking up after him, was likewise made of an assortment of beautiful glowing woods and depicted a variety of flowers in natural colors beneath the glossy seal.

"Bring that champagne in, would you, sweetheart...oh, God help me."

From a hall and some rooms away, Malin groaned and audibly collapsed into a bed. I hurried to obey him, plucking up the bottle once I'd hung his coat on a peg, carved to resemble the neck of a swan and mounted alongside the elevator door. With the bottle tucked under my arm, I hurried along the chessboard path and past a series of rooms that seemed designed to be quite different from one another. After several shut doors, I found Malin sprawled out on the bedspread of a bedroom that was predominantly red with undertones of gold and a rich, burning orange.

"Darling," he said, unbuttoning his waistcoat and sighing with relief, "would you resent me if I waited to ravish you until tomorrow morning?"

I set the champagne down upon the bedside table with a smile—the alternative to sighing in relief. In another day or so, the bruise would be healed to a point of complete invisibility. "That's all right," I told him, stretching out beside him on the bed and sliding into the arm he opened for me. "Whenever you have energy...I want to make love with you, but mostly I'm just glad you're home safe."

Smiling slightly, Malin drew my hand to his lips to kiss my knuckles. "Poor dear," he said, studying my palm, turning it before his face, running his thumb over my skin. "So impossibly soft... such a young woman, to be locked up by a wretched old man."

"I don't feel locked up. I feel proud to be with you."

"Yes, but I can't help feeling a pang of...I don't know... avarice." His thumb trailed down my cheek and toward the corner of my mouth, tickling softly across my lower lip and making me itch for a kiss.

"Look at this mouth, this face...look at your body, Thecla... you're such a talented, sexy young thing. Any man who had you once would remember you forever; you could have a parade of lovers at your door, all of them fighting and begging and dying for your attention, for the chance to please you. And here I am—some tired old man, putting you off until tomorrow."

I parted my lips to playfully sink my teeth into his thumb, suddenly blessed by a casualness I hadn't been able to make myself feel with him before Eleison and I made good our bond. He wasn't the only one changed by that week, I supposed.

"You're not old," I protested, my eyes fixed on Malin's through my lashes. My tongue lapped across the spot of my nip. He inhaled, the fire in his eyes blazing up all at once. "You're older than I am, of course...but..."

"If fifty-four isn't old, what is?"

Giggling, I bent past his hand to brush my damp lips along his mouth. "Sixty-four, obviously."

"Ah, good...so you'll be saddled with an old man in ten years...ah, darling—"

"Sh..." My hand roved down his chest, down his stomach. The buckle of his belt gleamed in the low light of the bedroom. "Just let me pleasure you, Master...I've missed you so much..."

At the first stroke of my hand along the front of his trousers, I knew I'd made a mistake. I was going to ache all through the night. His body excited mine so immediately that I wondered if the Rift Event, still unformed and a mere percentage chance, weren't already afflicting me. But, no—it was just Malin, the feeling and reality of Malin. Malin, back with me.

After Eleison had been with me, instead.

WHEN WAS THE right time to tell Malin the truth of what had happened in his absence? How could I say the words? Even more importantly—how could I explain what had pushed us to our breaking point, without simultaneously revealing how foolish I had been in ignoring Eleison's advice? Without revealing how dangerous Eleison had become with his overwhelming, primal instincts driving him to take me—one way or another?

Surely one of us would be punished, and I didn't want that. I wanted life to be simple, and happy. I wanted it both ways, as it were. Both Malin and Eleison.

So, no matter what I had originally intended for the night of his arrival, I couldn't tell Malin what had happened. But...I couldn't tell him the next day, either. He was so happy to be together with me—I couldn't possibly annihilate his happiness with the truth.

"Let's have a party," he said that day, in fact. Between the bruise's fading and my hair hanging around my shoulders, I was comfortably naked in his arms and still quivering with the last reverberations of our love. His thumb and forefinger catching the tip of my chin, Malin murmured, "You need to be debuted before the wedding if our union is going to be accepted, so let's show you off and at least announce the engagement. Oh, yes—and the permit form for marriage to an unregistered party is processing as we speak. It's really intended for immigrant riftborn who might be in a different database that isn't cross-referenced with our continent's, but...well, who really cares about the difference?"

I laughed a little, though I found myself anxious at his suggestion. Such functions were inevitable if I was going to marry a territory master, but I still found myself vaguely nauseous at the idea of meeting aristocrats, other masters, and whatever politicians would make an appearance in hopes of earning Malin's favor. "I'll have to ask Charlotte for etiquette tips."

"While that may not be a bad idea to give you some confidence, you'll do just fine, dear, don't worry. Have *fun* with it! It's a party, and it's in *your* honor. You can stick by me all night; I'll make sure everyone knows your name by the end of it, and I can help you remember theirs. All you have to do is be there and be polite—so yourself, in other words. Let me do the rest."

Though I was still quite intimidated, Malin's description of how things would go put me at ease. I nodded, my fingers curling through his sparse chest hair of graying gold. Eleison was forever linked to his otherworldly counterpart, but Malin felt to me like a more terrestrial animal: a battle-tested lion. I found myself wanting to put my lips on his facial scar before his hand slid over my breast and interrupted my train of thought.

"I think that's enough scheming for one day, though, angel… how was it here without me? Did you have a good time away from your dull old husband-to-be?"

"Would you stop…oh, it was a fine time, but it would have been better with you, of course…"

His hand trailed down my stomach and I quaked, realizing he intended to return the favor from the night before. My thighs prickled with anticipation as, amid the gradual lowering of his hand, he asked, "What did you do with all your free time?"

"Orena showed me the city," I whispered, my breath catching as his middle and ring finger slipped down the cleft between my thighs. He made no move to penetrate—he only petted me, his caress gliding along my arousal and increasing it by the stroke. I spread my legs, whimpering, "Oh—it's beautiful—"

"Isn't it? I want to take you everywhere…let's go to a gallery soon…Thecla, ah, you inspire the stamina of a man half my age."

I moaned slightly, the back of one hand poised against my mouth. As I bent my knee to ease his access and to delay somewhat my climax, I reached down to tease him and gasped to find him hard again. "I told you, you're not old…"

"At the very least, my cock forgets its age when you're around…what else did you do, darling?"

"I can't remember just now," I lied, half-laughing, then admitting with a bite of my lip, "but I did take myself to a play…"

"Did you? Which?"

I told him, and he smiled in that sensual, dark way that incensed my nerves to a new height.

"I didn't know it was running…what a lucky girl. Be sure to tell me about the production later…"

"I want to go back with you, sir…"

"Then we will. Did Eleison like it?"

Blanching deeply, I said, "Eleison didn't see it with me."

"Then who went with you?" The interest in his voice artfully concealed his concern, but I rebuffed it with another half-truth.

"Eleison and I had an argument before I left, because I wanted to take myself out, so we compromised...he followed me at a distance I couldn't see, and I enjoyed my night by myself."

Laughing, Malin asked, "You made him wait outside? And people call me cruel...you are a wicked little minx. But I'm sure he did it with a glad heart, if nothing else for my sake. Are you two finally getting along?"

I bit my lip to fight away my smile. "Uh-huh," I murmured, my leg shifting open just a little more.

His voice dropping to a husky note of lewd interest, Malin looked me in the eyes and slowed his petting to a torturous tempo.

"How well are you getting along?"

Moaning slightly, I stroked Malin's length and whispered into the kiss he laid at the corner of my mouth, "Very well, Master... oh, yes, sir...I let him fuck me all day, every day you were gone."

Chuckling, Malin gradually sped his pace again, the heat he coaxed from my body rising to unsustainable levels. "I was hoping that...every time I was alone in the country house and you two would cross my mind, I would wonder to myself if he wasn't making good use of this gorgeous pussy."

I was so afraid to ask him if he meant it! It was tempting—but very often, fantasies are desirable specifically because they are not reality. Controlled in some unseen realm, naught but words, they passed by to avail a pleasure soon over and forgotten. I suspected, given his history with his first wife, that this was the case with the games he indulged with me; I couldn't know the extent of his interest without asking.

But merely asking the question of how serious his fantasies were might have indicated something was amiss. Assuming I had the least inroad, I was too petrified of losing Malin to take advantage of it.

And so, biding my time, I kept the truth to myself, celebrated Malin's return by making love to him all day, and the next morning resumed a city variant of our old schedule. I retreated to my quarters, one floor below his; he came to fetch me in the morning; and, after breakfast, we would leave the apartment for a stroll around the little park roughly two blocks away.

The first day, though, I perked with surprise to find Eleison awaiting us outside.

"Good morning, old boy." Eleison stubbed his cigarette out in the dirt of the window box while Malin nudged him and went on, "Beautiful day, eh? Ready for a walk?"

I eyed both men. Both men who'd had me. It was so difficult to tamp down my lust well enough to ask, "Eleison's joining us?"

"Of course. Unfortunately, my love, the convenience of the city is balanced by a slight loss of privacy. Even in broad daylight, people like you and me need to keep a hired gun. Ironically, since the infrastructure is much better, Rift Events are less of a problem here...it's the people."

I was learning that. As Eleison tossed his stubbed cigarette into a trash can before falling into step behind us, I told him with telegraphed disapproval, "I thought you quit."

"Sorry," was his only response while sliding on a pair of sunglasses to combat the morning sun.

'Sorry.' One word. I knew he couldn't afford to say more, but it stung me. We had gone from so hot to so cold, and neither one of us could do a thing about it. Teeth grit, I turned away from him and slipped my hand around Malin's forearm. "There's a pond in this park, isn't it? It sounds lovely..."

And it was lovely. Lovely to be with Malin.

The agony of knowing Eleison stood twelve yards behind us, pretending to mind his own business, smashed all that loveliness to bits.

Every day took on these torturous characteristics. Now, every time we took our morning walk, Eleison was my guilty shadow. He was an inescapable phantom—one whose disappearance back into the aether of avoidance would have crushed me worse than his presence. We once more hardly talked, and his face resumed tensing into that hard mask whenever our eyes met.

But there were moments. Bright, hot spots, like brilliant solar flares ejaculating from the fiery lake of the sun.

The first time occurred at a museum. Malin brought me to an exquisite art gallery during its off-hours, with only curators and in-house security to be seen. Outside of prints in books and the many pieces on the walls of the country house, I had never seen paintings so extraordinary—statues, so lively. We walked hand-in-hand, our moods both merry, until I noticed something he had not.

Eleison had hung back a room or two behind us.

"I think I'd ought to freshen up in the lady's room we passed a moment ago," I told him.

"Of course, dear, go on. Take Eleison, if you feel more comfortable, I'll wait here with Sargent…"

Smiling at him, I turned on my heel and made my way back to the previous room of the gallery. Though the only presence there was a museum security guard, I distinctly saw someone else duck back around the corner to a short hall adjoining a pair of exhibit spaces.

Breathless, I walked as quickly as I could while not giving anything away.

Before I was fully around the corner, Eleison caught me by the wrist and dragged me into an alcove to steal love from my lips.

The madness was in his eyes again. I wanted to whisper encouragement to him, but our voices, I knew, would carry through the empty gallery too well. Even our kissing seemed dangerously audible within the realm of my own skull, but I didn't care. His tongue was so demanding, his hands on my arms so strong—

And then, pushing me away, he stepped out of the alcove and said casually, "I'll wait for you, Mistress."

Inhaling, I nodded and cleared my throat. "Thank you."

Behind the lavatory door, I nearly screamed.

Every few days, one of these little moments would erupt. Passing one another on an empty landing, he would catch me for no other reason than to hold me to his heart for a few long seconds. Ecstasy. Then, the pain of letting go; of seeing his back recede down the stairs.

His lips on my neck as I sat reading a book.

My hand grazing his when Malin looked the other way during our walks.

His eyes on me, drinking me in every time we were together for any reason anymore.

One way or another, Malin was going to find out. I had to find a way to tell him what was going on.

But things happened so quickly after that party. I'd been given many opportunities to tell the truth, and I'd let every single one of them pass me by because I arrogantly assumed there would always be more chances before the truth told itself.

I was wrong.

In amazingly short spans of time, Malin could wave a hand and accomplish anything he wanted. It was nothing to him at all for a party to be pulled together. Invitations would be artfully written and sent, catering arranged, music prepared, everything and anything all brought together by his will and the hands of those who worked for him in the house. By the time he had been in the apartment ten days and the occasion loomed large in the night ahead, I read over the guest list with some astonishment.

"Will there be *room* for so many people in this place? Did they really all agree to come? My goodness..."

With a chuckle, as though he found my naivete quite charming, Malin patted my hand. "Dear, dear, this is barely a social mixer...I'd tell you to wait until you see the wedding, but—"

His lips pursed and I squeezed his palm. "What is it?"

"Well—as tempting as it is to arrange an extravagant ball for the wedding itself, I wonder how you would feel about eloping a little more quietly."

"Thank goodness," I said, making him laugh and flashing him a shy smile of my own. "Yes—I'd much prefer that, please. Everything has been so outrageously busy these past few months, so wild all the time, I—"

I laughed a little, my eyes shutting as I smoothed my brow with my fingertips.

"I just want to celebrate my love for you with *you*. Then go to your vineyard with you and rest awhile."

"Yes, of course...which reminds me. Charlotte said something about a loom for that property? Consider it done...the sound of you clattering away in that old meeting room upstairs for the past three days has truly been beautiful. Especially when I hear you singing to yourself."

Flushed to the tips of my ears, I struck him in the arm and said, "You eavesdropper..."

"And a voyeur," he purred. "Two days ago, I opened the door to speak with you, but you didn't hear me come in, and you looked so lovely—I just admired you a moment and walked away."

"I didn't think I left the door open…if you want to stare at me, Malin, you don't have to be so sneaky about it. You're going to be my husband, aren't you?"

He smiled and drew my hand to his mouth for a kiss. I permitted it before slipping away altogether. "I'd better finish getting ready."

"Very good," he said, waving a hand to dismiss me and letting his attention turn elsewhere.

One of the things I most enjoyed about Malin was that the profundity of his desire could only be matched by the strength of his will and self-control. He could smolder for me while retaining a sense of his responsibilities, and I found the combination to be somehow erotic.

Not to say Eleison's lack of control wasn't equally exciting, of course.

Having taken a shine to the black dress from the night of the theater, I was grateful to find Charlotte had mended it herself and returned it to its hanger fully cleaned. I wore it for the party, not only because it suited me but because it gave me a little thrill. The memories rushed back. Eleison—brutal, beautiful Eleison. I applied my make-up over my flushed face and spent my maid's visit to braid my hair off in another realm, thinking time and time again of the moment our desire to make good our mating boiled over into action.

Perhaps that was why, when I took the elevator due to my heeled shoes, Eleison glanced up from his watch with a look of surprise at the opening of the doors. His lips parted, his eyes dark with lust.

"Hey."

I stepped inside, the breath shuddering from me as I returned his greeting. Eleison's eyes roved over me so wildly I was sure he remembered the same things I did. Other things, too.

The doors slid closed.

His hands found my hips and he shoved me back against the wall of the elevator car, his mouth pressing to my ear in a growl. "You look sexy."

"I can't kiss you," I whispered, a moan rising from my lips as his teeth grazed the line of my jaw. "My lipstick—I can't."

"Then let me kiss you." Amid his negotiations, his hands roved over my body and caressed my breasts. His mouth lowered down my neck, working there to excite the flesh while I panted and trembled. "Just let me kiss you, Thecla...you don't have to kiss me back."

"Eleison—what if somebody finds us?"

"I know, but—ah—"

Inhaling, then exhaling against me, he lifted his head and stared intensely into my eyes.

"I can't go back to using the Stabilify after you, Thecla. It's not even close to the same. You—when I'm near you, I feel truly human. I feel—*good*."

"You *are* good," I assured him, stroking his cheek.

Summoned from below, the elevator jerked into motion. Our eyes dropped from one another, mine shutting and his lowering. Both of us sighed, then slid apart to opposite sides of the car.

When the door opened to release us and Malin stood there, his smile lit up to see me. He barely noticed Eleison, who slipped out as my fiancé drew me from the car.

"Goodness, Thecla, how gorgeous you make this dress look..." While I laughed at his praise and let him kiss my cheek, he stuck his foot in the elevator doors and said, "I'm going to do a final few things before shutting down the elevator for the party. Why don't you meet me in the parlor, and we can start greeting guests?"

He said that as though greeting guests were some finite experience: one consisting of a definite start, middle, and end with respect to the rest of the party.

The reality was that it *was* the party...or so it felt to me.

For the first few minutes I worried we were going to be caught forever in dreadful conversation with the mayor of Saalast, who was a nice enough man but very visibly sweaty when talking to Malin. Soon, however, my worry evolved into another: that we would be absolutely crushed by people who wanted Malin's attention. When the party had been going for twenty minutes, guests poured in with their plus-ones, and I struggled to maintain control of my performance anxiety.

These people were here for Malin, I reminded myself. They didn't really care about me at all. I didn't have anything to worry about. Every interaction followed a pattern: Malin would whisk me to a guest, whether with a partner or a group, and introduce me to all present as, "Thecla, my fiancée." Generally surprised to hear such a thing, the guests would make enthusiastic sounds, ask questions that I cringed to answer, (I received strange looks about everything from our age gap to my hometown to the length of our courtship, but Malin of course did not get a second glance for any of it), then said guests would deftly navigate conversation to themselves, their concerns, and their accomplishments. Malin would nod and listen, genuinely entertaining them for a few minutes, and would smoothly end the conversation by making eye contact with someone else in the room.

"Well, goodness, that is fascinating. Congratulations again—enjoy the party, have a little wine. I should go say hello to some other guests."

The ballroom of the apartment was not quite as large as the one in the country estate, but it was very fine nonetheless, and its rococo walls a colorful pastel. I admired their artistry while pretending to listen, in truth barely able to focus on a single conversation and not very interested in trying. My feet were hurting, and I wanted to go to bed so I could sleep well and make more progress on Malin's tapestry the next day. The design I'd whipped up had poured out of me, and in only the first few days of work on the actual piece, I had made incredible progress. But this blasted party—

Someone tapped me on the shoulder, a sensation so unexpected and obtrusive—especially given the context—that I didn't even think to be annoyed as I turned around.

When I found myself face-to-face with Dr. Gall, however, my pleasant expression faltered.

"Why—Dr. Gall! Vivian." I flicked her a glance, then a second one. Again, she wore dark glasses; these, teashades. Although Malin was unable to extricate himself from his conversation, his head tilted toward me enough that I knew he was splitting his attention.

"Thank you for coming," I continued on politely, forcing myself to smile as I tolerated that weird handshake. "It's nice to see you."

"And you as well! I was wondering if Malin would bring you up to Saalast with him, considering how unsafe it is for unregistereds. But, I guess since you're his fiancée, you must have a pass, right?"

Just keep smiling. Politely smiling. "We're rectifying the situation. It's all just paperwork, ultimately."

"It's more than paperwork to the unregistereds who end up paying for their dishonesty in my labs," he said with an obnoxious wiggle of his champagne flute and a look that was inappropriately mischievous, given the subject. "I'm sure they would have been glad for somebody to bail them out, too. Oh, hey, uh, by the way—"

Malin's responses to the person who was talking at him grew increasingly short and noncommittal with his efforts to end the conversation. Even so, I wished he would hurry.

"Your mother," Gall picked up. "What was her name again?"

"Giselle," I repeated to him.

"Giselle," said the doctor somewhat loudly. "Giselle, Giselle. So, I had it right."

Curiosity piqued, I straightened up and asked, "Did you end up finding her file?"

"Well, it's funny. I took a look for files with it just this week, when I got the invitation for Malin's party here. Your party. Anyway...I searched her up, and I just couldn't find her."

"Was she altered by another corporation than Sigma?"

"Maybe, depending on when—but the strange thing, what keeps bothering me, is I swear I *know* that name. I guess not from my lab, but...Giselle...Giselle..."

At last, Malin ended his conversation with a curt smile and a quick, "Fascinating. Excuse me, I'm sorry, I'd really ought to— Hello, dear."

Turning deftly, Malin slid an arm around me and set his jet eyes stonily upon the doctor.

"Dr. Gall. Vivian. So good you both could make it, we're very happy to see you."

"A pleasure as always, Master Farrow." The derision oozing on the title seemed new to me, though I couldn't imagine its source. Perhaps Malin's choice to be with me had colored the doctor's perception. Frankly, I didn't care; I just wanted the wretched man gone, and tried to look bored as he prattled on, "Thank you for inviting me. This is some party!"

"Just a small celebration of our engagement."

"Yes, that's sure something. I was just telling your girl—your fiancée here—that she's lucky to have you! Most people in her situation, well...let's just say most riftborn don't get a chance to turn down being one of my subjects."

"That's quite true...then again, most doctors wouldn't have the audacity to pursue the issue with a woman I'm marrying."

Smiling, his little teeth bright white, the doctor shook Malin's hand and said, "I'm nothing if not audacious. Great party, Malin. Really, just great. Good night, Thecla...see you around. Tell Eleison we said 'Hello.'"

And with that, Gall and Vivian once more merged into the crowd.

Inhaling sharply, Malin tightened his arm around my waist and brushed his lips over my brow.

"How about we get you a fresh drink," he said with an understanding smile that promised later conversation.

Nodding, I relinquished my empty glass to him and let him fetch me a new one.

The party carried on forever. My mouth was dry and I was hardly able to think by the end of it, I was so bored and tired. I could see how I might learn to enjoy this sort of thing as time went on, but for the moment, coming into this network of politics with no context and little if any memory for names and faces, it was all intolerably dreary.

Except for Dr. Gall, who had been intolerable, period.

What had all that been about? I didn't like that he was so interested in my mother, and I regretted giving him her name at the Torea Festival, but it was too late now. He had clearly remembered it, whatever good it did him and whatever he intended to do with it.

But I didn't care for the curiosity, and Malin didn't, either.

"The staff will send everyone home when it's time. Let's retire," he said into my ear around midnight, relieving me and earning a rapid nod. Pleased, he patted my arm, then led me through the crowd and back around to the side hall. There, he unlocked the elevator with his key.

I limped in, intent on taking off my shoes as soon as the doors closed, but Malin hit the button for the seventh floor and caught my hands before I could.

As his forehead rested against mine, something I'd never truly seen before shown from the depths of his black eyes. They were endless pools of empty darkness; a sky without stars, without life.

"If anyone ever hurts you—no, Thecla. If anyone ever touches you, *looks* at you in a way you don't like, promise me you'll tell me even those slights. But if anyone ever, *ever* hurts you, or takes advantage of you...I hope it brings you comfort to know that I will personally see their head cut off and mounted at our gates."

Fear rushed over and through me, folding around me like a cloak as I remembered the power—and the reputation—of the man who wished to wed me.

Fear—and something else. Something that throbbed from my heart to my center and made me lean closer against him.

"Even only knowing me a few months?"

"And loving you," he said, "yes, absolutely. I would see Dr. Gall hanged from the public gallows before I let him near a drop of your precious blood."

As terrifying as Malin was, the matter-of-fact, cold insanity of the statement was also somehow deeply touching. I raised my mouth against his, my tongue just brushing between his lips as the elevator opened.

Then, drawing away from him with my teeth set into my lower lip, I led him from the elevator with a look full of promises.

WHAT FRIGHTENED ME about Malin was not how protective he could be at unexpected moments. Rather, I was forced to ask myself how that devastating power could be turned against me if he saw fit.

Against me, or someone I loved.

Malin meant every word he said to me, and I believed him when he promised to have the head of anyone who harmed me. I felt it again the next morning, when we ate breakfast on the balcony of his suite to watch the city wake up.

"I know you won't like to hear this, angel, but I think it's best if you take security with you in broad daylight as well as at night, for the time being."

My lips pursed. "Do you think I could be in some sort of danger?"

"Well—let's just say that I trust Gall far less than I need you. Ah—Thecla—"

He caught my hand, holding it so tightly I yelped in surprise. His grip relaxed into a firm but pleasant massage along my joints as he told me, "I just got you—I won't give you up, won't give you any reason to recoil from me if I can help it in any way. Besides… this is a crucial time."

Releasing me, he picked up his fork and knife to resume sawing into his ferato steak—a Rift delicacy. "I'll be calling today to push your paperwork through faster, and it will *assuredly* get put through faster, have no doubt of that. But, until you are registered, you are in danger here. If a police officer stopped you—I don't want to think about the headache we'd be in for, and the trauma for you."

Brooding, his knife tapping against the edge of his plate, Malin glanced down the long boulevard into Saalast and said, "I think the best thing to do is push up the wedding."

My spine straightened, an ache for Eleison passing through my body at the thought. The movement caught Malin's attention and he returned his gaze to me, brow lightly arched before he casually lowered his eyes to his plate.

"You object?"

"No—of course not. I just suppose that the urgency in your tone is nerve-wracking."

"I'm sorry to have to speak on these matters so seriously, Thecla. I would much prefer the subject of our wedding to be lighthearted, always. But it would be imprudent to deny that our union serves a number of practical purposes for you, not the least of which being your safety. From that perspective, the sooner we're married and you're registered as my wife, the sooner you can walk the streets without concern again."

Wouldn't that be nice! But there was no walking the streets

without some concern; not in my life. The possibility of a freak Rift Event hovered over our heads on even a 2% day, and we had been long without one since coming to the city.

The drought was not to last.

A handful of days after the party, Malin had an appointment and left the house in the company of a few officers who gathered at the foyer along with Eleison. I happened to be nearby and watched from the stairs to the second floor as Malin waved a hand.

"No, Eleison, I don't think that's necessary," he was saying in response to some suggestion. "You've been run ragged this week, I think two plus a driver is plenty... Ah!"

He had glanced away with his chuckle and now saw me on the stairs. Smiling somewhat roguishly, Malin opened his arms.

"A kiss good-bye? I won't be long, but I won't miss an opportunity."

Smiling despite myself—despite Eleison's presence—I hurried down the stairs and threw myself into Malin's arms. As he bent his head over mine, Eleison looked away in my periphery.

"I'll be back after supper," he told me. "An hour or so, I'd expect. Don't wait to eat."

When I nodded, he smiled, brushed a hair from my cheek, and turned to indicate the door. The security man to his left got it for him, and Malin stepped out while setting his hat on his head. "Be good," he told me with a wink as the door shut, leaving me to stew in the words.

With the two remaining security officers hovering around us, all I could do was stand looking at the door while my soul was immolated by Eleison's nearness. He was perhaps six feet away, and I was sure he was absorbing me at the fringes of his vision just as I was him; but, as the staff members lingered, he walked past me with an imperceptible brush of my lower back to summon my attention. Everything in me grew stimulated beyond reason, transfigured and primed by his slightest caress. Since he had taken me, it felt as though Eleison controlled my body...but, maybe it had been that way from the moment he bit me.

While he took the stairs, I took the elevator to the sixth floor and hovered nervously just within the door of my room.

His knock rang out seconds later, and I weakly called, "Come in."

The door bursting open, then very nearly slamming shut behind him, Eleison caught my face in his hands and pushed me back toward the window seat overlooking the city. I was on my back beneath him before I could even realize I was surprised.

"You like kissing him in front of me, huh?"

I moaned, trying to scramble up and only falling further back into the cushions with a cry of surprise. As my hair fell away from my neck, he swept down upon me to kiss my throat and the swell of my decolletage.

"I don't like it," I whispered, "but I won't deny him, either."

"You do like it...I can taste it on the air when you do." His lips parted and he slid his hands beneath my dress, roving along my calves and up my thighs. I struggled for breath under the pressure of his intense gaze, the hard jealousy of it pained and aroused and pained by the arousal. "I can taste it now, Thecla... just talking about it."

While I gasped and splayed my legs to receive his touch, he slid my panties aside and growled to feel how wet I was.

"Do you still want to pretend like you don't enjoy it?"

"All right," I whispered, smiling somewhat wickedly up at him while his lip curled in return. "Maybe I do enjoy it—ah!"

"Maybe." Eleison scoffed, one broad digit sliding into the pathway that waited for his attention. "There's no 'maybe' about it."

Moaning, I sank my teeth into the edge of my thumb and struggled to keep my volume down. The feeling of him inside of me, even if just a few fingers or a tongue, had a way of sending me into a state of animalistic abandon—and, as I hadn't enjoyed more of him than that alcove kiss since Malin had returned, I was afraid I might shake the house with my cries.

"I like it when you're jealous of him," I whispered, the pleasure mounting with my panted breaths as a second finger joined the first. While I pawed at Eleison's chest, begging for a kiss, he stared hard into me in a focused denial of what I craved. "Eleison, please—oh, please, kiss me, I need you to kiss me!"

"Sure you wouldn't rather kiss Malin?"

With a groan of frustration that fluttered through my body and down between my thighs, I whimpered, "Right now, right this second, I want to kiss *you*, Eleison! Oh, please—you're my mate—"

My legs twitched together while his head bowed over mine, vanquished by the words. I gasped his name, ecstatic, my fingers curling in his hair as his worked expertly between my thighs. As our lips parted, something wicked was in his eyes.

"Someday, Thecla, I'm going to chain you up and fuck you as I tell you about all the women I've been with before you."

Moaning in protest, I shook my head and fought in frustration the flutter of higher arousal. "You cruel man...don't act like you don't take some small hint of pleasure in seeing Malin hold me. You wouldn't look, otherwise..."

This next growl heralded another kiss, ferocious, his teeth

scraping over my lip with the barely repressed desire to bite. As his tongue surged in my mouth, pleasure surged through my body, and I burst through the peak of the orgasm with a violent cry.

"Eleison!"

"I love you, Thecla."

"Oh, yes, Eleison—I love you, oh, yes—"

While I whimpered in ecstasy, he kissed the edge of my jaw and slowly worked his fingers in me through the end of my climax. Then, sliding free, Eleison breathed deeply the scent of my neck and hair, raised his head, and kissed me.

Before I could trail my hands any lower, he drew his mouth away to say, "I hear you're moving up the wedding."

"He's moving it up, you mean."

"You haven't told him yet."

My face fell. I shook my head, whispering hoarsely, "I don't know how to. I can't."

Exhaling, not in disappointment but in understanding, Eleison lowered his head to my lap and lay his cheek there, his hands remaining under my gown to stroke my legs.

"I can't blame you. I don't know how to say it any better than you do, Thecla."

"Sometimes I think there's a chance he might be fine with it, but—like the night of the party—"

From downstairs, something crashed and shattered upon the wooden floor. We exchanged a sharp look and rushed out into the hall. I lingered at the banister, peering over the edge while Eleison hurried down a floor below us.

"I'm not normally so clumsy," called Charlotte at the sound of his footsteps, her voice half-drowning the annoyed call Malin took as he climbed the stairs.

"—can't help the weather, can I? Don't complain so much if you know what's good for you...yes, of course, we'll reschedule. I'll have someone call you. Yes...that's fine. Good—what was that? Ha, yes. Good day."

The conversation must have ended with that, because a few seconds later, Malin's groan rang out through the apartment.

"Looks like I'll be back for dinner after all," he called up the stairs. "Has the alarm rung yet?"

"Not—"

The RMS chime began before Charlotte could respond. Snorting, Malin said, "Very good...shutters down, etcetera. Where is—ah."

He arrived at the landing of the floor below mine, those serpent eyes on me at once. Memories of our last exquisite Rift Event no doubt rising in his mind, he smiled.

"Would you care to have supper with me in my rooms, Thecla? Perhaps we can make good use of the time."

Downstairs, Eleison's door opened and shut. I focused on Malin and managed my finest smile.

"That sounds grand."

I T WAS STRANGE, but the influx of libido from the Rift flowed into other avenues than sex this time. Not to sex alone, at any rate. I was still restless and insatiable; more so knowing that Eleison was just a few floors below us and quite possibly suffering symptoms of Rift exposure without having to go into the blasted Event.

But for two days, in those instances when his thirty added years won out and Malin yielded to a few hours of sleep before again availing himself of my body's excited condition, I struggled to sleep. My mind raced. The play was in it all the time, and the play became my tapestry, and soon enough I would wake from a daze at my loom, my robe haphazardly thrown about me and my shuttle flying back and forth beneath my hand. As I wove, humming softly, the design sat upon a small table by my elbow. It seemed like some unknown director—something outside of myself. An idea that had flown into me from the play and engendered something vital in my mind.

It was vital to *me*, anyway. Charlotte was right. Since my coming, I had lain down and received whatever Malin wanted to give me, which was in and of itself his desire.

I could not abide such passivity, however. With my guilty conscience pestering me, and our inevitable discovery hovering ever closer, I wished to pour my love into a tangible creation that honored Malin and my feelings toward him. I was a weapon with no purpose; an unmade blade, steel waiting for the forge.

So, I made my own purpose.

Though the intense lust for sex had abated slightly with the ending of the Event, the lust for weaving did not. It was more than the object that it would become that was my desire; rather, weaving was an act, moving and flowing, a verb crystallizing into physical being as fluid water solidified into ice. When I wove, I was returned to the play. My eyes far away—as far as those of the blind prophet who had shown me so much, and still left far more for me to question (for had he not said three men? I could see no third, thank God! I had problems enough with two)—I grew numb to the hypnotic vision of the loom's shifting mechanisms and instead turned my focus to some inner eye.

This vision within me took liberties. It stripped away the actors and their costumes for better suited figures, and their quite impressive sets were still no match for the Birnam Woods inside my skull. With each vivid imagining, with each pleasurable rumination over the story that had spoken to me so deeply, my fingers plucked these visions, and the shuttle channeled them, and days passed until I found I had barely thought of my troubles with either Malin or Eleison or the wedding or any other thing, because I was so happy and so purified by weaving what I chose for the first time in my life.

Yes—I found myself easing into happiness.

And that should have been my warning of danger ahead: for good fortune seemed to surround me when I was most resistant to it; while its embrace, like a magnet, inevitably drew along its opposite as though to challenge me. To prove oneself worthy of fortune was no small feat; but, looking back on this time, I would do nothing differently, and would still count my blessings every day.

One week turned to two, and two edged into three. Gagging with curiosity by now, as my lips had been sealed about the true nature of the project that seemed to fly out of me with something like supernatural speed, (truly—it would have taken most weavers months to reach the point I already had), Malin slithered in one fine afternoon while knocking on the edge of the door.

"Hello, Thecla...am I interrupting?"

"Of course," I said with a laugh, raising my feet from the pedals and turning toward him to smile. "But that's all right. Are you finished working already?"

"I am...I was just wondering if you might like to go out to eat tonight."

In our many excursions across Saalast, Malin had most relished bringing me out to various establishments that were infinitely finer than the one to which Orena had referred me. It was quite a shock to discover this, but there were tiers to these things, and a man like Malin was privy to the very top.

In other words...I never refused an invitation to dine out with him.

"That would be wonderful. What time is it?"

"Already two."

I laughed in surprise, shifting in my seat and stretching my arms out as he at last succumbed to his desire. Malin crossed the room and slowly gathered my hair back from my shoulders while I asked, "Have I been at this for six hours? When was the last time I took a break?"

"Goodness, you'll have to ask Charlotte. But...ah, I am dying of curiosity—"

Laughing in playful triumph, I threw my head back to grin up at him. "I knew you wouldn't be able to resist asking!"

"How can I help but wonder what's kept you so intensely occupied for half a month? And it looks like it's almost done, remarkably."

It was. I had reached the bottom eighth or so of the tapestry, and the image was clear. Malin slid his thumbs into the muscles of my neck, pondering my work for a few long seconds before asking, "Why, is that me?"

"You, playing a role. That play I saw—it was feminized, or, at any rate, reversed."

Intrigued, Malin bent past me to study my work a bit closer, then released me altogether to regard it from a different, more forgiving angle of the loom. I went on, explaining, "It transformed the story for me. Now, instead of a regretful man whose wife pushed him into spilling blood, it's the tale of—"

"A wicked queen," Malin observed thoughtfully, crossing back around behind me and peering at the design on the table.

"Yes," I agreed as he lifted the image, black woods arcing up and around the pair of central figures. "Of a noblewoman, seduced into darkness by her lord."

A low chuckle rumbling from his chest, Malin set the paper design down and rested a finger just below the couple. Silver-cloaked Lord Macbeth stood with his arms wrapped around his wife, holding her bloodied hands by the wrists and his expression one of consolation as much as desire. Rather than the raveling, screaming, traumatized Macbeth of the stage, mine wore an expression of coy devotion; and upon the tapestry, her face was half-turned as though in anticipation of her master's kiss.

"I am so eager to see the finished result, Thecla."

The tone in Malin's voice was low, almost breathless with insidious desire. As his hand slid over my shoulder, I smiled up at him and said, "I hope you'll like it. It's meant to be your wedding present."

Looking sincerely flattered and even a bit flummoxed, Malin asked, "*You're* giving *me* a wedding present? Oh—"

His brow unknit, and it were as though, all at once, he looked at me differently—as he had when I first spoke to him frankly on my interest in his proclivities. As his chest rose and fell in a deep breath through the nose, Malin consulted every inch of my face before daring to touch my cheek.

"Those wood panels in the foyer of my apartment would be perfect, I think...they could use some coverings. Could it be a series?"

Biting back a smile, I leaned my cheek into his hand and told him, "Let's see if you like this one, first."

His chuckle soft, Malin bent over me until our noses brushed. "I'll love it," he swore, his hand gliding down to the base of my neck while his mouth teased mine. I leaned up, unable to stand it, and allowed myself to wash away in the warmth of his breath until he drew back.

"If it's to be a series," I declared as he left to ready himself for the evening together, "I'll have to defy the play...I want them to have a happy ending."

Smiling to himself, Malin patted the doorjamb and said, "I'm sure they will."

With him gone, I turned back to my loom and considered the job so far. Although of course I kept a general sense of the size and scale of the piece, and had done a great deal of math to figure the amounts and types of thread, among other considerations, I had been running on automatic. I was simply engaged in the fulfillment of a vision, and I had not stepped out and away from it to really examine the thing with a critical eye.

Stretching, rubbing my face with a great sigh, I looked at my cold mug of tea, dragged myself stiffly to my feet, and pondered the city through the window of my workroom.

The RMS readout was not kind. We had just had such a drought that it felt like the world was being spoiled at the time, but it really just felt that way because we had switched locations. In reality, a Rift Event had struck Saalast about three days before our arrival, and of course we'd had our own around the same time. But there were periods where the Rift was persistent, and I was frightened that we might be on the cusp of a difficult few weeks. What would that mean for the wedding, or at least for its honeymoon?

And for Eleison, while I was on that honeymoon?

I sighed to myself, idling beside my loom with my thoughts on one matter and eyes on another. When I took in the whole image as a broad, general piece, I was satisfied; but, of course, the closer I looked, the more dissatisfied I became. I needed practice after a few months of stagnation, and I needed to work on a few basic elements of composition. But, for a first piece and a gift for my own wicked lord, I was satisfied. It was an odd detail to take pride in, but I thought I did an exceptional job rendering an impression of the trees: the thickness of the blackening woods, the gnarled limbs of evil birches beckoning the viewer's gaze toward the lovers. The crooked trunks, too, were quite evocative, and I was excited to trail them down into snagging roots at the base of the tapestry soon as a finishing touch.

But my pleasure in my work was interrupted by a cold clutch of fear.

I saw it.

A face, hidden in my tapestry.

My stomach twisted. Perhaps it was a strange thing to be frightened by, but—all artists, young artists, must labor for a time under the delusion that they are in control of the art they produce. They do not recognize the spell they are under, and do not understand how to consistently engage with creativity because they do not treat it as a living thing. It is like a bread dough that must be daily fed and reduced, to enhance its flavor and perpetuate its existence through time.

I did not fully understand such things then, but I was beginning to. The women I had worked with in Lescaut were extremely superstitious, and I was sure that this strangely contorted face would have been regarded by them as some ill omen. The error was subtle, but once recognized among the white and silver threads of the trees, it could not be ignored.

At least, I could not ignore it.

"A witch," I said quietly to myself, lowering my hand to the long white edge of one otherwise black tree trunk. It hung below the face-like assortment of threads as though it were a plait of hair over a shoulder.

I could not say why, but I found the abstract figure had a haunting beauty.

Shaking myself free of the tapestry, I withdrew my hand and laughed a little. The play that influenced me was regarded as cursed…perhaps I shouldn't have invoked it, or so I remonstrated myself with a slightly nervous laugh as I shut off the lights and left the room for the day.

In retrospect, I shouldn't have laughed at all.

THE WEATHER THREATENED, but did not break. 85% for three days, but no Events.

Saalast held its breath, and I held mine with it.

"You'll never guess who I'm meeting," Malin said, pulling on his suitcoat while I, on a break from my work, stood in the foyer to kiss him good-bye. Eleison had learned to arrive late, or at the very least to go do something else, and strode casually in about sixty seconds after our kiss came to its audible end. My mate and I exchanged a long glance, but dared not even nod at one another while I asked my fiancé, "Whom?"

"Only your favorite doctor," he responded, the roll of my eyes bringing him visible delight. As Malin checked his wristwatch and put on his hat, Eleison got the door with a fleeting glance of sympathy. "Eleison's favorite, as well."

"I love him so much that I made a target up at the range that looked like him one time..."

While Malin, poorly repressing a smile, tried to tut and noncommittally remonstrate, "Now, now," I suggested, "Maybe you can make one for me when we're back in the country!"

He laughed a little, glancing at his shoes, then over at me with a hungry stare that foreshadowed how much more extensive our future training sessions, our most private moments together at the dangerous edges of the woods, would be.

"Yeah," Eleison agreed lightly. "Maybe. See you…Mistress."

"Have a productive day, dear." Malin tipped his hat as he ducked out of the house and made his way to the carriage.

Looking like he just barely resisted the urge to kiss me, Eleison followed our master while I stayed behind. The only man Malin felt he needed that day.

As a fighter, a guard, a footman, Eleison excelled in all ways but one.

I sighed in exasperation to catch myself thinking of my dilemmas rather than the tapestry, then mounted the stairs while Charlotte was on her way down.

Seeing me, she stopped on the landing above me and imperiously folded her arms.

"No," she said. "Absolutely not."

"What?"

"You are not going back to clatter and bang on that loom all day again today."

Scoffing, I incredulously searched for an audience in the one or two security officers who were always lingering around the foyer these days. They didn't provide one, and I told her as she glided down the stairs, "I enjoy it—and, anyway, it's a wedding gift for Malin. I have a deadline."

"And you've worked on it close to eight hours a day, every

day, for the better part of a month. Do you know how many days off you've actually had?"

"Too many," I lamented with a sigh.

Her lips fighting off an annoyed frown, Charlotte told me, "Two—and one of them, you spent reworking some part of your design for three hours."

"I don't know why you're keeping count. And, anyway, why should I take days off when I'm enjoying myself so much?"

"It's bad for your body to spend all day on that bench, for one. For another, there are *terrestrial* matters. You haven't even tried on a dress, have you?"

A little staggered, I cleared my throat behind my fist and admitted with a glance away, "Well—no, but—"

"That changes today." Upon removing one of her many hats, a black cloche with a silver lining, from the deep coat closet situated beneath the stairs, Charlotte jerked her chin. "I've made an appointment for you; it's in twenty minutes. Ignatius is bringing us."

One of the security officers better known to me, Ignatius stepped forward from where he had been loitering in the foyer. "I will remain as unobtrusive as possible."

I tapped an impatient foot. Before removing her apron, Charlotte quite remarkably pulled a pair of slippers from its pocket. Infuriatingly, their burnt orange even matched my dress that day. "Before you find an excuse to make us late," she told me, setting them on the floor and shutting the door on her apron.

And Eleison liked to call *me* stubborn! Then again—I suppose if I were not, Charlotte would not have to deal with me so strongly. The fact of the matter was she was the *only* staff member who could deal with me, and Malin surely knew it. If Charlotte was annoyed about my time neglecting my chief wedding duties, it really meant Malin was pressuring her to set me into motion.

And knowing that he cared did give me quite a glow as we made our way to the appointment, I admit.

The day ended up being quite long, and the designer was interested in perfection. I had never been to a tailor or dressmaker of any kind, and of course the clothes with which Malin's staff had so rapidly furnished me were modified dresses once belonging to someone else. That all was fine at the time, but it also meant I had a minimum of experience dealing with a dressmaker of such extreme luxury.

Everything would be bespoke, so I had to know what I liked; and because I did not know what I liked, I had to try on many, many things. In on the secret that she was creating the centerpiece of the territory master's wedding, I suspect the designer was eager to dazzle me with her talent, her generosity, the sheer variety of the work she did. No doubt, she had much of it. A small, enthusiastic lady edging toward a well-kept sixty, she had been at her trade for all her life and clearly knew more about aesthetics than anyone I had met at the time.

But, between you and me, she was exhausting. I would come trotting out of the curtain with some laughable train still gathered in the booth behind me, and her tongue would flap with wild adulation for how suited it was to me; Charlotte would ask if I liked it; I would express reticence, or fail to summon a polite reply in adequate time; at once, the dressmaker's opinion would change, and she would deem her own creation a piece of retrograde trash.

"I wish you'd tell me what you *think*," I told her after two hours and what felt like thirty different example dresses of styles that just didn't suit me. With a wave of my hands down at the style she had referred to something like 'mermaid,' I hobbled forward a mock step and caught Charlotte fanning a laugh away with a hand and a glance toward the ceiling. "You're trying all these different things to please me, but you're going to get my money by being *honest.*"

'My' money.

Love changes people so quickly, doesn't it?

"I think you're too wide in the bust and hips for something so close-cut," she admitted flatly, adding with a tilt of her head, "and white's not your color."

"See? We're making progress."

From the way Charlotte looked at me, I knew she heard Malin in my voice just as I did. Biting my tongue—cursing it, really—I inhaled deeply and forced myself to smile at the woman who was surely just nervous about doing the best job. This was the sort of thing that could change her career, after all—for better, or worse.

"What color do you *think* would suit me?"

"Well, if we can go anywhere, maybe a soft green—sort of a moss, or a seafoam. Bring out that lovely green at the edges of your eyes."

"That could be nice," agreed Charlotte. I smiled and nodded along with them. The dressmaker seemed encouraged to continue along the route of questioning.

"That, or we could go the other way, and try something gold or copper... Forget the color, though, that's secondary to style. What about your *personality,*" she pressed me with interest. "What are you like?"

My mouth opened and closed.

I looked helplessly at Charlotte, who answered on my behalf.

"She's a weaver," answered my friend, "and a creative sort of person in general, I think. Reserved, yet"—her eyes flashed over me, seeing me straight through to the bone; perhaps as not even Malin or Eleison saw me—"thrill-seeking."

"Thrill-seeking," repeated the dressmaker, tapping her chin.

"Yes. But, over all, introverted. Getting to know her in these past months has felt like getting to know a woman from an old painting, or a medieval poem."

I smiled at her, somehow touched. "Thank you."

"You're welcome."

"Very interesting," the dressmaker pondered, a coy smile of her own expanding across her lips as she studied me. "Maybe we better start with color, after all...I think I have just the dress for you."

In the end, we went not with white or with green, but a lovely gold fabric that shimmered like metal. She brought out several samples of colors and held them by me in the light, and all three of us convened before deciding it was the evident frontrunner.

But I was not settled on the color until she showed me the style of dress she was thinking. After rifling about in the back room for a few moments, she appeared in the doorway with her arm hidden by the wall and a coy sort of hesitation written on her face.

"Before I suggest this...how would you describe your relationship with him?"

Blushing at the mere question, I laughed a bit and said, "Hm, well...I suppose as far as it pertains to the dress...we are eloping, so I must admit—I want to entice him."

Though I laughed at myself, and Charlotte smirked mildly at the floor, the dressmaker gave her first real smile of the appointment: pleased, conspiratorial. At long last, confident.

"Perfect," she said as she showed it to me.

I looked it over, frowning. On the hanger, it was shapeless, and she thrust it into my hands without regard for my skepticism.

"Try it—trust me. The slip, too."

With a glance at the nude slip she had included with the gown, I shut myself behind the curtain.

While I had it in my hands and on my body with no mirror in sight, I thought of it as a bit overly modest. It had a scoop neckline and full-length sleeves, and although it was form-fitting lace, the somewhat stern column silhouette that extended from the waist down to the floor made me feel button-up. Schoolmarmish, perhaps.

But then I stepped out, and Charlotte's fast-moving hand flew over her mouth to conceal a smile.

"Oh, my," she said in a knowing tone. "You're going to pick this one."

"Isn't she stunning," the dressmaker commented with pride so deep I suspected she was personifying her garment, rather than referring to me.

But—it, me, both. Either way, she was right.

What I had not seen in the dim light of the dressing room was that the lace of the dress was very nearly transparent, and that without the slip it would have seemed very crude. Even with the slip, it was quite evocative, and although it was serious in form, in practical function I knew at once how profoundly it would excite Malin's senses for the wedding night.

After so many hours, I smiled at myself in the three mirrored panels, laughing and turning to regard how the open back of the dress, a slit that extended from shoulder blade to shoulder blade down to the opaque band around my waist, furthered the illusion of transparency.

"I knew you had something," I said with delight. "It's perfect—you're right. It's just what I want."

The relief in the room was palpable, and the dressmaker, who had slowly been growing rather tired of us, perked and served us with great enthusiasm. Once I was changed out of the model dress, she had me come out and let her get my measurements by her own system and requirements. That out of the way, she jotted a few extra notes on her internal form, tore off some slip Charlotte took on for me, and told me with a wink, "Don't worry about the price, of course...we'll bill your husband."

'Husband.' Amazing how one little word could race the heart so much! In that regard, it was like the word 'mate.' Each had its own connotations, its own weight—yet each was equivalent. They seemed somehow equal but apart.

And, during an early supper with Charlotte on the way home, I wondered if it were possible—truly possible, by way of appeal to reason if not to emotion—that one might manage to have both.

The booth we had been given by the maître d', who evidently recognized Charlotte from years past and knew her employer, was an extremely secluded little nook of old wood in a far corner of the restaurant. There, we could eat and speak in relative peace while the poor security officer had to keep craning his neck around his own booth, one row over and several tables down from ours. It was the first time since she had taken me away that I'd truly been able to speak to her without some prying ear somewhere.

Upon setting down my fork, I wiped my mouth and asked, "Charlotte—do you think it's possible to love two people at once?"

"It happens all the time...but most eventually choose one or the other, or are forced to."

Lips pressed thinly, I asked, "Do you think the alternative could be maintained?"

"Openly? Perhaps." Wiping off her own hands, she settled back in her seat and sighed in contentment for the meal. "There are different kinds of love, and different styles of giving that love. It all depends on whether all involved individuals are in harmony, as in any household...and that can be more challenging when there are more moving parts."

Somewhere, a watch chimed out in the restaurant, and I reflexively glanced at mine to make sure it wasn't an RMS alarm. It wasn't. "I suppose that's true. But—I guess what I'm really trying to ask—"

"I detest speaking about men," Charlotte insisted once more, her sigh far more withering this time. "And I know what you're trying to ask. You want to know if I think your proposal will suit *Malin*. I can't answer that."

Though I nodded, I was far from satisfied. "But—well... could you tell me this, at any rate—"

Half-aware that Ignatius spoke in terse bursts too soft for me to make out, I leaned toward Charlotte and dropped my volume as low as I could.

"Has he ever—do you think he would punish infidelity with death?" My tongue darted over my lip. "Is that what happened to his first wife, when she died?"

A great heave overcame her bosom, and Charlotte looked at me with something I didn't recognize until the passage of a few seconds made it clear. Pity—but why?

"No, Mistress. He did not kill her...although I suspect perhaps he would have liked to, for a time."

I leaned back, comforted but still afraid. "And you don't suppose he's eager to have a chance at what he missed out on?"

"Oh, he most assuredly is eager for that—just not for the bloodier side of it, to my estimate."

Her gaze drew distracted, darting to my left and around the edge of our seat. "Excuse me a moment," she said, sliding out of our little corner and sweeping out of sight.

I turned; there she stood, half-bent at Ignatius's side, listening with such intensity that even though her back was to me I could watch her grow increasingly upset. Her hand tensed around the edge of the booth, her shoulders stiffening.

I heard nothing of their speech, and when Charlotte turned around, her face was illegible; but it was apparent something was wrong from the way Ignatius hurried up from his seat, let alone the intensity that imbued Charlotte as she stopped by my elbow.

"I'm afraid we need to leave, Mistress. Have you had enough to eat? If not—"

I felt myself pale. "Is something the matter?"

"We should go."

Feeling her emphatic tone deep in my gut, I set aside my napkin and stood from the table. While we briskly settled the bill, Ignatius fetched the carriage. It seemed we waited for him forever, and I was sure something was very wrong. Charlotte stood halfway between myself and the front door of the restaurant, a strange defensive posture that I didn't understand until at last the vehicle's door shut behind us and we could speak freely.

Her expression was grave.

"Malin's carriage returned to the apartment," she explained. "Without him—without Eleison. They're both gone."

I had never felt so sick in my life.

B Y THE TIME we returned to the Saalast residence, the place was already frantic. After being herded inside amid the communications of Ignatius with the remaining security officers who had not been dispatched to investigate, I was strongly advised to keep to my suite for the foreseeable future.

"Or why not work on that weaving of yours," Charlotte said, gesturing up the stairs. "I'll speak to you as soon as we hear from him."

As soon as we hear from him—as though it were a given Malin would eventually have a chance to return the many calls that had been uncharacteristically ignored. It was all so optimistic that I lied to myself on the basis of that statement alone.

Yes. Of course. It was some misunderstanding. Soon enough, Malin would call and explain what had happened. Eleison might even be the caller, confirming his security, too!

That, or they would just walk through the front door, and everything would be all right.

But even with those fantasies, I could not bear to weave. Certainly nothing of importance. I could not read; I could not rest. I paced my room, my thumb worrying over my lip, my mind whirling between terrible possibilities.

What was happening? What was *going* to happen? My entire body knew it, somehow, yet I denied my impulses as firmly as I had once repressed my desire for Eleison. A crawling fear tightened my stomach and my diaphragm, as though inch by inch my body petrified. Soon I truly felt like it, standing beside the window bench with my eye fixed on the glow of the sun setting behind the city. I could not move, could not think; I could only wait, feeling as the owl did while waiting for her mate's return after hearing a terrible scream.

The door to my room opened without warning. I twisted around, hopeful, grateful—

But it was only Charlotte.

"Where are they?"

"I think you need to sit down, Mistress."

"I can't—not until you tell me where they are. Are they dead?"

With a deep breath and a tightening jaw, she looked me in the eye and told me, "We can't be certain, but we have no reason to believe—"

"What do you *mean* "We can't be certain!"" I looked at her through surely wild eyes, amazed to find her speaking to me in a tone of such placation. "Can't be *certain*—did they just evaporate, Charlotte?"

Lips pursed, Charlotte shut the door behind her to somewhat dull my voice—on the cusp of a shout already.

"Security and city policemen are looking for him, and at least one of the latter is downstairs right now—so unless you wish to be interrogated, I suggest, Mistress, that you maintain your sense of decorum."

'Looking for him,' she had said. As though only Malin mattered. Though I seethed, I raised my chin and straightened my shoulders.

"Just tell me what you know." I couldn't soften the cold edge to my tone.

"We know that the carriage arrived at its destination at its scheduled time."

"The Sigma building, over the bridge?"

"Correct. From that point on, we're not clear. The carriage was evidently programmed to return home, and it arrived with Malin and Eleison's watches sitting on the seat. The trail goes cold very quickly."

Extending a hand to the back of a nearby armchair, I held myself upright and tried to clear my throat. It felt like it was full of razorblades.

"It doesn't sound particularly cold to me," I responded in half a whisper. "What does the Sigma Labs have to say for itself? They must be there."

Charlotte, though patient as anyone could possibly be in such a situation, looked at me with a twitch to her eyelid and a deeply repressed opinion. "You will be glad to know, Mistress, that while you have been waiting here for the past four hours"— Four! Four hours, already, yet *merely* four—"officers swept the Sigma Labs location."

"And?"

"They found no evidence that Malin ever arrived."

I was going to be sick. What did all this mean? "Then—they were abducted on the way to the building?"

"Or there is some kind of cover-up at work," she mused, her expression sharp with her mind's own rapid calculations in the face of a disaster. "For instance...I just overheard our officer friend downstairs tell Ignatius that the security scanners at the front gate of the Sigma building haven't functioned this week. In other words, there's no footage or check-in data available."

Teeth clenching, my hand twisting into a claw that nearly pierced the chair's upholstery, I barely restrained myself from shouting again.

"It's that vile scientist," I told her. "I know it is."

"Funny you should mention that. One of the reasons the police were able to move in on Sigma so quickly is that, evidently, Dr. Gall and his little bodyguard have also been reported missing."

As I looked at her, confused as I was shocked, she smiled mildly.

"That is the official word, at any rate...what Sigma Labs just so happened to call in to cover themselves around the same time the carriage arrived home without Master Farrow in it."

I didn't appreciate the way this was shaping up, suffice it to say.

Tongue darting across my lip, I asked, "What's next?"

"They're still turning over Sigma's building, and tomorrow they'll start visiting employee's homes if they have to, as well as related sites. If he's in the city, they'll find him."

"And if he isn't?"

"Then we will have to hope whoever has him reaches out to us soon."

"That's not good enough."

"We're doing everything we can." Charlotte looked at me firmly, a brick wall unable or unwilling to pressure the authorities. "However, that brings me to my concern."

I already knew I wasn't going to like it, but I forced myself to listen. To be polite.

"First thing in the morning, I'm sending you back to the country manor."

"No."

"It's not safe for you here—"

"I just told you, *no*."

"And I'm telling you, Mistress, that you do not have a choice."

Her eyes boring hard into mine, Charlotte defied me to argue with the bleak expression of a schoolteacher who had no fondness for the switch but could wield it like a terror.

"I will send you *hogtied*, if I must. Malin has made it extremely clear to me—if a hair upon your head is ever harmed, and I fail to prevent it, there will be nothing left for me."

Balking to hear this, I told her, "I don't need to be *coddled*."

"Nonetheless, Master Farrow sensed there was danger, and it's quite obvious he was right in one way or another."

"There *is* danger, and my fiancé is in it. Look—I don't know what that wretched doctor wants with him, but I know the two are connected in this. And, that Vivian woman—"

I inhaled a little, my lips compacting together when struck by Vivian's absence along with Eleison's.

What was going on here?

"I feel certain I can help, if you'll just let me. Please." I looked deeply into Charlotte's eyes, releasing the chair to unsteadily cross and draw her hands into mine. "Please, just let me stay here. I want to see him just as soon as he's back."

For a rare handful of seconds, Charlotte made no attempt to fight the frown that flattened down her lips. She rubbed my hands in a maternal way, patting them a little before looking up at me to say, "You know, it was Sigma Labs I worked for all those years ago, when you were born. You were the reason he hired me, but I was already on Malin's payroll. I was a scout for him directly, because it paid much better than recording and registering riftborn births like usual."

"How many valuable prospects did you bring to Malin's attention?"

"Only one," she answered to my surprise, "but in looking for that one, he paid me so well I never could have dreamed of leaving Sigma—even though I wanted to, and desperately. No one could find what Malin wanted except for a Sigma midwife, and I'm sure I wasn't the only one of us that he had moonlighting for him...but I was the one who found you, so I'm the one who was rewarded by coming here."

"Why are you telling me this?"

"Because I want you to understand that, no matter your fiancé's reputation to this point, and however dangerous he is regarded as being amid his fellow masters, I would gladly work for him eternally before I spent another day helping Sigma do what they do. That lab—that corporation—it's not something you should ever get involved with, Thecla."

At the sound of my name on her lips—foreign somehow, after only a handful of months of being called by a title—I folded my arms over my ribs and digested what she had told me.

Yet even with all that in mind, I still could not consent.

"Please reconsider," I said, the words hoarse.

Lowering her eyes, Charlotte turned to open the bedroom door.

"I'm sorry," she said, stepping through while I followed her in protest.

Before I could step over the threshold, Ignatius extended a hand across the doorway and pushed me back by the shoulder.

"I'm sorry, Miss," he said in his deep basso, the shortened title preferred by most of the security men somehow boiling my blood. "It's for your own good."

"Damn you! If you knew what was *good* for me, you'd let me out to go look for them! Stop—let me *out!*"

"Try to get some sleep," Charlotte advised while shutting the door in my face.

Quivering with fury, I tried the knob but couldn't even get it to turn before the lock clicked.

CHAPTER 50

Jack looked at Gaven the gnome. Daniel just looked.

"It's a trap," he said, apprehension loud in his voice.

"Danielle Alba," he said. "I think I know the answer."

"I'm positive we are all going to die," said, interrupting the thought. "You with your gun."

"But what if you knew that the good doctor, and I can hear me now to look," I think. "Stay close as can."

"There is something," Charlie. "Sounds," he said, standing. He had an eye level.

"On come," Charlie. Daniel, Sam and Gaven. They gave it a little bit of the boy, right.

ET SOME SLEEP, she had said.

What a crass joke.

I sat up, stood up, paced, sat down again. With my watch, I called every restaurant he had ever taken me to before they closed for the night to ask if they'd seen Malin or Eleison.

They hadn't.

When I think of these things now, I cringe in deep pain. It was stupid, of course. Such actions could have easily gotten gossip spreading; but, then again, I wasn't really concerned with the idea that people knew the territory master was unaccounted for.

I was concerned with his safety—and with Eleison's.

When I closed my eyes, my mind felt like it was made of jagged glass. Every thought pained me, and I could not even begin to approach sleep. I lay there for hours as I had once lain there fantasizing about Eleison and Malin, my dreams now directed to how I might possibly escape this place before they dared take me from my own home.

And as miserable and fraught as the night was, I was grateful that I spent it wide-awake when my pocket watch chimed at midnight.

I had never moved so fast. In a flash, I was up from bed and fumbling open the case, my breath held as I squinted against the sudden glow through my dark room.

UNKNOWN, the watch helpfully announced.

Afraid I might somehow accidentally hang up, I set the device down on the table and steadied my trembling hand.

When I answered, and the line exhibited that faint fullness of space heard upon an open call, I glanced over my shoulder to the shut bedroom door.

"Hello," I whispered, whisking the device to the bathroom and struggling to tell by the hall light beneath my door if Ignatius still waited outside.

"Who's with you?"

That voice. I knew it—low and rough. More so than usual.

Like an animal's growl rumbled beneath his every heartbreakingly familiar syllable.

"Eleison?"

I whispered his name as I shut the en suite's door behind me, then lay that same hand across my overheating forehead. No single thought could form in me for longer than a second. I was a cauldron of hope mingling with new, more overwhelming confusion.

"Just answer the question."

"No one's with me. I'm alone—are you all right? Where's—"

He started saying something—numbers, I realized. No—an

address. Gasping, I scrambled around the bathroom for a bar of soap and, in the dark, hastily scribbled what he said upon the mirror.

"Slow down, please—"

"Come alone," he said, "and come unarmed."

"Wait—Eleison, don't hang up—"

"Be here by sunrise."

While my heart froze in the tundra of his tone, the line clicked off.

The call dropped from the face of the watch, leaving me agonized.

Something was wrong. I *knew* Eleison—truly, I did. In our five days of relative freedom together, I had seen into his heart and found a man who fought a lifelong battle against pain. He was a gentle man forced to be brutal by instinct as well as by necessity, and those contrary impulses plagued him every day.

Whoever was on the watch sounded like Eleison, but was not Eleison. Even when he struggled to resist everything he knew we were, there was still such a blazing heat behind his looks and words to me that I couldn't help but think of him endlessly.

These words, they were so cold—almost bitter.

Unsure what to make of any of it, I flipped on the bathroom light and grimaced until my vision cleared. The address, scribbled across the glass as though in children's crayon, appeared to be for some industrial warehouse, based on the information on my pocket watch. What could be there, I hadn't the foggiest, but I did not hesitate.

In my room, I quietly dressed and tied my hair back from my face.

Then, feeling like a fool to do it, I knocked upon my own door.

Ignatius, with the sudden breath of a man stirred from sleep, produced a rasp as he asked, "That you, Miss?"

"Yes, Ignatius—would you please let me out so I can go to my loom?"

"At this hour?"

"I assure you, I have nothing better to do."

Sighing as he rose to his feet, the security guard said, "I suppose I don't blame you...hold on, Miss. I apologize for the indignity..."

I did appreciate the apology, but I wanted to say if he meant it, he would have let me go. Not wanting to reveal my intentions, I withheld my true opinion and managed to smile as he opened the door.

Not long later, I sat at my still loom with one goal accomplished—leaving my room—and so many more still ahead of me. My teeth ground unconsciously as I thought, the weaving all but forgotten in light of my current dilemma.

Three stories below, the quiet city outside my window beckoned me to find my beloveds.

There had to be a way I could get myself out of this room. Out of this house. It was not so far to the ground.

And if I had been capable of weaving so much of the tapestry in so short a time, perhaps I was capable of other rapid-production feats of the craft.

I had to be. I had no choice but to be.

My foot tapped steadily upon the pedals, pushing the loom into motion; and I hummed to myself, drawing threads from their spools; and I did in fact weave, long into that ugly night and through to its dark, foul morning.

But I did not use the loom to weave, and what I did weave was not a tapestry.

With the machine operating without production but my feet audibly working at the normal pace, my hands flew between threads. Using nothing more than my fingers, thumbs and teeth, I braided, wove, and bound thread after thread together into a fantastic, furling plait of rope. For the first hour, I worried it would never come together in the time I required, or be long enough, or hold my weight, and that the certainty I could do it was some hopeful delusion to keep me occupied through the night; but, as I found a rhythm set loosely double-time to the beat of the loom, I grew astonished with myself. The braid of threads wound on and on, and I, like some spider perched in the heart of my web, ignored the burning in all my muscles. Every doubt was pushed away, each reservation rebuffed.

The only option was to save them. There could be no other possibility.

I would not allow it.

By four in the morning, it was done. I set my foot upon one end of the rope and tugged sharply, satisfied it would not break. Then, standing beside the shut door of the room, I held my breath and listened for Ignatius's snores.

One sawed through the third floor, and I waited for the next before pushing high the windowpane.

It was high, but not impossibly so. Patting my coinpurse in my pocket to ensure it was where it belonged in case I had to pay ransom, I tied one end of the rope to an empty spool that hooked satisfyingly into the edge of the window without threat of slipping.

Then, with it grappled in place, I tied the hem of my gown around my thighs and tried not to think about the fact that I was crawling out of a third-story window.

Saalast had been cooled by its mid-spring night, its dark sky not yet softened by the coming morning. I had time—but would it be enough? I wasn't sure.

To this day, I preen and flatter myself when I think of the way that rope held. I was terrified at the time, my palms and forehead drenched with sweat, my muscles, already aching from the weaving, now tested by this foray into rappelling; but I did not slip, and my creation did not fail me.

Arms quivering, I lowered myself down two stories. It was the limit of the rope, which I had planned for, but I was still a little sick for the last bit. Dangling as I was above a hedge along the side of the building, I let go and forced myself not to cry out as branches snapped beneath me.

Unhurt, I scrambled up and rushed around the back of the apartment the long way. While the security officer guarding the exterior of the front door went around to respond to the noise, I crept out the alley on the house's other side and rushed down the street in my slippers.

I even made it to the end of the block before my pocket watch chimed with the warning from the RMS.

From sleepless hours spent in the small, rapid movements of weaving to the frightful climb down the rope, my nerves were frayed. I was neither mentally nor emotionally prepared for the deadly little noise. I froze, snatching up the watch and checking the estimated time of the Event.

Fifteen minutes.

I could still turn around. It was remarkable I had gotten so far, really. I could just turn around, hurry back to the apartment, and tell them what I heard on the watch.

And get Eleison shot by Malin's security.

I couldn't do it. I wasn't sure what was wrong with Eleison—blackmail of some kind, perhaps?—but I knew that, whatever his hand in this, it wasn't by choice.

So if he didn't have a choice, and if Malin didn't have a choice, then neither did I.

My heart in my throat, I rushed on through the city streets. In navigating the vague direction of the industrial building, I sorted through my options. There were carriage services I could call, but I was afraid that Charlotte could very easily trace me by them when she discovered I was gone—not that she couldn't find me by my watch, I thought with a grim glance down at the thing that surely served as a tracking device. Similarly, about half a mile of very brisk walking presented me with the tantalizing possibility of an officer who was clearly establishing himself in preparation for the event. He sat astride a horse, and looked young enough that I thought he could be bullied or bribed into giving it up to me; but if he resisted, one call to confirm my identity would end in disaster.

I hid my face and hurried on, those few individuals who I passed in the street looking for their own shelter—or, in more unpleasant areas of town, an undefended store to rob—as a mournful siren rang out across the city to wake it in its early hours.

Frightened though I was, I was hopeful. The Rift Event would buy me time. If I could avoid getting killed by a monster, I might just make it to the appointed meeting site before anyone from the household was able to locate me. Though I'd been concerned they could track my pocket watch, the Event would be a deterrent to any follow-up, and such incidents even jammed electromagnetic signals at certain levels of severity. I had never found myself hoping for a severe Rift Event before, let alone while planning to run through it.

But there were more dangers posed by the Rift than mere monsters.

The slowly rising tide of the headache became apparent in the five minutes before the Event, although I was sure it had already been gathering before that. I rested a hand upon my forehead, then looked up at the deepening purple veins of the sky. The mere sight brought a far more vivid pulse of agony, and I averted my eyes before urging myself to march on.

In commercial areas, most streets seemed deserted completely. Buildings had already been shuttered the night before, and in these areas there was little to do or protect that was not automatically tended by the city government. I stuck to these blocks as frequently as possible, relieved to know the police apparently took a sincere interest in maintaining the wellbeing of Saalast's residents.

I just didn't want them to lose focus on the truly pressing matter at-hand, and I kept my own mind sharp as I trudged toward my destination.

The sirens stopped. My headache spiked, a violent throb— as though a carpentry nail had been hammered up through my temples. I groaned and shut my eyes for a few steps.

When I forced them open again, the violet aurora of the Rift had already overtaken the city.

I fought back the nausea that came with the headache and pushed on, wondering if I might find some parking attendant somewhere who could be bribed into letting me steal a horse. There had to be a private stable lot somewhere near almost every residential area—if I could just find one.

But—oh!

That headache, so swift, so fierce—it was like no other. I struggled to see, the familiar crest of an aura hovering in the center of my vision, like a rainbow shimmering in an oil slick, before slowly expanding outwards.

It wouldn't have mattered if I went blind. I kept going. I grit my teeth and thanked good fortune the roads in Saalast were, with very few exceptions, straight and neat.

And I marched.

Saalast is a large city. Very large. It goes without saying that, even having stayed there a month or more, I managed to underestimate its scale in my mind the way I underestimated the Pont stadium until we were beside its entrance. I had looked at the maps before I left, and I continued occasionally consulting them with my one still focusing eye on my watch; but, walking at a normal pace, it would have taken me the full two hours to reach the address I had been given.

Half-blind from a pain that made it increasingly hard to function, I had not even made it halfway there after an hour.

My eyes filled with tears. Loathe to stop, both for lost time and for the greater possibility of being found by a monster unoccupied by garbage cans or the bait laid out by the officers before the Event, I was nonetheless forced to pause and gather myself. To catch my breath.

And the headache pulsed on, stronger.

The throbbing was so intense I wondered in a brief spike of fear whether I wasn't having some kind of stroke—a blood vessel eruption, or something even worse. It was a pain that might have caused a person to scream if they had the capacity for such a noise, but I was so crippled I could barely make a sound. Even the violet glow of the Rift-veiled sky above was too much light for me, and I collapsed on a stoop with a wretched cry of absolute hopelessness.

What was going to happen? If Malin died—if Eleison died— it would be my fault. All of this ugliness, all Dr. Gall's unwelcome probing: it all had something to do with me. Malin would not have been kidnapped if I were not some valuable specimen. I felt absolutely sure of it, and was overwhelmed by guilt.

Even more so when I considered that I still hadn't told him the truth. Malin still didn't know what was going on all this time, in spite of my many chances to tell him.

Tears ran down my hands from my covered eyes. I tried to moderate my breathing, astonished how even thought itself made the headache worse.

"If they die," I whispered to myself, "I'll die, too."

"You can't die here."

The male voice was so smooth as to be otherworldly. It shimmered in the air, flowing into me like shining mercury rolling across a petri dish.

"We haven't forged our pact," the unseen speaker went on while I, tense not just from the headache but from fright, tried to come up with an even neutral explanation for why I didn't hear this man at my left walk up until he was standing over me.

I kept my eyes shut.

"Go away."

"I wondered how we met in this entropic world," he told me softly. A sort of breathless wonder lightened his alien voice, and my terror only deepened. "It's hard to see here...you just don't realize until you do."

He laughed at himself. It was a beautiful, delicate noise that chilled my blood.

I willed my eyes to seal shut; willed the headache to blind me completely, if that was what it took.

The dharmine above me chuckled, a musical tone that signaled death.

"Madame...don't fight so hard. You'll look at me eventually... just like you'll forge the contract with me."

Trembling, I tried to ignore it. If I just waited, if I didn't give it what it needed to exist in this world, it might go away.

But if I opened my eyes, it would be *my* dharmine. It would solidify in whatever form it pulled out of me, its mist reflected by my consciousness into a person's shape. For many, it was a dead relative, or a friend. A form that would allow the dharmine to get close enough to feast on their human victims in one way or another. For Kyrie, it had been their mother. I never saw the dharmine that poisoned my father's blood.

But this voice, this breathless voice overflowing with desire—it was unknown to me. I was afraid of the form it would take, and more afraid that it would kill me when I looked. Harvest me at the peak of fear, when dharmines were said to find human blood the sweetest.

"So I see now how far removed we are from our pact...how little you know of it. You're right, of course. It *would* be so sweet to harvest you, Madame. But the rewards I reap from our contract are so much sweeter than any rewards I might gain from your death. For instance...this pain you suffer now...it is so much finer when you are alive."

Though I kept my eyes steadfastly closed, and my senses were deadened by the pulsing in my forehead, I could still feel the man-shaped animal crouch beside me. I recoiled away with a frightened cry, my body cringing, my arms raising to protect me. I had heard that they were deadly even if they went unseen—another reason to shun the streets during a Rift Event—and I felt my death crashing down upon me as the dharmine caught my wrist in its cold clutches.

The failure of it! Oh—my failure. I was sick with it, screaming and pulling away as the hateful thing drew my hand to its mouth. Soon I would feel the fangs, and if I survived, the blood sickness would follow. Though I pulled and twisted and cried out and kicked, its strength was effortless, and mine beside it was tantamount to a child's.

I was going to die.

I had to accept it.

"Besides," the being whispered, its lips brushing with anticipatory hunger over the back of my hand, across my knuckles, around into my palm, "I've spent so long waiting for you, Madame. Why would your loyal slave kill you now?"

There it was. Its mouth, just parted, pressed against my wrist. The vein would rip open, and the pain—

And its mouth lifted away.

I was in such a state of bewilderment that I did not perceive the dharmine leaning toward my face until its nose, as cold as the mist it would have appeared to be without an observer around, brushed against mine.

Though I stiffened, I could not evade it. My back was flat against the railing of the stoop, and the dharmine still had my wrist. I was sure it was intent on my jugular and cried out again, pleading.

But then those frigid lips, inhaling with pleasure, brushed over mine, and the copper fear became a live wire of electric pleasure running a circuit through my helpless body. It—he—sighed with ecstasy, a noise that was almost a whimper as his tongue slithered out across my lower lip. Shocked, I released a jagged little gasp, then willed myself to stop breathing altogether, as he took this for invitation. That evil tongue slid into my mouth, brushing mine, and drew back with it something that I swore I felt leave me in some strange, metaphysical way. Some energy that curled out of me like a wisp of cotton.

By coincidence, the pressure of my headache lessened just so at that very second.

"Forgive me, Madame...I know you hate when I take liberties. I had simply forgotten," he whispered, his head tilting away toward my ear, "how truly exquisite you are. My memory can boast of your evocation all it pleases...but, however detailed its emulations are, they are nothing beside the experience of tasting you."

I had no idea what was going on. I was sure this was all part of some charade designed to lull me for the kill, but why had he not killed me already, if so? Surely, if he could touch me, he could drain the blood from me—even devour my flesh, as I'd heard some dharmine prefer.

"There is simply no benefit to it, Madame, as I say again. The terms of our pact are clear. I will do a favor for you, and you will kindly host me in this world forever. It is that simple."

All its words were nonsense—truly, without any meaning to me at the time—but I prayed they offered me an inroad. "Then you must have the wrong woman—I've made no agreement with you. Moreover, my title now is 'Mistress.'"

"And when you marry Master, of course, that will change."

To say the fear disappeared on hearing such a promise would not be correct, because it was of course a dharmine telling me these things. But, as desperate as I was, and as gradually my sense of mortality gave instead to a state of confusion, all my fear was pushed into the back of my mind in favor of that golden orb of hope.

"Malin will survive the night? And I will, too?" I burned to also know about Eleison, but the dharmine went on only in response to my spoken questions.

"Of course. If you did not survive, we would have no agreement in the future, and I would not have been looking for you since long ago in the past. I would not be here to help you."

Despite myself, I laughed in the powerful being's face. "Why would you help me?"

"To make sure you enter the contract, of course...and—well."

His chuckle was alarming because it was such a beautiful, elegant sound that it made me want to open my eyes and see the man who made it.

But I didn't need to. I could see him in my mind's eye with inescapable clarity.

I knew what his face looked like. I had seen it in the forest of my tapestry.

"Perhaps I had ought not to overwhelm you with too much information. Entropic beings are delicate...and, for now, that is what you are. It would be better for me to help you tonight, and let you see for yourself."

"And what do I have to give you, in exchange for your help?"

"My love for you now is the debt of the future...hold on to me, Madame."

Before I could protest that I wanted the dharmine to go *away*, and that I certainly neither wanted nor needed its help or love, it released my wrist. I twisted to the side, intent on escape, but quickly it caught me by the waist and picked me up with unnerving ease despite my wild flailing. While it rose to its feet with me in its arms, fabric swirled around me, against me, and I found myself pressed to the being's chest.

Its *bare* chest, I couldn't help but note with an inappropriate flush—bare, and hard with muscles that surely rivaled Eleison's.

"I won't be able to truly help you until you look at me, you know," he said in that deceptively gentle, uncanny voice. "And not until you agree to let me feed from you again."

"I knew it," I said, crying out but nonetheless clutching him around the neck as he sprang into motion. Even as he darted into the sky with a thunderous flapping of wings, I could not help myself from calling him out. "This is all some perverse scheme to get me to yield my blood."

"Ah! What I wouldn't do for a taste, a pretty ruby drop or two...but, Madame, I will not be the one to cause a queen's blood sickness. That honor is another's, I recall..."

How I wanted to open my eyes! I was so shocked that I craved to see the speaker of this fantastical sentiment at once, if only so I could laugh in his face. I was sure he lied to acquire my cooperation.

"Queen! Ridiculous—there's no queen on this continent, and if there were, I wouldn't be her."

I could hear the ghostly smile in his voice as, ignoring my protest, he went on. "There are other methods of feasting more sustainable than blood, you know. That taste I stole from you just now was enough to let me fly in this form again, for the first time in so long...but, if I'm going to kill anyone for you tonight, I'll need to consume more from you."

If I'm going to kill anyone for you.

The dharmine's casual suggestion was the first time that night I had become aware of the gravity of my rescue attempt. Focused as I was on making good my escape from the house and across the city, I didn't stop to ask myself what I would do when I arrived at my destination. I did not interrogate my own conscience about whether I would be able to do what even the best-case scenario would have likely called for.

Hearing this evil being say it out loud made me ask myself exactly what I was doing—then I remembered Malin, and Eleison, and I realized without hesitation that I would have killed for either one of them if life called for it.

Even so, I was afraid to become a murderer. I lodged a protest against the dharmine who rushed me through the air, around and between buildings it would have sickened me to see.

"I don't *want* you to kill anyone. I want you to go away—I want you to leave me alone, not act on my behalf so I can be bound to you in some evil debt."

"But you already are, I keep telling you…"

"No," I told him, my tone as frigid as my hard denials. "No, I'm not."

"When you change your mind about my help tonight," he said, unruffled by my refusal to believe I could ever be in such a desperate state as to deal with a dharmine, "call to me, Madame. The pains racking your skull are exceptional. Let me take more than a taste of them, and I swear, your troubles for now will be ended."

Vaguely, I grew aware of descent, and of his slowing. My stomach tightened in disbelief. I wanted desperately to confirm he had actually taken me where I was due to be—where I had not told him in words I needed to go—but I refused. I refused to look at the dharmine, whatever help he would give me in exchange.

If I did, I would be bonded to him forever.

"You already are," he whispered, gently setting me down upon feet that found their steadiness and leapt back from him in seconds. "'Forever' is the past, Madame, as much as it is the future...never forget."

A cold breeze lashed the loose hairs across my face and neck. Something flew past me, and, in the distance, the gunfire of hunters or police officers signaled that Rift monsters were making themselves known across the city.

My hand extending into the empty space before me, I waited nineteen seconds, counting each number out slowly in my head.

When I reached twenty, I opened my eyes.

Nothing stood between me and the industrial building towering before me.

The dharmine was nowhere in sight.

My fear disappearing, I sprinted for the cargo door ahead.

ONCE THE HEAVY door had been dragged aside enough to inundate me with the heady and unexpected odor of animals, I slipped over the threshold of the building. Any relief I felt at the slight dulling of my headache, any confusion to hear the murmur of living creatures in the darkness around us—it was all drowned in a sea of ecstasy.

"Malin," I cried out, recognizing him even bound to a chair with a bag on his head. Oh! My heart screamed with relief, the night of his absence having passed like three agonizing days. As I rushed toward him, the bag jerked up and thrashed back and forth with Malin's muffled protests.

I knew he would be worried—even frightened or angry—to realize I had come, but I didn't care. By his side, I whipped the bag from his head and absorbed every feature of his face.

He was saying something frantic, but it was muffled by the gag tied so tightly around his mouth that it bit into the edges of his lips and pained me for him. After fumbling with the knot at the back of his head, I gave up and pushed the whole contrivance down around his neck.

Though he gasped in relief, that breath was only the precursor to his hard command.

"*Run*, Thecla—get out of here—"

The cargo door groaned as it rolled shut. Whipping around, I took two steps toward it only to be stopped by a firearm's ominous click.

"Don't move."

My heart sank. Hands raising, I turned my head to peer into the dark.

A bullet whistled through the air and cracked into the concrete at my feet.

"Eleison," I cried, stumbling back toward Malin in a convulsion of fear.

"I told you not to move," my mate said simply, stepping from the darkness of the warehouse around us.

My headache eased down another notable degree just to look at him, and my newly liberated brow furrowed with a love sharpened by confusion and pain.

Unable to help myself, I stepped toward him and the gun he pointed at me. He didn't fire, but tensed and seemed prepared to. The last puzzle piece of my circus premonition clicked into place to see him look at me this way.

After that step, I took no more.

Something was wrong with him. That much was obvious, but I mean to say that something was *visibly* wrong with Eleison.

His red eyes had been, by some means I didn't understand, transfigured into pools of shining silver.

"What's happened to you?"

"He's been converted, of course."

My head craned toward Dr. Gall's mocking voice, which echoed down to me from some unseen gangway above. A few of the ceiling lights snapped on to better illuminate both him and me.

From somewhere in the darkness that encircled us, animals squawked and snarled and cried at the sudden light.

"I'm not surprised to see you," I told him coldly.

"You're not?"

"No—much more surprised to see Eleison is involved in this."

"Don't you know anything?"

Another voice—Vivian. I should have known she was around and now looked sharply toward her as she prowled across the warehouse from the door she'd shut. Even there, she wore sunglasses, and they made it difficult to perceive her intent until she approached not Eleison, as I had expected, but me.

"Conversion is what happens when an altered loses their humanity...it's when the beast takes control of the human permanently."

Permanently. I cried out, insisting, "No—that can't be possible. He—he's Rift sensitive, but—"

I couldn't say it. I couldn't say I was his mate, and had been led to believe that proximity to him would help him recover from his ailment.

Thankfully, Vivian interrupted me with a cruel smile.

"It's very possible when you have someone like me around."

"Dr. Gall's toy here is a riftborn. A converter," said Malin, his tone oozing contempt. "He took a shine to her because, even before alteration, she was deadly."

Vivian chuckled. "That's right...I can empty out any altered and convert them if I have enough time with them...or if they're weak enough. Off their Stabilify, or denied access to their mate. Why, Eleison here went down so easily that I was shocked! He really must have been in an advanced stage of sensitivity. The last time I tried to convert him, he was still too willful."

Shame welling up inside me to think I might have helped fortify him against this fate if only things were different, I demanded, "Don't you care about him at all? Why would you do this?"

She shrugged. "Because I thought his silly human instincts were what was keeping him from me, of course...now..."

Her lip curled and she looked over her shoulder, lowering her sunglasses a few degrees to study Eleison. He had let his gun arm relax, but still appeared ready to shoot at a moment's notice.

"It seems like even in this condition, I can't get through to him...can't imagine why, but at least he'll obey me."

"Why would he do that, even now?"

"Converted are slaves to the Rift," Malin told me, his expression grim as he studied silver-eyed Eleison. "In an instance of true conversion, they exist to serve the Rift and its creatures. To trick humans out of homes for dharmines"—I tried not to look pale with fright at the mention—"or to work within governments to dismantle or corrupt infrastructure designed to control the Rift Events. But, when an altered is converted not by the Rift but by a person—"

"—that person becomes their master," said Vivian with a smug smile, bending before me while raising her hand.

Straightening up, Malin cried, "Thecla!"

"And all it takes—"

Vivian snatched her sunglasses down, her uncanny golden eyes fixing upon me.

"—is a look."

I glowered at her, waiting for her to expound on the thought. She didn't.

Five seconds passed.

Her smile faltered.

"I thought you'd been in the Rift tonight," she said in confusion.

"I just came in from it, of course."

Her stare continued. I folded my arms in annoyance, at last glancing away to find some clarity from Malin.

But, far from helping abate my confusion, he looked like he experienced some of his own—then, the epiphany lit his eyes.

The pure wickedness of his soul peeked out in the edges of his smile.

"Thecla," Malin said in a rumbling tone of appreciation, "you are a treasure, aren't you."

"Because I can last in a staring contest?" I waved my hand toward her. "Surely she can't convert *every* altered. She just said herself, Eleison's will was too strong—"

"But, weakened by the Rift," insisted Vivian, stepping aside to stay in my field of vision, "not to mention, an altered with a totally unexpressed beast should be so weak that—"

Her teeth clenched and she stared abruptly up at Dr. Gall, her good looks made ugly by her fury.

"How is this possible?"

"You know there's so much we still don't understand about

second generation altered." Gall braced his hands upon the rail of the industrial catwalk that formed his personal stage. "Perhaps they're too stable to be converted at all...I suppose we'll find out when testing starts."

"I already told you, I won't be your subject."

His smile gross and unpleasant, Gall condescended to reply to me.

"But that's why you're here, of course."

At the snap of Vivian's fingers, Eleison raised the gun again—this time, pointing it at Malin.

I had to spread my feet a little to keep from leaping between them.

"I can tell how attached you are to your master, and vice versa, so I just thought I might incentivize your consent using what I knew about you."

"Then you're an idiot, because you're going to die for it."

"Maybe...if I can be tracked down after tonight. Rest assured, Thecla...once you agree to come with me as a willing subject, you and Vivian and I will all be disappearing to a place where research can be done without interruptions by prying eyes. And, even if I have to spend the rest of my life hidden, well...it will be worth it when I think about all that we stand to learn on behalf of mankind."

"You're sick. I'll never go with you—I'll never be part of your experiments."

"If that's the case...Vivian?"

She raised her hand.

Eleison snapped down the hammer of the gun.

Now I did lurch forward with a cry, but Malin's stern intonation of my name kept me from getting fully between them.

"You refuse, and Malin dies." Gall stared me down, unsmiling as my hands clenched in fists at my sides. "It's that simple. You want to save his life? You really love him? Then you'll come with us."

I trembled. The throb of my head, which had never fully abated, seemed to race at the same speed as my pulse.

"You're despicable," I told him. "A disgrace to scientific research."

That thin, ugly little smile reappeared. "That just goes to show how little you understand about science. So, come on—we've already been here all night. What's it going to be?"

Hatred flashed through me in an instant of heat and quaking. If that awful man had been standing before me, I felt sure I would have wrapped my hands around his throat and wrung his neck. I wanted him dead.

But I refused to stoop to calling the dharmine—to willingly perceiving the parasite, and feeding it anything that came from me.

I refused, even though it was right. Forever was the past and the future, both...and, assuming I survived this night, I may have still had quite a long life ahead of me when living in the comfort of the territory master's lifestyle.

That was a long time. A long time, with many chances to slip—many wild and unforeseen reasons why I might become a desperate woman willing to sign such a nefarious contract, and all of them impossible for me to envision when I was so young.

Still so naive.

I felt sure there had to be a better way, and there was no question whether I would rather sacrifice my freedom or Malin's life.

"I'll do it," I told Gall, staring blackly up at him in what was then a pale imitation of Malin's most hateful stares. As my fiancé, with a shock that was the furthest thing from his usually composed manner, cried my name and launched into a protest, I spoke over him. "Take me where you need to take me, but let Malin live."

"I certainly will," Gall mocked, his air too pleased to be even slightly honest. As Vivian's arm relaxed and Eleison's gun lowered along with it, the doctor slid his hand into the pocket of his theatrically selected white coat.

And, with equal theatrical flare, the balance of the warehouse lights surged on. The murmurs of the animals around us rose to shocked cries.

The Rift monsters had fallen so silent in their cages I had nearly forgotten about them, but they weren't what surprised me when the flash cleared from my eyes and I could once more make out form and color.

All this time, I had assumed, perhaps stupidly, that we were alone—but the reality was, in that ring of darkness, I had been surrounded from the moment I stepped into the warehouse.

Every twenty feet around the perimeter of the great, cage-lined room, men with military fatigues and guns far larger than Eleison's waited to kill.

But kill *what*? Me? I was so shocked I actually did laugh now, the absurdity of it and the lingering adrenaline of surviving the dharmine leaving this but the tip of a very surreal iceberg for my poor sleepless mind.

"You truly are insane," I told Gall with a shake of my head. "All this is for me? What do you think I'm capable of? I've told you, Malin's told you—I can't *do* anything, blast it!"

Yet the doctor smiled thinly on, gesturing toward the one soldier who was watching him instead of me. That man, face unreadable behind his balaclava, turned around to unlock the massive cage behind him. It was so large I had mistaken it for a door, partly because I could not see beyond what seemed some wall of stone on the other side of a portcullis.

Then, that wall of stone moved.

I inhaled sharply, falling back a step as Gall told me, "Now, Thecla...I think we both know that's not true."

To my horror, the soldier lifted what I'd taken for a baton but was apparently some form of stun device. Rather than risking his life by stepping into the cage to shock the giganturn, the bastard touched the weapon to the wall to electrify that cage... and all the cages adjacent. As the great creature howled amid a series of other, equally urgent cries of pain from the harpros and ventil nearby, the almost ape-like giganturn thrashed about and stumbled, disoriented, into the light of the warehouse.

"What is this," I demanded while the soldier, defending himself as much as guiding the beast, shocked the creature toward the center of the warehouse—toward me.

"This is our first experiment," Gall explained. "I'm testing an interesting hypothesis I developed at the Torea...and I am *very* eager to see it tested."

As it stumbled over a black strip along the perimeter of the floor, unnoticed by me when it sat in the shadows, Vivian's clattering heels alerted me to her flight. I clenched my teeth, stepping after her, but Eleison's gun trained on me again, and my heart throbbed with agony.

I searched for any trace of my mate in those silver eyes, found none, and demanded of the doctor, "Let Malin go, at least!"

"All part of the experiment."

With Vivian safe, a static spark popped through the air and vibrated across the warehouse. I knew what had happened even before, furious, the giganturn wheeled around and propelled itself upon its fists toward its tormentor.

It stopped short with another awful scream—caught in the electric fence that interacted with organic matter passing over it, no contact required.

Howling in outrage to have been hurt again, the beast beat its second set of arms against its barrel chest and snarled, ears pinning back against its stone-textured skull.

The stun baton still in his hands, the soldier stood at ease not three inches from the boundary and the beast it contained.

"Eleison," I tried, catching his cold stare and taking one step toward him, "please—"

"Don't bother," said Vivian.

"If that beast is inside you when you're a man, then the man has to go somewhere beneath the beast."

Snarling, the Rift ape prowled back and forth before the soldier, rushed at another, and had its next nasty shock. Eleison said nothing, his mouth tight but his face otherwise expressionless.

"Listen to my voice, Eleison—can't you hear me? Can't you remember—anything?"

I wanted to say it. I wanted to say that I loved him—but Malin was there, struggling against his binds, and I hurried to his side with a frightened cry for the sight of his handcuffs. At the very least, he'd been fixed to the chair with a knot that could be undone.

If my hands stopped trembling, anyway.

"Hurry, darling," urged Malin, his tone urgent as the beast fixed its snarling attention on us.

Exhaling, inhaling, exhaling again, I reminded myself of every thread I had woven into my rope for hours that very night. Teeth clenched, I took a new look at the knot.

And with the next loop I pulled, it gave in an instant.

"Run," he commanded, thrashing out of his coils and stumbling up.

"No, Malin—"

The beast's roar was nothing compared to Malin's fury for my defiance.

"Go, damn you! I won't see you hurt!"

Crying out to see the giganturn launched into motion straight for us, I ignored Malin's command, his anger—everything but the threat that could destroy everything I held dear, along with my very life.

Because it was the only thing nearby, I snatched up the chair Malin had vacated and thrust it out before me as though it were some other object liable to shock the beast. All four prongs of its legs jutted out toward the giganturn, just as I'd seen the borro tamer hold a stool at our own dear circus.

"Stop," I cried, swinging the legs forward and defying pain and death alike with my step.

The beast, which had been but feet before us, stopped short with an almost frightened wave of its arms, a hammer upon its chest, another bellowing roar that echoed through the warehouse. When it landed down upon four of its limbs, it stared me in the eyes as giganturns were said to do when they intended to kill.

But it made no move to attack; and as we stared at one another, the beast's furious panting slowed to a steadier respiration that mine momentarily emulated.

"Stop," I whispered again, wishing it could understand me. "Don't let him do this to you."

The beast jerked into motion so quickly I gasped—but it wasn't intent on moving toward us. Instead, though it had shown no sign of knowing he was there, the giganturn raised its head as much as its squat neck would allow.

For the first time, it stared at Dr. Gall.

It snarled in a hatred that gave me a great sense of sympathy. To my surprise, the beast acted at once as though it had completely forgotten about Malin and myself. Beating its chest, sometimes even leaping across the floor as though energized by rage, the giganturn took to pacing beneath the gangway where the doctor stood.

"Excellent," Gall said under his breath, the word still managing to echo out above the snorts and growls of the animal. "That's just excellent. Can we add a few more?"

While the soldier with the baton crossed around the perimeter, the doctor went on in casual explanation. "You see, Malin, the behavior of the oris at the Torea really stood out to me. It wasn't normal...or maybe I just felt that way, since it sure seemed like it was heading straight for *me!*"

With the flick of a key, several cages were unlocked at once, and the static shifted in the air as the fence was dropped.

I would not have expected the giganturn to move, but somehow, it did. As though it understood it had its chance, the beast launched itself over the boundary before the yprons had even been forced from their cages.

The soldiers shouted and raised their guns.

I screamed above the gunfire, throwing my hands over my eyes. The creature was gunned down before it reached the metal stairs along the distant north wall.

"Too bad," Gall said, sucking his tooth, "that was a valuable specimen...oh, well. There's always more somewhere...not of your girl, though, Malin."

Though we were in the heat of danger, I drowned in my loathing for Gall. Even now, he couldn't address *me*, but instead addressed Malin. I interrupted before my fiancé could respond, telling the doctor with disgust, "That's because, even if I *am* altered, or riftborn, or both, I'm still a human—an individual, with a mind and a body." And a soul, I almost added before he interrupted me.

"That's right. And you gave your consent to be studied, didn't you? So shut up."

"I look forward to your death," Malin told him calmly, adding, "though, I get the sense I won't be waiting long."

Beneath electric batons and angry shouts, the ypron were herded into the boundaries of the fence and took far less coaxing to take note of us. Like so many Rift creatures, they were omnivorous, and I knew they would gladly eat us, bones and all—especially after spending who knew how long trapped in little cages with no prey to hunt, nothing real to eat.

I raised the chair again, crying out as one threw itself upon me without pause for the sudden alteration of my shape or size. The ypron's legs were stumpy, but its muzzle was massive as it was toothy, and it locked down on the leg of the chair before shaking it out of my hands altogether.

Struggling with his handcuffs, Malin said, "If you just push through the barrier, Thecla, it'll hurt, but it won't kill you."

"Malin—watch out!"

Gasping, I shoved him aside as a tusked male of the species charged right for us. The beast adjusted course and kept coming, intent on him.

I ducked between them, crying out as I was thankfully headbutted and not gored. The goring would have disemboweled me on the spot; the headbutt, though knocking the wind out of me well enough that I was an easy target for trampling, was something I could survive.

And it gave me the first glint of hope I'd felt in too long: for, along with Malin's urgent cry of my name, Eleison made a noise like a man choking on nightmares in his sleep. I even heard his step echo through the warehouse.

But Vivian, who had been listing against him while laughing at my plight, cried out with anger at him, "What do you think you're doing?"

As Malin looped the chain of his cuffs beneath one of the abandoned chair's metal legs, straining up against it with his hands in pale fists, I managed to scramble back from the hooves that stomped me and the tusks that tore at my dress to reach my flesh. One of the creatures earned a sharp kick in the nose and recoiled, whimpering. The rest were gradually surrounding me, and although one of the pack did seem to hold back with a look of fright—as if unsure how to stop his comrades from making a mistake, or how to help me, or both—I could not seem to influence them all at once. Dread filled my heart until, snapping apart his handcuffs in a great gasp that signaled the strain it had required, Malin retrieved the chair to fight his way through the pack.

This, of course, only made him a target for three yprons that whirled around and produced the uncanny noise—like a ship's groan—for which they were best-known.

Now we were both in danger again. Panic flooded me. I cried out as a tusk scraped a cut into my calf and struggled to get to my feet when I didn't even have enough floor space enough to push myself into a seated position.

But when all was lost—when I began once more to accept that this truly was the night of my death—the borro's snarl ricocheted through the building.

His name fled my lips even before he broke the electrical barrier.

"**E**LEISON!"

The borro my mate had become snarled in pain, his great paws digging into the floor as he forced his jackal-head through the wall of electricity.

When his snout plunged through, the rest of him was soon to follow. Soon, there he stood, teeth bared, fur still smoking, all three slender tails thrashing out straight as prongs.

At the newcomer's snarl, the yprons looked up in a panic from their intended prey. Though the males of the group quickly assembled to fend off the predator, they were outmatched. Eleison swept around, a shadow darting through space, and careened into the pack from the left with a great double swipe of his front claws. Squealing in terror, half the females dispersed around the massive space and soon discovered the electric fence. Suffice it to say, they struggled to understand it as quickly as had the giganturn.

"What are you doing, Vivian?" Gall was furious and waved an arm at his guard, commanding her, "Stop him! We want to see her powers at their full potential, as purely as we can while we still have access to somebody she wants to protect. This can't be interrupted."

"I'm trying," Vivian protested, looking shocked, herself. "I'm trying, but—"

Eleison roared, his silver eyes fixing on the next target once he shook his muzzle free of gore. The graying male stepped forward, head bowing low. But others rushed in even before the old one did, and Eleison turned to meet them.

This opened his side to the old ypron, who rushed forward and stabbed one cruel tusk up into my lover's flank.

The borro snarled in agony, raging toward his aggressor with claws extended once the tusk had slid free. The old ypron paid for this transgression with death, and its kin were dispatched with a new, vengeful relish—but I was in a panic.

Blood already covered the floor, so it was difficult to perceive how much was from Eleison. But it was plain to see in the lights of the warehouse that his black fur gleamed with the stuff, and more poured out of his deeply pierced side all the time.

Yet he fought on as though he couldn't feel it, intent on killing to the last creature standing.

Until we were safe.

"Somebody just shoot him," said Gall at last, indicating Eleison with great annoyance.

"No," Vivian and I both screamed.

At least she had a gun to point: I could only stand there impotently and brace myself for her to shoot me, or Eleison, or both of us.

Instead, she pointed it at Dr. Gall.

"Do it," she told the hired guns, "and you'll lose your paychecks."

"What the hell is this, Vivian?"

"You promised me I could have him, and now you're treating him like he's so expendable?" She stared hard at her employer, reminding him, "We had a deal."

"Your 'deal' is that you are paid and permitted to work in the gray areas of the law as you require. Anything else is just a bonus...and you should never count on a bonus."

While Vivian bared her teeth, my mind frantically flew through solutions.

I had none—at least, I could see none. We were surrounded by mercenaries, all of them heavily armed, and most of them capable of releasing deadly animals if required. Gall, meanwhile, was too far above us to be reached.

Worst of all: Eleison, from the way he panted and staggered on through his final kills, seemed to be dying.

As the final ypron whimpered its last sound on Earth or in the Rift, Eleison fell back a few steps and tried to catch his breath. His head bobbed, his silver eyes sweeping the area for more immediate threats.

Not finding one, they fixed instead on me.

He collapsed.

I cried out, tears filling my eyes. Malin had taken advantage of the scattered yprons to hurry to my side and help me to my feet, and as he embraced me, I sobbed with relief to feel his arms again. "I love you," I told him with a gasp.

But, when he released me, I dashed away from him.

"Eleison," I cried, the name flying from me with a sob. "Eleison, no—"

"See," said Gall with an arrogant wave. "He's dying, anyway."

Eleison whimpered as I slid my arms around his dark mane, his respiration shallow but discernable—and irritating his wound into leaking more blood with every breath in. Even so, his tails thumped to indicate how glad he was to see me, and they worsened my sorrow.

"Please," I begged, tears racing down my cheeks before I even realized I was weeping. "Please, no—you can't die, not like this—"

"Eleison," gasped Vivian, the pain in her voice as close to a genuine emotion as I'd ever heard from her. "Gall—you son of a bitch—"

Gall launched into some lecture about the costs of science, but I didn't hear him. I didn't hear anything anymore. The entire world, in fact, seemed to disappear in a great void of darkness. No sight, no self.

Nothing.

That was what the world would be without Eleison in it. Without Eleison's love, there was nothing. I would still have Malin—but somehow, without my mate, that husband's love would be tarnished.

My lips trembled.

"I want you to live," I whispered to him, stroking his muzzle as his uncanny, still tainted eyes struggled to focus on me. "Please, Eleison—please."

Breast heaving, speaking even with full awareness of Malin's shadow crossing over me as he came to stand by us, I bent my head over Eleison's jackal-face and kissed his brow.

"I love you," I told him, bursting into sobs. Malin produced a sharp little noise. Not quite a gasp, but neither a sound of dismay. I couldn't place it, but it drew my attention up to him even as I rocked the dying borro in my arms.

"And I love you, Malin—I love you both, oh, so much. Too much! And I would do anything for either one of you. Anything at all. I'd give my life—my soul."

As Malin, brow slightly furrowed, intoned my name with great tenderness, I tucked Eleison's beastly head against my stomach with one hand and raised the other in a fist.

"Sh," Gall hissed to his mutinous assistant, whose gun still seemed intent on ending him. Looking shocked to be interrupted mid-sentence, she straightened her aim against him but listened to what he asked.

"What's she doing?"

Vivian glanced at me for only a second, snarling, "Who cares?"

"Dharmine," I said, the words half a whisper under my breath, "I invite you into me."

Gasping sharply, Malin lurched down to take hold of my shoulders. "Thecla, no—"

"Dharmine," I repeated, my words raising to a shout that echoed through the warehouse, "demon with whom I have a pact not yet forged—come into me! Take a form in me!"

Eyes still blazing with tears, I fixed Gall with my gaze and let my fist extend a finger toward him.

"Kill them for me," I screamed, the animals in their cages raising an alarm even wilder than the one they had at all the death they'd witnessed that night.

Gall's mouth opened in shock, his face paling and his beady eyes darting around.

"She's bluffing," he said hoarsely. "There's no dharmine around here—and if there were, it'd be suicide to invite it in."

But the soldiers all tightened their grips on their guns. Vivian fell back a step, her eyes wide with fear.

Gall scoffed, his expression twisting in disgust. He even had the audacity to laugh.

"Come on," he began. "You don't really believe—"

The great cargo door, which had taken all my strength for me to open enough to slip inside, slammed all the way open so hard and so fast it sounded like an explosion—especially given the inundation of Rift-tainted morning light that flooded us with an almost blinding purple glow.

Someone—Vivian—screamed, and a soldier opened fire.

The dark figure in the massive doorway sprang like a blur across the floor, his body undetectable until he stood before me with his cloak still swirling around his black boots.

"Thank you," whispered the dharmine, bending to take my face in the long fingers of his hands and smiling as the Rift exposure steadily increased the pulsing of my head past a point of tolerance. Those lips were perfect, truly: as white as alabaster. White as the shining teeth beyond them. White as the long hair that had been carefully plaited back from his frighteningly gentle face, which gleamed in an archetypal manifestation of what it was to be a beautiful man. Its gorgeous silver eyes fixed upon mine, the dharmine took a great breath of the air between us.

All this happened in perhaps four seconds, it moved so quickly. Before Malin could tear me from its clutches, the creature sprang into motion without regard for the rain of bullets the soldiers around us sprayed wildly into the air. One by one, the men had their throats torn open in a fashion so effortless that one couldn't even see it happen. One moment, the soldiers would be shooting; the next, their throat burst into a fan of gore, their last breaths wheezing and bubbling out of them as they collapsed to the ground.

When six soldiers had died this way and the rest were beginning to get wise and run, Malin pulled on my shoulders.

"Come on, darling—can you walk?"

"Let's stay," I murmured, hypnotized by the death.

My eye raised to Gall, who watched all this while similarly transfixed.

Then, seeing me looking at him, he remembered himself and turned to scurry along the catwalk.

The evil little man made it two steps before he realized the dharmine was already done killing the soldiers. It now stood with an elegant smile not twelve feet before him.

"So, doctor," the alien asked, its eyes sparkling with mirth, "are you satisfied you've proven your hypothesis?"

Staring the dharmine down with the pale look of a man confronting death, Gall nodded.

"I hope it was worth it," was the creature's response.

It moved so quickly to Gall and back that it seemed to merely jerk an arm forward; or perhaps it really had some invisible means of surmounting that twelve-foot gap for the kill.

Either way, it but flicked a slender finger while the doctor gagged at the splatter of his jugular across the gangway.

Shocked, Gall raised a hand to his neck. He collapsed against the handrail, then sagged over it so topheavily his actual cause of death must have been his broken neck on impact with the concrete floor.

It sounded that way, at any rate.

A long, slow exhalation swept all the detritus from my body and mind. Everything Gall represented vanished without ambiguity.

"Madame?"

I cried out. Malin cringed around my body, having crouched behind me and now fully prepared to shield me from the dharmine who had arrived at our side.

"The woman, too?"

"Especially the woman," I told him.

The dharmine smiled at me in an almost mischievous way before saying softly, "It's good to see you're feeling more yourself, Madame."

Then, in a streak of black lightning, the disguised animal swept from the building altogether.

Vivian's scream indicated she hadn't gotten very far.

With a shudder, I returned my attention to what mattered: Eleison, whose small breaths were getting smaller all the time.

"Oh"—I stroked his muzzle and ears, devastated to think of him dying in this way, in this condition—"oh, Eleison, please—"

"Thecla…"

Malin's hands were still upon my shoulders. They tightened in a manner intended to be affectionate, but the love in that small gesture was more than my guilty soul could bear. Exploding into new tears, my shoulders shaking, I shook my head.

"I'm so sorry, Malin—we've lied to you. *I've* lied to you. Eleison, I—he's my mate."

"Oh, darling."

"He's my mate, and I love him, but I was already in love with *you* before I knew, and—and we tried." My chest heaved with a great, wet breath as I begged him to understand, "We really tried, Malin—to be good, to respect you—"

"I know you did, angel."

"And *he* tried. He tried so hard. But—but—"

"But some bonds cannot be defied, Thecla...oh, Thecla, darling...I know."

Sobbing, I nodded along with the catharsis that came when he did not respond to my confession by threatening to kill me or leave me...at least, not right away. "But we've tried to defy it, all the same," I whispered on, liberated too late, "and look what happened. This is all my fault. If—if I had treated Eleison like my mate, instead of like some lover to sneak around with, maybe he would have been strong enough to resist her. Maybe he would have been able to protect you like normal, and none of this would have happened. Instead, he's dying, and you must be disgusted with me—"

"No—"

"—and I couldn't even tell him I love him tonight," I added, bending over Eleison to weep against the thick fur of his neck. "I was so afraid of telling you the truth, Malin, that I couldn't tell Eleison I love him! I couldn't look deep into his heart and beg him to come out of his stupor. And now—"

"Kiss him, Thecla."

I hesitated, so taken aback by the command that I almost couldn't understand it. "What?"

"Kiss him," Malin urged me again, shifting to look into my eyes while maintaining a hand on one of my shoulders. "If you two are mates, your love is more than stabilizing—it's healing. Hurry—"

"But—"

"Damn you, girl"—he spoke in such a sharp tone of authority that excitement bolted my spine into a perfect column, and he must have seen it in my face, for those dark eyes of his glittered— "if you don't kiss your mate this instant, I'll forget all your favors tonight and whip you senseless the first second I get you alone."

Breath hitching—disbelief, awe, adoration all flooding in me—I looked at Malin and tried to decide what I could say. Thank you?

"I love you," I whispered to him instead, bending my head away from his to kiss Eleison.

Tears flowed on down my face, rushing into his borro fur as I kissed his brow, his muzzle, his jaw. My hand stroking through his fur, I whispered, "And I love *you*, Eleison—I love you so, oh, I love you. I still feel like I hardly know you...I want to know you better. Do you hear me? Please—I want to be with you. Your brother and I, and Malin—we all need you, Eleison."

Eyes squeezing shut, my fists clenching in his fur, I fought back another wave of tears and begged him, "Please, Eleison— wake up."

"Thecla—"

Malin's hushed voice drew my attention. I raised my head, the motion worsening the throb—but not so much that I couldn't see.

And I was grateful for that, because I was able to watch with bated breath as the tatter in Eleison's side slowly fused itself together again.

The image was so uncanny that it was horrible, but I kept on staring, unable to tear my gaze away. It were as if the film of some animal decaying had been run backward before me. The skin pulled taut and sealed itself; the muscles jerked and jumped beneath as they and the organs they'd failed mended together; Eleison's breathing, ragged in my arms, slowly gained in steadiness and strength.

Sirens rose in the distance. Malin jerked his head toward them, his hand resting on my shoulder.

"Did you tell anyone where you were going?"

"No," I said, remembering I had erased the address from the mirror, then laughing down at myself and the pocket of my dress with a little, "oh...my watch, though. I brought my watch."

With a sigh of relief, Malin said, "Thank God—we'll be saved before that dharmine returns...maybe. But, Thecla, it can find you now, and—"

"It won't hurt me," I answered him, watching Eleison's face expectantly, my hand stroking tenderly over the crown of his skull and down into his mane.

"And you're sure of that?"

No, I wasn't sure of it. I wasn't sure of anything the dharmine had told me.

But one word—"queen"—rang out above all the rest. Above whatever deal I would eventually consent to share with the creature; above whatever I needed to fear when it came calling.

"Trust me," I urged him.

Malin didn't hesitate. His hand rested gently upon the back of my head. "All right."

Let fear wait for another day.

Eleison's eyes cracked open.

They were red again.

THE FOLLOWING EIGHT hours seemed as harrowing as the previous sixteen, though our lives were out of danger and both the men I loved were safe.

Now, however, we were dealing with something far more sordid and alien.

Bureaucracy.

As soon as the police swept in, Malin and I were separated for our own medical checks while Eleison was rushed to a hospital—non-Sigma affiliated, at Malin's strict command. Aside from superficial injuries, we were both cleared immediately and given no more distraction from debriefings that seemed somehow like interrogations. At least, mine did.

First the police wanted to know how I had found Malin. Then, they wanted to know how I had gotten there. They interrupted me next, demanding I explain how I had gotten out of the house if I had been locked up, and after I explained *that,* they expressed incredulity over the speed with which I was able to weave a durable rope. I suggested they might see it for themselves if they let us return to our home, and the line of questioning was promptly dropped for other matters.

The *real* question, beyond even the matter of Malin's kidnapping, was how all these people ended up dead.

Malin, ever the professional and persuasive territory master, explained the way the door flew open, and the dark streak, and the blood, and the sudden deaths.

"It was awful," he said, affecting a grim expression and tone that I knew better than to believe. "I haven't seen anything half so horrible in decades."

I made sure I knew about as much as he did, and I was also sure to let them know that the painkiller the paramedics had given me for my headache was wearing off. Hearing this, Malin quite literally shook the hand of the officer speaking to him, excused himself from his own interrogation, and promptly inserted himself into mine.

"I think we've had really a very long day," he said to the officers standing over me, his smile tight as he slid an arm around my waist. "If you're really interested in my fiancée's perspective of the evening, you fellows had better book an appointment with her once she's had a chance for some sleep...but, do you want to know what I think?"

Both a little concerned to be asked such a question, they looked at each other, then to the territory master, all without speaking.

"I think," Malin said with a gesture, "that the person who kidnapped me is dead up there, and his cronies are all piled up over here waiting to be taken away, and his little girlfriend seems to be face down somewhere out there...so the case really is *closed*, wouldn't you say?"

"Well, of course," said the older officer quickly. "Of course, we just—"

"Want to do the best job you can. And I admire you for it! What's your name, again? And you? Very good...well, I'll be sure to commend you both when the Rift Event is over and I have *also* recovered. But for now, why don't you both do me a favor and help my wife—I'm sorry"—Malin laughed gracefully and flashed me a smile, his arm tightening around me—"my fiancée and I get home before we both collapse from exhaustion."

Unbelievably, thirty minutes later we *were* home. The carriage ride through the Rift Event gave me uncharacteristic motion sickness and exacerbated my headache, but as soon as we pulled around a corner and into more familiar streets, I cried. While I raised my hand to wipe away silently flowing tears, Malin, who had said absolutely nothing since we sagged tiredly together in the back of the car, took my hand very gently. His lips barely brushed the temple of my forehead, and the pain was worse on the contact, but I didn't care. The rest of me was so happy to be with him.

"I'm not angry," he cautioned me, which of course sank me down out of joy and into anxiety, "but would you mind if I had a few hours alone to collect myself? I have had...quite an ordeal, and I'd like some time to think. I'm sure you feel the same way."

"Of course," I whispered, trying to smile. Trying to tell myself he really wasn't angry.

Sensing my reticence, Malin smiled softly and bent his head over mine. Our lips brushed, and another tear slipped down my cheek at the tenderness of his kiss.

"Do you want to be with me, Thecla? Do you want to spend your life as my wife?"

"Of course! Of course, that's why I—"

"Then we'll be all right."

My mouth shut and I exhaled shakily, looking into his eyes as he asked, "All right?"

I nodded weakly, agreeing, "All right."

Patting my hand, Malin leaned back into his seat and shut his eyes for the last few blocks.

The earful Charlotte had coming for me was truly without comparison in all of space and time. She was at once blind with fury, relieved I was alive, and impressed with my industrious solution. Somehow, all of that managed to come across when she greeted us in the foyer by striding up to me, taking my face in her hands with a very hard look in her eyes, and drawing me down to her bosom to be embraced.

"I suppose I should thank you," she told me tersely, "but I'm just surprised that you're both alive."

"You should have more confidence in the women I pick, Charlotte...come with me a moment, I'd like to talk to you about something. Oh, Lord, let's all use the elevator..."

I rode with them to my floor and received Malin's comforting kiss as I left the car. After what had happened, my instinct was to spend hours nervously watching over him—and Eleison, too.

But, if ever there was a time to be alone, it was after the night I'd had.

So exhausted I was beyond feeling tired—beyond thought itself—I drew a bath and stumbled in with a moan of appreciation. Every muscle ached from the weaving, the rappelling, the walking and running and fighting. The cut on my leg ought not to have been submerged, but I just didn't care. Eleison had not been conscious enough for my body to be healed the way his had been; the only coherent thoughts I could form were about whether he was conscious *now*. Whether he was really all right.

Whether he was really, fully back to himself.

That thought—the memory of his cold gaze, and how I had failed him by letting him sink to that point—was what finally brought me to a new wave of tears. Alone, in the bathtub, I let myself go completely. These were not the tears of guilt I had wept in front of Malin, as though little pleas for mercy sat in each drop; they were not the tears of fear that had rolled down my face as the dharmine crouched over me, his mouth ghosting mine.

They were tears of relief. Pure, undignified joy to realize that Malin, Eleison and I were all still alive.

And they felt so good to cry.

I must have slept almost twelve hours after that, because when I was awoken by Charlotte's latest visit to my room, she was pushing a dinner cart.

"You really *have* been through an episode," she observed, her wry manner of speaking once more about her now that she'd had a day to process my heroic defiance. "I don't think I've noticed you sleep more than six hours at a time since you first came to stay with us."

I said nothing, merely sitting up miserably and sliding out of bed to meet her at the table. With a suck of her tooth, she set down my plate (roast rack of lamb, my favorite, among a panoply of delicious starches and greens) and said, "I would have thought you to be in a better mood than *this*."

"You should know as well as I do what's going to happen to me," I said miserably, sinking into my seat. "No—you probably know *better* than I do."

"What are you talking about?"

Snatching up my knife and fork, I asked, "Will he hang me? Cut my head off and mount it on our porch? No—maybe he'll just have me shot and stuffed, like a prize borro he's—"

"What has gotten into—oh!"

Scoffing, rolling her eyes, Charlotte looked at me sidelong and said, "You mean *that*, don't you. Goodness gracious. Of course, he's not going to *hang* you."

"So it's beheading," I observed offhandedly as I gave up on the fork and picked up a bone like a cavewoman. "Speaking of, my headache is much better now."

"That's good—I'm sure you needed that rest. Master Farrow *did* inquire about some...items of interest to me along with his explanation of everything that happened this morning, but I can assure you, at no point did he tell me to go sharpen an axe for him."

"Probably because I already wove him a rope," I said, turning the bone this way and that before tearing off a chunk of meat with my teeth.

Rolling her eyes, Charlotte pinched my arm as though I were her child and said, "I'll leave you to sulk, since you're in such an inconsolable mood, but I think you should be proud of what you did. Although—*never* do it again," she told me sternly.

"I hope I'll never have to."

Waving her hand in agreement, Charlotte turned to go before stopping on her heel.

"Oh," she said quickly, turning at the waist to drop the bomb. "And Master Farrow requested that I send you to his chambers when you're awake."

"Go on then, messenger, before you're shot..."

While Charlotte chuckled lightly and left the room without further comment, I stared down at my plate and tried to summon my appetite again.

Once I'd eaten, I washed up and dressed myself in a burgundy gown. Its straight silhouette reminded me of the wedding dress I prayed I'd still wear, somehow...although I could not imagine how. Then, keeping my hair down but fastened back from my neck as Malin most seemed to enjoy, I looked myself in the eye and was jolted with a sharp surge of surprise.

How different I looked after these last months! I had looked at myself, of course; but since coming to live with Malin, I had not really *seen* myself. Absorbing my own features, it was obvious I had changed. Training with Eleison had given me a svelte pair of arms that stayed toned with the constant motions of my weaving; comfort from Malin had kissed my skin with new luster, invigorated my hair, refined my clothes; the love of both men had brightened my eyes, given color to my cheeks, and changed entirely the way I carried myself

Now, I saw myself through them: and I saw a beautiful woman I wasn't willing to see escape me.

I just had to hope they felt that way.

The elevator to Malin's floor was interminably long for taking me only one story. I folded my hands before me, then decided it made me look too contrite and instead folded them over my ribs.

Too confrontational; defensive.

Sighing in exasperation, I let them hang helplessly at my sides just as the elevator lurched to a stop.

What was I going to say? Forget that...what was *he* going to say? I was so sick that I didn't notice the scent trail of flavored tobacco hanging in the air around the entrance of the foyer.

And when I did, I was already so close to the open doors of the sitting room that I saw the edge of his arm, and recognized him by that alone. Crying out, I rushed into the room and faltered a few steps in, my hand raising to my mouth just to be confronted with him sitting there.

"Eleison," I whispered, my muscles unwinding to once again meet those beautiful red eyes.

He rose from the davenport with a relieved smile, his nostrils flaring and his pupils full to rest upon me.

I rushed into his arms, on the verge of tears again as I held the man I had feared I never would again.

"Eleison—I was so afraid—I'm sorry—"

"No, Thecla, *I'm* sorry—"

"No! It's *my* fault." Drawing back, I swept my fingers beneath my eyes and laughed as he handed me a handkerchief he plucked from his breast pocket. "Thank you...oh, I hate crying as much as Charlotte hates talking about my romantic life."

Laughing softly, Eleison said with his forehead resting against mine, "I love seeing you cry."

"You scoundrel..."

"Maybe...but it's special. You're normally so guarded, Thecla. But, when you cry in front of me—I feel like I'm seeing something from deep inside of you. Ah—I wish I could kiss you."

"Then do it," I whimpered, "please—it doesn't matter anymore."

He didn't wait, or question. Eleison only fit his hands to my damp face, holding me still to receive the grail of his hot mouth; and as our breathing fell into alignment, those big hands of his shifted down to my waist. I breathed him deeply into my lungs, savoring every hot inch of his body pressing against mine—

And he stopped abruptly, his muscles freezing and his head raising from mine with a sharp, tight look that was all business.

"It's all right," Malin said gently from the doorway, tucking his pocket watch away. "I didn't mean to frighten you two. Sorry to leave you waiting here, old boy…just got a follow-up call from the sergeant. Sounds like the police are willing to do the right thing and allow my agencies to handle the investigation into Dr. Gall and Sigma, so what happened in that warehouse is just between us."

"More like between you two," Eleison admitted, releasing me despite Malin's kindness and lowering back down into the davenport. "I barely remember anything. Vivian meeting us in the parking lot, and locking eyes with her, and the kidnapping, I remember. All through—through pointing a gun at Thecla."

His eyes flashed toward mine and I bit back the memory while Malin stalked over. As my fiancé slid his great hand beneath my hair and fit it in that customary way against the base of my neck, Eleison folded his hands and said, "And then seeing her in true danger—it was too much."

"I don't believe you could have pulled the trigger," I told him in a whisper.

His eyes averted.

"Anyway," Eleison continued as if speaking to the lamp beside him, "everything after that is fuzzy. I just know the cops came, and—Thecla told you the truth."

"She did," Malin said, his hand patting affectionately upon my nape one time before his other extended toward the davenport. "And now that we've all had a chance to rest—a little, anyway—I think we'd better talk about it."

I sat down in the left side of the davenport, leaving room in the middle and expecting Malin to sit in the armchair placed to our right. Instead, he nudged me, and I glanced at him with some surprise while sliding over beside Eleison at his behest.

Malin took my vacated seat with a low sigh and a grave air, his hands folded.

How outrageous it was that, in such a serious moment, simply sitting there between them with all three of us completely clothed was enough to charge my body with lust!

"I suppose I'd ought to come out and say first that I do feel rather like a fool," Malin said, raising a hand when I began to open my mouth, "but that's all my fault. We have our little games, of course, but perhaps I should have realized they were coming from a place of true desire, if not of true intent."

I swallowed sharply, sliding my hand into his and glad he didn't reject the touch. "You couldn't have known—and we didn't want to give in to it. Not for a long time."

"When did things begin, exactly? Physically, I mean."

Unable to help telegraphing my shame, I studied his knuckles. "Here. When you sent us here, Malin."

"Really?" The sincere surprise in his voice was echoed in his face when I looked up, and he raised his eyebrows toward Eleison now. "I thought for certain it had to be that time with the flowers that showed up at Thecla's door."

"No, Malin. I wouldn't do that to you." Scoffing a little at himself, Eleison amended, "Well—I wouldn't *try* to do that to you."

"Nobody *tries* to fall in love, Eleison...and if they do, they won't. But, as I understand it, mating is something even more bone-deep and primal. That you resisted it at all is a testament to your sense of ethics, and your respect for me...that goes for both of you."

Malin, his hand still in mine, tightened his grip affectionately as he told me, "Be honest with me, Thecla. Do you love me?"

"Yes," I said firmly, the word rocketing out of me and producing a small smile from him. "Yes, of course, Malin. I love you—I couldn't live without you, not any more than I could live without Eleison."

"I suppose that's why it's been so hard on you, eh..." Chuckling, raising his free hand to work the edge of his index finger back and forth along his jaw, he stared into space for a few ticks of the clock before sliding back into focus on me.

"But you're probably going to have to live without me someday, Thecla," he said, looking carefully at me while the thought settled upon my face. "That's the devil's bargain, the true deal you're making when you let an old man whisk you off your feet—"

"You're not *old*—"

"Sixty-four will be, though...and seventy-four, even older. How many years will we enjoy together? Fifteen, twenty? If I'm truly blessed, and you're deeply cursed, perhaps almost thirty... but I would be very surprised if my life extended much beyond that. And these are best-case scenarios."

Those numbers seemed so far away at the time, when I was not yet twenty-five and hadn't felt how fast ten years of an adult's life could slip past. Even so—what he said frightened me, pained me, and I tasted bitter ashes in my mouth as I asked, "Why are you saying this?"

Caressing his thumb over my cheekbone beneath one rapidly blinking eye, Malin said, "Because I want you to think about it, and take it seriously...and I want you to know that I understand your plight."

His thumb and forefinger caught my chin. I gasped as he bent close to me, fire raging in his stare. What were the contents of his mind as he spoke to me, his tone so hungry? I shuddered to wonder; shuddered as he spoke.

"You are a ripe, gorgeous nymph of a woman, with a sex drive like few possess, and a body you deserve to enjoy while it's at its athletic peak. Moreover...given your rare and poorly understood cocktail of abilities, I would not be surprised to see your body *remain* at that athletic peak for a long, long time. Longer than I've already spent on Earth, perhaps.

"And, the particular needs and longevity of altered beings aside... Isn't it criminal to insist that such a wonderful creature suffer and deny herself for love? That she retire every single night with the same drooling old beast—"

"You're *not*," I told him, eliciting a slightly more visible smile from the corner of his lips.

"—and that she tolerate whims, bad moods, medical ailments and long naps without someone else to supplement her pleasure?"

I flushed as I fully realized what he was saying, searching the eyes that said 'Yes' to every way I could possibly ask the question.

"Then," he added, looking to Eleison, "there *is* the practical matter of it. My finest footman is dying, in essence."

Eleison balked. "How could you—"

"Please, Eleison, Dr. Singer tells me everything I need to know. I've been keeping up to date with your condition over the past two years, and it has been alarming for the past twelve months or so. Remember breaking your mirror two months before Thecla showed up? And we must be paying through the nose for your Stabilify prescription.

"Doesn't it make sense, then, that when a natural solution

presents itself, we all take advantage of it? Especially given—well, I suppose I was naive not to consider this, but Thecla *needs* a mate, doesn't she? Just as you do, Eleison. If there *is* a possibility of Rift sensitivity for her somewhere down the line, you are protecting her just as she is healing you."

Eleison took a deep breath, looking as moved and as shocked as I was. In a similar fashion, he searched his employer's face.

"Are you sure about this? I mean—really, Malin."

Spreading his hands, Malin released me only to gesture between us.

"We're all adults here. I care about you, Eleison, and value you highest among my servants; and I think you care about me in turn; and I know we both care very deeply about Thecla. Now that the truth is out, it's obvious you do. If somebody is going to be entertaining my wife, I'd prefer it to be someone I trust. Someone who I know has my best interests in mind, and who won't take her away from me."

With a glance his way, I placed a consoling hand on Malin's knee. He stroked the back of my knuckles, the veins of my wrist, then followed the trail of goosebumps along my forearm to my elbow.

"I thought I would always regret losing my ex-wife to her lover, but I don't, Thecla, because it led me to you. And, now that the situation that so affected me is held before me in this mirror, I see in part that it happened the way it did because I was so immature. I didn't treat her properly, or compromise with her reasonably, and I resented the man who did. When they were forced to repress any sign of their relationship for so long, it was natural that it should lead to flight."

Pausing for only a few seconds to collect his thoughts, Malin took both my hands in his. He looked me in the eye.

"Promise me, Thecla, that you will never abandon me if we marry."

"I swear it—I want to be with you, Malin."

"Then I trust you—and I trust that you've learned your lesson about lying to me, too."

I nodded, relieved that his lecture was short-lived and not condescending...although I did suspect I would be in for quite the licking when my next whipping came.

"I don't want to keep any more secrets," I told him. "I want to be truly intimate with you, Malin."

At his slight smile, Eleison made a noise of near frustration.

"How can you trust us so easily after we've lied to you?"

"I pride myself on being a good judge of character, Eleison, you know that, and I judge the lies have pained you both...and, as I see it, if you promise not to sweep her away from me, I don't think either one of us is intruding on anything of the other."

"That's not how most husbands would regard it," Eleison said.

"Yes, my friend, but that's just it...I will be her husband; you are her mate. There's a difference. It's a matter of two separate domains, Eleison...and I'm not convinced either one needs to be in competition with the other. Why not be partners in Thecla's love and security? It would certainly give me peace of mind, if nothing else, to know she'll be in good hands when I leave her a rich and powerful widow."

Inhaling somewhat sharply, mulling it all over while I held my breath and hopes inside my chest, Eleison contemplated me for a long time before going on to Malin.

"This is—a very profound gesture."

"I know you won't let me down," Malin said with a smile.

Eleison, though, not sure how to take the generosity of the

compromise even as excitement rose to warm my blood, said, "I promise, sir, we'll be very discreet. Nobody will—"

Laughing before Eleison even finished, Malin slid an arm around my waist while I thrilled—especially at the flash of Eleison's scarlet eyes upon the embrace.

"Eleison," Malin said, "please—there's not a thing that goes unobserved by the staff, let alone by the courtiers during the season. There's no point in hiding anything, and I wouldn't ask you to. I don't intend to hide my love for Thecla from you or anyone else; and you don't mind, darling, if you must occasionally roll your eyes and correct a bit of society gossip?"

The apples of my cheeks burning with my blush, I assured them both, "Malin's explanation makes sense to me, and has crossed my mind only recently...a mate is different from a husband. Is it so unreasonable to have one of each? Though—I feel a little ashamed. I'm so jealous!" I laughed despite myself, admitting, "Here I am, begging to have you both, yet I don't know if I could stand to see either one of you even look at another woman."

"I don't see why we would need to," Malin said, as Eleison quickly assured me, "No interest."

"This is about *you*, Thecla," Malin reminded me, his free hand lifting to tenderly comb loose strands back from my cheek. "You are extraordinary...a jewel. I would do anything to keep you, darling...give my hot little wife anything to keep her satisfied. Spoiled."

His knuckles tenderly stroked down my cheek and farther, along the line of my throat. The craving in his eyes made my jaw ache for the pressure of his kiss as he told me, "I won't give you up."

To think how deeply he meant those words—what he would do to keep me, if something happened to me or if I changed my mind about him—frightened me...and excited me. Face still flushed, I spared Eleison one quick glance before leaning in to offer Malin my mouth.

He took it unhesitatingly, his arm around my waist tightening as his tongue slid between my lips. Eleison's eyes upon us, though his glance was brief, deepened the intensity of the kiss's pleasure and sped my heart.

Then, lips drawing back from mine, Malin seared me with the coals of his hot eyes.

"Since all that is settled, darling...why don't you run along with your mate and celebrate your freedom."

Eleison, who had turned his eyes away from the scene after a few seconds, looked over in surprise as I asked, "Are you sure?"

"Of course. He almost died, and though I'm sure he's been pumped full of Stabilify all day, I am quite certain there's no amount of any drug that can substitute for a mate's caress. Spend a day or two with Eleison, dear, help him back to his feet...in fact—"

I had never met a man for whom ideas were such a visible phenomenon, but I could tell from very early on in my relationship with Malin when an epiphany came upon him. His lip and eyebrow quirked, his barely repressed giddiness transfigured into a low, lascivious note that inhabited the voice he bent to pour into my ear.

"Let's arrange to give him a little time off a few weeks before the wedding. I'm sure he'll crave you deeply when you're on our honeymoon. You two deserve some unbroken time together...I can wait until the wedding for more than your company."

Every breath, every word, sent goosebumps racing down my neck while nerves sparked in my ear. I smiled and nodded, glancing sidelong at watchful Eleison.

"Yes, Malin, you're right...Master..."

Malin's kisses had begun to gather fire against my neck, and he pulled himself away with a forceful sigh. "I ought not to get carried away. You two have fun, now…"

I smiled at him slightly, my greedy desire to love them both at once transfiguring into the heated dreams of *having* both at once. This, I figured, was surely impossible, as Eleison's bestial nature lit the spark of jealousy in him even with Malin's compromise.

But, though I turned an expectant smile upon Eleison while they exchanged a firm handshake, it did not end there. With the exchange of their meaningful look and Eleison's wholehearted, "Thank you," Malin chuckled.

"With pleasure. I fear I've been so cruel to you now! All this time, I've been rubbing our courtship in your face without knowing it. You must have been furious, Eleison…I wouldn't blame you if you fucked her in front of me, just to return the heartache."

Their exchange of stares continued another three seconds.

Eleison broke eye contact by leaning in to kiss me.

The gasp from Malin's lips lagged half a second behind mine.

The sweet heat of Eleison's breath, the sheer force of his body, the sensual command of his tongue sliding into my mouth— it was all sweetened intensely by Malin's hand, which unwound from me only slightly. Only to trail up my spine, then down again.

"What passion," Malin enthused, accepting me into his arms when Eleison's kiss pushed me back against his chest. "Ah—look how you submit to him, Thecla, oh, it's so beautiful…you always need breaking for me. But it's so natural with him, isn't it?"

I moaned, all structure to reality dissolving in a sea of pleasure. Eleison's lips left mine only to let him nuzzle into my hair, his nose and mouth brushing over the ridge of my ear as Malin's great hands caressed down my breasts.

"I guess we don't have to be quiet anymore," Eleison told me, his teeth brushing over the lobe of my ear and eliciting an ecstasy that was simply overwhelming. While I cried out at the unexpected bolt of pleasure, he added with a smile I could faintly feel against my throat, "Or gentle."

"No," I whimpered, raising a knowing glance at my riveted fiancé. "No—don't be gentle with me, Eleison, please! Fuck me roughly, pin me down and—ah!"

Made feverish by my words, Eleison raised his head from me and set his hands on the front of my dress. The fabric tore like paper, a cry rising from my lips as my bra and panties were effortlessly exposed. While Malin sighed with pleasure to deftly assist in removing the former, Eleison wasted no time yanking away the latter. I was completely in their hands and nearly wept for the ecstasy of it, wept knowing this was but the *first* time in my long life that both their hands rested on me at once. The first time both controlled me at once.

Looking into my eyes with that exquisite, consuming desire that made me feel like I was already being fucked, Eleison slid down to the floor beneath us and spread apart my legs.

"Oh, good," Malin observed, his thumb sliding under my jaw to crane my chin for his kiss. "A generous lover, too…what my pretty fiancée deserves."

The tenderness of Malin's kiss belied his lust, which I felt not just in the caress of his tongue but in the lap where I half-lay, exposed and available for whatever either man wished to do to me. I gasped into his mouth, then cried out as Eleison's nose and lips brushed against the cleft between my thighs. Next came his tongue, and as it trailed over me, Malin happened to lift his head from mine.

The groan that slipped past my lips at that instant was embarrassing—wanton, inviting. *Truly* desperate. My fiancé hardly seemed to mind, however, and watched with intense interest as my mate brought me to increasing heights with nothing but his mouth. Malin's hand slipped over my breast, then settled upon my stomach to feel it tense with every streak of pleasure. There was still a hint of shame to be so completely focused on my mate rather than my watching future husband, but oh…it was a shame that, like the pain and fear Malin brought me, sweetened my ecstasy to the greatest heights.

"Oh, Eleison! Eleison, yes, please—just like that, don't stop—"

He had settled on suckling, licking, and otherwise overwhelming that switch of pleasure that always left me trembling. While my body flooded, the slickness of my arousal indistinguishable from the slickness of Eleison's saliva, Malin stroked the escaped hair back from my face to make sure I could watch.

"Look at that, darling…he's quite good, isn't he…"

"Yes! Yes! Oh, God—oh, Eleison—"

At the sound of his name, Eleison stripped off his jacket and set about dealing with the buttons of his shirt without lifting his head from me. Finally, aggravated, he tore the shirt and tie off altogether.

When he at last lifted his head to work on his belt, I sprang upon him.

Somewhere, Malin gasped. Eleison caught me in his arms, staggering back upon the floor and falling on his haunches. Forgetting all reticence, I straddled his lap and excitedly fumbled open his belt.

The scepter that was revealed when I pushed away his

trousers and the boxers beneath made me groan—made me realize how long it had been. I bent my head and kissed it, nuzzled my cheek against it, the size of it as frightening as ever. How I loved it! The surface of Eleison's rock hard passion was smooth as silk, and intense with the aroma of his flesh. My mouth eagerly received him, and as he groaned, I felt another flood of anticipation between my legs.

"Gorgeous," murmured Malin, watching from the sofa with his hands folded and his posture listing toward us in fascination. "Isn't she enthusiastic…oh, darling, you look so pretty with your mate's prick in your mouth."

Moaning, I reached up to push my hair away and let him see better; Eleison gathered it for me, drawing it from my neck and keeping it from my face once he plucked the useless ribbon from it. As I drew back to run my tongue along the drops of precum dotting Eleison's head, he used that same grip of my hair to pull me off him.

"I can't wait anymore," he told me, the words laced with the growling timbre that told me he meant it.

While, whining, I slid my hand into his lap in search of what I'd been denied, Eleison ignored my craving and dragged me to my feet. Without effort, his gesture of stooping and slipping me over his shoulder unnervingly simple, Eleison picked me up and inspired a cry from my lips. Unready for the abduction, I struggled and half-laughed.

And then he lay me down over the arm of the davenport, so that my rear rested upon it and my back slanted down into Malin's lap.

Barely flicking more than half a look at his employer, Eleison took my splayed thighs under his arms and sighed as I wrapped them around his hips.

"If I were you, Malin," said Eleison, meeting my eye as that wicked weapon of his pressed steadily, deliberately, against the endless river of my body, "I would lock her up.'

That hard helmet at last made good its penetration, spreading me so sharply that I cried out and threw a hand over my open mouth. Malin, gazing intently down upon my face, groaned and moved my hand away while Eleison went on.

"I would keep her in a tower—I would kill any man who looked at her. I almost want to do it now," he added with a humorless chuckle, his hand sliding over my hip and up, all the way up my body, over my breast, upon my fevered face. The long, relentless first penetration went on, Eleison's cock filling me with such agonizing slowness I trembled and whimpered as though on the verge of tears.

"If I could, if it were her and me and she hadn't met you, she would be mine completely. You're crazy to share her with me—especially with me."

While his grip of my face tightened as though he wanted to crush me, Eleison drew back to establish the rhythm of his strokes. I moaned his name, twisting to kiss the palm of his hand before it slid away back down to my breast.

Seeing my hand was tangling up in my own hair, Malin once more took gentle control of it. This time, he simply held it, and I gripped him as Eleison's strokes found their way to becoming steady pounds up into the very core of my being.

"But look at her, Eleison…oh, Thecla—" His dark eyes tender with joy, with lust, with something like a dream fulfilled, Malin raised my hand to his lips. He kissed it, squeezed it as I cried out against the pleasure of Eleison's assault. "Thecla, darling, you look so hot with your mate's big cock in you…this is what you were made for, isn't it, precious?"

"Yes," I cried, rocked more intensely by each thrust. "Yes, yes, oh! I was made to be fucked by you, Eleison—oh, God!"

My mate lunged down upon me, his mouth finding mine, and I moaned as we slid together from the couch. Malin laughed at the sight, his hand releasing mine at the last possible second, as though I had slipped too far below water for saving. A snarl on his lips, Eleison pulled out of me for a few eternal seconds that made me nearly weep; but, pushing me over upon my stomach, then raising my hips until I scrambled to my knees to offer myself to him, he settled in behind me and soon drove his weapon home once again.

I cried out, my eyes nearly rolling into my head for as incredible as it felt to be overwhelmed by him, by his strength—by his size, which he re-introduced into me all in one powerful thrust. It might have hurt if it didn't feel so good.

"Say it again," Eleison told me, one hand gathering my hair around its fist, the other keeping my hips braced so he could fuck me as hard and brutally fast as he wanted to. "Say it again, Thecla."

"Fuck, oh! I was made to take your cock, Eleison—please, yes, oh, fuck, I was made to be fucked by you, I was made to be filled up by you and sent back to my husband's bed, your semen running down my thighs so he knows exactly where I've been, and who I've been with, and what you've done to me—"

Malin's heavy breathing occasionally reached my ears through our own, but it was his gaze that most sweetened it. I could feel his eyes on every inch of my body as Eleison took me.

A growl on his lips, that ardent mate of mine bent to snarl in my ear, "That's not the only way he'll know."

The sudden, sharp pressure of his teeth in the flesh of my

shoulder made me scream, truly scream, in fright and in pain—but it disappeared in an instant, and something altogether different happened.

My body lit up with pleasure, the bite of my mate echoing between my legs as though the sting of his teeth upon my shoulder stimulated some secret sex organ. I cried out for him, bucking up against him, desperate to feel his seed inside me, yet sure I wanted him to keep fucking me forever. His body against my back was so powerful I felt small, protected—yet the teeth that once more clamped down, this time upon my neck, reminded me I wasn't totally safe. That, if things were slightly different, Eleison could be deadly to me.

And of all the perverse thoughts, that was the one that at last pushed me over the edge.

As his teeth relaxed and his tongue slid along a row of marks to collect my blood, a shock of ecstasy as great as those his mouth provoked between my legs bolted through me, up into me, and was the catalyst for the final reaction.

"Eleison! Oh! Eleison, yes! Yes, yes, mark me—I'm yours, I'm yours, oh, yes, show him I'm yours—"

Groaning, the noise extending in an animal rumble, Eleison fucked into the convulsions of my body and pressed his forehead into my hair.

"I love you, Thecla."

"I love you! I love you, Eleison—oh, Eleison, please, give it to me, give me every drop of you—"

Another low expression of male pleasure rolled from him. His strokes became smaller and faster, but all were poised deep within me. I gasped, my fingers sinking into the rug where he kept me pressed. Each pant of his breath was sharper, more ragged—

And when at last he roared out my name, the hard hammers of his cock pushed me to an immediate second orgasm that took me by surprise. I cried out, trembling, barely able to hold myself on my knees. Sensing my weakness, Eleison slipped his hand beneath my hips and let his other slide beneath my chest. He pulled me up against him, his hand on my heart while his mouth pressed to my temple, my cheek, my ear, my jaw.

"I love you," He repeated to me. "I love you—Thecla. I wish I had you all to myself...but I'm glad that Malin loves you, too. I can't exactly blame him."

Breathless, looking as though he had just witnessed an extraordinary ballet, Malin sat with one hand upon his heart and his eyes still twinkling in a combination of love and lust.

"Bravissimo," he said. "I love you, Thecla."

"Oh, Malin...I love you more than I could ever say."

He smiled so warmly—I knew he could tell that I meant it. "Take your prize from me for now, conqueror...I'll see her again soon enough."

Though I bit my lip and could not help my reluctant glance toward Malin's tender concession, I searched Eleison's face to find not just love, but some lightening effect I hardly recognized until he gathered me in his arms to carry me to the elevator.

On the way down, I realized it was joy.

PICKED LAST MINUTE, the dress was finished last-minute, too. It was better that way, I thought. I was less tempted to talk about it to Malin, who still met me every morning for breakfast and our usual walk. He invited me up for an evening drink and a bit of heavy petting once every few days, but his avid hands never strayed beneath my clothes as he took advantage of my inebriation by slipping lurid details from my otherwise shyly inhibited lips.

He wanted to see everything. Wanted to press his lips to the livid marks of Eleison's teeth along my clavicle. Wanted me to show him, by raising my hem, where Eleison's fingers had bruised my thigh.

But, to my wild frustration, as my body grew hotter and my yearning to be brought to Malin's bedroom grew sharper, he would bid me good-night and send Eleison his regards.

"I'll never understand men," I moments later told one of the two who had stolen my heart, petulantly freeing my wrists of bangles and my neck of chains I left there on Eleison's sleek black vanity. "What? Why are you *laughing*?"

Eleison rubbed his jaw, his teasingly merry eyes fixed on me as I let down my hair. He laughed more often by the day, and each time I heard it, it was more honest. Perhaps that was how he felt about my tears.

"I don't know…for somebody who claims not to understand men, you sure do want to see a lot of us."

"Charlotte understands that dilemma, I can tell…it's *true*, though, Eleison! I really don't."

"Malin is still teasing you, huh?"

The language was beginning to change. I was never privy to their private conversations, but over the final three weeks of lead-up to the wedding, Eleison's reticence to acknowledge I'd be marrying Malin began to relax. It was as much a matter of accepting reality as it was of seeing that I really did love them both…and, of course, seeing that Malin was not going to murder him.

Either way, Eleison was starting to play along, and it gave me a twist of excitement to consider the possibilities. I initially feared that night of our menage's consummation might not be expanded upon, and that Eleison would forever want to keep his relationship with me strictly separated from his relationship with Malin. My mate was very possessive, and at that point I could hardly imagine him enjoying the sight of my future husband taking me. But the tone in Eleison's voice, along with his evocative choice of word—'teasing'—indicated yet another step toward a more open mind.

"He's not just *teasing* me. He's driving me absolutely out of my head." I nipped my underlip and turned in the seat to face Eleison directly. "I know, of course, that he just wants to wind me up so I'll be even more desperate to be taken by you than normal, but I'm quite sure he'd love to do it himself...and he just won't!"

"He did say he wanted to give me time with you. Sorry if you're tired of me—"

"It isn't *that*." I snatched up my hairbrush and ran it over my scalp a few aggressive times. "Such a sulky boy...I'd put you over my knee, if I could just overpower you."

Chuckling in low surprise, Eleison arched his brow and asked, "Did you just threaten to spank me? You really are wife material for Malin, huh..."

Biting back a smile, I tapped the brush against my chin and looked away. I hadn't been kidding, of course, but hinting...yet, I wasn't sure how to express the seriousness of these needs to Eleison. While he loved to treat me roughly, to bite and wrestle me and feel my nails sink into his back, I was not sure he had any appreciation for the intricate kinds of games Malin devised for us at the snap of his fingers.

"Do you ever, Eleison, think about—oh, I don't know, giving me a lash with your belt?"

The mere idea of him doing such a thing heated me beyond reason, but he smiled sort of shyly, crookedly, at me in response.

"You know how bad I feel when we wake up the next morning and I see you all bitten up..." He crossed to me, sitting down on the vanity seat beside me and forcing me nearly half-off it. I laughed a little, swatting him on the thigh with the back of the brush, and to my great surprise he took it out of my hand.

With his other arm, he flipped me over his knee, and I cried out in shock and desire while he applied the hard flat of the wooden brush to my rump.

"I think slapping your hot little ass or giving you a spanking on your birthday is about all I can handle," he told me above the stinging crack of the mean paddle down upon my rear, upon my thighs, upon my bare flesh as he pulled my dress up and my panties down. I moaned, my legs kicking and twisting, each sting worse than the last until my fire had grown in a blink.

Pausing, he stroked his fingertips tenderly along my sensitized flesh and said in response to my whimper, "See...you're so delicate. When I hear you make a noise like that, I don't want to hurt you more. I want to take care of you. I want to protect you. So... maybe"—he lowered the brush again and a new flurry of stinging spanks landed over the hillocks of my ass, leaving me to squeal and twist helplessly—"if you need more than this, Malin's the one to go to...tell him I said you should get what you deserve."

"Oh, yes! Yes, thank you, Eleison, you're right, oh—I deserve a whipping, a lashing, oh, I'm so wicked these days, I can't imagine what's come over me..."

The next day, at breakfast, Malin's eyes glittered with delight when I winced to sit down, but he said nothing out of the ordinary during our meal or our walk. That night, having been invited during breakfast, I joined him for a nightcap wearing a provocative green dress that clung tightly to my hips and bust and dipped low down my back, inviting his eyes to run along my breasts or spine each time I leaned forward to laugh or gesture. I was comfortable in the corner of the couch, and for a time, Malin savored his wine from the adjacent chair; but, after a half a glass and a few deepening stares, he slid into the seat beside me.

As he wrapped his arm around me, I stiffened and pouted, and my glance up at his delighted face through my eyelashes was as accusatory as I could make it.

"Goodness, Thecla, have I done something? You're usually so pleased to be touched, like a pretty little cat rubbing up against my hand."

Despite my mock displeasure, he persistently caressed me, his big palm fitting into my lower back and drawing me close against his body.

"I don't want to say…you'll have some foolish *reason*, like the rational man you are, and I'll be forced to agree with you. And I don't *want* to agree with this."

Looking intrigued and perhaps even slightly alarmed, Malin lowered his eyes to the drink he took from me and set aside. Then, his hand resting upon the arm of the couch to pin me there, Malin stared into my eye and commanded, "Tell me what's wrong."

"I want you to take me," I begged him, gasping just to say the words and pressing to him all the closer. While he inhaled, he slid his free hand from the couch down to my thigh and permitted my leg to curl into his lap. "Oh, Malin—I ache for you whenever I see you. My brain gets so hot with bad thoughts that I can hardly think of anything else…"

"You naughty little harlot…I'm just waiting for the wedding night, as a decent man does."

Moaning sadly, I sagged my head back, and the gesture invited his lips like the magnet invited metal files. His mouth and tongue caressed my throat while pleasure blazed in me, irresistible.

"I don't *want* you to be a decent man…I want you to be a cruel man. I want you to beat me—I want you to take me even when it's not my pleasure. Oh, Master"—his fingers tightened into my flesh, sliding up to take hold of my rear and squeeze—"Master, won't you whip me? If you won't fuck me, then please, please—give me just one thing before the wedding night. One spanking, one whipping. Anything!"

Looking amazed, almost spellbound to hear me beg for such a thing from him, he said with a roguish smile, "Dear, dear…the wedding is next *week*. You can't wait that long?"

"No! Please! I can't stand it anymore—I want you to hurt me, Malin."

While he groaned, his free hand lifted into my hair and gripped me at the scalp. I yelped, and moaned, and spread my legs just a little to steal a grind against his lap.

"You're sure that's what you want? I'm not going to fuck you until we're married, you know, even if you get a thorough beating from me tonight."

Toes curling at the mere thought of such denial, I whined and begged, "Why, oh, why are you torturing me this way?"

"It's only fair…Eleison had to deny himself your body for months. I thought it was gentlemanly to abstain for a few weeks, just to give him a chance to have you to himself before you bind your life to mine…but you're always up here in the evenings, panting, whimpering, clinging to me with hot pleas in your eyes. You're too much of a slut for me to stay away, aren't you?"

Nodding rapidly, I moaned and arched into the hard, sharp swats he laid against my ass through the fabric of my dress. "Yes, yes sir—oh, Master, I'm your dirty slut! Whatever you do to me, I love it…hurt me, tease me, be mean to me, oh, please, I need it—"

"Take off my belt," he told me, keeping his grip in my hair and his eyes fixed on mine.

Breathless, I obeyed. My fingertips brushed something incredibly hard in his trousers, and I ached to be split in two by him—but I was afraid if I even asked again, he would send me away without so much as a beating.

With deft fingers, I opened the buckle and slid the long leather strap free of his waist.

"If I bring you to my bedroom, I'm going to wind up fucking you, so we're going to do it here. Take off your dress."

Trying to hide how eager I was and instead play up my already quite prominent anxiety, I sprang from my seat and reached behind me, my eyes fixed on him.

When the dress slid away, he brushed the loop of the doubled over belt against the edge of his mouth.

"I'll make you regret leaving your underwear on your mate's floor, you harlot...bend over with your hands on the arms of the chair. Get comfortable."

Moaning weakly, I turned my back to him and did as I'd been told. His eyes seared over every inch of my body, over my backside and the swollen cleft visible between my thighs.

"I am quite excited for our wedding night." He rose to his feet and experimentally cracked the belt against his open palm. As I jumped, he added, "And the next night...and every night after. The idea of you being my wife for the rest of our lives in a week... just a week...ah..."

The belt cracked down against my left cheek, and I jumped and moaned with ecstasy at the sting.

"Yes," I gasped, "yes, thank you—one—"

"What a good girl you are...keep thanking me, slut. Let me know how much you need a nice beating from your master."

"Ah! Oh! Thank you...two..."

The endorphins rushed in soon, each crack of the belt against my backside perfectly timed and expertly aimed. Eleison had gone at it a little too fast, and had of course made up for it with lovemaking; but Malin had nothing to make up for. Being whipped by him was lovemaking from him. He knew just where to place every lash, when to wait, when to sidle up behind me and caress the welts while letting the front of his trousers brush my rear. Each strike made my flesh burn hotter; made the flame of desire between my thighs rage to a wild extreme.

Then, too soon, it was over. I realized he truly didn't intend to fuck me when, stroking my ass with a loving hand, Malin stepped away and fixed back a hair that had fallen out of place from his coiffure and the vigor of his strikes.

"There," he commended, the word growled from his lips as he dropped the belt and drew me back by the hips. "Exquisite... sit with me a moment, my darling...come sit..."

Dizzy, weak with desire, I let him draw me into his lap and made no effort to hide my wince as the welts encountered the scratchy fabric of his trousers.

He smiled, his thumb caressing the line of my jaw. When his head lowered over mine for a kiss, I felt as though I might dissolve into nothingness. The euphoria from Malin's whipping was truly something otherworldly; I felt it in all my limbs, in the front of my very brain.

"Is that better, angel?"

"Yes," I whispered, my lips parted to receive his next kiss. When his mouth and tongue at last drew away, I bit my lip and stared into his eyes. "Yes—thank you, Malin."

"That's good...because this is going to be the last time I see you before the wedding."

Gasping sadly, I clung to his shirt and begged, "No," but he lowered his head over my ear to kiss and nip the ridge.

"I know, angel, oh, I know, you're made to be caressed and fucked and loved every second of the day, by myself and Eleison, both...but"—unable to help himself when I parted my thighs, Malin took the liberty of sliding his hand between and discovering both how wet and, at my moan, how sensitive he'd made me— "oh, but if you come here one more night, I'll fuck you, and I'll forever wonder what's happened to my self-control...so here is what you are going to do."

Staring me dead in the eyes, Malin trailed his fingers over my slickened clit and made me whine with desperation to be fucked.

"You're going to get in the elevator and take it down to Eleison's floor, naked as you are now—"

Blushing furiously, I moaned and slowly arched against the touch he deigned to thrill me with. "Oh, but what if I run into one of the staff?"

"Then they'll just confirm what everyone already knows... that you're a promiscuous little tart. A nymphomaniac so desperate for cock she has to go back and forth between her men, begging that one of them satisfy her..."

His finger plunged down, sliding between folds of flesh, and pushed steadily into me while we both gasped. He worked it in and out of me, his mouth lowering over mine.

"But that's what I love about you, Thecla...I love that this gorgeous little cunt can't be filled, oh, yes, that you're always two degrees away from boiling. So why don't you take the elevator down and let your mate take advantage of the heat...and, when the wedding comes, I'll give you the night of your life."

Moaning as he drew his hand from me altogether, I told him, "You cruel man...you evil man, I love you."

"And I love you, Thecla...because I know that, one day, you'll be just as cruel...now, go on."

Slapping me on the ass, Malin dismissed me by sliding me into the cushion beside him and kissing my mouth. "I'm eager to see you again. Don't come to breakfast; don't come looking for me. I want to see you with fresh eyes when it's time for the ceremony."

The ceremony.

I trembled at the thought: at the initiation it represented into something more. As deeply as Malin had already introduced me to his libertine ways, I marveled to think there was another layer of intimacy that could be achieved—but there was.

As I slipped out of the elevator and down the hall to Eleison's quarters, relieved nobody was about at the time, I thought to myself that, in some ways, the union of husband and wife was sweeter than mate to mate. It was a choice of dedication, rather than a matter of some chemical fate. Matrimony was a true gesture of trust and intention—of free will—that made my body a live wire crackling with Malin's electricity.

Shivering with anticipation, I darted into the fifth-floor suite and threw myself into Eleison's surprised arms while he sat reading and waiting for me.

"Where'd your dress go," he asked, laughing, then groaning as I responded with a kiss. Growling in pleasure, Eleison let his book fall to the floor and set his whiskey aside. Free, his fingers slid over my body to drink it in by touch.

I made fast work of his belt, pushing the fabric of his trousers away without hesitation or invitation.

"Ah—Thecla...did he finally fuck you?"

I pouted and shook my head, drawing Eleison's tool from his boxers and stroking it while I said, "Oh, no…he wouldn't do it, even though I felt how hard his cock got…"

Eleison's twitched in my hand at this, but I made no comment on the positive effect his jealousy had on his libido. I just kept on, gazing into his face and slowly stroking his cock between us while I straddled his lap.

"He just made me take off my dress and his belt, and he whipped me all over my poor ass…he felt my pussy, too, and how wet I am…but he doesn't want to fuck me until the wedding."

I pouted on—but Eleison, smiling a tight smile that still echoed envy at the thought of another man stroking my pussy, did so, himself. He sighed, his fingers trailing through the dripping crests and flooded valleys while he murmured, "Well, I appreciate his generosity…it's helped to have some time with you to get used to the idea of …everything. But, I have to admit…"

He slid his fingers away from me when he felt me leaning forward, and I wasted no time impaling myself upon him with a cry that echoed through his suite. He gasped my name, going on with a staggered breath, "If this is how eager you are to be shared between us…I don't think I mind."

The next week passed in a daze, as if I viewed the whole thing through the gauze of my wedding veil. I was dizzy with frustration, miserable to miss out on my breakfasts with my beloved. I did not see him at all, in fact; Malin avoided me, it would seem. A task made easy enough by the way I spent my time.

I had been afraid to return to the tapestry; afraid to look into it and see the face of the dharmine there. But, with only a week left before our union, I had to complete the wedding present, and I retired each day to the workroom early in the morning to complete the piece.

It took three more days, and then it was done.

Glowing with pleasure, I found Charlotte and grabbed her arm before she could even greet me.

"It's finished," I told her, pleased by the understanding that brightened her stern eyes.

"Well, let me see it!"

Together, we rolled it up and carried it to the best-lit parlor at that time of day, not far from the weaving room. Looking at it in the sunlight, the richness of its colors became more apparent, and the unity of the composition struck me as being very professional.

I felt like I had finally made something great—the first great thing of many great things.

Charlotte agreed, I could see, although as always her praise was kept mild. "That's very nice," she said, obvious pride in her tone to combat the milquetoast sentiment. "Yes, you've done a good job! And you're going to do others? Goodness, well, you'll certainly be busy…let me know if you need more thread, of course. Would you like to wait to present it to him on the wedding night?"

"No," I said, certain there would be no time for such trivial formalities as the exchanging of gifts. "No—please, would you bring it up to him now?"

Nodding, Charlotte said, "I'll have a few of the girls bring it upstairs. It really is beautiful work, Thecla—I think he'll appreciate it very much."

Nodding, anxious, I believed her words but would not relax until I received word from him, one way or another.

That did not happen until the morning of the wedding.

I awoke in Eleison's arms to find him staring at the ceiling, pensive.

"Are you going to be a sulky boy on my wedding day," I whispered to him, drawing him from his thoughts and earning a little smirk.

"No, of course not. I'm happy for you...for both of you. No matter what, no matter who you're with, nothing can touch what we have, and I know that. No...I just—had a strange dream last night. I was thinking about it."

"What?"

"Nothing. It doesn't matter."

Worried for omens of the union, I draped myself over his chest and whined like a child. "You can't say a thing like that on my wedding day and not tell me, Eleison! What did you dream?"

He laughed, insisting, "It was stupid! Really. Like a kid's nightmare. I just dreamed of somebody looking in the window."

Paling, I looked over at the fifth-floor window and wondered what might reach such a height, even in the disjointed logic of dreams.

I didn't dare ask him to describe the person he'd seen. The thought that I might recognize it—him—was too chilling for me to endure.

The rest of the day vibrated with activity from the moment Eleison and I finished making love. The house buzzed with the ceremony, and because of its private nature I received the good wishes of many staff members throughout the morning.

And each thought was a kind gesture—but each drove me to a state of greater exasperation.

He was so close. Malin—my husband—was so close. We would be wed in the early afternoon, I had been told, to allow ample time to make it to the site of our honeymoon before dark. We were going to be at the vineyard house—alone, with the only help for miles in a guardhouse that Malin promised me was on-call, but out of earshot.

He would have me all to himself, and there would be no more breaths of air from him ever again. No more bookshelves to hide behind; no more magical thresholds to protect me from his desire.

I was very grateful, in a way, for the time he had given me to focus on Eleison. Eleison certainly deserved it; but, more than that, I realized as that morning wore on that I really *was* going to become Malin's wife.

Things would be different. The bed in my room; it would never be slept in again. Not by me; not unless I was quite upset at both husband and mate, or I was truly desperate to sort out my thoughts on some yet unforeseen matter.

But, as deeply as I had anticipated this day, I was shocked to find it had rushed up like a borro leaping upon an obliviously grazing ventil doe. I was on the cusp of transformation, in myself and my life.

And, though it frightened me, it excited me, too.

I spent the later morning in solitude, taking a bath that left me flushed and sensitive as if in anticipation of Malin's touch. I ached, my unoccupied mind twisting and turning through the night that lay ahead. The idea of spending the rest of my life available to Malin's use as it pleased him left me on fire, and the only thing that could even begin to fight the blaze was his body.

Afraid I might faint, I emerged from the bathroom to find Charlotte had been by.

My dress and its slip lay out upon the bed, the entire effect infinitely more wonderful than it had been in the store. The gossamer fabric glittered as I held it up to the light, my hand splayed flat upon its other side and visible through in a few artfully selected panels across the stomach, between the breasts and down the legs. It was in good taste, but so tantalizing I knew Malin would barely make it through the wedding.

Smiling, I inspected its caress of my body in the mirror standing in the corner of my room, then trotted to my vanity to touch up my brows without worrying over more intricate makeup, as Malin preferred me without even lipstick. It was a relief to be spare, though I was wondering if I might put on just a bit of eye shadow to compliment the gold of the dress when my eye fell on the other item left while I was in the bath.

A long jewelry case of some animal leather, with a note attached in an elegant hand and bearing my name on its surface.

The wildfire in my core reaching new heights, I inhaled the great plume of sandalwood and peeked inside the note to read its short but laden lines.

Thank you for the tapestry, Madame. It is truly perfect; I'm excited to see the others. I hope you appreciate this token from me. Charlotte has assured me it suits your gown...I look forward to seeing for myself.

Eternally Your Husband,
Malin

Lips curling into a smile, I pressed the note to my breast before setting it aside to open the case.

I wish now I had done so with somewhat more ceremony, but I was not prepared for what I found within, and I stood there gawking like a bumpkin.

It was the first gemstone I had ever seen up-close with my own eyes: a ruby the size of a child's eye, its flawless facets set in gold and complimented by rows of diamonds along either side. The necklace, designed to fit around the base of my neck like a collar, was so gorgeous I was afraid to touch it, yet I couldn't stop myself. My fingertips trailed over the chain and I marveled, my breath held with incredulity.

This was my life now.

The knock upon the door drew me from my reverie; I hoped for a moment it was Malin, hardly able to wait any longer, but I smiled all the same to find Eleison there. He looked crisp in his suit—marvelous, in fact, foregoing the usual blue jacket for black that somehow brightened his eyes. I couldn't help but hurry to kiss him. He hung there, sighing to have me in his arms, drawing from my mouth all the love I had to give before he released me and remembered to shut the door.

"You look—beyond words," said Eleison, laughing a little. "I admit…I'm jealous."

"Don't be. If you like, we could have some sort of ceremony of our own."

"I feel somehow like we already had that," he said, the dark, pleasurable glint in his eye harkening back to just what I also thought of as some kind of ceremonial entry point into our love— that was, the mock kidnapping that in the end had been so deeply animal. "But, I wouldn't mind going away with you for a week or two someday."

"We can," I said encouragingly, hurrying to the vanity. "I'm so glad you'll be there with us, Eleison."

"Seemed right. Somebody has to witness it, anyway…"

His eye fell upon the ruby displayed at my vanity, and his

astonishment was real and distinct when compared to his usual solemn affect.

"Wow," he said.

"I know." I laughed and shook my head. "I don't even know what's going on…"

"You're being elevated," he said, carefully picking the necklace up by one end of its chain and holding it in the light. Then, glancing at me, he looped it around my neck and told me, "Get your hair for me, would you…"

Two hours later, Malin's eyes flitted but briefly over that ruby when they set on me for the first time in a week. My left hand rested on Eleison's arm while the other bore a bouquet of roses as red as the gem. Malin's chest swelled within his tuxedo, everything in his face at once drawn by a kind of preternatural hunger that frightened and intrigued me as he received me from my mate. Of those present, Malin was just as much an ordinary human as was the magistrate that wed us; as was Charlotte, who witnessed our ceremony along with Eleison.

But the territory master's intensity was anything but human. His desire for me, in fact, was inhuman to diabolical extents.

And, as the magistrate announced our union, the slow, calculating pressure of the kiss he rested in my mouth was the most inhuman thing of all, for it twisted my insides and contorted my limbs, and it made the world shatter away from my feet so utterly that I barely realized we were out on the street, halfway to the carriage, until I heard Eleison calling behind us, "Have fun! Congratulations!"

Inhaling sharply, I laughed and swayed and asked Malin as he helped me into the waiting car, (driven by real horses, I noted— he missed no opportunity to wow me, not that day), "Did I sign the certificate?"

"My God, who can remember—driver, get us out of here."

Slamming the door, Malin wheeled upon me and took me fiercely in his arms.

"*Thecla*," he said as he'd never before, the word full of a kind of accusatory rage—as though he were incensed by my audacity to make him fall so in love. "Madame Farrow," he then murmured, the wildness giving into a kind of shock.

"Husband," I whispered to him, laughing in my own mad glee as he descended upon me for a consuming kiss. His passion pushed me back into the seat and threatened to dislodge the diadem of my veil from my hair. Neither one of us cared; he kept pushing, forcing me to lie back in the carriage so he could gorge himself with kisses over my throat and down the curve of my clothed bosom.

"Beautiful," he murmured all the while. "You're beautiful, Thecla, the most beautiful woman in the world—and you're mine—"

"Forever," I gasped, meaning the word. "My heart was always meant to be yours!"

"Oh, you tempting little witch! I regret my own desire to please you—I want to take you to the vineyard *now*, and—"

"But I thought that was where we're headed?"

With a mysterious smile, Malin raised his head and rested his forehead to mine. "We're stopping somewhere else, first...I have something I think you want to see."

"Oh, Malin—what more could you possibly give me?"

He refused to tell, no matter how I begged and pawed and blandished him. But oh, he was very pleased with himself when I stepped from our carriage and gasped to recognize the city block where we stood. A little girl passing by whispered to her mother that I was a princess while the mother, shocked to recognize Malin, averted her face and sped up out of the way of the guards getting out of their own autohorse carriage.

"Go in," Malin urged me at my curious look. "The show's about to start, I think…we're just squeaking in. Hopefully there'll still be some seats…"

There were, I discovered as we stepped into the familiar theater I had once visited by myself.

The entire thing, lit in anticipation of a crowd, stood empty.

"Let's sit in the balcony," he said with a casual nod while I turned my shock upon him. "I don't want them to make eye contact with me and forget their lines."

Malin made me feel like a small child experiencing the world for the first time. I laughed in delight and had to resist the urge to run up the stairs, maintaining a ladylike pace only by virtue of my husband's arm. It fit so well, so warmly against my hand! I never wished to be separated from him again, and pressed close to him when we took our seats at the balcony's very edge.

"I have to say," he murmured as the lights went down, "you were so inspired by this production that I've been quite eager to see it. I hope they're good tonight."

His free hand slid over my knee, up along my thigh, and rested so comfortably there in my lap that I felt I'd known him for longer than I'd been alive.

I kissed my husband, his mouth a dark cauldron that poured his love and wickedness into me in equal measure.

Still high on him, I settled against his arm.

The curtain raised.

DON'T MISS THE HONEYMOON!

Want more of Thecla's tale between now and Book II? Sign up for Ada's mailing list! As a thank-you, you'll receive the **ultra-steamy novella-length epilogue to CONSORT,** only available for subscribers.

Sure, you can enjoy the rest of the series without **experiencing all 20,000 words of "Honeymoon"**…but do you want to? Not if you're into dark romance…just look at these triggers: **BDSM, bondage, corporal punishment, suspension, erotic asphyxiation, service-oriented domination, struggle-fucking, mentions of homicide and torture, and sexualization of those mentions of homicide and torture.**

VISIT ADA'S SITE TO SUBSCRIBE!

http://www.adadartromance.com

OTHER WORKS
FROM PAINTED BLIND PUBLISHING

REGINA WATTS

INDUSTRIAL DIVINITY (2020)
WILD GIRL RUNNING (2020)
DOTTIE FOR YOU SEASON 1 (2021)
THE BURNINGSOUL SAGA (2021-2022)
I WAS AN OP DEMON LORD (2021-2022)
BE MY BULLY (2021)
SEDUCED BY SABINE (2021)
MAYHEM AT THE MUSEUM (2021)
IDOL (2022)

M. F. SULLIVAN

DELILAH, MY WOMAN (2015)
THE LIGHTNING STENOGRAPHY DEVICE (2017)
THE DISGRACED MARTYR TRILOGY (2019-2020)

ABOUT THE AUTHOR

Ada Dart is an author of reverse harems and romances with undercurrents so dark you'll only want to read them at night. Her brooding, intellectual heroes defy boundaries and straddle conventions: whether older or younger, commanding or sensual, the men Dart writes are sure to keep readers' imaginations going long after the final page. In addition to writing other pulp genres under the pen name Regina Watts, Dart enjoys spending time watching opera with her cat and her real life age-gap partner of over half a decade.

ABOUT THE PUBLISHER

Painted Blind Publishing and its erotic imprint, Painted Blue Publishing, are the brainchild of M. F. Sullivan. Founded in 2015 while Sullivan resided in Tucson, PBP is a house dedicated to bringing readers the finest in consciousness-expanding fiction. Be sure to check out the wide variety of essays available for free at paintedblindpublishing.com to learn more about the company, Dart, and Sullivan.

www.ingramcontent.com/pod-product-compliance
Lightning Source LLC
Chambersburg PA
CBHW071425190726
48292CB00001B/112